Girl Gone Nova

Pauline Baird Jones

L & L Dreamspell
Spring, Texas

Cover and Interior Design by L & L Dreamspell

ISBN: 978-1-60318-204-1

Library of Congress Control Number: 2010920746

Visit us on the web at www.lldreamspell.com

Published by L & L Dreamspell
Printed in the United States of America

I'd like to dedicate this book to my children
Whose courage in the face of challenges inspires me.

To my sister
Who is amazing.

To my husband
Who anchors me in reality while encouraging me to soar.

And to both L's of L&L for wanting to publish yet another of my BABs. You both rock! ;-)

Author's Note:

Following the release of *The Key*, it came to my attention that I didn't make it clear that my *Project Enterprise* series is set, somewhat loosely, in the present day. I did this deliberately. It is hard enough to create a whole new galaxy, without having to create an imaginary future. I've tried to go easy on adding too many present day details, in hopes the book will outlast this present time, but any references to present day things is deliberate and not an accident. ☺

One

It was a party on an alien planet in a galaxy far, far away.

It should have been the most freaking interesting party Doc—Delilah Oliver Clementyne—had ever attended. They were in the fabulous, alien-equivalent-of-marble reception hall. There was good food and soft music. There were pretty aliens in pastels and Earthlings in camouflage to provide contrast and conflict.

Both sides were humanoid, but that was the only thing they seemed to have in common—well, other than their mutual obsession with the mysterious and ancient outpost on the planet of Kikk. Doc was interested in it, too. She liked weapons and the outpost was supposed to be loaded with them, but she couldn't think of any reason she'd get the chance to play with them. She sighed, her gaze skimming the room again.

Maybe partying with ET was only fun in the movies. Maybe it was her fault. She didn't party well with others, though she could fake it when necessary. This wasn't necessary. And it made her antsy to be out and about without a clear objective. Knowing what to do, knowing how to act, having a purpose created a safe zone even when what she was doing wasn't remotely safe.

There were worse things than dying.

She should blend and mingle, not prowl around the perimeter, but it took more than great food and pretty aliens to keep *them* at bay. They circled inside her head, their usual menace mixed with something new. She'd have rubbed the back of her tingling neck, but that was a giveaway move. She didn't do giveaway moves—

particularly when her camo wasn't camouflaging. In their drab garb the Earth delegation stood out like the specters at this very pretty feast. What had General Halliwell been thinking when he ordered them to dress down?

Her gaze tripped over the General—the head specter at the feast.

He was a big man, and burly, with the rock-like countenance and aggressive stance of the seasoned military man. He owned his personal space and appeared to have no problem casting a blight well outside that space. His personal staff had to stick with him. Everyone else gave him a wide berth as he stalked around the room, stopping now and then to glare and stare.

Halliwell hadn't arranged a face-to-face meet with her when she transferred aboard the *Doolittle,* and looking at his stony visage, she wasn't sorry. She bet there wasn't a diplomatic cell in his whole body.

Doc wasn't a diplomat either, though she was attached to the diplomatic team on the *Doolittl*e, courtesy of her oft-used—or abused—cover as a United Nations doctor. It said something about human nature that no one had thought to wonder why a UN doctor had been sent into space. It did explain why she'd ended up at the party. Porter Rockley, head of the diplomatic team, had tried to put as many diplomatic bodies as possible between the General and the Gadi.

He'd have done better to go with a squad of well-armed Marines.

This was the first time anyone on the expedition had been invited into Gadi home world orbit, let alone been dirt side there, and the General still looked pissed. Was that the Gadi Leader he was glaring at?

The current object of his displeasure wasn't wearing pink, the official color of the Leader, and his body language didn't shout, *I'm the Leader of most of the galaxy,* so she doubted it. Though she'd heard Helfron Giddioni was skilled at projecting everything from goof ball to menacing, and he'd given up wearing pink—at least around the Earth expedition. A good strategic move, but it was a pity. Doc liked pink, probably because it had been missing in her life. Her mum had been against anything that smacked of gender typing. Doc had gone a bit nuts over pink when she started buying her own underwear. And she might again, once she got back to Earth and she didn't have to be military regulation from the skin out.

She paused her thoughts to nibble at the last something on her plate, almost sighing as the exquisite blend of flavors caressed a palate depressed by over a year of subsisting on MREs. When she'd deployed with the *Nimitz* she had expected to return to Earth when it did. Instead, she'd been transferred to the *Doolittle* and sent even further into space. It would have been nice to know why, but her new orders hadn't caught up with her yet. One thing she knew, the Major hadn't sent her here to party with the aliens.

She put her plate on a passing tray and then paused in front of a small orchestra, studying the instruments as well-bred elevator music filled any lulls in the muted conversations between the Gadi and the Earth expedition. In the two-plus years since first contact they still didn't know that much about them beyond the whole pretty vibe they had going. It wasn't her mission to parse the Gadi, but that didn't stop her from being curious about them. She tried to think of something that did stop her curiosity and couldn't. Well, dying would.

Her gaze inadvertently intersected with one of the Gadi men and he crossed to her side.

"I am called Naman." He extended a hand.

Doc met him halfway. "Doctor Clementyne." It made her twitchy to use her real name, but she didn't let it show. That was a giveaway, too.

He lifted her hand to his mouth, pressing it with his lips, his appreciative gaze holding hers through the whole exercise. Doc kept her smile, even though she didn't like to be touched. She got it from her mum. And her dad. It surprised her they'd managed enough touching to produce two children.

He studied her with a puzzling male appreciation. Oh, she knew she wasn't hideous, but it wasn't her hotness factor that earned her the nickname "Morticia." And she was dressed like a guy. Was he pinging on her like a laser guided missile because he liked her looks or because she was with the delegation?

She didn't like anyone pinging on her for any reason she hadn't made happen, but if he wanted to do it, she'd turn the ping back on him. She tipped her head to the side, the angle mathematically configured for flirtatious effect. Her hair shifted, falling in a neat line as she added a tiny curve to the edges of her mouth. Her lashes drooped to a careful half mast to hide the calculation in her gaze while her brain processed his reaction and made minute adjustments. One didn't want to over—or under—mess with his head.

Next to him stood a server holding a tray of glasses. Naman seized two glasses and handed her one with a slight flourish. It seemed she wasn't the only one who calculated effects, though he might not realize he was being calculating.

"Thank you." She deepened her smile and added warmth to her voice. His response was in the expected range of her output. She could have calculated how many cc's of blood had left his brain if she'd wanted to. Did it bother men to be vulnerable in that way? It would bother her. She lifted the glass and pretended to take a sip. Even a small amount of alcohol put her concentration at risk, and the Gadi concoction had more than a small amount.

"This is a remarkable space," she murmured, because small talk was an expected part of this social ritual. She used the tip of her tongue in a swipe across her upper lip and sent a few more cc's of his blood heading south. She didn't want him to notice her small talk was really small.

"Is it?" Naman sounded as dazed as she'd wanted him to.

Doc looked around, glad to break eye contact for a few seconds. It didn't take this much pretty to please the Earth delegation, not after several months in space, but the Gadi wouldn't know that. Or maybe they did and they'd still pushed out the boat. They wanted access to the Kikk Outpost pretty badly.

"I am surprised, though." She paused with intent to distract.

He arched a perfect brow and leaned toward her, bringing his personal scent in range of her nostrils. Lucky for her it wasn't unpleasant. Unlucky for him, it did nothing to her heart rate or cognitive processes. She'd been called a cold bitch more than a few times. It was a fair assessment. It could be the scientist at her core that focused too much on analyzing and not enough on feeling. It could be *them* snapping at her heels.

Or she was just a cold bitch.

"What surprises you, Doctor?"

"Well, I would have expected a beautiful staircase for more dramatic effect, I suppose." And why no chandeliers? She'd been sure there'd be chandeliers. The Gadi and chandeliers seemed made for each other. She made some vague hand movements to go with her words.

It wasn't a shock when his gaze followed her hands, since that's why she did it.

"The arrival of your delegation was quite dramatic."

If he hadn't smiled after he said this, she'd have suspected he was being ironic.

"A big flash and then a bunch of olive drab. It needed work." She shrugged, adding a hint of rueful into the calculated movement.

He laughed. No surprise it sounded pretty, too. "Whereas we arrived via the lift."

He indicated what she'd thought were floor-to-ceiling panels at the end of the room.

"I would like to have seen that." This comment had the benefit of being both small talk and true.

He edged closer. Doc shifted, her gaze holding Naman's, as she maintained the distance status quo. One thing Doc had in common with the General, she didn't like people in her personal space. She'd once done the shift/retreat all the way around the desk of a target, until she got tired of it and kicked his ass. That technique wouldn't work here. Kicking ass at a party wasn't diplomatic. Even she knew that. If the guy got too persistent she'd ask for directions to the ladies room. She might learn something, even if it was only that Gadi women peed, too.

She was unprepared for the chill that snaked abruptly down her back, like a finger tip tracing a path from spinal tip to base. The hairs on her body stirred, and then lifted, but still not in flight or fright. She was well acquainted with both. Her heart sped up. Her breathing tried to, too. She fought that. Panting was passé at a party. The struggle to control her breathing created a kind of roaring in her ears. Her hands tightened around her glass, as if it could provide the stability she needed.

Someone was watching her.

She'd been watched, studied, assessed many times in her thirty-plus years, but not like this. It wasn't creepy.

It *was* new.

☼

Helfron Giddioni—Leader of the Gadi people and defender and protector of most of the galaxy—knew to his bones how important this reception was. The complex relations with these people from Earth had reached a critical mass. If war were to be averted, he needed to pay attention to the newly arrived ambassador—even if Rockley was as mind-numbingly dull as his predecessor. Something nagged at him, trying to pull his attention from matters of state. He resisted the urge for several minutes, but as the impulse built, he gave in to the urge to scan for the source. If something were wrong, he needed to know this.

All seemed to be well with both party and guests—a moving figure on the perimeter grabbed his attention—even as the hairs on the back of his neck rose in warning. All women are dangerous. Hel had known this for as long as he could recall. Since avoiding them was impossible, one approached them with caution, and was never surprised by anything they did.

This one might surprise him.

Through partially lowered lashes, he studied her, wondering what it was about her that bothered him. The purity in the curve of her pale cheek, exposed by the angle of her head and fall of her deeply dark hair were perfect, too perfect, he realized, like a pose in a tableau. The hair hung straight and thick almost half-way down her back. It shifted as she did, sometimes hiding, sometimes exposing a profile that appeared to be without flaw. Her clothing was meant to disguise her female shape. It failed in this. And it fed the dangerous aura she wore like a cloak. The way she'd circled the perimeter of the room reminded him of a *panthric* on the hunt, each move an invitation, and a warning. She activated his hunter's instincts, though he had other reasons to be curious about her.

His gaze moved to General Halliwell, standing at least a head taller than the group that surrounded him. He'd arrived in the first group from the *Doolittle*, wearing his reluctance for the meeting like a storm cloud. Hel had hoped that time out in his own galaxy and a promotion would have mellowed him. He'd hoped wrong. The General didn't like the Gadi, and he really didn't like their Leader. No surprise he didn't want to be at the reception—or that he'd come anyway.

Halliwell was a strategist as well as a warrior.

The Earth delegation had probably come to the reception in camouflage at the general's order, in hopes it would annoy Hel into misbehaving.

It wouldn't.

Hel was also sure that the people chosen to attend were here for a purpose. That made the woman even more dangerous—and more interesting.

After two Earth years butting heads with the various leaders of the Earth delegations, Hel should have had a clearer understanding of them. In many ways, they were simple and straightforward, almost like children, but he'd learned never to assume he was seeing the whole story. No, there was a reason for the woman's presence, a purpose to be served.

"Look at that. Morticia has stopped stalking and is talking to someone. Color me shocked," one of the expedition members said, the voice behind Hel.

It was easy to conclude the man spoke of the woman. Other than the servers, she was the only one who had been pacing. The words had a malicious edge. Was there dissension in the ranks of the expedition? Why had the General brought her here?

There was only one way to find out.

☼

Doc's companion turned toward the watcher. She turned with him, even though one part of her overactive brain thought it was a bad idea. Then she saw *him* and her brain did something it had never, ever done.

It froze.

The sudden silence inside her head was as disconcerting as the raw power the Gadi man emitted like a blast wave. He could have powered the *Doolittle* with a look. Even *they* paused inside her head.

She should have been able to calculate his height and center of gravity to within an inch.

Instead, she couldn't do basic math.

She wasn't sure she knew her own name.

Her only clear thought: *what would it be like to kiss him?*

It should have freaked her out to feel thrust into a romance novel moment. She'd gone through a pile of them trying to find romance in her soul. She'd concluded she had neither romance nor soul.

Now she wasn't so sure. She *was* sure he was beautiful.

His powerful body was slim and narrow hipped. His shoulders were broad and nicely displayed by his neutral, but well-fitted garments. His slacks were cut to display long, strong legs. His coat reminded her of a Nehru jacket with its standup collar that framed the strong column of his throat and jaw line. It suited a body that moved as gracefully as a jungle cat toward her.

His skin was lightly tanned, just enough to deepen the contrast with his blonde hair.

She couldn't see a single flaw, not in the way his brows arched over his intensely blue eyes, or in the sweep of his nose, or in the full, sensual curve of his mouth.

She'd never used the word sensual, never thought it except when reading. Now it whispered through her mind, stroked her insides like a promise.

He made an elegant motion, like he was sweeping something to the side. She was somewhat aware that Naman bowed and moved away from her. He might have spoken, but Doc didn't hear it, despite the deep silence inside her head.

A wave of heat hit her nerve endings at the same time *his* scent did. It was as mysterious and heady as the man. On some level she knew he couldn't smell any way but this one.

There was nothing calculated, no geometry involved in the rising of her chin. No deliberation in the lift of her lashes so that she could meet his gaze. Her world rocked, and when it stopped, it was off its axis. She should have known how far off, but she didn't. Her brows pulled together as the remaining sliver of sentience in her brain produced a hypothesis based on her body's reactions.

Desire.

So that's what it felt like.

☼

Her eyes were a deep shade of purple, an eye color Hel had never seen before. This should have made her eyes cool, but they weren't cool. They burned in the pale oval of her face. The frame of black lashes intensified both the color and heat of her eyes, ramped up the impact like a sun going nova. He looked for flaws in how she was made and found none. He homed in on her mouth. It was well formed and pink—the Leader's personal color.

If she was Halliwell's secret weapon, the man was more subtle than Hel had suspected.

Color stained the sculpted lines of her cheekbones, and the

pulse at the base of her throat jumped into hyperdrive, pounding against the pale skin in a way that seemed to say, put *your lips here, now, before you die.* Hel almost answered that demand, as desire, thick and rich, stirred in his veins. He needed to do something, say something before he gave into temptation.

"Morticia." His voice emerged as a husky rasp.

He'd been sure her eyes could get no wider, no deeper, but they did. Then the thicket of lashes swept down to rest against pale cheeks, there was a forever pause before they lifted again. Purple was gone, though the blue was still intense and unusual. Her mouth curved into a grin that was nothing like the smile she'd directed at Naman. This look was real. He didn't know how he knew. He just did. He knew *her.*

"Morticia?"

A soft chuckle spilled out of her parted lips. "Right."

Her voice had a different inflection than others of her kind, giving an elegance to her brief response. Desire settled now that he had her attention, though it's current still pulsed between them, like a circuit seeking completion. Her smile also removed that lethal, almost other world quality. She was just a woman, he told himself, a lovely woman, but still just a woman. Even as his brain called him a liar, he wondered if he'd let himself overwork the problem of Halliwell and the threat that this woman had appeared to pose.

"That's not—"

The sound of voices rising in jarring conflict ripped across the surface tranquility of the reception. Before his gaze, Morticia shifted into lethal again, like a picture losing its focus and then finding it.

And he knew he hadn't imagined anything. She *was* dangerous, possibly the most dangerous woman he'd ever met.

The interruption, the altercation, was ill timed. Hel turned toward the sound. A member of the earth delegation appeared to be arguing with one of the servers at the service entrance.

Hel frowned, shooting a sharp look of command at his head of security.

Wilstead started toward the pair, breaking into a trot as the dispute grew louder. The server's voice rose to a shriek as the Earth man shoved her toward the doorway.

In the space between two beats of his heart, Hel's warrior instincts displaced diplomacy. He moved to place himself in front of Morticia, but she was already in motion—heading *toward* the disputants. Hel shouted a warning that was engulfed in a roar and in the bright, deadly light racing toward him...

Two

Cordite burned into her nose bringing Doc awake and into a low-profile crouch. She eased a weapon free from concealment, ears straining for threats in darkness lit by a half-hearted fire. Nothing immediate presented itself, but her gut refused to stand down and her senses twitched like live wires in water. Something bad had happened. People were down. Stuff was on fire. It took a few seconds to orient her memory, to reconstruct where she was, what had happened and why she was on alert at the cellular level.

What light there was showed her the remains of the lovely Gadi reception hall. Moans filtered in between the soft crackle of fire somewhere off to her right. Her brain noted aches and pains in a variety of places, and smoke stung her eyes and lungs, but it was a low level concern, all energy channeled to her stretched out senses.

No one had told her to come to the party armed, but no one had told her she couldn't. Truth was, even if they had, she'd still be armed. It was SOP—standard operating procedure—to expect the unexpected.

She extracted her infrared monocle. Not everyone could split their vision, but her brain liked it. It pulled more data from the combo of IR and real-time viewing. With the IR in place, she surveyed her surroundings again. Heat signatures popped out of the haze, all of them prone, bodies and rubble tumbled together.

She would have been one of those bodies, but she'd realized

she couldn't stop the attack and hit the deck before the blast. Still got her bell rung, of course.

She needed to find the General and not just because of his rank. He'd be one of the few wearing a radio. She wasn't officially military, so she didn't have one, though the *Doolittle* should be monitoring the contingent and seen the explosion on their sensors. There'd been at least one medical officer dirt side, but he'd been the one trying to push the bomber out of the hall. No way had he survived the blast.

Her brain needed more to do, so she set it to work estimating the general's current position, calculating trajectories and blast radius. Seemed a good idea to assess for structural integrity concerns, so she threw that into the mental mix, too.

She had a medical degree in her pocket, but black ops resisted going offline. It was a bit like having multiple personality disorder, but without the forgetting part. No persona ever completely left the building, preferring to jostle for attention inside her head, but if black ops didn't want to go back in the queue, maybe it shouldn't. Doc knew to trust her gut.

According to her calculations, General Halliwell had to be somewhere off to her left. Doc started that direction, pausing when a body in her path stirred and muttered something. She crouched next to him, but before she could do more than check his pulse, a change in the air current proved black ops had been wise to stick around. Her IR-free eye met the wounded man's gaze, a finger to her lips silenced whatever comment he'd planned to make.

Her backup weapon slid into her left hand as she went ghost. Both weapons were already silenced. She knew not to attract attention when she shot someone.

It was easy to locate the source of her unease. They were the only ones upright and moving. The bogeys split into two groups of two, using some kind of hooded light that extinguished any lingering doubt they were a rescue party. The lights passed over each body just long enough for an ID. They were hunting. Didn't take many of her brain cells to determine two possible targets.

Doc decided to go hunting, too. She attached herself to the team heading in the direction that should lead to the general and saw his prone figure when they did.

"Finish him off and let's get out of here," one of them, a male, said, looking back over his shoulder. His eyes widened as his gaze connected with hers, his mouth started to move.

Doc's silenced weapon ended that move. The other found a target dead center of bogey number two. She turned before either body hit the ground. Thanks to her IR, she spotted team two. Didn't look like they'd found what they were looking for yet.

☼

Hel woke to a world forever changed. Never had anyone, not even the Dusan at the height of their power, been able to strike at the heart of the Gadi home world, let alone within their seat of government. And only one very dangerous woman had come this close to killing him.

Rubble covered his legs, and when he tried to move, more debris tumbled down, surrounding him in a choking cloud of dust that set off a round of painful coughing. He could smell blood, felt it making a warm trail down the side of his face. There was pain, but it was manageable. To be without pain was to be dead.

He needed to free himself. It was not arrogance to think he was the target of this attack. Most plots were aimed at the top. If he were running this operation, he would have backup in place to be sure all targets were eliminated. Bombing was an imprecise assassination tool, but the inevitable chaos could be useful. Mingle assassins with rescuers and no one would know who died when.

As he tried to shift debris off his legs, he scanned for attackers in the shifting shadows caused by the fire and debris dust. Did he see movement? Heading toward him? It was possible they were the front guard of the rescue, but if they were here to help, logic dictated that they stop and help. He eased his energy weapon from its place of concealment. This loosed a small avalanche of debris, and the two figures ceased movement. They were vague shapes, but he felt their tension. He shared their tension. They wished to kill him. He planned to stop them.

Did they know the nature of the man they sought to kill? If so many had not been injured, Hel would have enjoyed this encounter. Though he was, of course, pleased the war was over, he missed the mental stimulation, the plotting and counter-plotting involved in fighting the Dusan war machine. The politics of leadership were not nearly as entertaining. In its own way, however, it was as dangerous or he would not be lying buried in rubble.

He pressed deeper into the shadows as the light began to move again, still heading his direction.

"If he's under that, we'll never find him."

Hel did not recognize the voice. He did recognize what was left of the ceiling reflected in the light that the man held. A portion of it hung crookedly, supported by a pillar—a pillar that looked eager to cease its supportive role. At its base was a large pile of debris.

"If it goes, they won't find us either."

Blood trickled down into Hel's eye, blurring his vision. He rubbed at it as he lifted the weapon and centered the sight on one of the shadows. His aim was not as steady as he would like.

A soft thud, followed by an echo, distracted them. The light turned back along the direction they'd come. Soft moans joined sounds made by debris shifting and the crackle of small fires dotting the area.

"He's dead. Let's get out of here." The holder of the light sounded jumpy and the way the light swung around increased the impression.

"We finish it, then we go."

Hel shifted his sight line to this voice, the dominant one of the pair. With a soft flick of his thumb, he set the weapon to kill. One did not leave enemies behind, not now, not ever.

He hesitated. The energy flash would blind him, rendering his second shot uncertain, and it would mark his position if he missed the second assassin. Uncertain was not desirable. Fitful light played against the walls, further impeding aim. This would be a good time for a silenced Earth projectile weapon. Since he did not have one, or his usual two weapons, he would improvise. He marked the position of both men. They were moving again.

He considered his options, studying the terrain with care. To approach him, they would need to go around a larger pile of rubble. This would force them to be parallel with each other, instead of side by side. He used the debris to support and steady his weapon, adjusting his sight line to that spot as the two men continued toward the intercept point.

When they moved into his target zone, Hel squeezed the trigger mechanism, not releasing it as was his usual practice. The beam of light shot forward, blinding him, but he could still hear. First came the sound of the beam hitting the first assailant, followed by his stagger back into the second man. Air hissed from the second man's lungs, caused by that impact. He would instinctively grasp his companion, seek to hold him upright, but death would make the first sag enough for the beam to then strike the second assassin. Hel listened for and heard the small sound of both bodies tumbling to the rubble-strewn floor.

As his vision cleared again, his senses twitched in the almost silence. Was someone watching him?

☼

The light from the energy beam was painful to Doc's eyes, but the IR eye got the worst of it. She ducked back behind an unstable pillar and yanked it off, cussing in her head. Her timing was good, as transport wash from the *Doolittle* rescue team added more light to the equation. This time black ops went dormant without a fuss. When she could see again, she moved toward the rescuers. Doc felt the mental and physical shift in focus; her body realigned by the time the first search light played over her.

"Are you all right, ma'am?" The voice was brisk and American. "If you are—"

"I'm a medical doctor. If you've got a spare emergency kit, I'm ready to assist."

The young solider hesitated. "Captain Evans—"

"—was at ground zero." She delivered the information without inflection. She paused a few seconds to let him process this, then continued, "You need to get some engineers dirt side ASAP. The roof is trying to come down over there." Doc knew how much authority to infuse into her voice and wasn't surprised when the young man activated his radio.

She looked back to where she'd dropped the bogeys, curious who'd used the ray gun, but the transport wash made it hard to see into the shadows. She suspected she knew who it was, though. The Gadi Leader didn't seem like the kind to get blown up or assassinated. Too bad they were unlikely to meet. She didn't like most people, but she might like him.

The soldier turned to someone behind him, requesting the med kit.

"You'll need transport tags for the wounded Gadi, too." The Gadi might not like summary transport, but there was no sign of Gadi rescuers yet and it had to be better than dying. Doc didn't wait to hear him pass this suggestion along, just grabbed her kit and headed for the closest body.

☼

The constant transport wash kept the room almost well lit. Hel could have alerted the rescuers to his presence, but there were others with worse injuries. And it didn't hurt for his enemies to remain ignorant about his survival until he was less vulnerable. No sign yet of his people in the rescue party. It looked like they were transporting all survivors to the *Doolittle*. Not diplomatic, but Hel felt no desire to protest. His people were getting care. Would he allow himself to be transported? So much depended on where this threat came from. He had many enemies, both in the galaxy and within the council, but not that many had the power and the skill to attack inside their seat of government.

Carig was his most outspoken opponent. And he'd lost a son in the final conflict with the Dusan. He blamed General Halliwell and the expedition for igniting the smoldering conflict to a conflagration. He didn't like suspecting the man, but facing hard realities went with the position. If Carig had managed to eliminate both him and the General, he'd have been better positioned to promote his agenda. The expedition had a strong position on the outpost, but if the Gadi turned against them, their ejection from the galaxy was inevitable. The Gadi outnumbered them in every way that mattered.

Hel had considered the move himself, many times during the negotiations of the past two years. What his people didn't know, what they couldn't know, was that the Garradian Key had gone to Earth. Hel had hoped for a return when Halliwell and the *Doolittle* did, but it seemed their scientists still thought they could figure out the Garradian technology without the Key's help. The Key was about more than access to the outpost. Miri, the Garradian Key holder, was both a legend and symbol for their people. Many among his people believed the peace would not, could not, last without the Key's return. If the Gadi ejected the Earth expedition and went to war, they lost all hope for a return.

And there were those in the galaxy who could and would use this to foment further instability in the galaxy for their own gain. Hel could not allow this to happen.

There was a slight chance the attack had not been instigated by his people. He had information of disaffected groups throughout the galaxy. He did not understand it. All had benefited from the defeat of the Dusan. Gadi efforts were focused on restoring order and freedom in the galaxy, not conquest. Unfortunately too many people didn't know how to function in peaceful times. The Earth delegation had been useful in diverting some of that aggression away from the Gadi, but if it appeared they were close to gaining access to further technology on the Kikk outpost, then he'd have to act—assuming he survived this "rescue."

Footsteps drew closer, heavy booted ones. The lights this duo carried were larger and brighter than ones carried by the first arrivals to the scene. They played across the main blast area, once again highlighting that part of the ceiling that had collapsed in the area closest to the explosion. They made no effort to approach him, nor did he see any sign of Gadi healers in the rescue party.

The part of the ceiling still supported by the pillar looked more unstable than his last view of it. Debris pressed up against it, including a large sister pillar, trying to bring it down.

"This isn't good." The voice was male, with that military inflection so typical of the Earth warriors, a combination of brisk and pragmatic.

Hel was forced to agree with his understatement.

"If that pillar gives way—" the other Earth man stopped.

He didn't have to continue. It was clear a collapse would trigger a wider collapse of the ceiling—something that would make survival problematic for all those beneath it. He waited to hear the men suggest a general retreat. It was a reasonable choice. Why risk more lives in a dangerous rescue?

"What if you tagged that?" A third light traced the length of the problem pillar. "Transport it somewhere else?"

This voice was *her* voice, but it wasn't just the unusual and elegant tone that intrigued him, though that did help. He had a weakness for unusual and elegant. She stood in shadow, separate from the two men and her voice, while confident, wasn't assertive. It reminded him of *jelem*, the inner guide. Earth people called it a conscience, or sometimes, the voice in their heads.

"Can something that big be transported? And where would they put it?" The Earth engineer didn't look at the woman, just continued to study the problem as if she *were* a voice in his head.

The other man was asking someone at the other end of the radio those same questions.

"Not into space," she said. "Don't want to litter an ally's orbit. See if they can find a large area dirt side, one without life signs or structures."

And then she turned, as if the problem no longer concerned her, her light playing across the ground. That light started to track his direction when there was yet another interruption.

Two more figures approached, their light falling on her like a blessing. It *was* Morticia. She was covered with blast dust and there were black marks, and streaks that might have been blood, on her face. He couldn't tell if it was hers. Despite her general disarray, she projected an aura of calm competence, and no hint of that lethal quality that had caught his interest. This woman had many facets to her, like a rare gemstone.

"Corporal?" She lit them up with her light, but avoided hitting them in the eyes. "Is there a problem?"

"She said she wants to help."

It was one of the female servers. Hel frowned. Why would a server be offering to help?

"Are you trained in healing?"

Part of him was surprised Morticia knew the right terminology, the rest of him wanted to provide the answer. Of course this girl wasn't trained to heal.

The young woman's chin lifted, as if the question puzzled her. For the space of several breaths the two women stared at each other.

Morticia smiled.

And hit the girl in the chin with her fist.

☼

The young corporal managed to catch the server, despite his shock.

"Ma'am?"

Doc pulled up her pant leg and extracted a knife from a holster strapped to her lower leg. "Lower her to the floor."

Her tone of command had the desired effect on her unwilling assistant, and he did as he was told. Doc knelt next to her and slid the knife under the edge of the girl's top, cutting it open in a quick, fluid motion. She pushed back the sides and the corporal inhaled sharply.

"Son of a bitch. I'll call EOD—"

Doc studied the timer on the bomb as her brain kicked into a predictable kaleidoscope of higher gears. Despite the surge of data, there was a precision to it, as if her brain were a Swiss clock on steroids. EOD—Explosive Ordinance Detail—wouldn't make it. She had maybe a minute to defuse it. The good news, a "Doc minute" was more than enough.

"Shine your light on that for me while you make that call."

The corporal did as directed, directing his beam on the woman's chest. "How did you know?"

"Know?" Her tone was absent as she studied the pattern of wires and explosives. It felt like time elongated and slowed, though she knew it wasn't possible.

"That she was wired."

"It was a woman who set off the first bomb. The insurgents in Iraq used to do that, wait for help to arrive, then send in round two." In the shifting patterns in her mind, the right one came to the front.

"Oh." Silence. "But how did you *know*?"

"Her eyes were totally dead. She was probably a Dusan 'companion' prior to the war. They were programmed to do anything they're told." Her mind tried to jump on the distraction and take her into this unhappy place, but it was easy to resist with the timer ticking down to the Gadi equivalent of zero. She felt no fear. One had to dread death to fear it.

"Even to blow herself up?" The young soldier sounded shocked.

"They probably didn't tell her that part." Doc's tone was dry. What she found even more disturbing than using these women—captured when the Dusan invaded their worlds and turned into slaves—as tools. Their C-4 was wired into the bomb. Like secondary explosions, questions without answers tried to erode her focus on the task at hand.

Behind her in an odd, background drama, the problem pillar disappeared in a transport wash. The two men turned to leave and then spotted Doc and the explosives. One of them started to curse. Doc ignored them, her attention on the woman and the bomb. Doc didn't fight against the multiplying thought streams, just let them spin around the core concern, her focus never straying from the heart: the bomb wires.

"How much time, ma'am," her assistant asked, a slight tremor to his voice.

"About thirty seconds."

The two men cursed again, but didn't move.

"Where the foxtrot is EOD?" one of them snapped.

"Do you know how to defuse a bomb, ma'am?" The corporal's tremor was worse.

The question was a good one, though a bit late in the asking. She found the wire she wanted, tracing it with her thoughts as the timer moved closer to detonation.

"No, but I stayed at a *Holiday Inn Express* last night."

The spurt of laughter from the men eased external and internal tension. Doc channeled the positive energy as she eased her knife under a wire and severed the connection. She cut the other side, lifting the detonator clear with five seconds to spare. She didn't use the spare time congratulating herself.

"Hold that." She handed the detonator to the corporal. "Need to check for secondary triggers."

"A *Holiday Inn Express?* Last night, ma'am?" Relief colored the young man's voice.

She smiled and shrugged, as she let her whirling thoughts move on to the next problem. One clear thought emerged from the clutter: when she'd planted the idea of transporting wounded Gadi to the *Doolittle*, she'd thought it would be safer. The attack had happened here. It was reasonable to assume the threat was here. But the presence of C-4 removed that certainty. She frowned. Though it couldn't have come from the *Doolittle*. It had been out of galaxy for the last two years. Still person or persons had been either selling military supplies and/or conspiring with someone among the Gadi. The secondary assassins who'd come after the bomb weren't from Earth, though she didn't know if they were Gadi.

"You're a pistol, ma'am."

She half grinned, even as her brain produced more areas of concern. The bombing had to have been planned to foment more distrust between the expedition and the Gadi. The conspirators hadn't meant for this bomb to be defused. Their investigators could have identified the C-4 from the residue, but would the Gadi have allowed them dirt side for that investigation if there'd been two explosions? And would the expedition have sent anyone—risking more expedition lives?

Doc had a feeling that if the Leader and the general were among the dead, the answer wouldn't just be no, but hell no. And if the General had died on Gadi soil? Bad enough that they'd lost people here, but in the confusion following the loss of the General, who would have assumed command? It would be useful to know chain of command—civilian and military.

A transport wash flashed in front of her, and when it was gone, six tough-looking men with strange gear stood there.

EOD had arrived to take charge of the bomb. Doc hoped they didn't "accidentally" lose it.

Three

Doc rubbed her eyes, but it didn't help any more than the last thousand or so times she'd tried it. Lieutenant Simmons, who looked a bit wavy around the edges, waited patiently for Doc to respond to her request. It felt like being back in medical school, which was kind of comforting in a weird way, though she couldn't explain why or how.

"I feel like I didn't sleep." Doc admitted this with a rueful chuckle.

"You haven't slept, ma'am. Sorry."

"Oh." So she felt like she was supposed to feel.

"Can I get you some go juice, ma'am?"

"Thank you, Lieutenant. Coffee does seem indicated." She tried the eye rub thing again, with the same result. "Where did you say I need to go?"

Doc had some experience with blast injuries so semi-autopilot was possible despite her fatigue. It was also not that dangerous to her patients, since she was being given the lower-tier patients.

Simmons paused in mid-point. "Shouldn't you get dressed, ma'am?"

Doc had used part of her curtailed break for a two-minute shower, which hadn't helped as much as she'd hoped. She looked down at her tee shirt and military issue drawers, exposed by the open bathrobe robe.

"It's laundry day. I'm out of ABUs, and I don't have scrubs." Scrubs weren't issued to diplomats, even diplomats who were doctors. She pulled the sides together and loosely knotted the ties, staring down at her bare feet without a sense of recognition. She needed to get tired like this more often. *They* were just a whimper in the distance.

"I'll see if I can scare something up for you. And put someone on your laundry problem."

Doc blinked. "Thank you."

After another period of inactivity on Doc's part, Simmons pointed toward a partially opened doorway.

"In there, ma'am. Your patient?" She held out a medical file.

"Right." Doc flipped it open, registering the details as she made her feet move toward the opening. The patient had been thrown by the blast, but lacked the telltale "butterfly" pattern in his chest x-ray that would indicate blast lung, a good thing, since it was usually fatal. No sign yet of abdominal or brain injuries, though he was being monitored for mild concussion and possible tertiary injury. Sutures required on various lacerations. No sign of infection. Vitals good.

Doc shrugged on her doctor façade and repeated in her head, "You're doing as well as can be expected." Didn't stumble over the words, but she hadn't tried the sentence out loud yet. Good thing she could talk the talk with her eyes closed. Now all she needed to do was walk the walk. Though better to do both with her eyes open. A sleepwalking doctor didn't inspire confidence. She straightened her shoulders, shook her head to clear it—that just made the hallway do a one-eighty—and pushed the door wide enough to allow her to pass through it.

"Hello." The generic greeting was necessary, since she didn't know what part of the day it was. "I'm..."

She was halfway to the bed when she realized the patient was "her" guy from the reception. She felt a tsunami of un-doctor-like pleasure at the sight of him, followed by a comparable wave of curiosity. What was it about this man that made her long-dormant hormones come online? In romance novels, the women feared the flood of feeling, but Doc only feared *them*. Feeling sparked her curiosity. Curiosity kept *them* busy, so curiosity was good.

"Morticia." His voice was rich and faintly accented. "I am pleased to see you are well."

The theme from *The Addams Family* started to play in the void inside her head. It always did when someone called her that. A smile tugged at the edges of her mouth, further eroding her doctor persona. She should have been analyzing and cataloging this new experience, and maybe she was, somewhere inside her head.

He'd said her name almost as if he savored the sound of it, while his eyes revealed he *was* savoring the sight of her. His gaze peeled back who she tried to be and exposed someone she'd never met. She wanted to analyze that, too, but he dominated the landscape inside her head. Her feet carried her forward, without help from her quiescent brain. A small flicker of self-preservation tried to wave a warning flag, but curiosity trumped that, too, as a flood of interesting and new sensations flooded through her.

Her hand was still extended for a professional handshake, but when both his hands closed around it, professional went missing in action. The feel of his hands around hers cut through the fog of exhaustion with the precision of a laser lance. There was heat, pleasure, a feeling of unfurling, as if her insides were creaking open after a long sleep. Maybe she did like to be touched, at least by this man. That took her full circle to, *why him?*

Skin slid against skin as he turned it to find the pulse beating at her wrist. Holding her gaze with his, he pressed his mouth to the pulse point. Her core body temperature increased. So did respiration. Logically she knew both were side effects of desire, but logic couldn't tell her *why*. She didn't like not knowing why, but she liked this. Interesting.

"Morticia." He breathed the word against her skin, making her pulse skitter.

"That's," she had to swallow once before she could finish, "not my name."

She knew the nickname came from her dark hair and pale skin, and that it wasn't meant to be kind. She bothered people. She bothered herself, sometimes. Just because she wasn't normal, that didn't mean she didn't know what it was.

He looked up, his head at a mathematical angle that delivered maximum impact to her solar plexus. His precision was impressive. Breathing became difficult.

"It's not?"

She shook her head, the movement languorous. "Morticia's a kind of nickname." Her voice didn't sound like hers. And it was unlike her to be so imprecise. Or to sound so dreamy.

"What is your name?"

His hands still stroked hers, the pads of his fingers abrasive in a good way. It didn't feel real. The words and feelings were right, but *she* was wrong. She tightened her grip on the medical file to keep it from sliding out of her weakened grip. For a few seconds she couldn't remember her name, but then it emerged from the fog of sensation, not unlike a lighthouse beam in a storm.

"Delilah." She hadn't meant to say that one. No one called her Delilah, though she did have much in common with her namesake. It was a bad idea to trust her.

"Delilah." His gaze fastened on her mouth, heat flaring in his eyes when she used her tongue to moisten her lips in a way that lacked planning, but filled a deep-seated need. For the first time in her life, she felt like a Delilah.

She wanted him to kiss her. She had since the first moment of seeing him. He'd be good at it. She knew it, felt it in a place deep inside, a place she thought nature had forgotten to give her. It was a shock to realize Delilah had been dormant inside her waiting for the wrong moment to make an appearance—not unlike the *Bible* version.

Warmth pulsed through her and with it a longing that had nothing to do with doctoring and everything to do with being a woman. Had she ever been a woman? She kept her backbone straight, though it was a near thing. She wanted to lean in and inhale his scent and feel his warmth wash through her in slow waves.

As if he heard her thoughts, his mouth curved into a smile that threatened the structural integrity of her knees. Her bare toes tried to curl into the floor. His gaze found them, then traveled up her ankles, lingered on legs exposed by the robe, took their time passing by the gap left by the loosely knotted tie, before returning to study her face.

Her eyes felt wide and dry. She sent a blinking order to her lids and they slid down, but took their time, reluctant to lose sight of him. Just that respite helped her bring a few more brain cells back into play. *She had a libido.* Later she'd have to figure out if that was good or bad. For now, she flipped open the file with one hand and pretended to study it while she ordered her heart to slow down.

There was no noticeable sign of obedience.

"How are you feeling?" That was kind of a doctor question. She felt almost stupid. It was new, so she couldn't be sure. She didn't mind. She liked new experiences.

"I am alive."

Her mouth curved up in a not-doctor way. "Being dead *would* bite."

Okay, that was *so* not doctor speak. For a minute her mind floundered, looking for something that *was* doctor-like. She freed her hand from his grasp and it crept up toward her hair, encountered her stethoscope. She grabbed it like the lifeline it was.

"Mind if I take a listen?"

He did this sweeping gesture with his hands, the graceful movement giving her unspoken permission. The discreet flare of heat in his blue eyes didn't help her sensory overload.

Doc eased back his gown and leaned in to listen. The scent of him filled her nostrils, making *her* heart go so crazy she couldn't hear his heartbeat. Or his breathing. Moving the scope didn't help. Even with bruises and contusions, his chest was impressive. Smooth taut skin, lightly dusted with blond hair, lay over muscles that weren't just for show. Proximity boosted his personal power factor to the *nth* degree. She slid the scope to a new location. This forced her hand to trail across hair-roughened skin in a way that sent lovely, hot sparks along her nerve endings. It took all her self-control not to bring her other hand into play. She wanted to explore the planes and angles more than she wanted to breathe. She was used to being at war with herself, but not in this battle.

It helped that she still held his medical file. Surprised her, too. Strength seemed to have faded from all her muscles. She chanted *patient* about twenty times and managed to put some distance between herself and his chest. Her body protested at the cellular level.

"You aren't going to do that to my back?"

There was an impish light in his eyes that indicated that he knew she wasn't indifferent, but then neither was he. Heat lurked behind his humor. To act as a distraction, she flipped open his file and looked down. The words danced and blurred on the page.

"Doc?"

The voice jerked her attention toward the open door. It took Doc a minute to recognize the young corporal who'd held the flashlight while she disarmed the bomb. She wrapped the tattered edges of doctor—and her dignity—around her. With lifted chin, she managed a cool, "Yes?"

He held up a cup of coffee. "The lieutenant asked me to give you this."

"Thank you, Corporal."

"She also wanted the card key for your quarters?" His gaze tracked down her body, then hastily returned to her face. "Something about your laundry?"

Doc patted her pockets and produced the card, exchanging it for the cup of coffee.

"Thank you," she said again, her tone a bit more professional. He left and she had to face *him* again. And somehow she had to keep her composure. She gave herself a mini-lecture, at the speed of an auctioneer, set the cup on the tray by his bed and turned back to her patient. To her surprise, she didn't melt on the spot. Maybe she needed repeated exposure to build up immunity. Or maybe her body was taking a time-out to regroup.

He wore a frown, but it didn't mar his face. Maybe nothing could.

"Why did he call you *Doc*?" He looked and sounded annoyed.

"I'm a doctor." Had she ever stated the obvious quite so obviously? "But it's also because of my initials. Delilah Oliver Clementyne. I've been called Doc since I was born." Since before she was born, in point of fact.

Except for Stan. He'd called her Ollie because he was Stan. It wasn't that funny, but neither was Stan. Her mum had always planned to call her Doc. Both her parents had held multiple doctorates. It wasn't unreasonable to expect their daughter to be a doctor of something. Her Mum liked to plan ahead, though nothing had worked out the way she'd expected.

Unbidden, unwanted, came the memory of her brother. He'd sometimes called her Del until he stopped calling her anything. But even he'd called her Doc most of the time. Robert had been "the Professor," even without initials. Until *they* took him. Then he became Robert again.

"Your names are very different from ours," her patient said, breaking into her thoughts.

Doc was happy for the distraction. Thinking about Robert made *them* close in on her, as if they sensed a sudden vulnerability.

"My mum wanted to name me for both my grandfathers, but Stan insisted on Delilah." She didn't know why. No Delilah's in the family tree. Hard to see him as someone nursing a flame for a long lost love, but he must have been young once. "My mum was kind of anti-gender."

Her patient's eyes widened. "How is that possible?"

Doc shrugged, her eyes scanning the file for *his* name. He

probably thought she knew it, which she should, since it was in the file—

Her thoughts fragmented. She took an involuntary step back.

"You're…the Leader. Of the Gadi." *And the freaking galaxy.*

Not to mention very, very married. Certainly the most married man *she* knew—as if *they* weren't a good enough reason to keep her distance and her wits about her. She took another step back, her doctor façade snapping back into place with an audible, embarrassed click.

"You didn't know."

It wasn't a question, so she didn't answer him. It was hard enough to marshal her scattered thoughts, not to mention trying to find her dignity—which might be hiding under his bed. Color scorched her face. It had to be a blush. Had she ever blushed before? She couldn't remember.

"This troubles you."

"No." *Yes.* Now that her libido wasn't clouding her thinking, she matched his personal power with his role. How had she missed it? She never missed anything. This was a man, not just used to command, but comfortable with it. She'd read the material from first contact, when he'd acted like a shallow goofball. Looking at him now, it was hard to believe he'd gotten away with it. It was a pointed reminder for her not to underestimate him, too. He had also run a ruthless insurgency using a second, secret identity, too much like *The Scarlet Pimpernel.* If he'd had access to the book, which he hadn't, she'd have accused him of plagiarism.

"I am just a man, Delilah," he said, as if he heard the lie in her voice. His chin lifted arrogantly. "You may call me Hel."

He said it like he was conferring a favor, which maybe he was. She hadn't been briefed on Gadi protocol. The Ambassador probably thought she already knew because of her diplomatic ID.

"No." She needed the distance of formality, the reminder. "Sir."

His brows contracted. "It is what I wish."

His tone was imperious. Doc found that stiffened her resolve more than his marital status. She knew how to shift his focus off her.

"There are people anxious to speak to you, when you're up to it."

"People?"

He said the word lightly, but Doc had a feeling he was homing in on the area of her unease. She didn't want him to. He might think she was jealous.

"The people you work with, I assume. And the drama queens." Okay, hadn't meant to say that out loud. Nor had she meant to sound so caustic.

His brows shot up. "Drama queens?"

"Your…wives." Doc couldn't bring herself to use the word "mates" to describe the drama queens. "They seem to think you'll die without their presence at your side. Only there's not room for them in here."

She took the excuse to look away from him, feeling red sting her cheeks again. A pity the room wasn't big enough to provide long-term distraction. In the end, she had to swing her gaze back his way.

He appeared pleased, amused and a tad guilty.

"I suppose that now I must confess I have been guilty of teasing your general."

Before she realized it, she'd taken one step toward him. "Teasing?"

"The drama queens, as you say, are not my bond mates."

"But you said…"

"…that I had many *mates*. But they are not *bond* mates. A bond mate is closer to your concept of wife. Mates are not."

So what were mates, she wondered. Concubines? Mistresses? And just how close was a bond mate to a wife? She was glad that this time she didn't voice the question.

"Your people have offered many criticisms on how we treat our women, their lack of equality," his voice chilled. "These women, the drama queens, are mated to the *position* of leader. It allows them to retain their status in our society, even if their mate dies. It protects them from a loss of home and support. My *bond* mate no longer lives. She died some time ago, not long after the birth of our last child."

"I'm sorry." Why didn't they know this? What was happening in the diplomatic corp that they didn't know this?

"As am I. She was a good mate, a good mother to our children." His heavy lids lifted, pinning her with their intensity. "I am not saying that physical bonding is unknown among a leader and the women who chose to be mated to the position, but it is not *my* way. My people also have a system of political bonding, to cement alliances, but again, physical bonding is optional—and must be mutual. Unlike the Dusan, we don't force ourselves on women. Ever."

Though he didn't quibble at kidnapping, she recalled.

"And you didn't mention this to General Halliwell because…"

"He did not ask."

The sternness of his expression reminded her that she stood in the presence of a very powerful man. And then he smiled, bringing back the charm. He was as good at hiding who he was as she was. Was that the source of his attraction for her, that combination of lethal and charming? That he was gorgeous didn't hurt, she conceded.

"And I will confess to not helping matters." A flicker of mischief further softened the sternness of his face. "He gets so beautifully angry."

And the Gadi did like beautiful. Doc found herself smiling back, again without a conscious decision to do so.

"Well, we can be a bit self-righteous." Her smile widened, even as the last sensible piece of her brain was pointing out that she still needed training wheels in the arena of guys and girls and hearts. For a bright girl, she was being pretty dim.

"May I ask you a question?"

"Of course." She didn't have to answer it.

"Your voice is differently inflected than others of your people. I wondered why?"

Not what she'd expected, but a question she could answer. "That's because my mum was British. I guess I caught a hint of her accent." It was the only thing British about her, since she'd been raised in the U.S.

He smiled, taking his time. It slid through her like warm honey.

"I like it." He paused. "I haven't thanked you for saving my life."

She blinked. "I didn't triage you."

"But you defused the explosive device."

"Oh." He shouldn't have seen her do that. "You're welcome."

His smile deepened, bumping up the sexy vibe some more. She should be pondering it, analyzing it, defusing its power, not enjoying it. Her body was mush, while her mind was aware of everything, right down to the microscopic level. It wasn't that her mind was blank. It was full to the brim with *him*. She looked at him. He looked at her. And the air around them crackled and popped, like water dancing on a hot plate.

"You are an extraordinary people."

Doc frowned. "How so?" Hadn't he just called them narrow-minded and judgmental?

"You have the ability to be a healer, and you defused the explosive device. And you joke while you're doing it. I assume the reference to the inn was a joke? And when you said you had not defused a bomb before, that was humor, as well, was it not?"

Doc preferred to dodge the questions she couldn't answer. A pity her lust-fogged brain wasn't producing an acceptable dodge. Or even a lame dodge. His face was mobile, expressive and yet very controlled, very focused. On her. She opened her mouth, but before words could emerge, there was a welcome interruption.

"Ma'am?"

Lieutenant Simmons stood in the open doorway, her presence spreading a calm balm into the room that soothed Doc's ruffled senses. Hel's eyes told her he knew she'd been saved by the nurse, but she'd deal with that later. After she'd had some rest.

"Yes?"

"The general would like to see you."

Okay, as rescues went, this wasn't Simmons best.

☼

Doc didn't expect to enjoy her first meeting with General Halliwell, but she had expected to survive it. Judging by the look on his face when she entered his hospital room, she'd set her expectations too high. Good thing Simmons had found her some scrubs to wear or who knew what the general would have done.

Did he know who she was? The Major wasn't above sending her places without anyone needing to know. He didn't even tell her what she needed to know until he had to.

The *Doolittle* wasn't as cut off from Earth this deployment. The expedition had positioned a series of relay satellites, with boosted transmit capabilities, along their course to this galaxy. The Major had managed to piggyback a coded, secure packet for her on the last transmission, so she knew more than she'd known five minutes ago, but it still wasn't much. The packet was sparse on detail, even for the Major. It did hint her objective had something to do with the Kikk Outpost. This wasn't a total shock. It was the only ground the expedition held in the galaxy. The thought of spending time there made her jaded senses tingle with anticipation—and anxiety. Despite the plethora of weapons, it was still a geek's playground. While Doc had serious geek credentials, she didn't play in the traditional geek end of the pool. Actually, she didn't play period. The Major tended to deploy her in places geeks feared to go and shooting was expected. Neither criterion appeared to apply to the Outpost.

With more questions than answers, now wasn't the time to think about that. She needed every brain cell she had for this interview. Since she had a lot of them, she should have been good, only she was still off balance from her meeting with Hel and lack of sleep. She assumed a military stance, because she was military, with or without a uniform. She added a touch of humility. It might not help, but it couldn't hurt.

Or it could. His basilisk stare should have burned her to a black crisp. It seems she'd donned her asbestos drawers this morning.

"What the *hell* were you thinking?"

She blinked. "That if I didn't disarm it more people would die?" She kept her tone mild and bumped up the humility factor some more. She liked exercises in futility.

"What are you talking about?"

"The bomb?" What was he talking about?

"Why would I be upset about that?"

Doc could think of several reasons, but if he wasn't upset about it, why provide more ammo for his outrage?

"Isn't that what you do?" the general snapped.

He thought she disarmed bombs? He must know some unusual UN doctors. Unless he knew who she was. And even if he did, the answer would still be, no, she didn't disarm bombs.

The Major, who'd taken her unique skill set and focused it for his use, called her a troubleshooter, because it didn't limit what he could have her do. None of which gave her a clue about why the general was pissed, no, make that apoplectic. It wouldn't take that much to bring on a full-fledged heart attack. On the upside, he was in the right place if he had one.

"I'm talking about you and the Gadi Leader."

Doc blinked again. She flipped through several responses and settled on, "He needed a doctor, sir."

"I'm talking about the reception. You aren't here to get googly-eyed over a man, particularly *that* one."

Color surged into her cheeks, but she managed to keep her mouth shut. Did she want to admit she'd never felt like this? Not bloody likely. And had the tough-minded general just said googly-eyed?

That thought must have hit him at the same time. Color washed into his face, well, more color. The anger hadn't subsided yet.

And his comments still didn't answer the basic question of what he knew about her. Was he pissed at her as a member of the expedition or because he knew she was the *Chameleon*?

"The Leader's reputation with women is," he paused, "unfortunate."

If she were forced to describe the Leader, unfortunate wouldn't make her list, but she knew better than to tell him that. Her lack of response didn't help his temper. The dressing down was thorough and unabridged. Doc bore it stoically. It wasn't the first time someone had ripped her a new one, and it wouldn't be the last. Though being ripped for getting "googly-eyed" was a first.

When he ran out of words—or steam—she ventured a comment.

"You're doing well, sir. Your vitals look good." Her gaze intercepted the heart monitor. "Well, they did."

His color faded to normal as he stared at her. She almost thought his mouth twitched. She'd heard he had a sense of humor, but there'd been no evidence of it until now. If that was evidence.

He needed to know what had happened after the bomb, but his gaze didn't invite confidences. She studied him from behind her harmless and misunderstood doctor face while she considered her options. His gaze narrowed. He wasn't buying it, she realized. That was interesting. On the heels of that came another realization. Whether he knew who she was or not, she needed him to know who she was, if only because she was in another freaking galaxy. What limited support she got from the Major wasn't available here.

"You have something you want to tell me, Doctor?"

Okay, that was kind of an invitation, though his tone could use some work. Nor did it answer the basic question: did he know the Chameleon was on board his ship? And if he didn't know, what would he do when he found out?

Doc tended to dive into the pool, but this time she tested the water with a toe first. "You and the Leader were the primary targets of the bombing, sir."

He didn't blink. "And you know this how?"

"Four men arrived before the rescue teams. They split up and went hunting. I followed one team to you."

He frowned, his gaze turning inward. His focus turned out again. "You dropped them?"

The bullet holes *were* a giveaway during the autopsy.

"I dropped two of them. Someone else took out the other two." Hel? She didn't say his name out loud. She never waved red flags at bulls if she didn't need to.

A slight widening around the eyes was his only reaction. "Who the hell are you?"

She let her aspect shift. "The Major calls me Chameleon."

He still didn't blink. Doc was impressed. He didn't look surprised either, which was interesting. That seemed to indicate he'd known the Chameleon was on board or he bluffed well.

"I thought your kind never broke cover."

His tone told her he wasn't a fan, but was his ire directed at the Major, the Chameleon or "her kind" in general?

"The Major allows me some latitude when I'm in the field." Though calling another galaxy "the field" felt wrong on several levels.

His stare busted her to her core—something that hadn't happened in a very long time.

"I wish you hadn't met the Gadi Leader."

Doc was glad he didn't appear to require a response to this wish. She was unable to agree with him, and it wouldn't be smart to point out it was his fault she had met the Leader. She tried not to do "not smart" and when she had to, only did it as an operational necessity.

"I want you to keep your distance, without looking like you're keeping your distance."

Yeah, that would work. Doc studied the general for a minute. "If I start staying away now, he'll wonder why." She frowned, considering what she'd learned about the Leader. "He'd expect everyone at the reception to be hand-picked by you, to have a specific reason for being there."

"But I didn't know who you were—"

"*We* know that, but he doesn't. He probably thinks you meant him to meet me. That you had a plan, a master plan." Doc felt a bit evil about winding him up like this. Of course, just because it was evil, didn't make her wrong. And he had ripped her a new one. Payback, even for generals, was a bitch.

"So if you don't avoid him, he'll be focused on why I wanted you to meet." The general's gaze was reflective now. "Is this what you do for the Major?"

Doc wasn't sure how to answer that. There was a hint of irony in his eyes that told her he sensed more than he was saying. He wasn't stupid, even if the reception hadn't been his brightest moment, and she'd be wise not to forget it.

"I do what's required to meet my mission objectives, sir."

"And have you ever failed to meet an objective?"

Doc might be a scientist, but she still had a streak of superstition running through her. She didn't like tempting fate, even when it was the truth.

"No." She made a face. "Not yet."

"You weren't much of a chameleon at the reception."

Doc's chin lifted. "Camo was not *my* choice, and I was off duty."

He gave a sharp nod that could have meant anything.

"If that's what you can do off duty, I can't wait to see what you do when you are."

Doc thought she heard fate cackling in the distance. What if the impossible *was* impossible this time?

Four

It pleased Hel that Delilah was his primary healer, though he was surprised that the General had allowed them to meet. Halliwell believed, perhaps with cause, that Hel had a weakness for Earth women. So why trail this one in front of him?

Apart from her appearance, there were other things intriguing about Delilah. The healer was very different in her—he searched for the right word and finally settled for—aspect from how she'd appeared at the reception. Women could be dangerous in a variety of ways, but Delilah had exuded a *physical* threat at the reception just before the explosion. Her aspect was harder to quantify when she'd been pacing, but it had shifted to sultry seductress when Naman approached. He'd felt the façade of each aspect. Why did he know this? How did he know this? He had seen her adapt decisively to each change in circumstances, but before this he'd felt he *knew* her.

The charm and her sense of humor were a nice bonus, something he'd never required from a female before. He hoped time would provide clarity—and if the general was throwing the dangerous Delilah at him, well, Hel didn't mind. Safety was overrated.

The uneasy peace had been difficult for him in the last two years and now he was tied to a bed with a government to run. A woman would be a pleasant distraction, though that was all she could be. They were galaxies apart in too many ways. His enemies had tried to use women to take him down in the past. Of course they had failed. His ability to use, without being used, might explain the more pragmatic approach of the bomb. Hel hoped his continued survival would be a lesson to all his enemies.

The distracting woman in question chose that moment to enter his room, and he felt an unfamiliar shock of sexual awareness blast through him with a fierceness that surprised him. If she were the general's weapon of choice, the general had shown unexpected cunning. Unless someone else was playing a game with him? The general had been injured, almost killed in the blast, too. He needed to think about this further, but not around the very perceptive Delilah. Her eyes saw too much.

"How are you feeling this morning?" Her voice was brisk, very healer this new ship day aboard the *Doolittle*, but her eyes had turned purple, a phenomenon that appeared to be reserved for him.

He smiled at her and the color got richer. An answering smile curled her mouth. He was going to have to kiss her soon.

"I am tired of this bed." Unless she consented to share it.

Today she was back in camo, but this version, he had learned, were called scrubs for a reason clear only to them. The fabric appeared softer and moved when she did, making it somewhat more pleasing than what she'd worn to the reception. Her feet were covered. A pity. The memory of her narrow, elegant feet, the nails a shimmering pink, made his body heat.

"There's no reason you can't get up. In fact, we're going to have you take a couple of short walks, one this morning and another after lunch. If it goes well, you can stroll as much as you feel like within the infirmary area."

She didn't say it, but they both knew it was a security issue. His people would not be pleased their Leader was on the Earth ship. If he remained cut off…

"Also, the General has made arrangements for some of your people to come aboard, once they've cleared security."

"That's very helpful." And most unlike the good General. Hel wasn't sure he wanted the accommodation until he'd isolated and eliminated the threat to his life. His well-honed instincts told him there was a link between whoever was after him among the Gadi and someone in this expedition. The General would top the list of suspects if he hadn't been wounded in the explosion—though it didn't totally clear him in Hel's mind. With some reluctance he had to include Delilah on his list of suspects, despite the bomb she'd defused. It would not be the first time someone saved his life to gain his trust. He would have preferred communication by radio, but his people would be concerned he was being coerced. If the Council believed the Leader was being controlled, they'd move to replace him.

"You are a head of state. There are diplomatic protocols already worked out. Just a matter of implementing them."

Her tone was pragmatic, but her eyes weren't. The purple would start to fade, their gazes would meet and it flared again. The effect, against her matte white skin, would have made his head spin if he were the kind of man to let a woman make his head spin. It was something of a relief when she glanced down at the tablet she'd brought in with her.

"And your children want to see you. Arrangements are being worked out. They should be here in time for your first stroll."

Hel frowned. His children? Did they want to see him? They didn't act like they did.

As if she sensed his unease, she added, "Your mother says they're upset. That they needed to see you were all right for themselves." She hesitated, then added without looking at him, "It's probably a natural reaction, considering they've already lost their mother."

"Is my mother coming with them?" Hel tried not to flinch at the thought of his mother visiting here. There were so many things about this ship she would dislike. And she would blame him for the bombing, or worse, she might think his condition would make him more open to taking a new bond mate. It seemed everyone around him had a woman for him. A pity that, since the death of his mate, he'd seen only two women he wanted. Was it coincidence they were both from Earth?

"She didn't want to try out the transport system. Sorry." Amusement tugged at the edges of her mouth. "My mum was a bit intimidating, too."

Rather than address the issue of intimidation, which he most certainly was not, Hel made a conversational side step. "Your mother is no longer living?"

Her eyes turned dark blue, as if a cloud had darkened her horizon. "She died when I was fourteen. Stan died a few months later."

"Stan?"

"My dad."

Hel frowned. "You called your father Stan?"

"And he called me Ollie." Her face softened, memory chasing away the shadow. "It's a bad Earth joke about some comedians. And it made him feel old to be called dad. He was quite a bit older than my mum and it bothered him. If I didn't call him dad, he could pretend I was one of his students."

"He was a teacher?" Hel was fascinated by this look inside her head. He had a feeling it was not typical for her to share this much of her past, or herself.

"They both were. They taught at university—that's an advanced kind of school—and they wanted me and my brother to follow in their footsteps and become teachers."

The shadows returned to her eyes when she mentioned her brother.

"But you didn't. You are here. Did your brother become a teacher?" He thought she'd ignore the question when she hesitated.

"My brother," another pause, "became ill, but I think he would have. He liked academia more than I did."

"I am sorry." There was more to it, but he didn't press. His curiosity was no match for the brief flare of pain in her eyes.

"Thank you." Her smile was tinged with sadness, but she was less healer, more real Delilah. She gave a tiny shake and held up her stethoscope. "We've strayed from the reason I'm here."

The purple returned to her eyes, as she positioned the stethoscope on his chest and took a listen. Her voice was light, professional as she discussed his progress, but the pulse at her neck belied her outward mien. They were both waiting. They both knew it.

"I would like to show you my home," he said, surprising himself as much as he did Delilah. Now was not a good time for a visit, as he had good cause to know.

She looked up from her notes. "That would be," she swallowed, "nice."

She dragged out the word, as is she also knew it would never happen. It stirred a desire to push the issue and after a very brief struggle, he gave into it.

"Then you will come."

"No, but thank you for the invitation."

The General would fight a visit, but Rockley would jump at the chance to get someone back on the planet.

"I will arrange it."

"You're very confident." She sounded more amused than annoyed.

"I am the Leader. If I wish it, it will happen."

She chuckled.

"What?" Had a woman ever laughed at him?

"I've just never met anyone quite like you before."

"And you never will." He spread his hands and shrugged. "I am unique."

"I won't argue with you about that."

"It would be wise not to argue with me about anything." It was a serious truth, but he kept his tone light and teasing. It wouldn't do to spook her.

His gaze caught hers, and he could see the purple building in their depths again. Perhaps he couldn't wait. But the move to reach out for her was halted before it began.

Simmons arrived. Her timing was impeccable—and annoying.

☼

Saved by the nurse again. Did Simmons have built-in radar for when Doc was getting in over her head? Doc headed for her temporary office and sank down in the desk chair, her hands on her cheeks. That had not gone as planned. It hadn't even gone as expected. She'd never told anyone about her family. Even the Major only knew the basic facts of their lives and deaths. He knew about her brother. It was a matter of record. He didn't know Doc fought the same demons that had put Robert in a mental institution. If he knew—

Don't let them get you, Del.

She could see his face the first time he said that to her. He was five years older and seemed fifty feet taller in her memory. He'd crouched to bring their faces level, horror in his eyes. Even at nine, Doc didn't have to ask what he meant. She knew. She'd always known. The thing she didn't know was why *they* hadn't got her, too. Robert was older and stronger, but *they'd* taken him down like he was a straw man.

She shivered, but not with cold. Thinking about *them* brought them in close. She shifted, needing something to do, something easy, something that required her to focus, something that would distract her from the racket inside her head, help her figure out how to get answers to questions spinning inside her head.

Her gaze glanced off her Wii remote. Of course. A few games of *Mario Kart* were just what the doctor ordered, well, this doctor ordered. She booted up the game, picked her character and kart, then started a Grand Prix, losing herself in its whacky reality. *They* and the din faded into the distance as she battled her way through the various maps to victory. And while she played, other parts of her brain sifted through streams of data, analyzing and assessing, looking for patterns.

Hel had been interesting. Lots of beneath-the-surface patterns to analyze, along with her own reactions to him. The banter had appeared light, but she sensed deeper currents there. She'd suspect he'd somehow picked up on her hidden reason for being in the galaxy, her new duty, but she didn't know what it was, so there was nothing for anyone to pick up on. Her orders had referred her to the General and *his* sealed orders. Whatever her new objective, she couldn't do it from here, but she couldn't think of a good reason to be sent to Kikk.

Not knowing her mission wasn't a huge problem, because knowing what she needed to do and not being able to do it made her antsy, something that always gave *them* an in. There were plenty of non-mission related things to think about. Her brain loved patterns and it had found plenty to play with here. It was always interesting what brought *them* in close and what pushed them back. If she could find a pattern in that, she might finally defeat them, like she'd just done to her Grand Prix opponents.

"Yes!" She jumped up and did a victory dance that turned her toward the door.

And the two small people watching her.

No, not people, *children*. She didn't do children. Their eyes were too intense, too unsettling; they saw too much. She'd faced down men twice her size and felt less nervous.

She cleared her throat. "Hello." Okay, quit sounding scared. Children can sense fear. She'd heard that somewhere, hadn't she? Or was that animals? "I mean, hi."

"What is that?" the older one asked.

Even if she hadn't known who they were through a process of elimination, his tone would have marked him as Hel's son. He had the "I am leader of the galaxy" intonation down perfectly.

"It's a game."

They both stepped deeper into the room, their gazes fixed on the screen. It was a relief to have their attention off her, but it didn't relieve her anxiety. Despite her unease, she recognized the opportunity the boys presented. She'd collected information from a variety of informants, had manipulated them without blinking, but these were *children*. Children could smell manipulation and knew how to instinctively block information-gathering attempts from people they *liked*. With strangers, kids were ruthless. Even though technically she'd never been a kid, she knew this.

Still, they did seem fascinated with *Mario Kart*. It seemed it had intergalactic kid appeal. She'd been using it to get inside her own head, so why couldn't it help her get inside theirs? She bit her lip, hesitated for a long moment, then asked a question she'd never, *ever* asked a child.

"Would you like to play with me?"

Doc may have had a grown-up reason for the question, but she'd never felt this young as she waited for their answer.

☼

Hel didn't know what was the most startling, that he'd managed to lose his children, that his children had managed to find their way to Delilah, or the extraordinary thing the three of them were doing.

They sat on top of a desk staring with fierce concentration at a screen of some kind. What was on that screen was so far outside his realm of experience he didn't know how to describe it to himself, let alone to anyone else. Tiny, bizarre creatures riding on or in wheeled devices appeared to be racing around a course that went in and out of peculiar structures.

Relsten held a strange white device in his small hands, and Hel could tell by his actions that he controlled the movements of one the creatures in a box at the top of the screen. Lorin sat between Delilah's legs and her arms circled him loosely. Lorin held a similar white device and controlled the creature in the bottom square, with assistance, it seemed, from Delilah.

"That's good, really good, Lorin. Hold your red shell…hold it…fire!" One of the wheeled vehicles spun in a circle and a puff of smoke rose above it. "Direct hit!"

Lorin shouted his delight. One of the small wheeled things crossed a line, and Relsten whooped in a way Hel hadn't heard since the boys' mother died.

"I won, Doc! Did you see that?"

"Way to go, Relsten! Come on, Lorin, let's take second for the red team. That's it, that's it. Yes!"

"First and second. You guys rock!" She held up her fist and

bumped it first against Relsten's small fist, then against Lorin's smaller fist. "Now we do the victory dance."

All three of them jumped up and did a bizarre dance without music that involved hips shaking and fingers pointing up at the ceiling, then at the ground. Delilah didn't see him until she'd done a full circle of her victory dance.

"Oh." She stopped, color surging into her pale face. She tried to look sober, but the color in her face and the glow of her eyes gave her away.

His sons saw him, squealed in ways most unlike their usual greeting and hurled themselves at him. With a son wrapped around both legs, they both talked at once about winning and these shell things that exploded and banana peels. He should scold them for wandering away, but they were happier than he'd seen them in a long time. He would, he realized, have been disappointed if they hadn't wandered off. He'd wandered off all the time as a boy. It was what boys did.

"That's," he had to swallow back something in his throat, "that's very pleasing, my sons." Two small fists were presented. Delilah mimed bumping for him. It felt awkward, but his sons looked pleased. Lorin wanted him to victory dance with them.

"I was not a partner in the victory," he pointed out. "I have not earned a victory dance." Thanks be to the gods for that.

"We can show you how to win, too, Father," Relsten told him, his tone sympathetic and just a bit patronizing. Hel saw Delilah bite her lip to keep back a smile.

"They are very like you."

Unsure if he were being complimented or teased, Hel looked at the screen and the bizarre creatures pictured on it and felt a fear he hadn't felt—he tried to find a comparable moment and failed. He sent a look that might have been of entreaty to Delilah. Her gaze was kind, but her lips twitched.

"So, I'm guessing you don't have anything like this on your planet?"

"No." Hel knew he sounded forceful. He felt forceful. They

had nothing like this in their galaxy, thank goodness. "What is the point of it?"

"It's a game. Surely your children play games?"

"Of course they play games."

"Nothing this fun, Father!" Lorin looked delighted.

Delilah looked guilty. "It's the novelty factor. Our children would probably think your games are awesome."

"It's awesome, Father." Their voices joined together to explain the complexities of the game. Their delight in mayhem shocked him—until he remembered how bloodthirsty he'd been at that age. It hadn't been that long. Perhaps he was still feeling the effects of the blast. He felt a bit dizzy.

"That one looks quite pleasant," he added, as a ribbon of many colors popped up.

"It's brutal," Lorin said.

Hel didn't know he knew that word.

"It is a bit dark," Delilah admitted, "but in a really cool way."

"Cool," Relsten echoed her and Lorin echoed him.

Hel could see them filing the word away for future use. This enlargement in their vocabulary was sure to displease his mother. He smiled at the thought.

"Can we stay and play, Father?"

Lorin raised a face filled with entreaty. Relsten's matched it. What surprised him was that Delilah had the same look of anxious hope on her face.

"Doc says we may go to *Mario's Party.*"

His sons called her Doc. He should say something, but what? His brow arched. "A party?"

"It's a different game," Delilah explained. "I've never had anyone to play it with. I'd love it if they could stay."

"Your work—"

She looked at her watch. "I'm off for a few more hours."

This was a new aspect of her personality and one that shaved off years. She looked...lighter, as if she'd shrugged off a weight of some kind.

"You could play, too, Father," Nelsten said. "Doc has four controllers."

Why had none of her friends played with her? He almost asked, but he recalled the malicious tone to the voice that had called her "Morticia." A nickname, she'd explained, but not an affectionate one, he now concluded. She lived on a ship teeming with people, but she seemed as isolated as he was as Leader. Again there was that moment of clarity, of knowing her and who she was at her very core, of feeling connected in a way that had never happened before.

"It's very kind of you to play with my sons," he said. Before he'd finished the sentence his sons were doing the victory dance again. They lacked Delilah's sensual fluidity, but made up for that in enthusiasm. She didn't look dangerous, not like she'd looked at the party, but Hel knew it was misleading. She was still dangerous, just not in the way he'd expected when he saw her across the crowded reception hall.

She had to know who he was, what he'd done two years ago, had to know why the General disliked him so fiercely, but when he looked at her he felt no judgment. Even from his mate, from his children's mother he hadn't felt this level of acceptance—an acceptance that seemed to be without condition.

It was as intriguing as her pink mouth and passion purple eyes.

Looking at her, he knew something else. Whatever reason brought her to the reception, it was not by the General's design. There were many things that puzzled him about these people, but this he felt in his core.

Delilah was the last woman on this ship the General would want him to meet.

☼

Doc was as sorry to see Relsten and Lorin leave as they were to go. Her office felt empty without the two boys, but their departure left some stuff for her brain to chew on. That made her brain happy. She'd been careful how she pumped them for information, not liking herself very much as she did it. They'd liked her, accepted her in ways that she'd never experienced. If she could have found another way—but there wasn't or she'd have already found it.

Hel would talk to his sons and find out what she'd done. He wouldn't be surprised, but would he understand? He was at least as ruthless as she was, but she'd used his boys, traded Earth slang for Gadi words. He might not forgive that. If she had children—which she never would—how would she feel about what she'd done? She hadn't hurt them, but she had picked their brains, used their innocence against them.

She could wrap it up in all sorts of comforting rationalizations, but it still smelled. She'd never cared what anyone thought about her, well, except for her brother and her microscopic—and somewhat recently acquired—circle of friends. She'd loved her parents, but detachment pretty much defined their relationship. It didn't help that they had no clue what forces they'd unleashed on their children with their desire to pass on their IQs and DNA. She'd learned early not to care what they thought, aware that most of their thoughts weren't about her anyway. Robert had dominated the landscape of all their lives, even after his fall. By the time they realized they had another child, it was too late for them to be anything but acquaintances.

Hel seemed awkward with his boys, but there was love and caring bubbling below the surface. They must look like their mother. She'd have been beautiful. He missed her. Doc heard it in his voice when he talked about her, felt him missing her in the subtext of his words. A strange sensation tightened her chest. She had no experience, no parallel in her past to identify the feeling. She rubbed the spot, which didn't help, and focused on the inputting what she'd learned from the boys.

After a time, as she ran the translation program she'd created, the tightness lessened, though it failed to disappear. The Gadi patients had talked freely, confident that none of the expedition spoke the language. There was a saying that eavesdroppers never heard good about themselves. What they were saying pretty much proved the saying. Kind of crappy of them, considering they were getting free medical care aboard the *Doolittle.*

This research was not part of her mission objective, but if they lost the outpost before she got there, her mission objective became moot. She frowned as her mission brief bubbled back to the top of her thoughts. Doc was a scientist, but her skill set was both broad and narrow. Usually her missions involved science *and* guys with guns. She went places where geeks were required but feared to go. Her mission on the *Nimitz* had fit her deployment criteria. The expedition still controlled the outpost, so she shouldn't have to shoot her way to whatever it was the Major wanted her to do in this galaxy unless they lost the outpost.

That *might* explain her presence, if the head of the expedition, General Halliwell *knew* they might lose the outpost, but she'd found no sign anyone knew their control was at risk when she browsed through the *Doolittle*'s computers. She didn't know what was in the General's head, but would he have gone to a party if war were about to break out? Would he have entered Gadi space? The Gadi had more ships in the galaxy and even with hyperdrive capability they were too far from Kikk and the only other Earth ship in many millions of light years.

If the Gadi launched an attack to take back the outpost, they'd take it. Even with help from the outpost defenses, the expedition would be forced to withdraw from the galaxy or be destroyed. Doc was surprised the Gadi hadn't already taken it back. Hel hadn't indicated this level of patience in his past dealings with the expedition. Doc could think of one reason for it—the Key.

Doc probably knew more about the Key than anyone *but* the Key, so it was a shock to realize the official record listed the Key as a *device.* Only one person could have buried the information that deep, which made the upright General Halliwell at least as devious as the Major and brought her back to her question: How could the General not know how close they were to war with the Gadi?

She wasn't here to advise him, but he needed to know. And he needed to find out who *wasn't* telling him what he needed to know.

But would he believe *her*?

☼

Doc finished her shift without finding an opportunity to talk to the General, at least not one that wouldn't draw unwelcome attention to the meeting. So far she'd managed to stay under the radar of whoever was gooning up the process, and she intended to stay there until it was time to act. On the upside, she'd found something to do while she waited to find out more about her mission on Kikk. If she could serve up the traitors, it might help her mitigate the downside of spilling what she'd learned to the General. The General wasn't going to like what she had to say. The war would probably happen whether he believed her or not, but if she could delay the inevitable, she might have a shot at completing her mission.

This wasn't about Hel and his odd effect on her. With or without a war, she wouldn't be paying a house call. She didn't plan on doing—she couldn't do whatever it was he wanted to do. If he wanted to do something. Which he probably didn't. If part of her wished he did want to do something, then it should stop it. It couldn't happen. This wasn't just a different way to say potato. They were from different freaking galaxies. And that was before she added in all of her baggage and his.

She should get some shut-eye, but she couldn't sleep. Too much noise inside her head, too much data to sort through. Her thoughts were chaotic, her worries too pointed, and *they* were too close for sleep. She needed movement. She needed focus. The right words were there. She just hadn't thought of them yet. She pushed her primary problem to the back burner. Her mind knew it, hated it, and would work furiously on the problem in the background, eventually assembling the pieces she needed into the right configuration.

That left a lot of stuff for the front burner. If the prospect of war with the Gadi weren't huge, she'd have saved the back burner for Hel. What he did to her was unsettling in a way unprecedented in her experience. It was as if he had the pin number that brought down her defenses. He walked into a room and she turned, not just into a girl, but into a *real* girl. Doc had been many things in her life, but she'd never been that. Even as a child, she'd just been a short adult who calculated everything.

The curious part of her found it interesting in a disturbing way. How weird was it to have a piece of brain enjoying watching the rest of her squirm?

And most of her was dying to kiss him, seriously dying for it. It hadn't interfered with her concentration yet, because she was at her best when multi-tasking, but deep inside she wasn't sure she could keep all those balls in the air when one of them was obsessed with a kiss. And what would happen if she got what she wanted? That scared her as much as the thought of not getting it.

The only way she knew to deal with it all was to get active, wear her body down to the point where exhaustion took down her brain. She was reaching for her iPod when Briggs strolled in the ship's gym. He was a big man with an imperfectly squared face. His skin was reddened by his years in the sun and his hair had been cropped to the point of near invisibility. His gaze had a piercing quality that made her feel like he saw all her secrets. If he did, they hadn't scared him off.

The retired Sergeant Major was the closest thing Doc had to a friend on the *Doolittle*. Sara, Doc's only other friend in several galaxies, had introduced the pair not long before Doc had been deployed on the *Nimitz*. While the friendship with Briggs had been orchestrated by Sara, the friendship with Sara was accidental. Doc happened to be there when Sara went into labor. Doc had no experience with friends, so it took her a while to figure out what was happening. She wasn't an easy person to befriend, but Sara didn't know how to quit. Doc trusted her more than anyone and that included the Major. Not that she trusted the Major. That would be stupid.

The trust between her and Sara was mutual and a surprise. Doc was, she knew, one of a handful of people who knew Sara's story. And Sara, and her husband Fyn, were the only ones who knew Doc knew. Doc didn't know what Briggs knew about her or Sara. The truly weird part: she didn't mind.

"Haven't seen you for a few days," the laconic Briggs said, looking her over as if it had been longer than a few days.

Doc half expected him to tell her she looked like hell, but he didn't. He never did what she expected.

"I've been helping out in the infirmary." He probably knew that already. There wasn't much that went on that Briggs didn't know.

"Then you probably need a workout."

"I do," Doc agreed. She docked her iPod and selected "their" play list. Dancing with Briggs even made *them* tired. And it was fun, a benefit missing from most other aspects of her life.

☼

After a quick shower, Doc headed for her office to check her email. An update was due through the communication array. Maybe she'd received something more from the Major. By this time he'd know the *Doolittle* had detoured to the Gadi home world. Surely he'd have a comment on that. He had a comment on everything, even if it was just one word.

Doc opened her door, her hand going to the light switch, but before she could flip it, she sensed a presence. Doc froze, her whole body poised to spring, every cell abruptly, lethally online.

"I was hoping you'd come back before I had to leave," Hel said.

Her heart pounded with adrenaline that had no place to be expended. She'd have bet money that her workout with Briggs had left her with nothing but a butt load of tired. And she'd have lost.

"I'm sorry. I was working out." Her voice was thin with the strain of keeping herself in check.

"I startled you."

Startled? "A bit." She uncurled her fingers and flexed them. The fading adrenaline left a series of tremors in the wake of its retreat. She needed to do *something* or she'd explode. And then he was so close she could feel his body heat, could see the glint of his eyes in the dark.

"I am sorry."

Was he sorry? He didn't sound sorry. He sounded, well, not sorry. She wasn't sorry either. In the dark she wasn't Doc or Delilah or the Major's creature. She was a girl wanting to kiss a guy, if she could figure out how to make it happen. The Major hadn't covered kissing in her training. Doc didn't know if he sensed her thoughts or just heard her breathing pick up. Maybe he was just a guy doing what guys did with a girl. His hand, warm and strong and big, slid along the side of her neck, cupping her nape. This cause had the effect of tilting her head to the side just enough to be encouraging. That it was also the right angle for kissing was an added benefit and one he took advantage of, though he didn't rush it.

His lips brushed across one eyelid, then the other, found the tip of her nose and stroked across each cheek. Part of her wanted him to hurry, but most of her was lost in mind-reeling sensation. She thought she knew chemistry, understood biology, the mechanics of attraction, but this wasn't mechanical or scientific.

She didn't understand it, didn't want to study it. It was enough to *feel*.

His mouth finding hers was a shock and a shocking pleasure. No amount of study had prepared her for this, her first kiss. His mouth was warm, his lips firm and gentle, confident and inviting. There was taste *and* texture and magic. Lots and lots of magic for a girl who didn't believe in magic.

The smell of him so close made her head spin. She found his shoulders, gripped with her hands and that helped anchor her in a moment that felt a bit like slow dancing. His other hand found its way to her waist. They flowed together, as if to music, her hands sliding up his shoulders and into his hair, as his mouth stopped teasing and settled onto hers with confident authority.

So this was hugging.

So this was kissing.

She'd read the books, the poetry, seen and studied the science and none of it had prepared her for the reality of being held and wanted by a man. To feel safe and not safe, to feel powerful and out of control. A wonderful insanity that explained everything and nothing.

The hard wall of his chest, the feel of his arm holding her close, the grip of his hand at the back of her neck felt incredibly *right.* His mouth left hers and she almost moaned, but then his lips were against her throat. That was good, too.

"I knew you'd be good at this." She sighed and angled her head as his wonderful hands smoothed her hair back so that his mouth could slide across her neck.

"I am the best at everything I do," he assured her, his voice a husky growl.

Doc believed him and she believed in learning from the best—

The intercom on her desk buzzed, popping them apart almost a whole inch. The smell and taste of him still held her in thrall. She should do something, if only she knew what that was.

His blue eyes burned with desire, like high beams in the dark. Doc was a person who had to believe the impossible, in order to do it on a regular basis, but it was still hard to believe that look was for her.

The intercom buzzed again. Doc felt her brain do a partial reboot. She put as many inches between them as the small space allowed, found the switch and turned the light on, blinking in the sudden glare. That was good, because it meant she didn't see Hel right away. Of course, when she did see him, her brain almost seized up again. Questions about why he was the one to find her inner girl swirled in her head, but for once answers didn't matter.

"I think you fried my brain." She wasn't embarrassed, just curious. Curiosity always trumped everything, well, until now. Clearly passion ruled, even in her world.

The intercom made itself heard again.

"I should answer that."

"Yes." Hel stepped back, as if he, too, knew that touching would be a bad idea if answering was going to occur.

Doc sank into her desk chair and pushed the button. "Yes?"

"Have you seen the Gadi Leader, ma'am?"

"Yes." Her eyes met his. Heat scorched through her like a carpet bomb. "He's here in my office."

"It's time for rounds, ma'am."

"Of course. He's on his way back now. I'm sorry. I didn't notice the time. Please give the Colonel my apologies."

She sat back, trying to find her way back to mental certainty. She didn't regret the kiss, but it couldn't happen again. He had a galaxy to run, and she had an impossible mission and *them* on her heels. Even she sometimes found the impossible well, impossible.

Hel half turned to leave but stopped, his face not quite facing her, as if he didn't want to look into her eyes. "I'll be returning to my planet in the morning."

"They are releasing you?"

"I must return to my duties." He seemed to hesitate. "You could visit."

The words were weighted with what he wasn't saying. He didn't know she knew what he couldn't say, what he feared, but she couldn't let him know what she knew. He was loyal to his people, his agenda. She had to be loyal to hers. It wasn't the only thing that divided them, but at the moment, it was the one that mattered.

"You know that's not possible." She hesitated. Based on what she'd heard, he could be in trouble, too. "Please take care of yourself."

He opened his mouth, but nothing came out. He finally nodded.

"You, as well."

Five

Nights had always been a tough gig for Doc. In the twilight world of ship life, she'd hoped to break the link between *them* and the darkness, but maybe it wasn't the darkness that gave *them* their strength. It had, she'd decided when she got old enough to consider the problem, something to do with the way her mind worked. It was her personal theory of relativity. As she closed on a solution, her thinking patterns kicked into light speed, and time slowed as thinking sped up. This effect increased in that place between sleeping and waking, becoming a trap that allowed *them* to close in on her, perhaps hoping to take her down while she was in the no man's land between sleeping and waking.

And since she slept in four-hour or less increments, it happened as she was drifting into sleep and as she started to wake. The down side was balanced by high productivity between her short stretches of sleep, but she'd never had quite so much to think about and even worse, so much to *feel* about.

She spent too much of the night pondering chemistry and biology with little to show for it. There was no explanation for why Hel had been the one to unlock her libido. There never would be an explanation. Her brain didn't like dead ends, but it would have to live with this one. On the upside, the dead end made her brain so frantic it came up with a plan to deal with the general—though she was still uncertain about the outcome. The general was a long shot. That shouldn't be a problem. She dealt in long shots on a regular basis—but he could be a long shot across her bow.

While she waited for rounds to start—and her visit with the General—she opened the first patient file. She was about halfway through the updated data when her door opened and her speakers started playing the theme for *The Addams Family*. It was her spin on the singing trout on the wall. Contrary to common opinion, she did have a sense of humor. It would have been funny if it had been one of the many people who deserved the tail yank.

It wasn't.

Even dressed in infirmary issue pajamas and robe, General Halliwell managed to look intimidating. Doc scrambled to shut the music off, trying to get past feeling like she'd been caught with her drawers down.

"Sorry, sir. I was expecting someone else."

His brows arched. "I'm not going to ask who."

That was good. She hadn't planned telling him.

He studied her in unnerving silence for ten seconds that felt like a really long minute.

"I guess the nickname comes from the hair and skin."

Doc blinked a couple of times. "I thought it was because I'm creepy."

He almost looked startled. "I guess some people could confuse lethal with creepy." He frowned. "You're a very dangerous young woman."

She took it as a compliment and sat down again.

He eased himself into the only other chair the tiny room boasted. It should have helped equalize their positions but it didn't. He was a man who knew by instinct how to dominate.

"I'm being released today." A hint of relief broke through stern.

Doc had never met anyone who *wanted* to stay in a hospital, so this wasn't a shock.

"I had some sealed orders I was supposed to open when we got to the outpost. I decided to open them now."

That didn't surprise her either. Generals weren't immune from curiosity.

He pulled a folded sheet out of a pocket in his robe and tossed it at her. Doc opened the envelope and unfolded the page, an out-of-character tremor in her hands. What level of impossible would the Major expect this time? She read it through once, then again. She didn't need to, but it gave her time to think. She needed to think. She was pretty sure the General wouldn't be impressed with a, "What the—"

This wasn't just impossible, it was totally whacked.

She studied the General through her lowered lashes. It wasn't that she didn't know how to deliver bad news. She did it all the time—even when she completed a mission it wasn't always a good news situation, but she didn't want him to kill the messenger.

"So, you can do it?" he asked with obvious impatience. "Can you suss out the technology on Kikk?"

She stared at him for ten seconds, counting it out in her mind. It was a power thing, just as his pause had been. "Probably not."

As in, not just no, but hell no. Though she could admit that the idea of trying intrigued her. Her brain loved puzzles and the Kikk outpost was loaded with them.

His brows jerked together in a fearsome frown. "What?"

Doc expelled a silent sigh. "I'm called in when a situation has been deemed impossible. By definition that means it is *not possible*. I don't promise what I don't know I can deliver. Not ever."

Not to mention there were at least six scientists with a better chance at it than her—not because they were smarter. Her IQ was seriously high, higher even than the Major knew. Higher than she knew. Robert had taught her how to manipulate IQ test results before *they* got him. At the time, she'd thought it was interesting. Now she knew he did it to protect her.

"But you said you've never failed."

She'd been afraid he'd bring that up. "No."

"Then—"

"That doesn't increase the odds of success. Each time the impossible gets more impossible. I am going to fail sometime."

She knew this intellectually, but her gut didn't believe it. She had to believe she could do the impossible to even try. It was an odd contradiction in mental terms, and if she weren't already a mental freak, it would make her head explode.

"They want you to figure it all out. I just want you to get our people home."

A puzzle piece clicked into place. "The space-time portal."

The portal had been accidentally discovered during an assessment of the Kikk Outpost's technology. At first look, it had appeared to be an intra-galaxy transportation system, connected to a series of strategic outposts all over the galaxy. But further study had revealed it to also be capable of traversing both space *and* time. In hopes of finding safety from what appeared to be certain defeat at the hands of the Dusan two years ago, some noncombatants, guarded by a team of combatants, had opted to evacuate through the portal and hadn't been seen or heard from in time or space since. One of the scientists who tried to work on it after the fact—one of them with more credentials for the task than her—wrote in his report that it was "an intergalactic bitch of a Rubik's Cube." And he was the optimist.

"We don't leave our people behind."

Doc had guessed she was being pushed by the rock, but hadn't realized her situation included the proverbial hard place, too. If the Major was playing games with both of them, had he considered the ramifications of pissing off her ride home?

"But—" She stopped and frowned. She'd read some of the reports when she hacked the computers. "Who briefed you about the portal, sir?"

"Dr. Smith. Tobias Smith. Did you know him?"

Doc shook her head. The Major liked her to stay clear of the geek squad. They might notice she was one of them.

"He told me there was a way back."

Doc frowned. He'd been the on-scene expert. It was more than possible Smith knew something, or had discovered something *she* didn't know. None of which explained why the Major was letting this man think she could do what Smith claimed was possible, despite the fact that a lot of more qualified geeks hadn't managed to figure it out.

"That's the only reason I let him and his team go through."

"I'll need access to his notes." The request was a formality. Whether she was given access or not, she intended to see them. Interesting she hadn't found them before now. She put the lid on another frown—it seemed to upset the General—but the feeling that prompted the need to frown didn't fade.

Just because it felt wrong, didn't mean it was wrong, she reminded herself. Dr. Smith was a brilliant scientist. He'd been an important component in the success of the intergalactic space program. He'd been on the outpost and had a chance to study the portal. The Major liked to keep her skill-set broad and her brain agreed. It was why they got along as well as they did, if you could call what they did getting along. By having a working knowledge of a wide variety of scientific disciplines, she was able to see past mental boundaries sometimes created by specialization. It was kind of like being a scientific general practitioner. But she could also get quickly up to speed, when specialization was needed.

And she was always up to speed when the situation involved ass-kicking.

That didn't seem to apply here. Usually, once in the situation, Doc could figure out the Major's real objective, the asses that needed kicking. She hadn't yet, and it made her twitchy. He'd buried his goal deep this time, about as deep as the General was going to bury her if he found out the Major had another agenda—if he had another agenda.

At least now she understood why the General was hanging onto the outpost so fiercely. *We don't leave our people behind.* She hoped he meant it—and that she was one of "his people." A pity clinging to the outpost was working against him. She'd given him the bad news. Time to deliver the worse news.

"If we weren't on the brink of war with the Gadi, it would lessen the impossibility factor some." Doc chose her words with care. She didn't want to lie to this man.

Her words got his attention.

"What? What are you talking about?"

Doc kept her gaze steady and cool. Her calm was absolute—on the outside. Bluffing was SOP for Doc. She'd been doing it as long as she could remember.

"I didn't think you knew." She waited a few beats and then added, "There's a lot you don't know."

His face darkened. "I don't know what kind of game you think you're playing—"

"I'm not the one playing games. I leave that for the real diplomats."

That stopped him. She could see the momentary anger gave way to thinking.

"Tell me what you think you know."

He was a tough old man, she'd give him that. She'd also give him this truth unvarnished. She just hoped he believed her before it was too late. She thought about the look on Hel's face.

If it wasn't already too late.

There was an upside to too late. If they got kicked out, maybe he'd never find out the Major had been planning to use her to screw him over.

☼

It all made sense, but that didn't mean Halliwell accepted it. He stared at the empty wall of shelves. The small office was almost as unsettling as its occupant. The only personal item was a game console and monitor, her other visible equipment, an expedition-issue laptop. No pictures, no books that he could see. His gaze made its way back to the messenger. Throughout her recital, through each bombshell delivered with pinpoint precision, she'd looked and acted as if she was discussing what he should order for lunch, not implying he had traitors onboard *his* ship.

"He fed you this to get me to let him onto the outpost." No one on this ship could have withheld information critical to the survival of the mission, to the survival of this ship, to their own survival. They wouldn't. They couldn't.

"The Gadi Leader is not my source."

"I don't believe you."

She didn't flinch. Just a flick of her lashes and a hint of color in her cheeks, but it brought back a memory of a meeting with another young woman who'd had the same carefully blank eyes and too many secrets. The doctor was so damn young. How had he missed that?

He rubbed his face.

"What's your evidence?" It wasn't an apology. Those were against his religion.

Her face didn't change, but he felt an easing of her wariness, a cautious acceptance of his non-apology.

"I'm afraid I eavesdropped on our patients in the infirmary. No surprise it wasn't flattering, despite the free medical care."

"They talked in front of you? Not possible."

"In Gadi." She pulled a small device out of her pocket. "I kept a voice activated recorder on me and then downloaded it to my computer. I was able to find some patterns in the words, but the real breakthrough came through the boys."

"The boys?"

"The Leader's sons. They played video games with me yesterday afternoon. I taught them some Earth slang and they taught me some Gadi."

Halliwell almost smiled at the thought of Giddioni's boys learning ghetto slang, but he was too worried. "If he talks to them—"

"He will, but I suspect he'll be pleased we're finally figuring it out. The reception was probably an attempt to bridge the gap. The bombing an attempt to blow up that bridge before we could cross it."

If she was trying to remind him she'd saved his life that day, it worked. He had the autopsy report on the two men she'd terminated. Two head shots. He'd like to know how she'd managed it in uncertain lighting and her melon still ringing from the blast. And how she'd arrived at the reception armed to kill. That she was the Major's creature was a huge strike against her. They might be on the same side, but that bastard always had a hidden agenda. She could have two sets of "sealed" orders, and the fact he wanted to trust her just made his gut twitch harder.

"Did anyone tell you that the position of Leader is elected?"

He stiffened. "No. I did wonder why we never seemed to know anything about them, but I thought the Gadi were—"

He stopped. She knew what he thought. If she was right, he'd trusted the wrong people. He'd been a fool. Which didn't mean he could trust her or Giddioni. Just thinking about the Leader made him want to hit something. Too bad everything around him was metal. He wanted to break something, but not his hand.

"The Leader didn't do much to help the situation, sir."

Could she read minds? He gave her an annoyed look and found something like sympathy in her eyes. It was such an ordinary look, it surprised him again. How did she do that? No wonder they called her Chameleon. Which begged the question: What was real? Was any of it real? And just because Giddioni wanted to talk didn't mean he wasn't covering his own ass.

"If you knew what he'd done—" He stopped again.

She hesitated. "I do know what he did."

He slammed his gaze into hers and she didn't flinch.

"You couldn't know. I'm the only one who knows except for Giddioni, and he wouldn't talk about it."

"The...Key knows."

He flinched. "No." She wouldn't talk. He'd ordered her not to. If anyone found out how much he'd covered up, his ass would be grass.

She stared at him.

"Why would The Key tell you anything?"

Now she shrugged.

It didn't matter. What did matter... "The Key trusts you."

Another shrug. A flicker of a charming smile.

Halliwell gave a slow nod. "How did you find out about it, I mean about the misinformation campaign?"

He would admit to being impressed she'd made the connection between the second suicide bomb attempt and insurgent tactics in Iraq. And chagrined he hadn't thought of it himself. It had taken the insurgents time to adapt their tactics, as the Americans learned to block their moves. But the second bomb attempt hadn't been a reaction. It had been part of the plan. It wasn't outside the realm of possibility that terrorists in this galaxy could come up with the same plan as terrorists in their galaxy. It did stretch credibility, though, considering any type of terrorism was new to the galaxy. Her elegant brows rose. It was kind of relief that it was both of them. Just one would have been too Spock.

"It's what I do."

It wasn't enough, and he let her know that with a look.

"I look, I listen, I gather information, I find patterns, connections, and put them together to create hypothesis, then I try to find out if I'm right."

She didn't mention using lethal means and neither did he. It still shocked him that *she* was the Chameleon. It had taken his superiors the better part of his refit to get the Major to agree to her deployment on the *Doolittle* and then only because she was already doing a job onboard the *Nimitz*. The Major didn't like his asset being so far out of his control. He'd pretended he didn't know about his sealed orders, hoping to find out what skin the Major had in the game, but if she knew, she hid it well.

Was her disclaimer sincere or SOP? While Dr. Smith couldn't have known about the Chameleon, his description of the needed skill-set to bring them home had led them to the Major and this asset.

"How would you find out about my information problem? You weren't in the galaxy when it started." In a small way it helped to know it wasn't limited to his ship, since he'd been on Earth for refit since the end of the battle two years ago, but it still pissed him off.

Her lashes swept down, a pause and then they rose. "I got curious. Hacked into the *Doolittle's* computers. Tracked some transmissions. Once I knew what to look for, it wasn't that hard."

Ire did a comeback. "Into mine?" He could almost see her consider whether to tell him the truth.

"I needed to know, sir."

She made insubordinate seem reasonable. He wanted to stay pissed, but why bust her chops for taking a short cut to knowledge when he was the beneficiary?

He rubbed his face. "I hear what you're saying, Doc, but you don't know him like I do."

"You think I'm naïve." Now she sounded amused.

She couldn't work for the Major and be naïve. He knew that. "I think you like Giddioni. I think that might cloud your mental clarity."

Color tinted her cheeks, but her gaze stayed fixed on his. "I'm sure he'd come after me without blinking if he knew my mission. He's ruthless and clever. He'd have to be to keep his position, to do what he did during the war with the Dusan, to lead the counter insurgent Ojemba."

She hadn't denied liking Giddioni. "And you want me to let him, or his people on my outpost?"

The first hint of frustration broke through her calm. "It suits him to have you controlling the outpost right now."

"And you know this how?"

"They have more ships and men than we do. He could have taken it any time the last year."

She had a point.

"So why hasn't he?"

She shrugged. "I can think of several reasons, but I don't *know*. I'm not a mind reader."

Could have fooled him. Felt like she was browsing through his at will. The quiet reason in her voice made frustration spike again. "Share a few. It's not so obvious to me."

"If you'd been properly briefed it would."

Halliwell gave her his Look.

"The bombing targeted the alliance and *both* of you. Maybe there's an internal power struggle he's dealing with. Lots of unrest in the galaxy. Could be he thinks it's better for him if people are pissed at us and not the Gadi." She frowned. "Has to be a point when that won't work. And he can't afford to let us figure out the tech, or he'll piss off his people and lose the leadership."

"So you think he thinks we can't do it?"

"I don't know what he thinks, sir." She gave him a mildly exasperated look. "He might believe no one can do it. Even if we never figured out the bulk of the technology, what has been unlocked is remarkable enough to want to control. No question that securing the outpost would solidify his credentials with his people in an election cycle."

"Which is when?"

"Not clear. Soon, I think."

"So I pretend to give them access because he's our best ally until he decides he's not?"

"You can't pretend. It's not like you won't know when he makes his move." A pause. "And you need to tell him about our people." This in the cool, neutral tone again.

"No. Absolutely not."

"Sir." She rubbed between her brows, the crack in her calm oddly endearing. "Him understanding your motives would be useful for a couple of reasons."

"And they are?" He was still skeptical, though he could admit, she'd impressed him—which was what she'd intended.

"If he understands that your goal is to get your people back, he'll learn something important."

"That's what I'm afraid of."

"He learns that you won't be easily dislodged. He has to know how we feel about leaving people behind." She stared at him for a long moment. "He's seen how we fight, that we don't give up. Information about the capabilities of the outpost has been controlled. He knows some, but not all it can do. If he commits to this war, before we get our people back, we might not go quietly back to our own galaxy. Maybe he is afraid we've figured out more than he knows. He could attack and we could hold our ground. He has to know that there won't be a second chance to be friends. He has to know that would cut him off from—"

"—the Key will never return to this galaxy, no matter what he thinks he knows." It was his turn to rub his face. "You think he's still hoping?"

"A belief in the power of the Key is deeply buried in their myths and psyche, sir. A return of the Key is tied to peace in this galaxy."

"If I let them on the outpost, they'll find out what it can do."

"They'll know what they suspected all along. That it is impressive and challenging."

"What if it makes him want it more?"

She sighed. "He wants it bad, sir. Not sure he can want it more."

Halliwell released breath he didn't know he'd been holding. "He's a devious bastard."

"Yes."

"But you still like him."

Her eyes widened. She shrugged.

"And the Major?"

"He doesn't like us to get attached."

Halliwell almost smiled at that. That wasn't what he'd asked and she knew it, but he didn't push the issue. "You shouldn't get attached to Giddioni either."

"I don't get attached, sir." A flicker of a smile, then she sobered, her gaze connecting with his appeared filled with resolve. "You've got to buy me more time to do what I was sent here to do."

"I'll talk to him." It embarrassed the General to sound so sulky. He took some satisfaction from the fact that the Leader was under attack from his people, too, though he shouldn't feel this way if she were right and Giddioni was the only thing stopping a war. Just how vulnerable was the Leader? He wanted to be well clear of Gadi space if things went south. "What will you do?"

"I need to get to the outpost, sooner rather than later."

He nodded. This was a plan he could get behind. The people they'd lost through the portal haunted him. "I'll assign a driver—"

"I can drive myself."

He started to frown. He didn't send his people out alone.

"I'd rather keep my departure low key. I fixed it so that the infirmary staff thinks I'm back with the diplomats, and the diplomats think I'm still in the infirmary."

"You already planned to leave the ship? Before you knew what I wanted?"

She didn't sigh, but he could tell it was a near thing. She gave a slight shrug.

"But you couldn't know what I wanted."

"I didn't have to know what. I knew where."

She was right. She was a bit creepy.

"And if someone presses to talk to you?" Like the Leader.

"I'm sure you'll think of something, sir."

She frowned, considering things he couldn't begin to suss out. Her waters ran still and deep.

"I already set up a paper trail."

"Why?" If they had a traitor or traitors on board he didn't want her exposed to them.

"Outpost security won't let me stroll into the secure areas with my current ID, but I made sure the trail was muddy." That almost smile flickered on her face again. "No one tracks me that I don't want, sir."

"I believe you," he said, dryly. He wasn't sure he trusted her yet, but he did believe her.

"It is how I earn my pay, pitiful as it is."

This time the grin stayed put long enough for him to study it. She wasn't just young, she was lovely. How did she manage to hide that?

"Is there anything you don't do?" His almost indulgent

tone surprised the hell out of him. She worried him, though he shouldn't feel that way, knowing who she was, who she worked for. When was the last time anyone had her back—if they ever had? And with the sympathy, came the question: Was she playing him? How would he know?

She thought for a minute. "Windows? I always streak them."

"Anyone in ship who is likely to notice you're gone?"

"Just Briggs. I'm his dance partner."

If she'd told him that first, they'd have got along better and faster. No one got anything past Briggs. Not that he trusted her yet. The Chameleon could fool Briggs, too.

"He'll know anyway. He's the person we need to get your ride." Briggs had a couple of the Garradian ships they'd pirated parts from before the war. An unofficial craft would be a good choice for an unofficial trip.

"You have a devious mind, sir. I like that."

That explained why she liked the Leader. He scowled, thinking of the upcoming meeting.

"Best get it over with quickly."

She had to be a mind reader, despite her protestations. He gave her a look. It bounced off.

"This isn't the first time you've sat down with the enemy and played nice. And try to remember that, whatever he did two years ago, anything you've heard since isn't necessarily true."

"Most of it probably is." He had another thought. "Doesn't it bother you he has all those wives?"

She even had an answer for that. Her explanation of Gadi mating practices interested him, though he wished they didn't.

"I hope they all give him hell."

"I'm sure they do, sir." She paused, her expression turning serious. "About your leak..."

"I want to know names, Doctor. I want to know who gave *our* C-4 and insurgent tactics to terrorists. And who's been feeding me false information." And he didn't want any damn qualifications or excuses. She was on his turf now and she'd damn well deliver. What he was asking *was* possible.

She came to military attention with a jerk. "Yes, sir. If you'll check your computer, I did make a start. As far as I can tell right now, it's limited to the diplomatic corps, though it's not clear who all is involved yet. You'll need help from the Leader with the Gadi connection, though I did mark some interesting video for you to look at."

"It's been three days since the bombing, Doc."

"I know. I'm sorry. I'm not usually so slow. I'll try not to let it happen again, sir."

Slow? He looked forward to seeing what she could do when her time wasn't cluttered up with a bomb and patients. His nod was short, but approving. "You're dismissed."

She saluted, then turned with military precision and headed for the door.

"Doc?" It wasn't relevant, but he was curious. "What's your rank?"

Her hand on the door, she gave a half shrug. "Must not be impressive. The Major is always pulling his on me."

"You don't know?" How was that possible?

"It's not need to know."

"Bastard."

An almost smile twitched the edges of her mouth. "Didn't realize you'd met him, sir."

No reason to wonder why she and Sara Donovan were friends.

☼

Hel looked around the small healing room, not looking for forgotten items. He'd arrived with just the clothes he'd been wearing and he hadn't accumulated much since. There was nothing to forget but the drab colors and Delilah. He had a sinking feeling that both would be difficult to get out of his head.

Whatever illusions he'd had about a casual encounter with

her had been burned up in the heat of the kiss they'd shared in her office. Something in him had shifted when his mouth had covered hers. He could, he would shift it back. Helfron Giddioni would not allow his destiny to be ruled by a woman, no matter how interesting she might be.

His mind was adamant on the subject, his body not so much.

He wanted her. This was not a surprise. He'd wanted her since the moment he'd seen her at the reception. If circumstances had been normal, he'd have pursued an alliance mating with her and satisfied his craving, put it in its proper place and moved on, but the General would never agree. Beyond Halliwell's dislike, was the reality that Delilah was not just a woman within the Earth expedition, she was a *resource.*

She'd been brought to this galaxy for a reason. Hel felt this to his core, though the reason was obscured by Delilah herself. She was multi-faceted, constantly shifting, dangerously clever and, he conceded, the female version of himself. Was that her appeal? Was it just a need to assert his dominance?

The thought was almost a relief. It was something he could live with. It would, he decided, be good for him to get off his vessel and back into his normal life. This place, these people—Delilah—threatened his certainty that he had his world, his life, under control. No, not them, the bombing had done this. He would give no ground, not inside his head or in his life. He turned toward the door, determined to leave.

General Halliwell was the last person Hel expected to see in the opening. Even more surprising, he entered and shut the door behind him. When Halliwell crossed his arms over his barrel of a chest, it was almost a relief. That was normal.

"Can I help you, General?" Hel rose to his feet, meeting the power play with one of his own. His senses were tingling with warning. If the General wanted him dead, now was the time to do it.

"I will support your request for access to the Kikk outpost. Assign someone you trust to liaise with my security officer and start picking a team."

Just like that. Hel studied his face, looking for the deception, the trick. The General had fought this from the moment the outpost had been located. He could not, he would not, concede without a good reason.

"You are serious." Hel didn't make it a question, though it was one.

"I am." He looked at his watch. "I've given orders to start transferring your people to your medical facilities. I understand they are ready to receive the wounded?"

Hel nodded, still wary.

"Send me your people's ETA when you know it." His gaze bored into Hel for a long moment. "The recent bombing was a failure of both our security efforts."

"Yes." This was a concession he hadn't expected. He'd been sure the General would use it as another reason to keep them out. He wanted to ask what had changed, but the General wouldn't tell him. At the moment, it was enough to know he felt partially culpable for the incident.

The hard gaze studied him again. His nod was short and sharp. "I'm going to arrange secure, direct communication. For now, I'd prefer to bypass the diplomats."

Hel's eyes widened at that. "They are the bane of my existence as well." It was illegal, of course, but legal contact hadn't worked. Hel was willing to take the risk. This might, just might, be enough to stave off war. Then again, his unofficial sources were sending him some very disturbing reports about power brokering on the Gadi ruling council. He didn't need those warnings to feel a chill down his back. He'd allowed himself to linger, to get distracted; now it was time to refocus on his political priorities.

"You're leaving for Kikk soon?" His tone was curious, none of the anxiety he felt bleeding through into his words. He didn't think his enemies would make another try at the General or his ship, but he hadn't expected the attack at the reception either. His world had changed. He needed to start expecting the unexpected. Hel believed he still controlled most of the fleet, but that could change if his supporters thought he was too weak to lead.

It would be interesting to see the next move, assuming he survived his arrival on the planet. He'd survived worse than this, but he would take nothing for granted. He'd already begun to make discreet arrangements for the safety of his mother and sons, not that his mother would thank him for it.

"As soon as your people are dirt side," the General said, his hard gaze hitting Hel's.

Hel held his gaze as he said, "That is wise."

The General's eyes widened, signaling the warning had been received.

Hel thought he'd leave but he stood there, letting the silence build.

"Was there something else, General?"

"We have some people missing."

The words sounded forced, unlike the General. Hel felt like he'd missed something. "Missing? Since when?"

"It happened during the battle with the Dusan." The General paced toward the door, paused and turned to face him, his hands clasped behind his back. "On the outpost, there are these doors, portals, we call them. You go through and end up—"

"Where?" Hel was curious now and not just because he was hearing about the outpost. At last. The General was not usually so hesitant in what he said.

"We aren't sure."

That wasn't the whole truth. Hel felt this in his core.

"At the time, it seemed a better option for our civilians. If the Dusan had won..."

He didn't need to finish. They both knew that mercy wasn't a Dusan trait.

"Our people, our scientists, think they were originally set for two-way transport, but were reset to one-way when the

Garradians abandoned the outpost. We haven't figured out how to reset them."

So this wasn't about where, this was about getting the technology to work, which meant they hadn't figured it out yet, just as he'd suspected.

"I see." Hel did see. Many things were clear, such as the reason for the General's unwillingness to abandon the outpost. He'd assumed it was the weapons they were after—and Hel was sure they still were after weapons. How could they not want the weapons? But he also knew their attachment to their people. His thoughts spun with possibilities and questions.

"Do you think your scientists could help?"

The General didn't choke on the words. It was something of a surprise.

"I will direct them to try." If bringing the General's people home would speed their departure, he would order his people to try.

"Good." He still hesitated.

This was not a General Halliwell he was familiar with. Hel resisted the urge to shift in unease.

"We've made some progress on your people's request for a political mating. Finding someone willing to make the sacrifice slowed the process down." If anything the General's face got stonier.

"Sacrifice?" Perhaps the General should have left this discussion for the actual diplomats.

"Don't you think it's a sacrifice to leave your own galaxy and adopt a whole new life and culture?"

Hel hadn't thought about it quite that way.

"My people tell me you've met Gretchen Bilstead?"

Met her and remembered her. Her name was as unattractive as her person. He tugged at his shirt collar.

"I have met her. She is," he swallowed, "willing to make this sacrifice?" He tugged at his shirt collar again. It still didn't help.

Perhaps they shouldn't have pressed so hard for the alliance. It had been amusing until now.

The silence seemed long and then the General did something Hel had never seen him do. He smiled. Hel hoped he never did it again.

"I thought you liked teasing, Leader."

"You were," Hel swallowed to ease his dry throat, "teasing?" He gave a weak smile. "Point taken. I will only make serious requests."

"And I'll try not to get *beautifully angry.*"

Hel tensed. There was only one person who could have told the general that comment.

"Then we are in agreement."

It was a rare moment. It wouldn't last, but Hel felt he should enjoy the moment.

"I'll say good-bye. I need to ready the ship for departure."

"Of course. I must go as well."

The general looked like he wanted to add something, but in the end he just nodded and left.

Hel's brain sifted through the scene as he waited for the summons to leave the ship. He'd learned much from the brief encounter, perhaps more than he'd learned since their arrival in the galaxy, some of it information he was sure the General hadn't meant him to learn. It was a short, though interesting list.

The General did not trust his diplomatic channels, didn't trust what they were telling him about the Gadi or that accurate information was being passed on to the Gadi. Did he believe the security breach was related to this problem? Probably, Hel concluded. It was possible he had the same information blockage with his people. For a conspiracy of this magnitude, complicity would have to be on both sides. Unlike the General, he wasn't surprised. The Gadi liked plotting even more than they needed beauty in their surroundings.

The General hadn't mentioned anything about the outpost

except these things they called the portals. There was a reason for this brevity, Hel was certain. Did he seek to distract attention from their progress related to other technology there? Or was his purpose to avoid admitting they could do nothing with any of the technology? He rather thought it was both, and not just because he wanted both those things to be true. The General wasn't that devious, though he seemed to believe he was.

He'd been frank and open in the information exchange. The General must hope Hel would accept the information as it had been delivered, and he might have, if the General had ever been frank and open in their past dealings. And if he'd stopped before resorting to clumsy teasing to make a point. He'd made his point—this was a serious situation and it needed Hel's serious attention—but in the process he'd also revealed his source of information.

It wasn't just that Delilah had told the General about Hel's teasing, but that she had *access* that allowed her to pass it on. The *Doolittle* wasn't a small ship. If he were to make an access comparison with his people, it would be as if he'd sat down with the helper of Council member Carig's personal aide's assistant. The Earth hierarchy was more relaxed than theirs in some ways, but it did have strict military protocols. She appeared to be non-military and was working in the infirmary. She could have been assigned as the General's healer, but in what context would such a revelation occur between Delilah and the General?

The General must have noticed Hel's interest in Delilah and had warned her about Hel, though when he could have noticed was a puzzle. The only place they'd been together publically was at the reception, and that was a brief meeting interrupted by a bomb. Why would the General bother with such a warning anyway? He and Delilah were going their separate ways. There was little chance they'd see each other again, particularly if war broke out.

This thought hollowed out his chest in an unsettling way and he felt regret at what might come. He didn't let his focus be split with attachments. It had served him well during his years leading the Ojemba, though not as well in the matter of Fyn and Sara. Thinking of Sara was a good reminder of what happened when he left himself get distracted by a woman.

At least, he thought with a wry grin, the women who distracted him were extraordinary. The long war with the Dusan had taught him what he could change and what he couldn't. As for the rest, his enemies better hope they killed him sooner rather than later.

He needed to think on it some more, but first he needed to get off this ship.

The ever efficient Simmons tapped on his door before poking her head in. "Are you ready to transport, sir?"

He gave Simmons a cool smile. "I am ready."

Six

Briggs was ready for Doc when she arrived in the repair bay. As usual, it was in pristine condition, despite the dirty work done there.

"You're late."

"I had to pack." She'd also decided to get a haircut. She needed one and she hoped it would change her appearance enough to confuse things if someone noticed her in the shuttle bay. Her hair was terminally straight and, if she believed the stylist, the chin length cut suited hair and face. Perhaps the shorter length would also minimize the Morticia comparisons, though she wouldn't count on it until it happened. She lifted her chin when Briggs gaze lingered on the new do for what seemed like a long time.

She'd also taken time to pack an overnight bag—and had something to put it in thanks to the efficient Simmons arranging for her laundry to get done. She didn't need much. The *Doolittle* should be right on her heels. As much as the General had wanted to keep the Gadi off the outpost—he now wanted them on it. It was no surprise when Briggs refrained from comment and led her to a storage bay. He had three Garradian ships for her to consider.

"They have missing systems," Briggs explained, "but they'll fly. This one still has some weapons, but none of them have a cloak." He cocked a brow in an unspoken question.

"Shouldn't need a cloak," Doc murmured, looking at the craft. Two were sleek and deadly looking, though in a different way from the expedition's fighter craft. One looked like some kind of shuttle craft, clunky compared to the fighters. The fighters would be more fun. "I suppose I should take that one."

She pointed without enthusiasm at the shuttle.

Briggs gave her a look. It was the same one he gave her when she missed a dance step.

"That's no fun."

Her lips twitched. "Am I allowed to have fun?"

"I could make it an order."

Doc grinned. "One I'm happy to obey, sir. I'd like to leave sooner, rather than later."

"You could already be gone," he pointed out, then added, "You shouldn't be out there alone."

Her brows shot up. She'd never have pegged him as protective. "I always am."

Now she'd surprised herself. Had she ever said anything quite so revealing? Or so true?

He scowled. "You're not as tough as you think you are."

She considered this. How tough did she think she was? "True." She smiled. "Thank you."

His scowl deepened. "For what?"

"For worrying." Something in his face prompted her to add, "About your ship, I mean. You wouldn't worry about *a girl*. I know that." Sara had warned her about Briggs so-called prejudices. He was cute in a tough, scary way.

He grunted. "I'll prep the one with weapons."

His tone told her not to argue it. She could have told him she didn't plan to. She liked traveling with weapons, the bigger the better.

"Colonel Carey is waiting to issue your gear."

As she walked away from him, she shrugged on fighter pilot, her smooth stride turning into a military swagger. It felt good, felt comfortable and she liked that, even if it wasn't real. There wasn't much about her that was real. It was an uncomfortable thought, so she pushed it away, turning her attention to the Colonel.

Doc hadn't been around Colonel Carey that much, but she knew *of* him, knew Sara's Fyn liked him more than anyone but Sara. They both trusted him. Obvious that Briggs did, too. He couldn't get better recommendations in her view. Maybe someday Fyn would trust her, too. She wasn't holding her breath while she waited. He'd made it very clear what he'd do to her if she betrayed Sara's trust. It was cute that he thought he could take her.

She didn't expect Carey to recognize her, so she wasn't surprised when he looked at her like he felt he should, but didn't. She could've told him he did, but what was the point? Anything she told him now would be a version of not-her-real-name.

"Ma'am?"

"Colonel." She waited while his gaze did a thorough, very guy-like once over. Maybe she looked a little while he looked. He wasn't hard on the eyes.

The Colonel had a deceptively boyish look that hid an inner toughness. Dark hair tumbled onto a strong forehead. He had a mild blue gaze and nice mouth. His hotness factor was high—something she hadn't considered in her assessments of men until she started working around the military. There was just something about tough men in uniform that required the use of the word "hotness," even if getting heated had eluded her until recently.

Why didn't she want to kiss *him*? It would be less complicated. And he was probably as good as Hel. He looked like someone who got lots of practice kissing. He probably didn't even have to work at it. Ship life was like a never-ending reality show. All of them. Except maybe *Top Chef,* not with MREs a constant on the menu. Normally male/female interaction would be officially forbidden, but with civilians on board, and everybody single because of the long-term nature of the expedition, nature could take its course without fear of charges being filed as long as it didn't interfere with good order and discipline.

She pulled on her flight suit, running preflight procedures in her head, and trying not to think about kissing Hel. Not a good plan to get hot and bothered while pulling on speed jeans.

☼

Hel was the leader of half the galaxy, technically in control of most it. He was feared by his enemies and revered by his people. High born women on every inhabited planet in the galaxy sought to become his mate and his staff lived to serve him. He was a highly trained, skilled warrior, and able to navigate the shifting loyalties of Gadi politics. He'd fooled the Earth expedition and the Ojemba organization about who and what he was. With a single word, even a lift of his brow, he could start a war with the expedition and send them packing to their own galaxy.

So why, he wondered with an inward sigh, did one look from his mother leave him feeling like a child again? She was ageless in that she looked the same now as she had when he was young. She'd never been young and would never be old. Hel suspected his father had died to annoy her. Hel annoyed her by surviving. It was a double benefit that it also irritated his enemies.

Her cool, level gaze stripped away all the trappings of a leader, inducing in him a need to tug at the collar of his shirt. He resisted this urge. He couldn't escape how she made him feel, but he could refuse to let her see it. The sooner he moved her and his sons to a safe location, the better, though it was tempting to consider just moving his sons. Anyone who knew her would know she was not a leverage factor in Hel's life. Still, his sons were fond of her and she appeared to be fond of them.

"You look well, Helfron." The censure in her tone was not a surprise. Her swift scrutiny was most likely to ensure the transport had not left him missing key body parts. Her faint air of disappointment came from being proved wrong about the safety of the method.

"I am well, Mother." He bent and kissed the cheek presented with a haughty tilt of her head, catching a fleeting look of sympathy on Naman's face. His personal aide knew his mother better than most. He was the first assistant to last more than a few seasons as his primary gatekeeper. He did enigmatic almost as well as Hel.

His mother didn't gush and his near death experience was no exception. Having asserted her rights as mother of the Leader, she made her exit, the soft swish of her mourning clothes the only sound until she'd passed from sight. The mourning wasn't for his father. She'd worn it prior to his death. Audible sighs of relief were almost unanimously released upon her departure. She did have a rare gift for temporarily emasculating any males within sight or sound. Prolonged exposure was not advised.

Carig, leader of the opposition party, waited to greet Hel. Carig produced a welcome that almost sounded sincere—if one had an over developed imagination. He was eldest son of family Osteone. Until Carig's rise to power, this ruling class family had not managed to seat a member on the Council for many seasons. Gadi society placed great value on both brains and visual appeal. Carig had no visual appeal. It wasn't his height or his dark skin. There'd been short, dark Leaders in their past. He was ugly, both inside and out. And he was stupid, the worse crime in Hel's opinion. An ugly man might be able to convince people he was handsome, but a stupid man could only persuade himself he was smart. It bothered Carig to be short, and he believed Hel looked down on him because he could.

There were people both in and out of government who were taller than Hel. His ego did not require height, though he wasn't above letting people think it did. Hel always preferred to let others think they knew what he thought. It kept them from knowing what he actually thought.

Carig was cunning, but not teachable. Hel had provided much evidence that Carig lacked insight into his Leader's thoughts and still Carig thought he understood Hel.

After the required exchange of civilities, Carig said, "Leader, we need to speak privately."

Hel made an assenting gesture, allowing the man to fall into step beside him. Their route through the building had been cleared, an unprecedented event in Gadi history. Hel didn't trust anyone in the ruling class, since they were always after his job, but there'd never been trouble from the serving classes until the bombing. Hel had reviewed reports on new security measures implemented while he was still on the *Doolittle.* How wrong it felt to create security measures at the end of a successful war, measures not needed during that long war.

The combination of soothing and pleasing vistas and accoutrements was a relief after the stark functionality of the *Doolittle.* To his entourage Hel indicated a need for distance, giving Carig his opportunity to speak.

Carig looked around, before lowering his voice to say, "I have information about the Kikk outpost, Leader."

Despite the heavy use of lotions, Carig had a faint, but distasteful base body odor. Someone, somewhere in his family's past had cross-pollinated, Hel thought cynically, and not in a good direction. He arched a brow in inquiry. One needed to be careful with words in this man's presence.

"The *Doolittle* carries a scientist who they believe will be able to unlock the technology. We must act now, before this person succeeds." He paused, perhaps hoping for Hel to comment. "I haven't told the Council…yet."

Hel expected the threat. Carig could be counted on to not disappoint. Predictability was his only good quality.

"Does this scientist have a name?" Hel kept his tone indifferent.

"Only a code name, Leader. *Chameleon.*" He stopped, as if only now noticing his Leader's lack of surprise. "You knew. And still you choose not to act. One wonders whose side you are on."

Carig didn't wonder. He thought he knew. Hel stopped, turning to look down at Carig with a hauteur learned from his mother.

"I am, as always, on the side of my people." Hel paused, holding Carig's gaze until he shifted uneasily. Finally he sighed. "Oh, Carig, Carig. You are too easy to play."

Carig, as expected, puffed up like an angry *panthric.*

"My contact—"

"It is not enough to receive information. One must also understand the subtext behind the information." Hel waited, watching Carig try—and fail—to understand Hel's meaning. "If this Chameleon were the key to unlocking the outpost, do you not think he would have been brought to the galaxy sooner, rather than later?"

Hel used the male designation deliberately. For himself, as soon as Carig mentioned the scientist, this chameleon, he knew it was Delilah. He'd seen her in action. Now he needed to know how much Carig knew. The man used blunt force for every problem. Hel didn't want that hammer directed at Delilah. This uncharacteristic urge to protect was easy to explain. She had saved his life. He owed her this. That was all.

"My contact was quite sure—"

"Contacts are always sure of the information they pass on until they are no longer sure." He turned, resuming walking. "Tell me about your contact."

"I have promised confidentiality."

"Of course you have. I'm not asking for a name. I want to know why you trust someone so willing to betray his own people. What is his motivation? His end objective? One would expect your contact to want his people to succeed. He appears to want them to fail. This does not trouble you?"

Now it did. He noted that Carig didn't correct Hel's assumption that his contact was male. His contact would have been attached to the diplomatic group. Someone would have noticed Carig talking to a member of the security detail or a female.

"If this chameleon succeeds, we will never be allowed onto the outpost."

Hel paused again, this time signaling his entourage close.

"How interesting that you believe the Earth expedition will never allow us onto the Kikk outpost, Carig." He paused, to make sure all were within hearing. "You seem to be misinformed." He didn't add *again*. He didn't need to. "While I was on the *Doolittle* General Halliwell asked me to assemble a team of scientists to work with his people on the Kikk outpost. I have recalled my flagship for transport. I intend to travel with them and tour the outpost."

Carig stared at him, his confusion and anger apparent to all. "Why do you let them *allow* us to visit when we should control the outpost?"

Hel leaned in, concealing his distaste at the proximity. "I allow them to think they control the outpost until it suits me to intervene. Surely even you can see the tactical advantage in studying the layout and capabilities of the outpost prior to any military action?"

"You plan to betray them?" Carig's voice was thick with disbelief.

Interesting how people heard what they wanted to hear, not what was said.

"I plan to do what is best for our people, as always."

"Why wasn't I informed our people had been invited to the outpost?"

"I informed all Council members. Have you read my briefing for today?" Hel knew he hadn't. He'd made sure to send it just prior to his transport dirt side, after Carig had already left his quarters.

"I...no, Leader." Dull red suffused his face. It was not his color.

Hel looked at his time piece. "I should hurry, Carig, so you can be prepared for the emergency council meeting. It will have to be short, so we can all be at the death ceremony for our fallen."

Naman stepped forward now. "We have a few items to discuss before the meeting, Leader. If Council member Carig is finished?"

The wording was unfortunate, but to the point, at least for the moment. Without further word, Carig spun on his heels and stalked off.

"A clumsy man, Naman," Hel murmured, for his aide's ears only.

"Indeed, Leader."

"I need to know how he's getting his information from his contact. Is it through diplomatic contact or by covert means?" If Carig had to wait for diplomatic meetings, his information wouldn't be current.

"And if his contact is covert?"

"Find a way to listen in, Naman." He paused at the doors to his quarters, as his security team moved in to do a sweep. "This is more than political maneuvering, my friend. The bombing wasn't planted to get our attention."

"No, Leader. I'll do my best."

"I know you will, Naman. You always do." With a brief, charming smile, Hel swept into his quarters. It was good to be home.

☼

General Halliwell was on the flight deck to see her off. Doc wasn't sure whether to be surprised or touched, since she didn't "do" either. Not that she'd had a lot of opportunity. Her mum had taken the British stiff upper lip to ridiculous lengths and then there was the Major. The only way he'd see her off was with a boot to the butt and that was during his warm, fuzzy moments.

They were using a secondary flight deck and they were the only ones there, though she was careful to keep her back to the security cameras. She didn't need anything pointing a big arrow at her with a possible conspiracy on board. The General was a big arrow, though he didn't appear to realize it.

"Be careful out there." Halliwell had returned to his grim expression. Grim was probably his mother ship.

Doc considered his request. She was never deliberately careless, though that wasn't quite the same thing as being careful. She met his gaze and gave him a fighter pilot nod. Something odd happened when her gaze connected with his. He looked the same. So did Briggs, but she felt something unfamiliar seep into her, or possibly out of her? She wasn't sure. Her brain flipped through the memory files, but she had to go way back to find anything similar. *Roots?* Surely not? She twitched her toes, wanted to lift her feet from the decking, just to prove her brain wrong. You couldn't put down roots in a space ship. She couldn't put down roots anywhere. She hadn't put down roots on the *Nimitz* and she'd been aboard it longer than the *Doolittle.*

Was she in denial? Her thoughts were pretty defensive. It was possible she might be deluding herself. She relaxed her brain and felt tendrils that might have been roots reaching down through the soles of her feet and going, not just into the ship, but reaching out to these men.

She didn't panic. She didn't *do* panic, but it was a good thing she was going.

She made herself come to attention and saluted again. "Permission to—"

This was a ship, but an Air Force ship, so what was the correct Air Force term for "can I get the hell out of here?"

"—kick the tires and light the fires?" Did the slang work when there were no tires?

Briggs gave a grunt that could have been disgust or approval. He had a one-note grunt and made no apologies for it.

Halliwell jerked his head toward the craft. Doc took that as permission. Carey walked with her and helped her get settled in the cockpit. He hooked her up to the ship's communication and oxygen, while she ran her systems check. When everything was a "go" for launch, Carey stepped back and gave her a thumbs-up.

She echoed the move, then hit the control that lowered the canopy. There were some whirring sounds and a secondary canopy rose and locked in place. It was, she knew, the backup ejection system. If the main canopy was compromised, it protected the pilot in an oxygen nil situation. She'd had a chance to study the parts of the system at Area 51. Their people were working on a version of it for their ships.

She tapped her radio. "This is Test Flight One ready for launch. Do I have a go launch?"

Her voice was steady, but her hands gripped the controls. She'd never been at war with herself before. It was uncomfortable. But it would get better when she was gone. Roots might be put down, but they could be ripped up. People did it all the time. If people could do it, then she could, too. She was better than people at most things.

"Test Flight One, you are go launch."

Heading and course appeared on her avionics. Coordinates had already been preprogrammed into the hyperdrive systems. Doc tested the controls, felt them respond, took a deep breath, and eased the ship off the decking. A pause and then she put the figurative pedal to the metal. Her reflection in the canopy was cool and calm as her ship shot down the launch tube and out through the force field, but inside she did an exultant *yeehaw*. She was in motion. That always pissed *them* off. Whatever pissed *them* off was good for her.

She did a tight turn, a quick couple of loop-the-loops, and then turned on her heading before someone could tell her to settle down.

"Control, Test Flight One preparing to enter hyperspace window in five, four, three, two, one." Everything outside the ship turned into bright, golden blur and her speed jeans inflated as the *g*'s hit. A period of adjustment, then bright settled to a muted glow.

She was alone in space in a galaxy far, far away. That tiny ache around her heart was just from being so alone, so far from the familiar. It was normal to have a period of adjustment, even if she hadn't needed one before and had never thought she *was* normal. She should be moving fast enough to stay ahead of her demons, but there was moving and there was *moving*. Whatever was going on inside her head, she couldn't sit here and let *them* get on her case. She needed to focus, to concentrate. She needed to control the chaos starting to stir inside her head.

She let her fighter pilot shift to the back burner, bringing theoretical physicist to the front. She pulled up what she'd heard or read about the portal and began to sift through the data. There had to be holes in what she thought she knew if Smith had been convinced retrieval was possible. Without access to the original equations, all she could do was theorize. It seemed obvious that the Garradians' hadn't planned for one-way trips, so returning *was* possible. Without a way back, they would never know if the portal operated as expected. The Garradians had locked down the return controls before they left, apparently to keep people from returning to the outpost following the evacuation.

This tracked with what the Key had told her about the original Garradians' reasons for leaving. They'd opted to shut the outpost down, rather than destroy it, so that all the scientists working there could evacuate safely. It also indicated trust issues with some of the evacuees, but mulling that was far outside her mission brief.

There had to be a way to turn it all back on, but Doc suspected that turning the switch wouldn't be enough. Traversing time *and* space was more art than science. When Doc first heard about the portal, she'd wondered how the Garradians had managed to overcome the distortion factor of travel through time and space. Even assuming they'd learned how to fold space, there were other variables. Planets rotated and orbited. There were no truly fixed points in space. A wrong calculation could drop a body into an ocean or on a mountain top. Simultaneous arrival would be even more difficult, even if people went through seconds apart.

What had Dr. Smith discovered that made him believe the group *could* arrive at the same time and place? And then come back? She hadn't been able to find his notes in the ship's computers. Hopefully they'd still be available on the outpost computers. She'd have used communications to hack the computers, but she didn't want to leave a trail anyone could follow. That was against her religion.

Two years ago, when the Key was turned and some of the outpost systems came back online, the scientists on-site assumed everything would eventually start to work. It took time to realize that some of the technology had activated, but most hadn't. There were two camps of opinion on why. One postulated that there was something else the Key needed to do to activate the rest of the outpost. The second theory was the "different scientists, different solutions" hypothesis. This one presumed that each technology needed to be understood before it could be activated or operated.

Was it this theory that had resulted in her arrival in the galaxy?

It was possible that someone believed Doc's multi-tasking brain would be able to find the various threads and pull them all together, i.e., do the impossible. What didn't seem possible is that the Major would care. She frowned. Unless he'd been promised something for her participation? Would fancy, high-tech weapons tempt him? What Doc knew of him was all about stealth, but she didn't kid herself she *knew* the Major well enough to draw a conclusion about that. She'd bet his own mother didn't know him that well.

Doc still thought it interesting that none of their people seemed to know that the Key was a person and back on Earth. The General had kept a tighter than tight lid on that information, and he'd been unhappy she knew it. It didn't surprise her he didn't wholly trust her, considering she was associated with the Major—who didn't inspire warm, fuzzy feelings in anyone.

The General had good reasons for protecting the Key's identity. He knew, none better, that the Key had earned her freedom the hard way. Being a part of the small circle *in the know* affected Doc more now, than it had when she'd heard the story. It was all more real here, where it had played out. Doc felt the weight of that trust and touched that her friend had known what Doc hadn't realized at the time: that Doc would never, ever give her away.

It would have been nice if General Halliwell had been filled with equal certainty. His distrust stung in a way Doc had never experienced before. She wanted to deliver the desired outcome, even as her gut told her it wasn't possible and would never happen, despite Dr. Smith's assertion it could. Doc could ponder and hypothesize until the cows—or the Key—came home, but would be low on answers until she had a chance to study the portal herself and get a look at Smith's notes.

At the same time she pondered the portal, another channel in her brain mulled the possible consequences of launching people into the unknown. It would be interesting to know who, besides Smith, had gone through the portal. If, as everyone believed, they'd gone into the Earth's past, the impact of their contamination on civilization should be apparent, particularly if one had insight into their personalities and knowledge bases. They'd been ordered to minimize impact on the time line, but minimize didn't equal *no* impact. It was possible someone had tampered with the settings before the decision to use the portal had been made. The place had been crawling with geeks and geeks, by nature, loved to touch stuff. Inadvertent touching had been how the portal had been discovered in the first place.

Her brain loved this. With so many unknown factors, it was like giving a dog a rubber bone to chew on. But that didn't stop it from also bringing Hel to the forefront. Her brain was as much of a bitch as she was.

Was Hel already back on his planet? Had the General told him yet that he was giving them access? What if Hel chose to come with his people to the outpost? How soon could they put a team together? And how had thoughts of him snuck into her head again?

She rubbed a spot on her temple that wanted to ache.

This would be a good time to for a brutal workout.

And that made her think about Briggs. He'd seemed worried about her. And the General, too. Their worry made her feel strange and unsettled.

It made her *feel*.

And that made her head ache more.

✡

Hel was certain that Carig had approached him after transport wearing a listening device, what the Earth people called "wired." Had the man thought that Helfron Giddioni would beg him to stay silent for any reason? The Earth people had a word that Hel found appropriate to the situation: smackdown.

Carig had received a smackdown. It wouldn't stop his plotting. Hel had reports from his contacts that he'd sent surrogates to suborn Gadi fleet ship's commanders. The Gadi had eighteen large cruisers patrolling the galaxy. He'd not approached the eight commanders Hel knew would remain loyal, at least for now. There were two ship's commanders of the old guard who would be neutral in a dispute until it turned official. Then they'd come in on the side of the Leader, whoever it was at that time. If Carig managed to turn the others, he could use that to apply pressure on the Council. No one wanted a civil war—except Carig.

He would never secure the Leader position through an open election. There was deep-seated prejudice among the Gadi towards Carig's family in general and his mental acuity in particular. His appearance didn't help. The Earth expedition would consider it shallow, Hel supposed, if they knew how much appearance played a role in picking a Leader, but appearances mattered in the galaxy. The Leader represented the Gadi. He wielded great power. He attracted alliance matings. It was necessary he look the part. Being the part had never been enough.

Hel could play the part required. He needed to play many roles to survive and thrive in a world where war was a way of life. Safety at home had been elusive, too. He shifted easily among whichever persona he needed at a given moment, but the meeting with Delilah had been different. He felt jerked all the way to his center, as if she'd honed in on his core—a place he had not visited in many years. He kept that man buried very deep, and she'd unearthed him with a sweep of her lashes. She'd tapped into the passion he used to drive him through the rocks and pits of Gadi politics, the passion he'd used in his fight with the Dusan.

He'd felt passion for his mate, but this was different, though he had not yet discovered why. A man's passion for a woman was expected, but he'd needed to use care with women, no matter what role he played. Everyone and everything in his life could be used against him. He walked a path that required him to appear just competent enough to do the job, so that his enemies would underestimate him. Two years since the end of the war and most of who he was, was still hidden in the shadows.

Delilah lived there, too. Was this how she'd found him? How he'd found her? And why did this bother him, when he was unlikely to see her again?

He had to force himself to concentrate on the council meeting. Despite his inattention, it was not going as Carig planned and the funeral ceremony would not help Carig's position as much as he'd hoped. It was true the bombing had been a severe blow to the people's confidence in the leadership. But because Hel had been injured, the people had chosen to blame the Council, rather than their Leader. Hel may have helped nudge that perception along. His political instincts had not let him down yet. Because of the Dusan defeat, the Council had been preparing to lift the War Powers Act, which had been in place since shortly after war began. The measure would have hampered Hel's ability to monitor Carig's communications and meetings—not to mention diminished the power of the Leader overall. Carig should have waited until after that meeting to make his move, but he'd always been clumsy.

Carig wasn't Hel's only problem. If Halliwell wasn't getting critical information, then it was equally true that information getting to Hel would have had to have been filtered or altered as well. The false feeding had gone both ways; otherwise Hel would have bypassed the process much sooner.

His enemies had timed it well. In other circumstances, he'd have picked up on the problem before now, but he'd been distracted by the chaos that had ensued after the fall of the Dusan. This level of tampering was beyond Carig's reach and abilities. It was possible that someone on the Council was using Carig to do their dirty work. He could think of several members devious enough, including his cousin, Glarmere. The man took after his mother's side of the family. Their father had been dangerous and devious, which is why Hel's grandfather had arranged the mating between the two families. His motto was, keep your friends close and mate with your enemies' daughters. His mother had never forgiven her father or her mate, though Hel's father had redeemed himself somewhat by dying. If Glarmere was working with Carig, had he been party to the bombing? The blood tie was supposed to be sacrosanct—otherwise marriage was useless—though Glarmere wouldn't cry at Hel's funeral. The attempt to discredit him had Glarmere's fingerprints all over it, and Hel suspected the bombing would, too.

Hel looked at his time piece. It was time to end the meeting, if they were going to make it to the death ceremony in time.

"If there is no further business," he raised the meeting stone, but Glarmere rose in his seat.

"There is one more item, Leader."

Glarmere had inherited the family stone face, but Hel could tell he was pleased. He'd lived with his mother long enough to excel in reading stone.

"Are you sure this can't wait until the next session? We have the death ceremony."

"I will be brief, Leader."

Hel's eyes narrowed. "Proceed—with brevity."

"Since the Earth expedition is unwilling to proceed with a mating contract, I would like to propose a mating with the Carnarions."

It was a clever move. The Council had been pressuring him to take a bond mate since the official mourning period for his bond mate had ended. The war had provided some distraction. What good was an alliance mating if the world disappeared to the Dusan? And the Carnarions lived on the distant edge of the galaxy, along the corridor that fronted Dusan territory.

If he refused to meet with the Carnarions, they'd be offended and the Council could use this to unseat him. Alliance mating was the duty of a Leader. His father had been happy to mate when and where he could, but Hel had managed to dodge that trap. The women his father mated with had elected to remain as Leader mates so the alliances continued.

A Leader was only required to pursue one alliance mate at a time. Even among the Gadi it didn't look good to be courting more than one woman. Their women weren't as oppressed as the General thought they were. The fall of the Dusan had raised the issue again. The Earth expedition had been a useful delaying force, since they didn't seem to understand the concept. He could just give in and engage in negotiations, but that would require him to travel there or bring the prospective mate here. Either move would limit his ability to leave the planet.

Hel didn't like limits and he did not like the Council forcing his hand.

"Leader? Is there a problem?" Glarmere had a pleased glow in his cold eyes.

"I'm curious to know where you heard the Earth expedition had decided against a mating alliance." It was a gamble. This new, uneasy alliance with General Halliwell might crumble if Hel pushed too far, but all he needed was the appearance of negotiation. He didn't want a mate from Earth anymore than the General wanted to give him one. Hel kept thoughts of Delilah locked in a compartment inside his head. He never allowed himself to want what he could not have.

Glarmere lost a bit of his glow. "At the final diplomatic meeting before their ship left our space."

Hel put the tips of his fingers together and leaned back in his seat. "Would this be the same meeting where you were told we weren't going to be allowed onto the Kikk outpost?"

Glarmere lost a bit of his stone face now. "Yes, Leader."

"I'm open to discussing the Carnarions—when I'm sure negotiations with Earth *have* concluded." He lifted the stone and dropped it on the pad. "This meeting is adjourned. It is time to mourn our dead."

☼

It was a nice, tight little ship, Doc decided, more than halfway into her journey to Kikk, but she could have used room to move. Or more noise. She'd pulled up every problem she'd ever wanted or hoped to think about and still the journey dragged by. The way her mind worked, in some ways, she was almost an android, except with time. She knew that time couldn't slow or speed up, that it passed the same for everyone, but that failed to change her sense that it was not fixed, that it changed its pace with willful intent to give aid and comfort to *them*, but only when she was vulnerable. It was if it *knew*.

Just thinking about it made her feel paranoid. Most of the time she could keep time, and time thoughts, on her back burner. She'd have beaten her head against something, if there were something she could safely bang it against. Shouting just made her head ache.

She leaned back in her seat and tried not squirm. She hadn't been squirmy when she was little, and it was too late to start now. She should have brought her iPod. She could have drowned out her thoughts with loud rock music. As if *they* knew she was in trouble, they closed in, closer than they'd gotten in a long time. She had to focus and she needed to do it now—a warning light flashed on her flight control panel. Most people would see that as a bad thing, but she welcomed the distraction. She leaned in to study the incoming data. She was being scanned? She entered a query to identify the scan.

Unknown. But they knew everyone in this galaxy, didn't they?

Two could play the scan game. She initiated one at the source. A HUD—a heads-up display—appeared, showing her the area of origination, and with it some sort of energy signature, emanating from the surface of an uninhabited, class-five planet. According to the Garradian database, it was just off her course for Kikk. She'd blow by it in a few minutes—

Her ship slowed so abruptly it made her speed jeans inflate.

"What the crap?" That wasn't supposed to happen. She did a systems check. Hyperdrive was online and functioning well within optimal ranges. The window was stable, but her ship continued to slow. If the ship was fine, then it had to be something *out there* slowing her down.

Doc keyed in a more detailed scan of the energy signature, increased shield strength to max and got ready to kick on her sub light engines. On the HUD, the energy signature looked like a giant hand reaching out from the planet surface. She was at its outer edge. The ship's defenses weren't reacting badly yet, but Doc felt something clench in her gut, a premonition of trouble incoming. She keyed on her radio.

"This is Test Flight One declaring an emergency." She activated her beacon and sent her coordinates to the *Doolittle* and to the outpost. "I repeat, this is Test Flight One declaring an emergency."

"...Test Flight One...nature of the emergency..." The voice came through in pieces. The field was interfering with the signal. Doc didn't know why. She worked the controls, trying to clear transmission.

"Hostile energy field is interfering with my hyperdrive." It sounded weird, but that's what was happening. She felt the ship shudder as the field engulfed her ship, then a lurch, as if she'd stood on the brakes. Only her straps kept her from hitting the canopy—which didn't mean the sudden stop didn't hurt.

Okay, now they'd pissed her off. She kick-started the sub light engines and threw them into reverse. The ship shuddered, danced and shimmied as she fought the field's attempt to drag her toward the planet. All that did was slow the drag.

Another system pinged a warning. The field was attempting to pierce her shields. *What the freak*? Based on her scans, it would have had the same effect as getting hit by a stun weapon. She checked shield strength. Holding for now. Interesting that they were attempting to disable ship and pilot.

She used the scanners to pinpoint the source of the beam

and brought weapons systems on line. Targeting failed to lock. The energy field interfered with it, too.

Warnings began to blare about almost every system. On the HUD, she could see the field tighten and wrap around her, like a hand closing into a fist. If she could break free, she might be able to open a hyperspace window and get clear before they could expand it again. She transferred power from everywhere she could find to sub lights. She did some quick mental calculations, her hand hovering over her thrusters as she watched the field tighten.

"That's right, shrink yourself down nice and tight..."

She hit the thrusters, not sure if the tearing sound was the ship coming apart or her overactive imagination. More warning lights kicked on, but she didn't have time to shut them off. On the HUD her nose started to clear the edge of the field. She got a targeting solution and fired. Metal shrieked. The ship shuddered again, and she saw the nose go, felt the vibration as her engines sheared off. Her HUD flickered and went down.

"Pod deployment initiated," a mechanical voice informed her.

"No shit," Doc muttered, switching her efforts to gaining control of the pod's descent. It was her last chance to elude whoever controlled the field, if it was still impacting her. Without her HUD it was hard to know anything.

She recalled the pod had a semi-flat side, almost like an egg, that was meant to be turned away from the atmosphere during entry. If that was down when she hit the atmosphere at the right angle—she did the calculations inside her head—she *might* bounce off. It was a long shot, but better than getting caught like a rat in a cage by a hostile bogey.

The pod's autopilot resisted being turned off, so she found the wires and ripped them out. The pod bitched, but submitted. At least it had moved past the shimmy stage. Now it was more like a cha-cha.

Her gaze moved back and forth between the very basic

tracking screen and the controls as the pod slowly turned its egg-shaped ass toward the planet.

More warnings blared. Did it think she'd missed the memo about being screwed?

"This is going to be bad," Doc said, not sure if she was talking to herself or *them*. The angle still wasn't right. And then it didn't matter.

The pod hit the atmosphere.

It didn't bounce. It might have splattered.

☼

Hel still felt the chill of his mother's outrage at being sent into hiding. It *was* inconsiderate of him to have his life threatened. Other Leaders had managed the plotting and counterplotting without almost getting blown up. Clearly he took after his father's family.

He flexed his fingers, but the chill went deep. He'd felt warmer on Aris, the winter planet in the Zindi Quadrant. He almost wished he were back there.

At least he was finally alone. The last "Leader, if I might have a moment," request had been dealt with. The Gadi sun was long gone. Most everyone was in their quarters, either sleeping or plotting against him. He rubbed the aching spot between his brows. He almost wished he were back on the *Doolittle*. Thinking about the Earth ship led, inevitably, to wondering about Delilah. Was she making rounds in the infirmary right now?

He closed his eyes and let himself remember what it felt like to hold her, to kiss her. Heat washed through him. Heat and something more. He opened his eyes, rubbed his face. If the General were reasonable—but he wasn't and he never would be.

He could take her. He had the power. He was the Leader, but he had other ways to get what he wanted. He didn't often think about his other life, his secret identity, not even here in his quarters. He was careful to keep the parts of his life separate, even in his mind. The one time he'd let the parts touch had been disastrous. His attempt to secure the Key for his people was the root cause of the problems with the Earth expedition now.

But he was tempted. What would happen if he sent his Ojemba after Delilah? He almost smiled, seeing his image reflected in the night-darkened windows. Even his Ojemba, as highly trained as they were, might find her a challenge.

He sighed, pain from his injuries gaining ground now that he was tired. He needed to sleep, but he felt uneasy. He turned, studying the familiar surroundings. This peaceful room was usually his sanctuary, the place where he sought solace and renewed vigor to face the challenge of leading his people. Tonight, solace was missing. It frustrated him to realize he'd felt safer aboard the Earth ship. This was *home*. Had it changed? Or had he?

Something, something more sensed than felt or seen, had him pulling his weapon from its hiding place against his back. He brought the lights down, moving so that he was no longer silhouetted by the moonlit windows. He knew the room, could move around it with his eyes closed. He drifted toward the door to the sleeping chamber and melted into the shadows.

No movement. No sound.

Still he kept still. He knew how to wait.

Cooler air began its scheduled flow from concealed vents. With the moving air came the scent of something, or someone, alien to this space. Hel had learned to use all his senses. Now he homed in on this smell.

It teased his memory. Not something recent. Something from the past…

A slight, barely audible rustle of clothing.

He keyed on the sound and sensed unease, perhaps rising anxiety.

Waiting took iron nerves and a strong will.

Hel considered triggering an alert, bringing his security into the room, but he was tired of being acted upon. Tired of reacting to events. In here, all alone, he did not have to play Leader. Whoever was waiting in there might wish he had called security.

A slight creak of wood. Hel knew now where the watcher

waited. He avoided that spot when pacing. His mother looked for it when lecturing.

His eyes had adjusted well to the reduced light. His night vision had always been excellent. The door to his sleeping quarters was ajar. If he were the one inside and he had to come out, he'd nudge it wide, fire, then drop and dive out, firing multiple directions. In the dark, each shot would mark position, so continual movement was necessary.

It would be wise to assume this assailant was well trained until proved otherwise. He padded quietly to a tall chair. It would give some cover, depending on the type of weapon being used.

He could go into his quarters and remove the threat, but it amused him to string out the tension. He could almost feel the frustration of the intruder building to a boil.

Did he catch a sigh as the cooling system shut down?

He rested his weapon on the decorative edge of the chair, sighting the center of the door and waited. Not long now.

The door kicked back. A flash came from the darkness. Hel used it as the sight line for his shot.

A gasp was followed by a heavy thud.

It could be a ruse. He kept low, made his way to the dark rectangle. Pressed against the wall, he listened, thought he heard the rasp of air in and out of lungs. He reached around and flicked on the light and jerked back. Nothing happened. He waited longer than that, then eased up to the opening, put his weapon around first, then took a quick look.

It looked like the blast had caught her square in the chest, throwing her back a few feet. He still approached with caution, kicked her weapon aside, before kneeling to check her pulse.

Unease spiked again. He reached up and ripped her bodice down to her waist.

The bomb's timer showed bare seconds to react. He hit the alert on his wrist as he spun and raced for the hallway. He met his security coming in.

"Bomb." He snapped. They spun to cover his exit as he

counted down the time to the blast.

"Now!"

He dove for the floor. His team covered him as the building shuddered. He lifted his head. Rubble spilled from the door of his quarters, but it appeared the blast had been contained. One of his men helped him to rise.

"How far out is my flagship?" he snapped.

"It just broke orbit, Leader."

"I want transport as soon as they are in range."

He sighed. If someone was going to assassinate him, they could pay him the compliment of being marginally adaptable. Two bombings? If he weren't so annoyed, he'd be bored.

Seven

The *Doolittle* had just cleared Gadi space when the distress signal from Doctor Clementyne was picked up. Halliwell, about to exit the bridge, switched directions, coming to a stop at the communications station. The doctor's voice was calm, characteristically cool. Halliwell imagined her expression would be similar to the one she'd used giving him the bad news about a possible war with the Gadi. While the communications officer tried to determine the nature of the emergency, they received a data burst containing her coordinates.

"Ask her for more details about the energy field," he ordered. His gut tightened with worry and guilt. She was out there alone because of him. He didn't remember reading any intell on unusual energy sources. Was this something new? Or something else left off the briefings? Why had no one on Kikk noticed the energy field? "See if Kikk has anything on it, too."

"There's a lot of interference with the signal, sir."

He waited tensely until the officer said, "I've lost contact, sir. Sorry."

"How long before we reach those coordinates?" Halliwell's voice was calmer than his thoughts. He'd lost many of his people in a variety of ways. It was always a blow, but loss went with any military command. They were hours behind her. It didn't matter that she requested the fast egress. He'd let her leave alone so she could get to work on *his* problem faster. Giddioni had been planet-side for several hours now, and their secure communication setup ready. Could he have something to do with this? It was hard to see how, since Doctor Clementyne had covertly left Gadi space. Halliwell entered his private quarters and opened a channel—video and audio.

"General?"

Giddioni looked calm and inquiring, as if he weren't expecting the call. That didn't mean he wasn't

"We have a situation." It was an effort to sound calm.

Giddioni's eyes narrowed. "What has happened?"

"We had a small fighter in transit to the outpost. It appears to have been," he paused, "intercepted."

Giddioni frowned. "You let a small ship travel alone so close to the Dusan frontier?" His frown deepened. "You did receive our reports of raiding on the fringes of the frontier, did you not?"

Halliwell tensed. "I received no warnings." Who had stopped it? One of their people or a Gadi? He had to hope it was a Gadi. If one of their people had done this, heads would roll. He shouldn't have needed warnings. He *knew* that Kikk existed on the fringes of the galaxy, close to the no-go zone that had been Dusan space. It was the first planet they'd found upon arrival in the galaxy and considered an uninhabited backwater until the discovery of the Kikk outpost. That didn't explain why someone would attack a small fighter craft. Surely raiding parties would go after targets that promised a useable cargo, such as food or arms?

"Our pilot mentioned an odd energy source interfering with the hyperdrive," Halliwell said, watching the Leader. "We've picked up nothing unusual from the outpost."

Halliwell had a feeling something he'd said interested Giddioni, but he didn't know which part.

"I still have some resources from my Ojemba days that I can tap into for information. I will need you to transmit photographs of your missing crew members to distribute with the information request. I'll attach a reward to the bulletin. That will increase interest."

Halliwell didn't want to mention Doctor Clementyne, but

Giddioni would know it when he received the transmission.

"Doctor Clementyne was the only crew member on the ship." Halliwell hesitated, not sure if it was possible to head off Giddioni's curiosity, but felt he should try. "It was a Garradian fighter ship she was running some tests on."

If it bothered the Leader in a personal way, it wasn't obvious on his face. This was, the General reminded himself grimly, a man who'd fooled them and his own people into thinking he was a shallow idiot, while he covertly ran a dangerous and ruthless counterinsurgency. He'd managed to get his agents aboard the *Doolittle*, and they'd almost accomplished their mission of securing the Garradian key for Giddioni.

"I did not realize the doctor was part of your military."

"It was a civilian test." Would he buy that? Halliwell sighed internally. When had Giddioni ever "bought" anything Halliwell said? "And she had business on the outpost. At the time we didn't realize we'd be so close on her heels or I'd have insisted she wait."

"Where was her craft intercepted?"

The question was logical, but it still galled Halliwell to give him any information, galled him to have to ask for assistance in the matter.

"I'll forward coordinates from her last transmission. We're heading there now, but we're still hours away."

Giddioni looked down for a long moment, before looking at the screen again. "Your doctor is most resourceful. Perhaps you will find her waiting for your arrival. Of course, you will let me know if she is safe."

It was a logical request, but it still made Halliwell uneasy. How much did Giddioni know about the doctor and how much did he think he knew?

"Of course. Everything all right there?"

The Leader's brows arched. "Of course. My science team should be heading for Kikk in the next couple of days."

"That's good." He almost meant it. To get his people back,

he'd do a deal with the devil himself, and now that Doctor Clementyne was missing, the Gadi scientists might be his only hope for getting the portal working again. Halliwell reached for the switch to cut the connection, but Giddioni lifted his hand.

"I have information on our mutual problem."

They had a mutual problem? Halliwell frowned. "We have a lot of mutual problems."

"True." A slight smile appeared, then disappeared. "This one concerns the flow of information, or should I say lack of flowing information?"

Halliwell tensed.

"One of my minister's passed on a name."

"Oh?" It took considerable effort not to visibly tense.

"Chameleon." Giddioni's brows arched. "Does the name mean anything to you?"

"It's a lizard, a small reptile found on my planet. "

The brows stayed arched. "I have heard the word used to describe someone who disguises who they really are, General. Could this use be a code name, perhaps?"

"Due to security imperatives, I can neither confirm nor deny that, Leader." It was, he knew, an admission, whether he wanted it to be or not. "I would be very interested in knowing who told your minister that…word."

The Leader shrugged, the movement very French. "As would I. All I was able to ascertain was that it is a male in your diplomatic corps. Do you retain security video of the meetings?"

Halliwell nodded. In his spare time, he'd been looking at the video the Doc had tagged for him.

"I will send you an image of my minister and his entourage. It may help you trace the connection on your end. I haven't determined if they have covert communications or rely on their physical meetings for their exchange of information."

"Would your man use a surrogate?"

"Probably. He is not a risk taker." Again that slight smile.

"I'll get my people on it, see if we can plug the leak." Halliwell, after a brief struggle, added, "Thank you."

"We both have, what is the phrase your people use? Skin in the game?"

Did he have skin in the game? And how long would his skin stay in the game?

"I do have a favor to ask, General."

Halliwell tensed again. *Quid pro quo* wasn't a shock, but it was a worry.

"Political intrigue is SOP with my people."

The Leader had picked up a lot of slang in the last two years.

"You must be aware that there is a divide in our ruling class. Allowing us onto the outpost has helped quell some of my people's concerns."

"But not all of them?"

Giddioni's look was rueful.

"There is an effort being made to restrict my movements. I'm aware of your people's dislike of our alliance mating practices."

Halliwell felt his gut tighten.

"If I had the time, I would explain the process to you, but I don't. I will just tell you that my freedom of movement is important to both of us."

Halliwell wasn't sure he believed that, but he was curious about the favor—and worried.

"I need you to reconsider your refusal to countenance an alliance mating between our people. I need you to reopen discussion on the subject."

He was asking for his trust. Halliwell knew this, knew he had to make a choice. No, he'd already made it he realized. His choice was based on trusting the Doc.

"Done." A discussion wasn't an agreement.

That put a hint of surprise on the Leader's face.

"Thank you."

"Was there anything else we need to discuss?"

Giddioni shook his head. "Please keep me posted on your search for the doctor."

Halliwell nodded and cut the connection. Just in time. Being polite to the Leader was hard work.

☼

Doc opened her eyes to a world that looked like it had been turned on its head. She looked up and saw ground. Even dazed, she knew that was wrong. She gave a tiny shake and realized *she* was upside down, not the world. Except...shouldn't she be dead?

She ran the data. Based on pod damage, angle of entry and impact with the atmosphere, she shouldn't just be dead. She should be bits and pieces drifting in space, but all her pieces appeared to be intact.

Okay, she had a vague memory of the pod holding together against the odds until the secondary pod could deploy, but that should have only changed *where* she died. The thrusters designed to slow the pod's descent had taken heavy damage. Plummeting to the ground still added up to dead.

She looked for a reason and found lines and a bright red parachute tangled in tree branches. No one had mentioned parachutes in their examination of the Garradian fighters, but there it was. An honest to goodness alien parachute and her first involuntary nylon let-down. That explained the not-dead part. Blame the tree for being upside down.

Gravity pulled her against her harness, and the pounding of blood inside her head suggested she make a change in orientation sooner rather than later. The ground wasn't far and there were no visible threats. She released the harness and dropped to the ground in a cautious crouch. Heat came off the ground in waves, and beads of sweat formed on her skin. She wrinkled her nose at plant smells just enough off ordinary to let know she was on an alien planet—in case the purple moon hanging low on the horizon wasn't enough of a clue. She eased upright, still wary, and looked around.

Her LZ—landing zone—wasn't that interesting. Green stuff, brown stuff and rocks. If this was Earth, she'd have known names and the edibility/survival potential of the flora and fauna, thanks to her SERE—Survival, Evasion, Resistance and Escape—training, but it wasn't Earth, rendering the "living off the land" training useless to the situation. A long stay might be a problem, but she'd deal with that if she had to. At the moment, the muggy heat was her biggest problem. The flight suit held it in like a sauna, so she shrugged it off. This also put her weapon within easier reach, which was always good.

She pulled it and did a quick recon of the immediate area, crouching to study the ground for signs of wild life. The dry, hard-packed ground yielded few clues. Only bug sounds broke the dense silence. Doc secured her weapon and turned back to her rig. A pity about her clean drawers. They were floating in space now. There was a survival pack in a compartment at the rear. She found it and tried out the compass, got a magnetic pole. That would keep her from walking in a circle.

She extracted a packet of water and sipped it while she considered her situation. She wasn't sure if her emergency beacon had been in the pod or in the seat. The whole ejection system had taken heavy damage, so the beacon might not be broadcasting her location. She did know the *Doolittle* had received her distress call, so sooner or later someone would come. They knew her course, speed and time of distress call. This was the only habitable planet within the search area they'd identify from that information. That was the good news.

The bad news: whoever had been behind the attack was already here.

The energy beam had originated from the planet surface, but that didn't mean they couldn't track her from space. They could have a cloaked ship.

Doc checked the spare magazines for her weapon and frowned. She didn't have enough for a sustained firefight. Time for the "evasion" portion of her SERE training. She stowed the spare magazines in her vest pockets and finished her water, retaining a small amount to make mud. She smeared this on her face and hands. She used her knife to cut some branches from the tree and tucked them in her pockets, waistband and cap. If the bogeys had heat-sensing capability the branches should break up her silhouette. Though, since she was using alien mud and tree branches, she couldn't be certain of anything.

She shouldered her pack and headed into the underbrush, heading due North, or the alien equivalent of North. While she'd often *felt* alone, she hadn't, she realized now, *been* alone. Not even during her SERE training had she been *this* alone. It was easy to feel self-sufficient when your comfort zone was the whole Earth—or a ship full of very competent military types.

Even *they* seemed subdued.

I'm always alone, she'd told Briggs, but she'd been wrong.

This was alone.

Normally calm worked against her, but for now the isolation quieted her overactive mind, leaving her free to hear every little sound, magnified a thousand times by her edgy senses. Thanks to the Major she had HD vision and had trained blindfolded in order to heighten her sense of smell and hearing. Her brain began to auto-filter sounds and scents. She needed a handle on normal to know what wasn't normal. After a few minutes of hiking, she spotted a small, rocky bluff and angled toward it. She'd always liked the high ground. And if someone was following her heat signature, a rock cave should mess that up.

The heat and humidity increased as the sun arced higher in the sky. Good thing she'd shed her flight suit. While it felt good to be in motion, her sense of unease built. She pulled her already silenced weapon. Her pace slowed as wary grew to near critical mass. If someone was tracking her, they were as good at being quiet as she was. Or they weren't dirt side yet.

Something changed, though she wasn't sure what. A tingle across her skin or a shift in the way the air moved? Her heart thudded slow and heavy, and adrenaline began a slow bleed into her system. Her feeling of being watched went into overdrive. Someone was out there. She was certain of it.

The underbrush shifted beneath her boots, the sound loud

in the deep quiet. Even the bugs seemed oppressed into silence by the heat. Doc stopped by a large tree and eased her pack off with her free hand. It would suck to lose it, but it would slow her down if she had to move fast and it increased her silhouette. She kept the tree on her six while she did a perimeter scan.

Her body was a coiled spring, her senses so attuned to subtle shifts in the airflow, she had dropped and rolled before her brain processed the subtle whine of something incoming. It sizzled along her back before slamming into the tree where she'd been standing.

Doc fired in the direction of the shot, rolled and then fired again. Energy blasts hit the ground on either side of her. She did a fast, low crawl through the dense scrub toward one of the bogeys while she processed the attack.

Three shots from three directions. They had her ringed, not easy to do unless they'd been tracking her from space. Was that what she'd sensed? Remote transport? Drop in and shoot?

Not the way to make first contact with her.

Face close to the ground, she concentrated on filtering out the normal ambient sounds and smells, her brain now screening for what had changed.

"We wish to help you," one of them called out, the sound coming from her three o'clock. His scent drifted toward her, too. That upped the opposition to four bogeys. "We observed the crash of your ship and we wish to help you."

By shooting her?

"We mean you no harm."

This was a new voice, coming from nine o'clock. That put the bogey count at five, though she wouldn't count her bogeys until they were all unconscious. *Never assume.*

As silence once more settled in, Doc began to sort bogey sounds from nature sounds. They were pretty good, but not good enough. The subtle shift of feet on grass. Soft inhale and exhale. Different scents drifted in, too. They had edged closer, trying to tighten the ring. Did that mean they were able to track her or were they overconfident? Her hand brushed a small pebble, her fingers closed around it. She tossed it, the movement small, but directed.

It hit the ground a few feet to her right. The sound was minute, but the response wasn't. A light flashed from one of the positions she'd identified, striking the ground near her pebble. Firing revealed their positions.

Time to find out if they could track her.

She turned ghost as she low crawled through the dense ground scrub, heading straight toward the most recent shooter. She studied him through a shrub screen. His camo was of the *Conan the Barbarian* variety, and he was built like a tree trunk. His neck was the only missing body part. And he looked about sixteen.

She cussed silently. The Major would expect her to use her knife and make sure the kid ceased to be a problem, but she didn't kill babies, even ones too stupid to live. She studied the terrain for a moment, then moved to his right, careful no sound gave her away. He showed no sign someone was feeding him her movements. He seemed to be focused on where she'd gone down. He could be a decoy while someone came up on her back. She checked her six, with sight and ears, then worked her way around to his. She knew her physics, knew she had to work with his weight and size, not against it. She stowed her weapon.

There was a tree branch hanging down at about the right height. She jumped at it, her body swung up, her legs hooking his neck. A quick twist and he hit the ground so fast only a choked cry escaped his mouth. His hands came up, clawing at her legs. She took his ray gun, shot him with it, and was back under cover in the scrub before his body quit twitching.

She hoped it was set to stun, but if it wasn't, they *had* shot first.

"Cadir?" This voice was new, but it came from a previously marked position.

Doc was already low crawling to the next bogey. She did wonder why they didn't just transport her up to their ship when they spotted her. Only reason not to, they didn't want her to see their ship, but that was stupid. She knew it was there. It had yanked her out of the freaking sky. She frowned. Cadir's clothes were pretty low tech. Was it possible she was dealing with a different adversary? No, that didn't make sense either. They claimed to have seen her ship crash. Since it had crashed against the atmosphere, they'd have had to be up there, too. None of it made sense.

She hated that.

"Eamon, check on him," the bogey directed. So this bogey gave the orders. Good to know. A young barbarian eased through the scrub, almost stepping on her as he moved to kneel by the downed Cadir.

"He's been stunned," Eamon said. "She has his weapon."

She? How did they know that?

She heard a muttered curse. She was pretty sure she was outside their perimeter now. She'd caught no sound or scent of further movement. If it had been darker, she'd have been tempted to let them flail around while she played ghost somewhere else, but the alien sun was high and bright, despite that low hanging purple moon.

She had a ray gun now, too, but if she fired it, it would give away her position, unless...

Doc felt around until she found another pebble, about the size of a quarter and continued her low crawl until she spotted another bogey. He looked a bit stressed.

She liked stressed bogies better than happy ones.

She sighted the ray gun on the center of his back, using a V in the scrub branches to steady the weapon, so she'd have a hand free. With a flick of the wrist, she sent the pebble sailing into the center of their perimeter. Doc was pretty sure they all fired. She knew she did. None of them appeared to notice her shot, except the guy she hit and he wasn't talking. She didn't take time to gloat. Only people who wanted to get caught took time for gloating.

She almost didn't see the next guy. He must have moved while they were all shooting at the pebble. He stopped right in front of her, his body alert, his head angled for listening. It was the one called Eamon. He turned, putting her at his back.

Doc came up out of the scrub without making a sound and tapped him on the shoulder. When he spun around, she applied her knee vigorously to his groin. His eyes crossed. So did his hands—over the affected area. Some blunt force trauma from the butt of the ray gun took him the rest of the way down.

Doc had moved on before his body hit the ground. She found a big section of scrub and worked her way in to a depression hidden by the low profile branches.

The eerie silence had returned in spades. She wished she'd dared pause to search the bodies for radios. Whoever had set this up was a decent strategist. These boys had been trained. They just hadn't expected her to be, well, her. Doc doubted they'd ever met anyone like her. They might have the brute strength, but she'd been trained by the best—and she'd eventually kicked their asses. The Major thought it was because she could think so fast, the whole genius thing. He might be right.

Now that they were getting a clue, how would they react? And how many of them were left *to* react? Right now if she were them, she'd be trying to smoke her mark into the open, trying to take back control.

She saw one of the boys emerge from cover. His back was to her, but there was a self-consciousness to the way he moved that made her roll her eyes. They knew they could mark her position if she fired the ray gun. She hadn't used lethal force, so whoever was running this op didn't mind using the kid as bait. The bait didn't look happy. She'd heard the stun setting hurt like a son of a bitch, so she wasn't surprised. He had his ray gun out and was making wide sweeps from side to side.

Doc set down the ray gun and eased out her hand gun.

Doc did another pebble toss and when he jerked toward it, firing in multiples, she used the confusion to cover her shot. The bullet hit the barrel just above his hand. He jumped like he'd been shot, his ray gun went flying, he said something that sounded like a curse and dived into the scrub. That was four, well, three-and-a-half identified bogeys down. Number four wasn't unconscious yet.

She caught a flicker of something sailing through the air in her direction. She pushed her face into the dirt, hands over her ears. She felt the flash, heard *and* felt the bang. Dang that was close. So the aliens had their version of a flash bang. When the smoke cleared, four bogeys moved into the impact zone, their thrashing loud enough to cover a military band moving through.

If she'd expected to encounter this type of problem, she'd have been packing flash bangs, too. She didn't even have a stinking grenade. Too noisy. She low crawled back to one of the unconscious bogey's and did a quick body search. She didn't find anything that looked like a radio, but she did find two unfamiliar devices hanging off his belt and took them and his ray gun. She did a quick check of the search effort. Four bogey boys all still bunched together. Bad idea.

It took her ten seconds to figure out how to activate the alien flash bang. She tossed it into the middle of them. One of them managed to get out half a curse before they all went down. Something sizzled past her position, but other blasts were going off in other directions, so she didn't think they'd made her. Several blasts hit close, though. The idiots might take her out by accident.

She felt that odd tingling feeling again. Had they transported out? Or in? Reinforcements or strategic retreat? The rocky bluff might provide some protection from a low orbit scan, but she'd have to expose herself to get there.

She'd decided to stay put, when another wildly fired shot sizzled down her back. She stowed her hand gun, still reluctant to use lethal force. She gripped both purloined ray guns, counted to three and came up out of scrub, firing from both weapons. She lay down a line of fire, turning in a circle to clear her perimeter, and then took off running toward the rocky bluff. Her legs weren't as long as Sara's, but they were long enough. What she couldn't go through, she went over, training and adrenaline working in perfect synch.

She saw the bluff, the fall of rocks just ahead and put out an extra burst of speed. It surprised her she still sensed the transport while running full tilt, still felt the change, the tingle of awareness. She almost cannoned into the stolid young man that materialized in her way. He tried to get his arms around her, but she had momentum and training on her side. All he had was his tree-like size. Even as she dealt with him, she knew he was the decoy, a distraction. She twisted, trying to turn to face the real threat.

She saw the bogey, but the ray's blast was already tracking toward her. Even she couldn't move faster than light but that didn't stop her from trying. The beam caught her full in the chest. Hurt a lot worse than she'd expected. She felt her feet leave the ground, a short flight, and then the jolt as her body hit the ground. That hurt, too. Her body jerked as her overloaded senses began to shut down, the light around her shrinking to a small circle. She fought to stay alert and felt herself losing the battle. She had time to see a face swim into view, had time to learn it before the circle closed with a decisive snap.

☼

The General had given Hel much to think about. At some point, he would need to tell Halliwell that Delilah wasn't the first woman to go missing in the last year, but he needed more data. He sent a request for full details on each woman that was missing and then leaned back in his seat.

His quarters aboard his flagship were as comfortable as those planet side and felt considerably safer. Security was even now installing transport inhibitors, not to mention organizing repairs to his quarters. He didn't mind the forced shift in location. It would be a lot harder for his enemies to track him. Oh, they could track his ship, but he had his own ways of dealing with that. In the meantime, he needed to decide what to share with the General and how much.

The General had been unexpectedly cooperative, though it was still a struggle. He hadn't wanted to tell Hel that Delilah was missing. And he'd been shaken that Hel knew about Chameleon.

Early on, one of the diplomats had given Hel a dictionary. Before contacting the General, he'd looked the word up. What had interested him the most about the definition was the lizards "synonymous ability to change color."

The first time he'd seen her pacing the perimeter of the room, he'd tagged her as lethal. Then she'd shifted to seductive and then, what? In their brief interaction prior to the explosion, she'd been aroused, then surprised into ordinary when he called her Morticia. For that moment, she hadn't been anything but herself. And then?

She'd dealt with the roof collapse and defused a bomb. Two very disparate skills, but they did have one thing in common. She'd solved two *problems.*

She had business on the outpost.

The General was worried about his people, missing through the portals. If Delilah was supposed to solve that problem, then her hasty departure made sense. She'd need to tackle the problem before war broke out. If she was the Chameleon Carig's contact had spoken of, was it possible her ship had been intercepted by someone from the Earth expedition? They could have hired someone to do the intercept. Except the General had contacted Hel. He was suspicious Hel had been involved. That suggested the General considered her cover secure—at least until Hel had informed him that her cover might not be secure.

Just because Carig didn't know the sex or real name of the Chameleon, didn't mean the contact didn't know. Hel rubbed his face. The General would have to pursue that angle and he would. He was no fool, even if he was easily riled.

Hel's communication system alerted him that his reports had arrived. He opened the reports and read each one. At first glance, the only thing Delilah had in common with the thirteen missing women was that they were all female. All earlier abductees had been well under twenty Earth years in age. Delilah was at least thirty. That was a significant age difference. This seemed to imply she'd been intercepted by someone from the expedition, except for the other connection with some of the intercepts: the energy field.

Only five of the ships' captains had reported interference from an outside source, only three had named an energy field. The rest had reported malfunctions with their hyperdrive. The ones who identified an energy source claimed it had interfered with hyperdrive transport. All had reported a period of unconsciousness following the attack. None had managed to send out a request for help until the attack was completed.

He finished the input of data collected from the reports and waited for a map to appear. He leaned back, his elbows on the chair rests, his fingers steepled as he mulled what he knew and what he sensed he knew.

Halliwell hadn't wanted to tell him that Delilah was the missing crew—no, the missing *pilot.* Could it be her skill diversity that gave them hope she could unlock the technology?

Hel had been sure they would fail to figure out the technologies on the outpost and have to bring the Key back. If they believed Delilah would do the job, why had they waited so long? It could be simple, scientific arrogance. The people who'd been working on the problem might have been convinced they could do it. It took time to get people to admit defeat. It took more time to devise a new plan. Was Delilah the new plan?

But Delilah couldn't do it if war broke out. She needed time, she needed access. And the General had arrived at Hel's door full of helpful information to get her that time. Primed by Delilah? That last part, the so-called teasing, was off script, he was sure of it. If she were pulling the General's strings, she wouldn't want Hel to know she was the source of the General's information. She'd been moving among the Gadi wounded for several days. To his knowledge no one on the expedition knew the Gadi language. It hadn't been necessary when both sides spoke Standard.

But what if she were a linguist, too? And the words she couldn't figure out? That time with his sons hadn't all been spent having a party. His mother was still complaining about the words they'd learned during the visit. It would have been an easy matter to "trade" words with two small boys.

She'd liked him, wanted him, even as she plotted against him. He chuckled. He'd thought he could live without her. Now he was not so sure. He might just have to have her. And the General had almost handed her to him on platter.

He just had to find her first.

☼

The woman lay on the bed where he'd dropped her. Vidor Shan stared at her pale, mud-smudged face, noting that even unconscious there was a willful curve to her mouth. He wanted to know why she'd done that, smeared mud on her face. How she'd managed to elude them. He wanted to see her eyes again, to see if the intense blue color was real, but her lashes lay stubbornly against her pale cheeks. His body remembered her scent and the silk of her hair brushing against his face as he carried her. She was both smaller and lighter than he'd expected, based on the ferocity and precision of her attack on his men.

She was, Vidor Shan acknowledged, unlike any of the other women they'd taken. Is that what made her interesting? Both Eamon and Cadir were dumbstruck by her—and a little fearful, though not as much as they should be. Knowing this, why had he brought her into the camp? She dressed like a soldier, and worse, fought like one and they had little time to process her into compliance with their needs.

"Why doesn't she wake?" Vidor asked, letting his frustration break free.

Bana shifted at his side, as if fighting impatience. Vidor scowled at the old, lined face.

"Each person reacts to the stun in their own way." Bana's tone was respectful, but with a hint of irritation. There was a pause.

"She is too old and there is no time for one such as this.

You should have thrown her back." Another longer pause. "Or killed her."

He hadn't done either and that troubled him. His mission was proving challenging without introducing someone destined to be difficult into their group. The other women had adapted quickly to their new reality, but targets had dried up in the last few months. They'd used care in harvesting women, but word had spread. Convoys had formed or ships had ceased using women or providing transport for them. This was the first ship carrying a female in some weeks.

That she traveled alone surprised him and made him suspicious. He'd almost let her pass, but time was short, as Bana had pointed out. They'd brought her gear back with them, but it had yielded few clues to her identity. He had not planned to take a woman for himself, but this woman might change his mind.

His gaze tracked from the top of her head, down to her feet and then back up again until he reached her mouth. It was soft and pink. His hands fisted at his sides. He should eliminate the problem, but he couldn't do it. Not yet.

"She interests me," he said, as if his insides weren't clenching. Her features were clean and classic, her mouth a frustrating temptation. He tried to imagine what her name might be, but he couldn't. He wanted to trace the shape of her mouth and then take a long taste. Would she taste as exotic as she looked?

"You're thinking with the wrong body part, Vidor, though it gives me hope that you can." Bana sounded more amused than annoyed now. "Come, leave her to wake when she's ready. If you are to change our history, you must learn how to wait."

Not for the first time, he wondered why he'd been cursed to live now, why it had become his burden to change not just the course of his life, but that of his people. His gaze traced the length of the woman one last time. There was strength in her body, in the line of her jaw, but was strength enough? Could her will be turned for their purpose in time? He needed to know quickly.

☼

There was pain, but not a kind she recognized. It hurt to breathe in. It hurt to breathe out. Doc tried to slide back into the dark, pain-free void, but it faded like mist in the sun, leaving her aware and hurting in places she didn't know it was possible *to* hurt.

She'd heard them talking, speaking what they called "standard" in the galaxy, realized she was the topic and translated it into playing possum, even when she wanted to moan. It was a relief when she'd heard them move away, but hearing hurt, too. How could hearing hurt? It was an odd kind of pain. It didn't throb or pulse. It was more like an electric charge brushing across her nerve endings, a muted thrum, except when she moved. Then it wasn't muted.

You should have thrown her back or killed her. The phrasing was interesting. Wasn't "thrown back" a fishing term? And if it was, what had they been fishing for? And what about her that "interested" him?

She lifted her lids. That hurt. So did blinking—looking not so much. She considered what she could see, which wasn't a lot. She appeared to be in a tent, lying on a bed. She wasn't a fan of tents, even ones with beds. The blanket against her cheek was coarse. Not a fan of that either.

Not Kansas or Oz. Hell was on the short list of possibilities.

She studied the bedposts. They looked rustic. It wasn't fun, but she managed to sit up and dangle her legs off the edge of the bed. Her vest and her pack were on the table across from her, a table that was more rustic than the bed. Someone had rummaged through the contents. If the painkillers were gone, someone was going to die.

She looked down. The floor was dirt.

Doc was not a fan of that either. She could accept it had its place in the cycle of nature, but not as flooring.

Hell was fast moving up the list of possible locations.

She stood and her legs held. That was encouraging. She headed for her pack, a bit of a totter to her gait. That wasn't so encouraging. If she couldn't walk, how was she going to kick ass? Her ribs hurt, too, recalling the moment when she'd slammed against the ship's harness.

Pain meds first. She found a packet of water and the tablets she needed. She also snagged a power bar from the mess. It eased the gnawing in her stomach and helped clear her head.

She did a weapons check. They'd taken her sidearm and spare magazines, but missed the stuff strapped to her body. Interesting they hadn't searched her. She didn't remember them looking sensitive, so that left clueless. She liked clueless opponents.

There was a way out of the tent, but she wasn't sure who to *be* out there. It was no longer a secret that she could kick ass, so that took being underestimated off the table. She didn't mind that much. She didn't like pretending to be scared, not when fear was as close as *them* all the time.

She heard the softer tones of women, the deeper tones of the men. She padded to the flap and eased it back, trying not to wince as her careful footsteps set little shockwaves across her nerve endings. It was like pain sparklers going off inside her. Through the small gap she could see more tents and a few people, but not much else. She took a shallow breath and stepped out into light that was either fading or building. Not enough data to know which. It took a moment for anyone to notice her. Doc used that moment to expand her SA—her situational awareness.

It was an encampment, with too much emphasis on *camp*. The series of tents were arranged in a rough semicircle in a forest-like clearing. Doc wouldn't have called them a loud bunch of people, even before silence spread through the group. She waited a half beat, angled her chin and stalked into the center of the encampment. She felt them study her, but Doc ignored them. Her gaze swept the surrounding flora and fauna. It was green, brown and rocky with bug sounds just like where she crashed. She looked up. It had sky, but this sky had *three* moons, none of them purple.

Three blue moons. Didn't seem like a good omen and didn't take much to conclude this wasn't where she'd crashed, even if their ship was playing least in sight. So why the primitive pretense?

The campfires in front of the tents were part of the whole bad sign motif. The men were still doing the *Conan the Barbarian* theme she'd noticed when they attacked her. She easily picked out the ones she'd "interacted" with during her capture. It helped somewhat to know they were hurting, too. The women, young girls actually, looked like Moonies in coarse robes and one-size-fits-all braids. A couple of the girls were pregnant. One guy stood next to each woman in front of almost all the tents. The ones not in pain looked smug. The girls looked varying degrees of shell-shocked. No sign of commerce or crops, no tools, no children out of wombs.

Boy, girl, boy, girl, boy, girl…

She turned from the thirteen boy/girl combos and found three guys near a table so archaic it could have belonged to the Seven Dwarves huge cousins. One of them was the guy who shot her. She avoided direct eye contact with him, so she wouldn't be tempted to kick his ass. Boy, boy, boy, and one old woman with shrewd eyes. She studied Doc as intently as Doc studied her. She took a step toward her with a smile that was probably meant to be reassuring creasing her lined face.

Doc didn't feel reassured.

"Hello."

Doc frowned. That was weird. Hello was an Earth word, wasn't it? For no reason she could quantify, Doc shifted from her usual 'say little' policy to 'say nothing.' People were uncomfortable with silence and often rushed to fill it. Filling this silence might provide her with useful information. She'd slid into scientist, she realized. Oh well, she *was* a scientist. She looked past the old woman, giving in to the temptation to assess the shooter. It was easier from behind the scientist screen. He'd packed a wallop before he shot her. That hadn't changed.

The boys were big, but this guy was bigger. His lean, hard

body was poured into black leather and then accessorized with a hefty serving of arrogance and an array of weapons that were a bit sexy. He had a thin, cruel mouth. His dark hair hung around his face as if he'd shoved it out of the way when he woke up and then forgot about it. His face was all sharp angles and he needed a shave.

Looking at him, her hope for plumbing dimmed even further.

He had the wild and untamed look down cold. Despite the grubbiness, he was good-looking if one liked barbarians.

She didn't.

His icy green gaze burned over her, but Doc couldn't get a read on his thoughts. His expression was a minor rock formation. Good thing she didn't need to know what he was thinking to kick his ass. It would be a challenge to wait, but she needed a challenge, she reminded herself. Her gaze flicked around the technology *nil* environment. She also needed plumbing, but that didn't seem to be on offer. Did everyone dig their own hole or just find a bush?

"See to her, Bana," Conan ordered, his voice as cold as his eyes. His voice had a hint of an accent that reminded her of a Slavic language. He and Bana exchanged looks that would have made Doc wary if she weren't already throbbing with wary.

Doc followed Bana to a tent set apart from the others. It wasn't a shock to find it contained a pit toilet.

It was a disappointment.

Eight

When the Key activated the outpost two Earth years ago, all the Garradian outposts with scanning capabilities had become active, boosting tracking and scanning ability throughout the galaxy. It wasn't perfect coverage. There were still data holes in the scans, caused by planets, moons and other orbiting rock masses, as well as areas the Garradians had either not got around to watching or didn't consider interesting.

Since his fleet had been upgraded with the "new" technology, Hel had tried to position them to cover scanning holes, but his ships were also required for escort and protection duty. If they hadn't had ships already being built before the war, he couldn't have replaced the lost ships so quickly. Their numbers had doubled from pre-War, because no one had been shooting at them since the defeat of the Dusan, but it wasn't possible to cover all vulnerable areas all the time. If someone knew the scan capability of the outposts and ship movements—and many of the pirates and raiders in the no-go frontier did—a rogue force could hide in plain sight. But they might also grow careless as time passed without detection. And if mistakes were made, they could be found, analyzed and maybe they could be tracked.

Hel combined all available data to create a galactic map showing the abduction/interception points of the missing thirteen women and all ship movement energy signatures from before the first abduction. Delilah's abduction was close to one of three areas of activity. All three areas were interesting. All were close to shipping routes and partially hidden by large planet masses. A ship would have to be almost on top of them for detection to occur.

He honed in on the area where Delilah had gone missing, keyed in additional search parameters, and put the map in motion. His search revealed a faint, but unusual energy signature in the area. It was muddied by Delilah's ship and the *Doolittle's* rescue craft. He marked that signature and turned his focus to the other two areas of activity, neither of which had been as impacted by search ships. The pattern was in both those areas, as well. He keyed in a galaxy-wide search for that pattern. It would take time, but it was a place to start.

He found it interesting that there was no information or alert on a ship or ships of unknown designation during the time of the abductions. Did that mean that the unknown ship had the ability to cloak in a way that even the Kikk outpost couldn't track? Or did it mean that someone had suppressed the information for their own purposes?

If no one was concealing this information, there was a new player in the galaxy—one with the ability to hide from everyone.

The energy signature could be from their hyperspace drives, or the anomaly could be occurring when the ship or ships dropped cloak or used their energy weapon. Their ships also had to drop cloak for transport. It was possible to use an adversary's weakness—such as the scanning holes—to hide this activity. If the signature was from using the energy beam, they were going to be much harder to find. They wouldn't need to, or they would take care not to, use this beam near their bolt-hole.

Hel assumed that the General's people were doing the same assessment he was doing. Delilah had managed to run a scan on the tractor beam. This information had been pulled from something called a "black box." The General had included some of that information in the data burst. He wished he knew if he had all available information. The energy signature was close to the one he was searching for, but not a perfect match. He added this energy pattern to his search parameters.

He pulled up the abduction reports again. None had been able to send a warning. Interesting that Delilah had managed to contact her people, and provide information about the nature of the attack. He considered what he'd learned—and what he still needed to determine. He would have to tell Halliwell anything he could find out through other means. With their new friendliness, it was important to appear helpful. He flipped through the reports. He would provide all of them to the General, just not all at once.

He picked out the abductions closest to where Delilah went missing. Those would interest the General, while providing an incomplete picture. His report as complete as he wished it to be, he sent it to the General as a data burst using their secure communication channel.

Next, he needed eyes on the galaxy. He needed to get his people scanning for that energy signature and for unknown ships in the blind spots. He pulled up maps on Gadi ship deployments. He'd tagged the commanders he considered loyal and noticed that there'd been some unreported shifts in some deployments. For some reason, suspect ships were now positioned closer to the Kikk Outpost. Ship's commanders had a certain amount of autonomy. It made no sense to tie their hands and inhibit their ability to respond. It was assumed, however, that any change in position would be reported as soon as possible. He searched through his communications and found the notifications buried in inconsequential chatter.

Someone had hoped he wouldn't notice.

He ran a deployment scenario for maximum scanning ability, noted prime positions and sent orders for the new deployment grids, including scanning instructions with the patterns he'd identified. He tagged the order as high priority. It would be treason for any of them to ignore the orders without contacting him to explain their position.

He did have one other resource he could use.

In the time before the defeat of the Dusan, in the days before the Garradian cloaks, he and his Ojemba squads had used planetary bodies to hide their movements. Now—as then—his Ojemba allowed him to do things that the official Gadi Leader couldn't. The scan holes he didn't know, his men would. But he needed to decide how little he could get away with telling them. He wanted good information but didn't want them to know what he was looking for. Since the fall of their common enemy, his men's loyalties had become…flexible. They followed the money and had an instinct for going where the rewards were greatest.

A missing expedition crew member could command a high price. He could outbid others interested parties, but if he went too high, it would start a feeding frenzy—and tip off his enemies. If Carig knew of the Chameleon from leaks via the expedition, it wouldn't be long before someone figured out it was Delilah.

With traitors on both sides, betrayal was inevitable.

Hel smiled. It felt good to be back in the plot and counterplot zone.

☼

"She is—" Eamon stopped, unable to find the words he needed to describe the woman.

Vidor could have finished it with "dangerous." When she'd come out of the tent, she'd worn lethal like a coat. He'd seen many soldiers in action, but none had sent a chill down his back in quite the way she did. And then she'd shifted, that was the only word for it, into something else. She'd looked curious, assessing, almost harmless—until he realized how little she revealed of her thoughts.

There was no outrage, no tears, no trembling demands to know why she'd been taken. Just that quiet assessment of everything and everyone. Her study of him had been thorough and detached. But he had confirmed the usual intensity of her eye color. And he'd noted that the color seemed to change with her shift in moods. Her expression stayed remote and indifferent, as if they'd inconvenienced her in some minor way. It appeared as if she was learning, but what was there to learn? They'd taken great care to disguise who and what they were. Loyalty must be taught before knowledge could be shared.

Cadir rubbed his aching neck. "She looks so small."

Eamon would make no comment on her size. He was still having some difficulty walking. Or explaining how she'd been at his feet without him noticing.

Vidor would not soon forget the ruthless efficiency with which she'd taken down his men—even turning their own weaponry back on them. He'd surprised her and he'd still almost missed her.

"I will toss you for her," Cadir said, his gaze fixed on where she'd passed from sight. He was too young to hide his desire, and he lacked Eamon's reason to control his thoughts.

He was the youngest. Based on seniority, the woman should be Eamon's, though Vidor, as leader could claim any woman he desired at any time. None had tempted him, but this one did. He didn't like admitting it, but he must.

"She will choose." They'd allowed all the women the illusion of choice, but this one wouldn't be fooled by illusions, nor would she be interested in boys. They'd learn. This was one of the reasons they were here.

☼

Doc distracted herself from her gnarly surroundings by mulling what she'd observed so far. These people spoke Standard, but with that hint of Slavic accent that made her feel like she should recognize it. Logically she knew she couldn't, but it still nagged at her.

The encampment *looked* dug in, but without commerce it couldn't be anything but temporary. It appeared they were fishing for women and weren't in a hurry about it. One of the girls was seriously pregnant, the other medium well. The other women could be, too, based on the smug expressions on the faces of the men with them. Good thing she had her own birth control. It didn't appear to be on offer, though any guy who tried to take her to bed had more to worry about than her ability to conceive.

Their expedition had no intell on the group. No way would Halliwell have let her fly alone if he'd known about the girl hunt.

Interesting that they had the technology to bring down ships, but expected the women not to realize they had this technology. In fact, they seemed to have pretty low expectations about women. That wasn't that unusual in this galaxy, but she was sure they weren't from this galaxy. They knew all the players here and this bunch wasn't one of them.

It was kind of funny they were going to all this trouble to find women when all they needed was match.com.

Doc finished with the pit toilet and emerged to find Bana waiting with a bowl of water, a piece of nasty-looking soap and a coarse, primitive towel. She also had one of those Moonie gowns over her arm.

The woman touched her chest. "I'm Bana." Then she pointed to Doc. "What's your name?"

Doc blinked a couple of times and turned to wash her hands and face, turning the water a dirty brown from the mud she'd smeared on her face and hands. She took her time. She didn't plan to be mute forever, just until it no longer served a useful purpose. She was smarter than these people. It wasn't arrogance, but a biological fact. She'd find their ship and take it. Payback was a bitch, but totally deserved in this case.

She turned to find Bana holding out the robe. Doc stared at her until she sighed and tossed the robe to one side.

"We'll *talk* about clothing later."

That sounded like she suspected Doc understood her. Doc bumped up her IQ a few points, as she studied her with more care. Her pale blue eyes were calm and a bit amused, as if she knew a joke that Doc didn't. Doc didn't let this bother her. At the moment, there was a lot the old woman knew that Doc didn't, but that would change because *she* didn't know Doc. After a long moment of clashing gazes, Doc gave her a few more IQ points. Better to overestimate, then underestimate. She could afford to be generous.

Outside the light continued to fade, so it must be moving toward nightfall. She didn't think ahead to how she'd deal with that. No sense borrowing trouble until it got here. The encampment looked more dispirited than before. It wasn't fair. Sara Donovan got shot down and met a hunky alien who fell in love with her. Doc got yanked out of the sky and ended up in 2000 B.C. with three barbarian morons.

But she wasn't bitter.

She looked around.

Okay, she was bitter.

The three barbarians were still huddled around the dwarves' dinner table like they were waiting for her. The youngest showed some rather obvious signs of interest. It didn't surprise her that the other guy had his body parts under better control. She'd been pretty emphatic with her knee when they first met.

Quick-draw Conan frowned. "Where is her robe?"

Doc wasn't surprised they wanted to get her out of her clothes. They *were* guys.

Bana and Conan exchanged a look that lasted long enough to be interesting. There was a curious dynamic between her and Conan. He gave off "I'm in charge" vibes, and yet it appeared Bana could exert some control over him. Doc filed it away for further consideration as Bana pointed to a stool and indicated Doc should sit. Doc hesitated long enough to be annoying. When she complied, she was unable to suppress a wince of pain.

Conan snapped his fingers and the henchman with the blood flow problem hastily filled a crude mug with an amber liquid. He shoved it toward her, some of the fluid sloshing onto the table. The wood smoked where the fluid hit it.

Conan mimed drinking. "It will help with the pain."

She wrapped her hands around the cup, noting the intent way they all watched her. With a flair for the dramatic she didn't realize she had, she waited a five count, then pushed it away.

Conan pushed it back. "*Drink.*"

The rest of them gave her encouraging nods. Why didn't they just say, "Please drink our booze and get mindlessly drunk. When you sober up, you'll be the girl half of a boy-girl combo, living in a tent, and stirring a pot filled with my dinner." It would have been more subtle.

"It will help you relax." Horny boy's smile was almost charming—a bit of surprise considering what she'd done to him.

Relax was the one thing she didn't dare do, and not just because of the barbarians. She could feel *them* pressing close, as if they sensed her vulnerability in this tech-deficient environment. She needed more than what they were offering to survive. She needed to multitask more than she needed air, food and water. Fear helped her focus, but *their* presence created other problems with her concentration. It left her stuck in place, when what she needed was to *move.*

Don't let them get you, Del.

"Drink," Conan said again.

Doc picked up the cup and dumped the contents on a bush. It shriveled down to a wisp of smoke that drifted toward the sky, until a slight breeze caught it and whisked it away.

She looked at Conan, her brows arched.

Conan grabbed her gaze, as if pleased him to have it, and held it as he asked Bana, "What's her name?"

"She hasn't said." Bana acted like they were best friends, allies against the boys.

Had the other girls fallen for this parlor trick? Doc thought about it for a couple of seconds and decided they probably had. They'd have been scared and needed someone to cling to. Bana couldn't know Doc didn't cling to anything but her sanity.

The space between Conan's brows creased in a fierce frown.

"Perhaps she can't." This contribution came from horny henchman.

Bana appeared to consider, before saying, "She can speak."

She wasn't surprised when Conan kicked a stool out of the way and crouched in front of her, his gaze boring into her like a laser.

"What's your name, woman?"

"Vidor?" There was a warning in Bana's voice.

Doc blinked. Had anyone ever called her woman? If the truth were told, she'd never felt female even when she'd gone vamp for an op. By the time she left her mum's gender neutral world, it was too late for her to be a real girl. *Pinocchio* with female accoutrements and an oversized brain, only she was a better liar.

She could even lie well to herself. Because she had felt like a girl once. With Hel. But she couldn't afford to think about him right now. She felt a quiver of something in her gut at the thought of Hel, at the thought of never seeing him again. It kicked on her senses.

Smell came first. Conan—she refused to use his real name, even inside her head—didn't smell as bad as she'd have expected, given the layer of dirt coating him. He smelled of the earth and the sky and of guy, she supposed. She could see the texture of his skin under the dirt and beard, and she could feel the intensity of his will. The guy might be as stubborn as she was, but the lack of plumbing scared her more than he did.

"Tell me your name." His tone was softer, as if he sensed the change in her.

It was enough to bring her defenses crashing down with an internal clang. The barbarians were at the gate. Not the time to lose focus.

He touched her chin with his finger, lifting it until their gazes intersected. "Your name?"

He thought he'd won. It was there in his eyes. There was something else there. Names appeared to be important. She flicked her gaze over him, let a hint of dismissive in and then mainlined bitch and beyond, just to make sure he got the message.

He did. His face hardened, sending an icy chill down her back and not in a good way. Doc tensed, bringing her inner warrior online, just in case.

"If we can't name her—"

A look from Bana cut off the words, but not in time. A hint

of chagrin in Bana's expression confirmed Doc's initial hypothesis. Names mattered.

"I'm Eamon."

The gabby one pointed to his chest, just in case she didn't realize he was talking about himself. It was a pretty good chest, but she didn't want to take it home with her. Or live in a tent with it.

"I'm Cadir," the horny one said, defiant for reasons that weren't clear. Her gaze shifted between the two men. They could have been brothers, probably were. Maybe age mattered, too. Eamon got first dibs?

Cadir was grimy cute, but also not enough to tempt. They were both young enough to qualify her as a Cougar. While it was always good to have a goal, getting it on with younger men had never been one of hers and adding it to her to-do list seemed contraindicated under the circumstances. She couldn't decide if Conan was closer to her age or not. The dirt hid a lot, as did the pissy expression, and he had the added air of command clouding the issue. It also wasn't clear if he were a contender for her hand or an enabler for his henchmen.

Doc stared straight ahead for a few seconds and then blinked. She didn't yawn, but it was implied. All three looked annoyed. Nice when cause was followed so closely on effect.

Conan huffed as he rose, staring down at Doc. He had imposing down pat, but at least he wasn't touching her anymore.

"Make her understand."

Doc could feel Bana mull over whether to out her or not, like there was a question about which side she was on.

Only the guys were surprised when Bana said, "She understands."

"If she understands, why doesn't she speak?"

Bana met her cool look and upped the ante. "Do you wish to tell them or should I?"

Doc waited a ten count, shrugged. "You're doing so well."

Conan puffed up, like an angry cat, but without the cute factor.

He was more like a sabertooth tiger, but Doc didn't know if they puffed up. That was the problem with using an extinct species in an analogy, not enough information to be sure it was apt.

"Why would you do this?"

Doc gave him a cool look. Her tone was flat, indifferent. "You shot me."

He crossed his arms over a chest Doc had to concede was nicely put together. "I stunned you."

"By shooting me."

It was habit to evaluate the impact of her words and tone on a target and she had no reason to make an exception with Conan. Susceptibility was an unknown but could be estimated with reasonable accuracy. Based on limited observed data, this was a guy who hadn't been crossed too often. Lack of exposure to annoying behavior would increase his inability to maintain patience and focus.

She wasn't surprised when smoke almost came out his ears, and she was pretty sure sparks did come out of his eyes. She *was* surprised he didn't shoot her again. He had better self-control than observed data indicated.

She pointedly rubbed a sore shoulder.

"The mead would ease the pain," Eamon pointed out.

Doc looked down at the dead bush and then back at him.

"It is not for plants."

"But useful in lowering inhibitions." Should she have said that? Hard to act stupid when she wasn't.

"It is true that we hoped it would ease your transition into our community," Bana said, giving the three men yet another of her warning looks.

Maybe she should just tell them to shut up. It's not like Doc couldn't see "the look." Maybe she'd upped the old woman's IQ a bit too high. Doc looked around the encampment, taking her time before returning her attention to their little grouping.

"Your *community* is a bit too rustic for my taste. Even getting drunk wouldn't help me *transition*." Doc felt like she was channeling her mum, she sounded so coolly British. It was kind of comforting.

"You don't like my home?" Conan growled the words. The guy had all the finesse of Hitler, minus the great personality.

"I haven't seen your home."

Conan frowned, like he was puzzled. Perhaps she'd been too subtle.

"This isn't your home."

"This is where we live." Again, Bana's tone contained a warning.

Doc wasn't sure if it was for the guys or her. "I wouldn't call this living."

Cadir leaned closer. "We mean you no harm, woman."

Yeah, she already knew what he wanted to do and it would do her harm, even if he didn't know it. She hadn't been created to sit in front of a tent and stir a pot. Her gaze shifted to the other women and she almost felt envy. It was no gift to be her.

She returned her attention to Cadir. "You shot me."

"We were trying to help you," Eamon corrected.

She wouldn't have needed "help" if they hadn't yanked her out of the sky, but it seemed they were all pretending that hadn't happened.

"By shooting me?"

"I think she's upset you shot her, Vidor," Eamon said, his delight a bit too obvious.

He was like a large, untrained dog. She'd never had a pet, but he didn't look house-trained.

"Neither of you stopped him," Doc pointed out. In point of fact, they'd tried to shoot her, too.

That wiped out the grin. Now he looked like a sulky dog. "You hurt *me* and I am not upset with *you*."

"You haven't been beat up by a girl before, have you?"

"I haven't done anything with a girl," he admitted with a frankness that was kind of cute, in a lame way. "When we are married—"

Married. Not mated? Doc rubbed the tight spot between her brows. Usually it took *them* and the impossible to make her head ache, but they'd managed it in four, short minutes.

"Are you hungry?" Bana seemed to think a change of subject would help.

She was wrong. Doc sniffed the air and then wished she hadn't.

She made a face. "No."

"You lack manners," Conan growled the words. Perhaps he only had the one tone.

"You shot me."

He slammed his hands on the table between them, making the mead cup bounce along the surface. He leaned in until his face was inches from hers.

"Tell me your name."

Menace quivered in the air between them, his hot, hers cold.

"Vidor, let the girl breathe."

He waited almost a whole minute, his gaze locked on hers, before straightening. Doc lifted her lashes, holding his stare as he moved back, determined not to be the one who looked away first.

"Vidor." Bana's voice was more insistent.

Conan broke the look-lock. Doc didn't sag in relief on the outside, the inside was another story. The guy must have been a steamroller in another life.

"Sit." Bana's tone was soft, but Conan sat. "We'll eat now." Her gaze shifted to Doc. "All of us."

Doc realized that someone had set a bowl in front of her during her stare down with Conan. It didn't smell any better up close. And it looked worse than it smelled. Pit toilets and gray sludge. The facts were in. The hypothesis confirmed.

This was hell.

Nine

Hel knew that even with reduced access to information, the highly motivated General Halliwell would be close on his heels, in both planning and in action. They were a resourceful people. The General had forwarded him the report from the search team, most likely a carefully edited version. It noted that Doctor Clementyne had been apprehended by unknown hostiles some distance from where she'd touched down. Hel could fill in the missing parts. He'd faced down those with hostile intent many times during his Ojemba operations.

If she had survived the encounter, Delilah would find a way to aid in her own rescue. And when she did, he needed to be closer to where she'd been taken than the *Doolittle.* It would be difficult to accomplish in a Gadi ship, but he had a way—and a ship—that would let him move freely about the galaxy. He'd improved this ship with a Garradian cloak—and modified it so that it would be undetectable by the outpost's sensors.

There were concerns with leaving his ship. He could stay in constant contact, but if his enemies moved on him, it would make his life interesting. He did not know when his enemies would act again, or how. He just knew they would.

He pulled the Gadi deployment map back up. All but two ships had obeyed orders—the two closest to Kikk. He'd need to deal with them before dropping off the grid.

☼

Halliwell may have only recently become acquainted with

Doctor Clementyne, but it didn't take a lot of interaction to know that she was a resourceful young woman. He knew in his gut that Giddioni knew this, too. He didn't know where the doctor was, but he was sure of two things.

Helfron Giddioni was going to bust his butt to find her first and forget to mention it if he did.

The Doc would do her damndest to help someone find her.

It hadn't escaped his notice that the person most equipped to find Dr. Clementyne was Dr. Clementyne. Her mind was both agile and devious. Could he get some of their geeks to think like her?

He'd have to assume that they hadn't been told everything the Gadi knew and that Giddioni had a head start on the search. He knew the galaxy and had resources that the expedition lacked. But they had some information Giddioni didn't have: the black box from the Doc's ship. He'd had the geeks send some of the data, but not all of it. He had to look like they were one big cooperating family, but didn't mean they had to *be* that family.

He waited until the geek squad was seated around the table in his ready room before strolling to the head of that table. He stared at each geek long enough to make them tug at the necks of their tee shirts. It was a fine line, scaring them enough to make them think, but not so much they went brain dead.

"You've seen the data shared by the Gadi. How is it possible for someone to be operating so brazenly in the galaxy and we don't know about it?"

When the excuses trickled to a stop, there was one geek with a decent brain, but an addiction to big words and an inability to shut up. Halliwell let him go on for a few minutes before he cut him off.

"So we have holes in our scanning that someone has been exploiting?"

The geek, with the forgettable name of James, considered this for far too long, then pushed up his glasses and nodded.

"How do we plug the holes?"

A geek without glasses looked up from his computer screen. "Maybe we don't have to. Looks like the Gadi are already working on it."

Well, color me not surprised. "Show me," Halliwell ordered.

Glassless geek did something to make what he was looking at show up on the HUD. Then he added in scan capability based on Gadi ship deployment.

Halliwell studied the HUD. It didn't make him happy they were thinking along the same lines as the Leader—not when they were behind. He noticed something.

"What about these two ships? What are they scanning?"

James did some checking, then looked up. "Us."

Halliwell stiffened. "Is this a new deployment?"

More clicking of keys.

"No, sir, well, not for them. There used to be a cluster of nine ships there, but seven of them have moved into the new configuration."

Two Gadi ships didn't scare him, not with the outpost at his back.

"When is the Leader's flagship due to arrive?" He walked up to the HUD.

"Not for five days, sir. They aren't rushing it."

Also not a surprise. Giddioni needed time to find the Doc first.

"Which ships were among the nine? Show me where they are now."

When one of the geeks did, Halliwell studied the deployment. Interesting. Giddioni had moved them to the outer fringes of the no-go frontier, the corridor between what used to be Dusan and the free section of the galaxy. *I wonder whose ass he's trying to protect with that deployment.*

"Is there any way for us to tap into the Gadi scans without their knowing about it?"

Glassless geek looked the most surprised. "You want us to hack the Gadi system?"

"They're looking for something specific, and I want to know what that is so we can look for it, too." Halliwell turned to give him his signature Look. It had been known to make some men wet their pants. "Is that a problem?"

More tie tugging. "No, sir."

"I also want to know if there's any covert contact between those two ships and our ships or the outpost."

James, the smart one, swallowed visibly. "You think someone is—"

He couldn't say it, so Halliwell said it for him. "Betraying us? I don't think it. I know it." He paused, bumped up "the look" a notch. "If you can't find it, then I'll have to assume you're the leak. And you don't want to know what I'm going to do to the stinking traitor when I find him. Is that clear?"

Both visible and audible swallowing was followed by wide-eyed nods. Nice when they were all on the same page. He moved to his next round of questions.

"I want immediate update on *any* ship movements, particularly any movement close to the Dusan frontier. I want a list of habitable but uninhabited planets in or near the frontier." He paused, wondering how to phrase his last request. "I want to know if anything unusual has been or is detected near any of those planets."

"Unusual how, sir?" a different geek asked.

"We know the pilot was removed from the planet following the attack." Why was it that smart people were sometimes not that smart? "Had to have been moved by ship, but we showed no ship on tracking."

The man frowned. "So you think the ship was cloaked?"

"Obviously." Halliwell tried not to sound as impatient as he felt.

"I thought the outpost could track cloaked ships?"

Halliwell took a calming breath. It didn't work that well. "Obviously this ship isn't Garradian or the cloak has been modified somehow."

"But if it's cloaked so we can't see it, how do we find it?" This from a third geek who should have known better than to say this out loud.

"We could search for unusual energy signatures," James put in. "We've been studying the Garradian cloaks, to see if they can be tracked and found they do leave a slight energy pattern when they are used." He shoved his glasses up on his nose. "It's probably what the Gadi are looking for."

That had occurred to Halliwell. He didn't want to wait for the hack into the Gadi systems to begin searching. They'd need every edge they could get if they were going to beat Giddioni to the Doc.

"Even if we identify an energy pattern," the glassless geek said, "it's a big galaxy."

"If they are using holes in our scanning to evade detection, isn't that a kind of trail we can follow?" For the first time Colonel Carey joined the discussion. He moved up to the HUD. "We knew they were here." He pointed to the Doc's acquisition point. "There can't be that many holes in this one area. And they had to know we'd be looking for them once we got the SOS from—"

"Our missing crewman," Halliwell cut in, giving Carey a "keep your mouth shut" look.

James looked excited. "That's not a bad idea, sir."

"We can look," a geek with a clue said, "but all they need to do is nothing and we have nothing to search for." The geek wasn't an optimist.

"Bread crumbs," Halliwell said.

"Excuse me?"

"Didn't you ever read *Hansel and Gretel*? Bet our crewman did and he'll be trying to leave bread crumbs for us. Count on it. Watch for it. See it when it happens. And no one knows about it outside this room. I don't have to tell you what I'll do to you if this leaks out, do it?"

The geeks might have turned pale. It was hard to tell, since they started out pale. They all nodded.

"Then get to work."

They filed out. Colonel Carey didn't go with them.

"Sir, about the...crewman?" He hesitated, maybe hoping the General would remove the need to ask the question

"Yes?"

He hesitated, then said, "She remind you of anyone?"

Halliwell grinned. "Oh yeah."

"Do you think whoever took her has figured out how screwed they are yet?"

☼

Morning failed to make the encampment look less dreary to Doc's admittedly jaded gaze, though it had been a relief when she'd learned she was to bunk in Bana's tent. Doc had refused to share the same bed, even if it meant she slept on the rustic tabletop. Doc didn't sleep a lot anyway.

The three barbarians made it clear they considered that a temporary situation and that their lame courting efforts would break down her resistance. Bana was hoping for that, too. Doc was a lousy roommate. She didn't like spending nights with herself, so why should Bana? Interesting that it was possible to low crawl like a ghost, but a few calisthenics sounded like stampeding dogs. Course, she hadn't tried that hard to be quiet. She'd offered to go outside several times but had been ignored.

At one point Bana said, almost impatiently, "You are very headstrong."

"You're not headstrong enough," Doc shot back. Doc felt and heard her response in the dark of the tent. A sort of tensing and a sharp inhale, as if Doc had shocked her but she needed to hide it. It might be part of her mind games as enabler-in-chief, but Doc still felt uneasy about the innocuous exchange, though she couldn't explain why.

Even if Doc was tempted to give in to pressure—which she wasn't—she couldn't *do* this. The only way it could end was badly. Of course, if it was going to go badly anyway, it might be good policy to give bad a nudge in a direction that was bad for them instead of her. But, what was the right nudge in the bad-for-them direction?

She spent the insomnia portion of the night working out and considering various nudging options, while Bana put a pillow over her head and plotted her death. One idea was to play the three men off each other. Conan was hanging back, but giving off jealous vibes that he thought no one noticed. If she'd stopped to think about this, she'd have been stuck in shock at the idea of three men vying for *her* attention, so she didn't.

The problem with playing the men off each other was *her.* She'd observed the process, but she had no practical experience. She did know her science. These men weren't just an unstable element, but an unknown quantity of unstable. There was a less than ten percent chance of a positive outcome and that might be an optimistic projection. Even if she were close in her outcome assessment that left a ninety percent chance someone would get hurt.

Not that she minded hurting any of *them,* but it should serve a useful purpose. Doc wasn't an assassin, nor was she into revenge, well, she tried not to be. She wanted a way off this rock. If she got to kick Conan's ass in the process, that was a bonus, not the end game.

There were other ways to stir his pot. Conan looked like he'd hate uncertainty.

She had a gift for creating it.

Conan seemed certain he had the upper hand, that he had her boxed in. Changing that perception was as good a place to start as any.

She paused, not in doubt, but in an honest assessment of the risks. Bana had suggested killing Doc. It was a concern that she might push him too hard and trigger a hard termination, but that wasn't the worst that could happen to her. If she doubted that, all she had to do was think about her brother.

Don't let them get you, Del.

She added hard termination to the list of escape options. With a little experimentation, she should be able to determine Conan's breaking point, though she might die doing it. She grinned. Dying doing something was the primary risk of any of her operations. The more her life changed, the more it stayed the same.

When they went through her stuff they left the stuff that looked harmless to them. A small, but powerful pair of binoculars lurked among the harmless stuff. She'd tucked them and her compass in a pocket of her ABUs before she left the tent.

The guys sans women were eating more sludge for breakfast, joined by Bana. She ignored them and the bowl waiting her attention. For the moment she was subsisting on her emergency supplies. Instead, she studied the trees surrounding the compound. She needed a big, sturdy one, kind of like the barbarians, only taller.

She identified a good prospect, then slanted a look Conan's way through her lowered lashes. As soon as her gaze pinged on him, he pinged back. Interesting that he seemed to be so aware of her. It might prove useful—and annoying. It went against both training and personality to attract attention, though she wasn't above doing it for operational necessity.

Once she was sure she had his attention, she crossed to her designated tree in long swift strides, not wanting to give him time to stop her. Her brain was already calculating the amount of thrust and the best angle to get her body on that lower branch. She hit the sweet spot, bent her knees and then surged forward, leaping at the optimal moment. When her hands hooked around the branch, her body swung up and over. Her legs straddling the branch, she held back a grin at the looks of shock on the various barbarian and girl faces, but it was Conan's reaction that concerned her. As he approached, she lifted her legs up, then rose to a stand on the branch. Didn't want him to yank her down until she was ready to come down.

"What are you doing?" His tone seethed with a frustration out of proportion to her action. He was an uber unstable element.

"I'm going to climb this tree." She met his frustration with a cool tone and cooler gaze.

"Why?"

"Because it's here." She could see him consider the activity and conclude it was harmless, though he was still uneasy. She broke eye contact and started up, not stopping until the limbs were too small to hold her weight. She wedged herself in place and looked down. Conan waited at the bottom, staring up at her with what she was coming to think was his only expression—a scowl.

"Come down." He'd ramped up again while she climbed, but it eased off when she looked at him.

That was interesting. Was he calmer because she wasn't moving or did he like it when she looked at him? She broke eye contact and looked around. It was early, but the heat was already building. The humidity was in play, too. She wondered idly, because it wasn't an operational necessity, what kind of variations there were in the climate. It had been freaking hot since her arrival. Her ABU jacket upped the heat factor, but she wasn't comfortable stripping down to a tee shirt in front of three horny guys.

It wasn't about her desirability factor, she'd decided sometime in the night. There was some kind of female deficit, either in their expedition or their society—and a huge arrogance surplus. Thinking about what could be happening and why with this bunch sent her mind into a tailspin of theories and spin-off questions.

Doc's hands tightened around the branch, the pain a place to use to regain her focus.

"You are not well?" His voice was sharp and anxious.

That helped her get her focus back. She needed to learn their pressure points without giving away hers. She relaxed her body, then her hands and looked down.

"I'm fine."

It was her attention that eased him. She could see it happen. She looked away, counted to ten and looked back. Tension eased back again. It was like a yo-yo, though she wasn't sure who was doing the best job of playing whom since the intensity of his scrutiny made her feel on edge. Normally living on the edge helped her cope with *them*, but this was different. It had a draining component that was troubling. She felt a need to adjust her internal shield strength and integrity, if that was possible. There was a lot going on inside her head, even for her and not much was that useful.

Doc put the problem on a back burner, wedged herself to free her hands and pulled out the binoculars. As she studied the terrain, the intensity of his scrutiny faded to the back burner, too. The annoyance factor of her actions wasn't the only reason to do this. She did need to know about her surroundings.

She felt his gaze leave her and took a quick look. Now he paced back and forth under the tree. He wore his rock-like expression but his body radiated tension. He tensed, as if he felt her watching and started to look up. Doc returned her gaze to what she could see through the binoculars.

They seemed to be deep in a forest. The terrain was diverse. There was a lake a couple of clicks to her right. It was pretty, but she had a bad feeling it doubled as a bathtub, so it was hard to appreciate it properly. Mountains loomed in the distance. No sign of any other human habitation. What she *didn't* see was troubling. There was no clearing larger than this one where a ship might be parked.

It could be parked in a low orbit, if they had a remote transport device similar to the Garradian one. It could even be Garradian. It would also need a cloak if it were in orbit and not just any old cloak. Everyone had assumed the Kikk outpost could "see" cloaked ships, but evidence suggested they couldn't see this one. A ship hovering over a habitable—but not inhabited—planet would have prompted a visit to check it out.

Doc was pretty sure this planet was located somewhere along what used to be the Dusan frontier. It could be in Dusan space, but it seemed unlikely. If this were about women, well, there were Dusan women left from the war, but they weren't good breeding stock. None of the brides showed signs of having been Dusan companions, though Doc would need to chat with them to be sure. She was sure they'd been culled from the non-Dusan side of the galaxy.

Granted she could only see a small portion of the planet, but it appeared uninhabited and probably was. Conan and his merry band were hiding out and doing a pretty good job of it for Cro-Mag men. Using the frontier between Dusan and Gadi space made a kind of sense in the bride hunt, so lurking close to it made sense, too.

The planets on the fringe of no man's land near the Dusan frontier were still pretty sparsely populated and isolated, though the inhabitants all had access to space travel and interplanetary trade resources. They'd be easy targets for someone jumping in from the Dusan frontier, and many of them were still fearful of traveling in Dusan space—with some cause. Pirates had quickly filtered into the void left by the Dusan defeat.

But a small settlement, protected by a cloaked ship, with inhabitants that were careful not to draw attention to themselves? And if pirates did notice them, their primitive profile would indicate a low profit potential not worth the bother. It was moderately clever, though the underlying premise was seriously flawed. There were better—and faster—ways to get girls.

She honed in on a rocky bluff, maybe twelve clicks from the encampment. If there were caves there, or even overhanging rock, it might screen her from the ship's sensors. If their ship was in orbit, they needed a control device. Survey complete, she lowered herself down onto a sturdy branch and stared ahead, letting her mind spin with what she'd learned, looking for patterns and clues she might have missed in her initial assessment.

Her mind, happy with new input, was less fractious than normal, though that wouldn't last. This place was too quiet, too bland. Her mind hated a vacuum and upped the input streams—

"What do you think about?" His voice cut into her thoughts, shattering the forming patterns with his frustrated curiosity. "What do you see?"

She blinked away bits of equations and data streams as external awareness returned. Her temples ached, which was not a surprise. It was one of the downsides of being her. She looked at Conan, letting placid settle over her like she was a cow chewing a cud.

"I'm getting a fix on my location."

She started down, moving from branch to branch until she reached the last one between her and the ground.

"It will make it easier for my people to find me if I can tell them where I am."

He smiled. It wasn't a pleasant smile, but he did have good teeth. It was very anti-barbarian and another clue he wasn't what he seemed to be.

"You have no way to contact anyone."

She stared at him, so placidly she irritated herself.

It annoyed him, too. "You have no transmission device."

If he believed that, why did he look so worried? Again, she said nothing as the air achieved sluggish movement. She loosened the top two buttons of her ABU jacket, letting that air slide in around her neck and provide minute relief.

Conan pinged on the small action. He was so anxious to see a little skin she was embarrassed for him. His gaze burned into her, trying to find a way past placid to where her real self lived—a person she wasn't sure *she* knew, one she hadn't known existed until she met Hel. Was it all just sex or was there something else in his scrutiny? Did he see her when he looked or just a *woman* to fill his bride quota?

She had learned all she could watching them watch her. Now she needed them to leave, she needed them to go to their ship so she could figure out how to take it from them. He wouldn't want her to see it, but she planned to do a lot of things he wouldn't want her to do until she got away or he killed her.

The two other barbarian boys were watching her now, too. She was pretty sure they just wanted sex. Could she let Conan think she was softening toward him? If the boys thought they weren't going to get what they wanted from her, would that bring back the bride hunt? Thirteen girls grabbed and it had taken at least nine months, possibly longer. She was gauging results by the two pregnancies, so her data could be flawed. But if she was correct, that was a bit more than a bride a month and she'd been in camp one night—give or take how long she was out and the travel time between where she went down and here. She might not be able to get them to go hunting for some time.

Though Bana had said something about a lack of time when they'd thought Doc was still out. Was there a ticking clock? If there were, it would help her more than it would them.

Her attention shifted to the brides. How much force had been applied to achieve their compliance? They might be content with their lot or suffering from Stockholm syndrome. Doc slid deeper into detachment as her thoughts went further along this path. It was reasonable to assume there would be a tipping point where Conan would force the issue. She knew the mechanics, so didn't dwell on that. Marriage appeared to be the goal. Naming was important, but what would he do if she refused to give her name? Would it matter? She couldn't get pregnant—at least not for several months, but there were signs they could be patient, when they had to be.

Of the three men, Conan was the most unpredictable. If she toyed with his libido, she might get more than she could control. His expectations were murky, as well. It was obvious they wanted women, and that sex was part of that want, but their overall purpose was unclear. Why choose *this* course of action? If one were looking for the biddable and downtrodden, they'd come to the right place. But if downtrodden was the goal, then why did it appear part of Bana's job was to enlighten the men on how to treat the brides?

If one of them got impatient or seemed unkind to his bride, she was on him in a flash. And these big, tough men subsided at a word from her, even the nasty Conan backed down after two or three words from her. All of them were careful of the pregnant women. Doc assumed this meant they needed children, as well as women. But again, why chose this way to deal with it?

Doc sighed silently. The brides were so freaking young. Even a geek didn't like feeling old and neither did she. What had possessed them to bring her here? Her biological clock wasn't frantic yet, but it was getting pissy. It hadn't figured out that she had no intention of having a child.

Don't let them get you, Del.

Her parents had wanted a couple of geniuses and that's what they'd gotten, but they'd also gotten a freak and whack job. No, she would never have a child.

She might suspect they'd targeted her because of her association with the Earth expedition, but they didn't act like they expected her to know anything except her name. They could be trying to lull her into a false sense of security, but they appeared to have a point-shoot-and-take mentality. They *thought* they were being devious about their ship, but there was a big difference between thinking you were devious and actually being devious.

She needed more information, but the brides were skittish and unhappy despite Bana's "support." They had no clue how much power they had over the grooms, because no one had broken down the sexual math for them. A little girl bride rebellion would build the boys' character faster and better than Bana's etiquette lessons. Doc smiled to herself. She may not know much about sex, but she was great at math.

"Why do you smile like that?"

His fascination with her colored his voice, while his expression retained its rock-like impassivity. She fell forward, doing a complete flip in mid-air and landing on her feet in front of him.

"If you return me to my people, they might be willing to help you with your problem."

His eyes narrowed. "We have no problem."

"You have so many problems, it's embarrassing."

His hands fisted at his sides. "You know nothing about us, woman."

His gaze bored into her but she gave no ground, waited a ten count, then arched her brows. Fire flamed in his eyes. She'd gone too far. He was going to hit her. She shifted body alignment, prepared to take him on. The moment wasn't optimal, but she could work with what was. She always did.

☼

This was his flagship and everyone on board should be loyal, if not to him, then to the position of Leader. Hel was learning, though, that what should be and what was could be quite different. It would be a relief to disappear for a while. He'd chosen to board his flagship because he was expected to stay out of sight and let the ship's commander command. He could board his Ojemba ship and, using the phase cloak, leave without being seen. He would remain in constant contact with this ship and his people on the home planet, but it would appear he was secluded in his quarters, as was both proper and expected.

But first he needed to do something about Carig. He couldn't be allowed to run around making problems for Hel while Hel cruised the galaxy making problems for the General. One thing he'd perfected during his time leading the Ojemba was how to make people disappear.

He also had the issue of the two rebellious ships' commanders to deal with. He wasn't ready for an open confrontation with them, and he suspected they weren't ready for that either. He was supposed to contact them and ask why they hadn't moved. Then they would explain they had information of a threat on the Leader's life and had stayed to act as escort to the Kikk outpost. It was so predictable, it was boring. While he was glad the Dusan had been defeated, he missed the mental cut and thrust of those times.

He looked at his timepiece. His men should be securing Carig for an unscheduled rest about now…

The signal came. Carig had been neutralized. This would force whoever was playing Carig to act or go to ground. Hel was almost certain it was Glarmere. Either choice had good points and bad. Now he needed to speak with his commanders. He opened a channel to the two ships, saw both commanders appear on his view screen.

"Leader." Their voices were neutral. Both men were new to commanding ships, had been recruited after the war.

"I am pleased you were both delayed from making the ordered deployment, gentlemen." Hel smiled blandly. "Minister Carig has disappeared. I wish you to return to our home world and oversee an investigation. It is possible it is connected to the other two attacks."

Many worries were clouding their thinking right now. With Carig out of the picture, moving on the elected Leader or the outpost was pointless. How much did the Leader know about them and their relationship with Carig? To plot against the Leader was treason, punishable by death. And what was the Leader going to do about it?

In the end, they both acquiesced. They had no choice with the ground cut from beneath their feet.

It would have been more enjoyable had they been more interesting.

☼

Vidor stared at the woman, rage licking through him like a fire burning out of control.

He wanted to shake her.

He wanted to kiss her.

He wanted to kiss her more than he wanted to shake her. That made him angry, too.

She was dangerous in a way he couldn't explain or understand. She shifted from one way of being to another—he groped the right word to describe what he saw and failed to find one—as she reacted to only she knew what. She changed as he stared at her and then changed again, as if this were a waking dream. He sensed her need to elude him. He feared to blink and find her gone, wanted to grab her and hold on.

Could she contact her people like she implied? Bana thought

she did these things to annoy him. If so, she had succeeded.

He was annoyed.

Now that she was out of that tree, he could see the pale skin exposed by her loosened clothing. Was it as soft as it looked? Would she taste as enticing as she smelled? His hands relaxed as his annoyance faded, replaced by something else. A pulse beat against that skin just below her stubborn chin. He reached out to touch the spot, but she blocked him, her hand a blur of controlled movement. Wrist against wrist, she stared at him. He stared back. Her other hand was raised in defense, both hands curled into serviceable fists.

He made as if to pull back, but instead twisted his hand around and grabbed her wrist, holding it just hard enough to let her know he was stronger than she was. He wanted her to feel *his* control. He wanted her to know he was in charge.

She didn't tug against his hold, but he felt her resistance in her utter stillness and saw it in the way she shifted yet again into someone new. He tugged her closer, hooking his free arm around her waist. She didn't fight him, but she didn't relax.

He wanted to push his hands beneath her enveloping clothing and discover her shape, but she was tense, like a weapon ready to fire. If he pushed too hard and she pushed back, he might have to kill her. He wanted many things—but not her death. There was still time to bring her to heel, not much but some.

He withdrew his arm from around her waist, but placed his fingertips on the pulse point she'd tried to deny him. Her skin was soft and warm, her scent a unique enticement that threatened his control. Her pulse beat an urgent, primitive tempo beneath her skin. It was an interesting contrast to the complete detachment of her gaze.

"Tell me your name," he ordered, his voice husky.

The sides of her mouth edged up, though he wouldn't call it a smile.

"You can call me Morticia, if you want."

He fought the urge to crush her against him. "That is your name?"

"No."

He bit back an oath. "Why should I call you something that is not your name?"

She shrugged. "You don't seem to have a problem calling me *woman*. At least Morticia is *a* name."

Vidor almost laughed and he didn't remember the last time he'd done that. He also wanted to pull on his hair.

"Can I go now? I need to pee."

He didn't know what this pee was, but he would get one concession from her. "Call me by *my* name and I'll let you go."

The narrowing of her eyes was slight. If he hadn't been staring at her he'd have missed it.

"I'll wet my pants before I say your name, Conan."

He realized what she meant and felt heat flush his face. He stepped awkwardly back. "That is not my name."

"I know." She spun and stalked toward the sanitation quarters, shifting from casual to lethal as she passed both Cadir and Eamon and then back to casual. They both turned to watch her. Vidor wondered if he looked as girl sick as those two.

"One of you needs to take the girl and put us all out of our misery," Bana said.

Vidor looked down at her. "I thought you were against forcing marriage on the women."

"Then kill her."

He was against that, too, but he didn't say it. He didn't need to. She had known him a very long time.

Bana sighed. "*Think*, Vidor. She is learning you, learning about us. Learn about *her*. Find her weaknesses. Find out who she is."

Vidor wasn't so sure she had a weakness. It had taken ten of them to subdue her during her capture—if one could call her subdued. Still, Bana had a point. If the woman were a military objective, he would use different tactics. A frontal assault didn't work against a heavily defended front. If he shifted tactics, would he find a way past her defenses? It was worth considering.

Bana huffed out another sigh. "If she doesn't start eating, you won't have to kill her."

She almost sounded like this was the option she preferred. It was a change that should have surprised him. She'd been very adamant about how the wives would be treated if she participated in the collection. It was their lack of care of the women that had precipitated the crisis. While the collection wasn't the main thrust of their mission, it was an important side goal.

Interesting that the woman had also managed to alienate Bana in the passing of a single night. Vidor felt frustration spike again. He waited until the woman emerged and stalked over to her.

"Why won't you eat?" He fought an urge to call her Morticia. In a way, the name suited her. She was unusual, it was unusual.

"That sludge stuff is seriously nasty."

Yes, it was, but, "It contains nutrients necessary to sustain life."

"Only a life not worth living."

She tipped her head to the side and studied him in a way that made him shift uneasily.

"So are you all vegetarians? Have religious problems with meat? Lousy at hunting and gathering?"

"Hunting and gathering?" How did she manage to shift the conversation away from herself like that?

"Where I come from, men bring home *meat* for their women." She frowned. "And chocolate. *That* makes life worth living."

He would prefer meat as well, but it was not possible.

"No one else complains." That wasn't entirely true.

"Have you *asked* them what they like?"

Asked who? The women? Why would he ask them what they liked? Bana's words came to him, "You have much to learn about women, Vidor." It appeared she was correct.

"If I bring you chocolate, you will tell me your name."

He knew the tone was wrong when her brows drew together.

"You wish."

"You *must* choose." He leaned toward her, hoping she would understand what he was telling her.

"And if I don't?"

He waited for a few beats of his heart, his gaze holding hers with deadly intent. "Then you will die."

She *shrugged.*

"Everyone dies."

Frustration spiked again.

"Is that your wish? To die?" He kept his voice hard, though the thought of her death made him feel hollow inside.

"Not this minute." She stared at him, her gaze speculative. "What if I *tried*?"

He tensed. "How do you *try* to choose?"

"I need time to get to know—" Her gaze shifted in the direction of Eamon and Cadir, "them." Her tone lacked enthusiasm. "Maybe we could go out or something." She looked around. "Though since we're outside, maybe that would be a need to go in—only in somewhere better than this?"

"Out?" He didn't like her looking at them and sought to shift her gaze back to him. It worked.

"On a date? It's the way my people *choose*."

Her gaze left his, returning to Cadir and Eamon again.

"They're awfully young, but statistically women *do* live longer than men." She sighed, tipping her head to one side.

What was she looking at?

"They're both built. Good shoulders. Nice ass on the younger one." She looked at him. "What's his name again?"

"Cadir." The word almost didn't make it past his gritted teeth.

"So what's your time frame?"

The question took him by surprise.

"Time frame?"

"Do I have to choose right now?"

His gaze narrowed. "You are up to something."

"It's called negotiating terms, Conan. You've given me two options, neither particularly great, by the way. I'm just trying to negotiate a better deal. It's not unheard of in *civilized* societies."

Her eyes were wide, her gaze clear, maybe a bit annoyed, but overall she projected an air of calm reason. He wanted to shake her again. He wanted to tell her she had no choice. She belonged to him. So far neither man had noticed her looking at them. How was that possible? It looked like she was studying Cadir's ass again. He wanted to kick it.

"The leather is nice. And I know he's strong as an ox."

"He went down like one, too," Vidor growled, deep in his throat.

"Did you say something?" Her wide-eyed gaze shifted toward him again.

He was not fooled by her air of being puzzled. Her attention started to shift again. To stop it he spoke.

"You may have two days to choose."

Now she blinked. "Two days to choose a husband? The person I'll be spending my nights and days with for the rest of my life?" She frowned. "This is life we're talking about, isn't it? Because that would change things. If the marriage lasted only a couple of weeks—"

"Of course it is for life. What else could a marriage be?"

"Which brings me back to *what the hell*? Two days to make a decision this huge?"

He gritted his teeth again. "How much time do you think you need?

She changed again. "Oh wow, that's a tough question. I mean, a lot depends on the guy, of course. There are compatibility issues, which are already a bit iffy. I mean, we've got that whole, different culture thing going. And then there's the age issue. Shared interests—"

"Shared interests." He had to cut off the flow. It made his head hurt.

"Well, has either of them read *Harry Potter*? Because I

couldn't be happy with someone who hasn't read *Harry Potter.*"

"You read." He didn't know why this surprised him. Nothing she did should surprise him.

Her eyes widened. "You mean they don't? Oh wow, that's a major deal breaker for me."

"We all read."

"*Harry Potter?*"

"No. You will have to find other *shared interests.*"

"Which brings us back to the need for dates."

"What are dates?"

"Where I come from we go out to eat or to a movie. Since those things seem to be missing in action, I guess we'd talk."

"Talk." He stared at her, trying to understand what she was saying.

"To each other, like we're doing, only different."

"How?"

"How what?" She stared at him and then blinked. Her lashes drifted down slow, rising slower.

"How would talking to them be different than talking to me?"

Her eyes widened. "For one thing, they haven't threatened to kill me."

He gave up resisting the urge to touch her. His finger brushed her cheek, pushing a strand of hair back. Her skin was soft as a flower petal and smooth as the finest silk. She shifted just enough to end the contact. He let his hand drop, but he felt the connection linger. "I don't wish to kill you."

"And I don't wish to be here. Obviously, one of us isn't going to get what they want."

Frustration evaporated like mist in the sun. He smiled at her. "I always get what I want."

He didn't like the change that came over her. Why did his comment amuse her?

"And which one do you *want* me to choose?"

The shape of her mouth when she said the word "choose"

sent warmth flooding into his body. He stepped close to her, his gaze fixed on her soft, pink lips. She started to step back, but he stopped her, his grip loose on her shoulders but able to be insistent if needed.

Her chin lifted and her mouth lost its shape and softness as it thinned with her gaze.

"You feel it, too, woman, deny it if you can."

"The only thing I *feel* is a need for more meat in my diet and better plumbing."

His grip on her tightened.

"You're hurting me." She shut down, retreated to some place inside where he couldn't reach.

He flung his hands free of her, spun and walked away, heading for the edge of the woods. He fought it, fought turning around, but it was as if this was as far as he could get from her. She waited until he was looking and then turned to join Eamon and Cadir. They both offered her a chair, but she jumped up onto the edge of the table, her legs swinging.

"So what do you do for fun around here?"

Ten

The exterior of Hel's ship was as scruffy and deceptive as his other identity when he used it. Both concealed more than they revealed. The exterior hid powerful engines and enhanced sensors and shields. As the trappings of a Leader fell away, Hel felt his personal power surge closer to the surface, too. He endeavored not to think about why he was doing this, focusing instead on how to accomplish his goals. In the past, this had worked for him, but in the past, he had not switched identities for a woman.

As Leader, he believed he could retrieve Delilah and remain detached. He could spin himself useful lies about neutralizing the threat to eventual Gadi control of the outpost, but in this ship, as this man, it was not so easy. This place brought him closer to the core of his power, his passion, and brought back the past when he had last made a mistake about a woman. He did not spend time regretting past mistakes, he just hoped to learn from them and move on. All life was an education of some kind.

Here, now, he found it difficult to maintain proper prospective on the problem she posed. Did he want her because of what he believed she could do or did he want her for himself?

This was a question that needed answering before he brought her on board this vessel.

But he did not have to answer it right now. With relief, he shelved troubled thoughts for practical matters. His scanners were up and operating within expected parameters, as was his cloak. He saw no sign of interest in his movements from either the Earth ship or the Kikk outpost. If the unknown vessel twitched out there, he'd know about it, either through his own scans or through the ships he'd strategically placed around the galaxy.

His flagship was on course for Kikk, but not hurrying. He hoped to be back on board before it reached Kikk. No one would believe he'd stay on the ship once they reached the outpost. He'd spent some communication face time with each commander before going underground. At least eight were solid, seven could go either direction, and the two Carig had suborned? They weren't as solid in his direction as Carig thought. They left for Gadi space without hesitation, and they didn't contact anyone before leaving. It wasn't totally good news. Their support was solid for the *Leader*. Most of the support wasn't personal. He wasn't offended. Military commanders were supposed to be loyal to the government.

Would they be as certain if a governmental transition weren't the result of a vote of the people, but action of the counsel? Doubtful. Military commanders came from all levels of Gadi society. While they might support the ruling class in theory, in action, most would side with the Gadi people.

Hel rubbed the stubble emerging on his chin as he plotted a course to the Quindo sector. It was off the main space lanes, but because it had good access to the frontier and trade lanes, space pirates and off-the-book traders used it as a place to buy information and trade in illegal goods. His former first commander, Hilber, called Quindo home. Like many in the galaxy, the fall of the Dusan hadn't opened a way home, since the Dusan had made sure there was nothing to go home to. Some were the only ones of their kind left. Hilber was one of these survivors.

He had used his old Ojemba channels to arrange a meet. One didn't arrive unannounced at Hilber's quarters. Like all good Ojemba, he shot first, thus eliminating the need for questions. Hel trusted Hilber as much as he trusted anyone: not at all. None of the Ojemba knew Hel as the Gadi Leader, but that did not mean they wished him long life. That Hel knew *their* identities was enough to make them restive.

Quindo had the additional benefit of being close to the region where he believed the unknown kidnappers were hiding. It met the criteria he'd identified. He'd been all over the frontier and this was the sector he'd choose if he were looking for optimal concealment and maneuverability. Everyone was looking for the unknown group now, not just the *Doolittle* and the Gadi. They'd need to hit fast and then go to ground even faster. There was a higher risk of pirates discovering their presence and following them home, if they spent too long in the space lanes, even cloaked.

He'd tapped more resources to track the *Doolittle*. If it moved, his Ojemba would let him know. His men knew what to do, though they didn't know why. Hel trusted one man and he was dead.

What would Gaedon think of this move, he wondered? He still missed his old friend and commander of the Gadi forces. His death at the end of the battle with the Dusan had been a blow Hel had yet to recover from. Gaedon had liked the Earth people from the beginning. He'd been hopeful, despite the many years of war with the Dusan. If Hel had followed his advice back then, would things be different now?

He gave serious thought to the question. He had time for it. Considering General Halliwell's personality, Hel could see slight differences between what would have been and what was. It was certain that the Key would still have left the galaxy. He'd had to try to keep that from happening and he still hoped for a return. Even beyond the technology on the outpost, there was the issue of his peoples' history. The outpost and its contents were their heritage, a lost part of their history. They deserved access to it. If the General followed through on his promise, then they had made a beginning, but would it last if Delilah figured out how to use the portal to secure the return of their lost people?

Was this a real outreach or a bid for time?

And would gratitude over a rescue make Delilah helpful or

hostile? The way she had kissed him indicated she was open to persuasion. Still, he had underestimated the will of a woman once before. He would not make that mistake again.

☼

Memo to self: don't ask horny guys what they do for fun.

Even Eamon had managed to rise to the occasion, though the area must still be tender from its interaction with her knee. Doc didn't let it go to her head. It was easy to be a ten when there was no competition. And she had other things to think about, like round two of yank Conan's chain.

She wasn't sure if the two days was a hard deadline or not, though it felt like it was. Bana had mentioned a lack of time when she thought Doc was unconscious, and her gut sensed a ticking clock, even if time seemed to have stopped in this place. No, stopped was too optimistic—something she wasn't usually guilty of. Time had rewound, had rolled all the way back to primitive. Time had never been her friend, but it wasn't always the enemy. It just was, just as *they* were. It was the place she lived and coped and did and until recently she'd lived without an overabundance of angst about it. No wonder she was cranky. She sighed. Whether the deadline was real or not, she'd have to act as if it was. Just like they were pretending he wanted her to choose one of the boys.

Following their earlier "interaction" he'd settled into an uneasy orbit around her. He kept his distance, but it was always the same distance. She moved and so did he. It made the day long and exhausting. Doc had fended off an effort from Bana to give her cooking duty, pointing out that the boys could stir their own sludge. She didn't want to eat it or see it. She'd also ignored another attempt to get her out of her clothes and into a Moonie robe. Bana didn't try the "you stink" argument. She'd probably already figured out that Doc wasn't interested in smelling sweet for the boys.

Bana interested Doc almost as much as Conan did. She was more complex than the guys. Doc could almost feel her thinking, and she watched Doc as closely as Conan.

Some of it Doc could understand. She had a brain, eyes in her head. She'd figured out Doc had the power and the will to upset the dynamic of their group. So why did Doc get the feeling she wanted her *dead*, not just gone? She went through the motions of helping Doc assimilate, but her heart wasn't in it. Which made it odd that Doc sensed *liking* in the old woman's manner, sometimes to the point of fascination—a fascination quickly hid when her gaze met Doc's.

Why would she like Doc *and* want her dead?

Doc had managed some conversation with the brides, used it to drop a very small pebble in the pool of the men's control over them. It didn't take big rocks to make big ripples.

She smelled pretty rank from her periodic outbreaks of exercising in the heat multiplied by the hours since her last shower, but that didn't stop her from doing some stretches while she waited for night. No one had suggested a stroll to the lake, so she didn't stink enough yet. Movement released mental and physical tension. She felt Conan watching as she slid into the splits, then bent forward until her face was on her knee.

The retreat of light brought some relief from the oppressive heat, but not enough. She missed air conditioning and showers—even short ones. Her seventy-two hours worth of supplies was running low and the energy bars didn't make much of an impact in the hollow that was her stomach. The camp was too quiet, too peaceful. She needed loud music and loud thoughts, something impossible, something mentally challenging and very physical to do. Inside her body screamed with the effort of maintaining her outward calm. She wanted to claw at her head and release the pressure swelling inside her skull. It was too big, too much. She couldn't even work on the problem of escape when she had nothing to work with.

Time had paused, or so it felt. It was a kind of reverse tornado, with the eye out there and her playing the part of the storm. As the fury roared inside, she wanted to take it outside, take someone down. But then what? She needed a ship, not to kick ass. They weren't outsmarting her. That wasn't possible. They were...out-stupiding her. They didn't have to plot and plan. All they had to do was sit on their asses to win.

Two damn days.

Now was a bad time to remember her unease, her sense of fate laughing when she'd told the General that each time the impossible gets more impossible. That she would fail some day.

Was this that day?

The sun hung on the horizon, as if mocking her desperation for it to sink from sight. It also wasn't like her to long for nightfall. The last rays slanted across the encampment, unable to soften the harsh edges. The brides moved silently through their night preparations. Was it her need for change that made them seem more thoughtful than downcast tonight? A small breeze ruffled through the camp, easing the damp heat on Doc's face. She sat up, sliding her legs into the lotus position. She rested her hands on her knees, searching from beneath lowered lashes for signs of the slight power shift she thought she sensed.

Light began to pull in, giving way to night, but just before the curtain fell, Doc saw one of the brides say something to her man. That wasn't the surprising part. It was the look on his face.

The worms had started to turn.

She knew Conan still stared at her, so she didn't smile, just came fluidly to her feet and headed for the table. He shifted, too, moving with her. This time he didn't stop when she did. He moved into closer orbit as she climbed up on the table and lay down on her back. She tucked her arms under her head for cushioning and stared at the sky as the stars came into view one by one.

"Now what are you doing?" His tone was more tired than annoyed.

Doc couldn't stop the tiny, pleased twitch of her lips. "I'm studying the sky."

She intended to be very clear about what she was doing, but he needed to work for it. He'd distrust a gift. With her peripheral vision, she saw him look up, saw and felt his gaze return to her.

"Why now?"

"You can't see the stars during the day."

"Why do you wish to see the stars?"

He was suspicious, but she didn't mind, since that was the plan.

"To get a fix on my position." She wasn't totally yanking his chain. She was curious to see if she could figure out where she was. She'd studied the Garradian star charts on the trip out, because they were there. And because she thought she might need to know. She never knew what she'd need to know, even with a good briefing, and she hadn't gotten a bad briefing for this trip.

The three moons were hanging on the horizon opposite the fading sun. They wouldn't start their climb until later, and they'd linger into the morning. There was a magnetic pole here, too. Her compass had moved when she'd tried it out. The moons appeared to orbit a tad south of that pole. It wasn't that helpful to know that, but her brain didn't always care about helpful. It just liked data.

She lifted the binoculars. They couldn't replace a telescope, but Conan wouldn't know that. And they were better than nothing, but that wasn't saying much. She could mentally search every damn chart, but it would be more efficient to narrow the search parameters. She was pretty sure they were somewhere in the old Dusan frontier. She knew where she'd been and ought to be able to come up with where she was.

Star charts rotated through her head. She discarded some as too far away from her flight path. Homed in on one that looked promising. Was it possible she was on Feldstar? There were some other possibilities but her gut liked Feldstar.

"Why do you need to know your position?" Conan sounded almost indifferent.

Had Bana been counseling him? They'd been joined at the hip for a while today. Doc would bet she'd tried to get him to deactivate the buttons Doc had been pushing. Time to see if it worked.

"So I can let my people know my location." She looked at him, her brows arched in mock surprise. Should she name drop?

He propped a hip against the side of the table. "And how do you plan to contact them?"

She fluttered her lashes. "If I tell you that, you'll try to stop me."

"Or you don't have a way to contact your people. You just want to mess with my head."

Okay, that was very Earth sounding. She needed to think about that, but later. Her "sort that out later" list was getting long.

"That is a possibility. Or you missed my transmitter when you searched my stuff." She sat up and studied him. "Your transmitter is hiding fairly well."

He frowned, stopping just shy of outright scowling. Nope, hadn't disconnected that button yet.

"What transmitter? I have no need of a transmitter."

"Does your ship read your mind or just come when you call it?"

"There is no ship."

Doc ignored this stupidity and jumped off the table. She walked around him. "If I were your transmitter, where would I hide?"

He threw his arms wide, his enjoyment of her attention a little too obvious.

"There is nothing to find, but please, look your fill. Touch if you desire."

Doc didn't blush, but it was a near thing. The dark helped. He had a transmitter on him somewhere. He wore a lot of leather. What if it was built in? She touched one of the decorative metal rivets. He didn't stop her. He shifted so her finger brushed his bare arm. She shifted so it didn't. It might be as simple as an ear bud. She moved to the side and then the other, but his hair straggled over both of them. And if she shifted that hair, he'd enjoy it *way* too much. His wrist bands were pretty thick and had no obvious function. She didn't want to touch him, but it was necessary.

She slid her hand along the back of his and heard his breathing ramp up at her touch. Just how long had these guys been without girl time? In the deep dark, his eyes gleamed, but he didn't move. She kept her touch light as her fingers curved along the edge and then turned his hand so the palm was up. The underside of the wrist band appeared to be irregular, though in the dark it was hard to be sure.

"Clever." Doc stepped back, pretty sure she'd figured it out. And because she had a feeling she'd pushed him as far as was safe.

He kept his cool. Didn't reach for it, like she'd hoped he might. He frowned, though, because his eyes got closer together.

"There is no transmitter. There is no ship."

"So how did I get from my nylon let-down to here?" The barbarians hadn't tapped the heels of their boots together and said, "there's no place like hell," three times.

"You crashed here." Sounded like he was gritting his teeth again.

"No, I didn't." Doc stepped back. "You should look up more. You'd learn when to bluff and when to fold a losing hand."

He looked up. He had to. It was human nature. "You seek to confuse me."

"I seek to enlighten you." She hesitated. "You can count, can't you? See one, two, three blue moons." They still hovered on the horizon like they were shy. "I crashed on a planet with *one* moon. Right after you messed with my ship." She leaned close, but not too close. "I'm sure you're relatively clever for a guy. But even if you aren't, you have to know it's easier to build a ship than add moons to a planet." She stepped back, but added an extra layer of evil to her voice. "And you're going to learn what happens to people who mess with *my* ship. Now if you'll excuse me, I have a call to make. My people will be very interested in Feldstar soon."

If that didn't get him to initiate a scan for her transmitter, he was too stupid to live.

She could almost hear his jaw working in the dark.

"Go to your tent."

Doc could sense how close he was to losing it. She turned without a word and walked away, but she felt the familiar shift in the air flow that indicated transport. She spun around.

He was gone.

"Gotcha," she murmured under her breath. Chalk one up for the girl. Now she had to hope someone was looking this way with feelers out.

It gave her a reason to hope while she plotted her next move.

☼

Hel found the Garradian transport system a definite benefit. In the past, he'd had to try to find secure place to land on a planet teaming with thieves and pirates. Many times he'd had to fight his way back to his ship. A low orbit worked well for space parking. Drop cloak just long enough for transport. The phase cloak eliminated space collisions, too. He did have to check and make sure his ship wasn't inside another ship prior to lowering the cloak, but his remote device allowed him impressive control of his ship. If he'd had the Garradian ships in his arsenal, the Dusan would have been defeated much earlier.

He contacted Hilber and got approval for transport. Life signs readings showed Hilber was alone in his quarters, but there were ways to block the infrared scans. Hel readied a stun bomb and transported it. He checked the life signs readings once more, pulled his weapon and initiated transport.

As soon as transport was complete, Hel did a perimeter scan, with his weapon and his personal scanner. The room appeared clean, but his Ojemba instincts were twitching. He edged up to the prone figure. As he'd expected, it wasn't Hilber, but another former Ojemba named Corstin.

He'd heard that some of the ships' cloaks, pilfered from ships damaged in the battle, had been converted to personal cloaks. It would have provided some protection from the stun bomb. Hilber's problem was, he couldn't shoot while cloaked. Hel backed into a corner and scanned the room. He even knew what to look for.

He aimed his gun at the spot where the faint energy signature registered.

"If you are not going to come out and talk, Hilber, I will depart."

A long pause, a ripple in the area and Hilber appeared. He'd holstered his weapon and looked resigned.

"I keep forgetting what a crafty bastard you are." He grinned, the action friendly enough if you didn't look at his eyes.

Hel always checked the eyes.

As if he knew it, Hilber turned toward a cabinet. "A drink?"

"How much?"

Hilber hesitated, then turned back with a shrug. "You heard?"

"Don't I hear everything?" And what he didn't hear, his instincts filled in. It wasn't a stretch to guess someone had put out an agreement to kill the man they thought Hel was. The Leader disappeared and problem solved. That Carig and Glarmere had made the connection between Hel and the former leader of the Ojemba confirmed their alliance with someone on the Earth Expedition. That they'd chosen to kill rather than expose him indicated that the power of his other identity had not waned in the past two years. The Ojemba may have been hated by the rulers of planets whose convoys they pilfered for supplies, but the people honored them for the way they'd fought the Dusan. No, Glarmere would not want to add "hero of the Ojemba" to Hel's Leader credentials. "Corstin your source?"

"His timing was good." Hilber kept his hands well clear of his weapon. "It's not personal."

"You need the money."

"I always need the money." He named a sum that made Hel's eyebrows rise.

"I had no idea my dead body was so valuable." He nudged the unconscious Corstin with his foot. "You going to share it with him?"

Hilber arched his brows, did not bother to reply.

Hel was unsurprised Corstin wanted to kill him. His relationship with his men had always been more hate than love.

"They wouldn't have paid you."

Hilber's eyes widened, lost their calculation.

"Bastards."

"The enemies of my allies usually are." Hel considered the man. "If you've got anything interesting on the other matter, I'll pay you half of what they weren't going to pay you."

Hilber's eyes gleamed with sudden avarice. "You got it on you?"

Hel gave him a look. "If it's interesting you'll get paid. I may be a bastard, but I honor my word. You know this about me."

Hilber rubbed his face. "Fair enough." He kept his hands in sight as he moved to his desk. He pulled out an information tube and tossed it to Hel. "You aren't the only one who's curious about these people. One of the girl's father's is paying big money for information."

"Bigger than I am?"

"He's spreading it around more than you." Hilber grinned, one that reached his eyes this time. "Any problem if I resell it to him?"

He'd do it, whether Hel had problems or not, but he shook his head. No way was some land tiller going to beat him to the prize.

Hel grabbed the tube and pocketed it. "I'll check this out. If it's good, you'll get your payment before I break orbit."

☼

Vidor paced the central corridor, circling his ship as his thoughts circled the woman. He didn't, he couldn't think of his larger purpose in the galaxy. The only way to deal with raging impatience, the only way to deal with his roaring desire to go home, was to not think about it at all.

He took the steps and each one took him, took them all closer to what he wanted, what they needed to do.

Until the woman.

Seeing her, dealing with her was a battle he had not expected. Fighting was not a problem. He liked a fight, a good fight was a bonus. But this…this was different.

His pace slowed as he reached a view port where he could see the planet below and the moons she'd talked about. A planet with three moons. He'd seen many wondrous things since he left his home, since he'd embarked on this quest to restore to his people what they'd lost.

His father had given him many reasons to do this thing. His mind had supplied others. Most revolved around duty and honor. He rubbed his chest. His heart was an organ, like the other parts of his body. It served his body by circulating his blood. Hearts, he had always believed, did not feel. They were. If what he believed was so, then why did the sight of the woman make his ache in way that was new to him? Why did he feel linked to her like the three moons were linked to this planet? Why did he feel?

He tried to push the thoughts away, wanted to shove these *feelings* back into the dark place they belonged. He knew how to control himself, how to hold the reins of his own nature and direct his energy to what must be done. Step by careful step.

Even now, he had to fight the need to return to the planet, to be where he could see her.

He turned with a jerk and resumed his pacing. Had he always known he would come here? He rubbed his face. It felt—he didn't *feel*, he was not a man who felt, but he had *known*. Knowledge had lived inside him, the knowledge that he would come here. And did this knowledge include the woman? No, his mind said. His heart disagreed, even though he had not given it a vote. He'd come with the knowledge of what he needed to see, but not knowing when he would see it. The wife hunt had kept his men happy while he watched and waited. Neither he nor Bana had expected it to take so long, but now the signs were there. The time of acting was close. The pieces were in place. It was a bad time to be distracted by anything, but—he paused again and felt a new knowledge rise up, not from his heart, but from lower and deeper, from his instincts.

He would claim the woman.

As soon as he made the choice, the decision to act, his insides eased. This was right. And with this right came a new knowledge: the woman was part of the whole in a way that would become clear. Bana feared she was a distraction, but now he knew better.

She was as much a part of what had drawn him here as the other.

☼

When Halliwell's intercom buzzed, he slammed his hand down on the button to activate it. His day had been long and discouraging, and it looked like his night would be more of the same.

"General Halliwell, sir?"

Who the hell did he think would answer his intercom?

"This is Dr. James."

The geek with a clue. "Yes?" He tried not to sound as impatient as he felt.

"I've made some progress on that matter we discussed." The tone dropped to secret-sharing level.

"Your office or mine?"

"Better if you came here, sir."

"I'll be there ASAP." Halliwell pushed back from his desk and headed out into the corridor, turning in the direction of the lift. Maybe it was exhaustion that sent him back to the first time he'd boarded the *Doolittle.* It was an amazing achievement and a heavy responsibility. He'd felt equal parts awe and overwhelmed then and he felt it now. Just like him, his ship didn't carry any scars from the battle with the Dusan, though he'd had to limp her home after the battle. He flexed the arm that should have given him trouble, but didn't. The Key had healed him and many others of his men. Still made his brain twitch to think about how. His ship had needed the yard to put the pieces back together. It had emerged from refit better than before, too.

In the past, when he stalked his corridors, he'd felt connected to the people who served with him. This was a joint enterprise, a shared adventure. It should have brought them together, not spawned a stinking traitor. When the Doc got snatched, he'd brought his senior staff into the hunt for the bastard. They were working the problem, but they also had to brainstorm damage control plans and do it without knowing all the damage that had been done. He did know that the Gadi had the Doc's code name. That was bad. He didn't know if the traitor knew the Doc or if he or she had passed that information on, too. Right now, only a handful of people knew she was missing. His prime suspects, the diplomats, thought she was still helping out in the infirmary. Since she had no defined job with them, no one needed face time with her. And as predicted, the infirmary staff thought she'd returned to her primary job.

It added to his frustration that the Doc had been his best hope for sussing out the traitor and getting his people back. And he'd sent her out there alone. The fact that it was women being targeted didn't help his anxious thoughts settle. She was a tough cookie, but even though it was old-fashioned, he didn't like a woman being at risk. And this one was at risk in a damn, different galaxy.

He swiped his card to open the door and strode into geek central. Smith and his team were huddled over their stuff like a bunch of women over a chocolate dessert. For them, maybe it was dessert.

"Doc?"

James looked up, pushed up glasses still sliding down his long, straight nose. "We managed to hack into the Gadi scanning system." He sounded a bit surprised and maybe a touch impressed with himself.

Damn, he missed the Doc and her matter-of-fact delivery.

"They know you're there?"

He blinked a couple of times as his glasses did a slow slide down his nose again. "Doubtful."

Halliwell arched his brows.

"They'd shut us out if they knew, sir. Much of what they have technologically speaking, they can use and fix, but I don't sense they understand it."

"Okay, so we're in. Learn anything?"

"They are scanning for two specific energy signatures. If they find them, then we will, too."

"You could have told me that over the intercom."

"Yes, sir, but I wanted to show you this." He tapped some keys and pulled something up on the geek's version of a HUD. It looked like one of the Gadi ships. "What am I looking at?"

"It's the Leader's flagship, sir. The one heading here."

Halliwell's gut tightened at the thought of Giddioni going dirt side on Kikk. Doc said it had to be done and on some level, he believed her. But he also believed that Giddioni was hoping that the Key would return to this galaxy. He didn't know that would never, ever happen. If the right people knew about the Key, she would already be here. They wouldn't have risked an asset like the Chameleon if they'd had another, more likely option.

A ship launched from the Gadi ship. The general frowned. Looked like it emerged from an area that wasn't a launch bay. Ships with phase cloaks could do that, but why bother?

"See that ship?" James paused, his voice going thin with excitement. "It's cloaked."

"It's not that unusual to see a cloaked ship, doctor." Halliwell kept his voice calm, but it took effort.

"Yes, sir but this one's cloak has been modified to hide from our sensors. I modified our cloaking settings to see if I could track one and this popped up." He pushed his glasses up. "We're the only ones seeing this. This ship is invisible to the outposts and our ship's sensors."

Halliwell straightened. He could think of one person who'd

be leaving the flagship using a modified cloak that they weren't supposed to see: Helfron Giddioni.

He could think of only one reason Giddioni would leave his flagship in the middle of a crisis, but it still surprised him. Did he consider the Doc that much of a threat to his eventual control of the outpost? It couldn't be personal, because the Leader didn't *do* personal unless it fit in with his non-personal goals. He'd liked the Key, maybe even wanted her, but he wouldn't have tried to grab her if she hadn't been the Key. Too bad he hadn't heard the Doc outline her chances of unlocking the rest of the outpost. He knew too much and too little. And, like always, he knew just enough to be a pain in the ass.

"Keep tracking it, but only you and I know about this." He hesitated. "Where do you think he's going?"

"His course took him here." A geek finger touched a spot on the galactic map. "It's the Mos Eisley of this galaxy."

"What?"

"The place Obi Wan called a den of thieves and pirates? Where he and Luke went to meet Han Solo?"

"Oh." A place where information would be exchanged for money. "Right." So the Leader was tapping into his information resources. Well, as long as they could keep tracking him, then he could use the Leader to lead them to the Doc. "What about back tracking the bogey using the scan holes? Any progress there?"

James beckoned one of the geeks over. "Tell the General what you found."

The man looked nervous, but Halliwell wasn't sure if it was him, the fact they were in another galaxy, or his normal state of being.

This geek pulled up a different screen, though it was the same galaxy. Halliwell wasn't sure he'd ever get used to how different it was from the Milky Way. It always gave him a jolt seeing where they were—and where they weren't.

"I was able to find several holes in our scanning in the region where the crewman disappeared and I was also able to connect some dots. We can narrow our search grid to three zones, sir."

Three areas lit up on the screen. Halliwell studied the three areas.

"Habitable planets?"

"Again, each one has a planet or planets within the parameters you specified."

"Have you scanned these areas using the patterns the Gadi are using?" Halliwell wasn't expecting the blank looks he got for that question. These guys couldn't seem to climb out of their box, let alone think outside it. The Doc had ruined him for dealing with ordinary smart people. The two men exchanged sheepish looks. Halliwell ruminated while the two men bent over a single laptop, their elbows bumping. He might not know the geek stuff, but he did know strategy. Before he could voice his request, another geek at another laptop jumped.

"I got something here." He had glasses, too. His had tape over the bridge of his nose. He co-opted the HUD. "We got a match on that energy signature."

"Where is this?"

James did something with his laptop. "It's known as Feldstar. Uninhabited because it was too close to Dusan territory and it has a crappy climate. It's one of the areas we identified from connecting the scan holes."

It would be a good hiding place. Halliwell rubbed his chin, but before he could decide on a next step, the scanner pinged again.

"Got more of that signature in some other places, sir."

The HUD changed, reflecting the new locations.

"Any of these in the three zones you identified?"

James frowned. "One, in addition to Feldstar."

Made things more challenging, but that wasn't new.

"You see anything in either place again, I want to know immediately." James nodded agreement. "And I need you to adjust the cloak settings on some of our ships, so they can't be tracked."

The three men's jaws identically dropped. Before they could

ask him why, he quelled questions with his signature Look.

"Anything else I need to know?" he asked and got three slow shakes in answer. He turned and left, his thoughts still sifting through all he'd learned, trying to integrate it with what he already knew. Did the Leader think he could turn the Doc if he got to her first? He remembered her matter-of-fact assessment of the Leader. And the Doc saying she liked the Leader. Maybe in the world she operated in it was possible to distrust and like a person at the same time. He'd worked with people he didn't like. He'd even worked with people he didn't trust. Had a bunch of them onboard the *Doolittle* right now. One thing he'd never been able to do was like someone he didn't trust.

Were they tracking the Leader or was he using an agent, perhaps an Ojemba? A surrogate made sense, but the Leader's trust issues were as deep as Halliwell's. Logic said the Leader wasn't in that ship, but his gut said he was. Logic had let him down, but his gut never did.

Eleven

On his scanning screen, Hel studied the three-dimensional image of the energy anomaly from the frontier planet known as Feldstar. The *Doolittle* would have seen it, too, but since he'd had a couple of his Ojemba standing by to transmit the same signature in two different places, he wasn't surprised when the *Doolittle* failed to respond. The General would wait for more definitive data before committing resources to investigate.

Feldstar, he recalled, could support life, though it would not be a great life. The climate was either hot or cold, with little moderation to ease the pain. There was edible plant and animal life and good cover. They'd launched several Ojemba attacks from there, though he'd learned to choose the hot weather cycle. And even then, they'd had to be careful of severe weather, blowing up without warning. Thanks to the Garradian transport system, the weather was not an issue any longer, though he would not like to attempt transport during one of the bigger storms.

It troubled him that the two energy signatures were the only sign the unknown combatants were using space-capable transport. The nature of the attacks indicated the group *was* highly space capable and appeared to have some ability to track even cloaked ships. Hilber's information supported this supposition. He'd earned his money and a bonus. Hopefully he'd think twice before trying to kill him the next time Hel needed something from him. Knowing Hilber, it was a faint hope. He needed to adjust his shields, but he would lay down a false trail first, just in case someone was able to track his movements. He tried to shift his cloak settings each time he traveled like this. He'd never felt tracked, but this time he had an itch between his shoulder blades. He'd drop into a scan hole he'd purposely left in place and make the change before heading in the direction of Feldstar.

He was certain that Delilah would find a way to send another signal. He worried he would arrive, too late if the group decided to shift location. He could be wrong, of course, but this didn't feel wrong. All he could do was follow his instincts.

☼

Three days. She'd been in camp for three endless days and three longer-than-endless nights. And in those three days she'd managed to change too much, Vidor thought grimly. He'd believed that claiming her would solve the problems she'd created. Claiming her removed Eamon and Cadir as weapons for her use. She'd never intended choosing one of them anyway. They were, naturally, frustrated. They couldn't secure wives until the tractor beam was repaired, and they were almost out of time. He still didn't understand how the woman had managed to fire on them. Or how she'd managed to stay conscious during her retrieval. He had many questions and few answers to show for three days of talking that felt more like a battle than a conversation.

He'd told her she must choose by this evening, but instead of considering her options, she had chosen to use the time to disrupt the even tenor of the camp. She'd drifted around, chatting with the women. It seemed harmless. Until the women had revolted against the food. It seemed a minor thing. The food was better. Everyone was more cheerful. The women now talked and laughed as they cooked. This change was not so terrible, though Bana seemed to have fallen into disfavor. Vidor could see a clear shift in the power balance between the women and the men.

If she'd stopped there—but she seemed unable to be content.

Did she think the men wanted to observe the women's baths? Of course the women deserved privacy, but they were vulnerable while bathing. The men did not need protection during their baths. It had nothing to do with the cold or their male pride. He'd made one concession for her—she could bathe alone. He would stand guard alone. Had she been grateful? Not visibly.

"If you want to get me out of my clothes, you're going to have to do better than this," she'd informed him. And before he could stop her, she'd turned and strode into the water fully clothed.

His men had accepted the changes without a fight. He'd wondered why, until he learned that their participation in the marriage bed depended on it. Vidor, contemplating his own empty bed, wasn't surprised that they'd given in. And he had no doubts who had educated the girls to this sexual reality. Or turned them against Bana.

Bana appeared to find her fall from grace more amusing than annoying. "You wanted them to learn. They are learning."

"Talk to her."

They both knew who he wanted her to talk to.

"I can talk, but will she listen?"

"I won't give her up."

"You can't make her tell you her name or name you, Vidor."

"Then I will find another way."

"She will fight you."

"And she will lose." Morticia didn't know it, but she'd already lost. He'd scanned for her so-called transmission device. It had been a bluff, and it hadn't taken him long to figure out her purpose. She'd hoped the scan would reveal their position. It wouldn't. He knew how to use planets to block scans. His ship was well cloaked. He'd operated in this galaxy for longer than she knew without being detected. Even the vaunted Garradian scanners had failed to penetrate their cloak.

"She will never adjust to our world, to our ways. If you bring her back, she will undo all we have accomplished, all we hope to accomplish. She is wrong for us."

The words increased the pain in his heart.

"She'll do what she must." She was female. Females adjusted. It was their way.

"She won't, Vidor. Think with your brain. Don't do this."

He hesitated, something in her tone, pierced his thoughts. Was it fear? What could she fear from this woman? Their people feared one woman and soon he would take care of her, too. Bana needed to trust him.

"I do what I must, old friend. Trust me in this."

She sighed. "It's not you I do not trust. She worries me."

"Let me worry about her and the other. I will deal with them both."

Tonight he would give her a choice, but not the one she expected. She didn't fear death, so that was off the table.

As if she sensed his thoughts were on her, Morticia met his gaze. She deflected his effort to pierce her thoughts. She revealed only what she wanted to reveal. He got that now. He'd learned the lesson. It was her turn to learn that everything was going to change.

And then a cry broke the happier sounds of the encampment. While he and his men reached for weapons, Morticia turned toward Riven's wife. The girl was bent, her hand at her back, her face showing distress. Morticia crouched next to her, her hand on the girl's distended stomach.

"Has your back been hurting a lot today?"

The girl nodded, her eyes wide, her fear obvious. Vidor and Riven both stepped back, and he saw a flash of annoyance in Morticia's eyes.

"Did you have a plan for when the babies start coming?"

"Bana." Vidor nodded at her to help the girl.

"That's your plan?"

"I don't want her! I want my mother!"

Morticia's gaze chilled. He might as well have been dipped in the lake again.

"You're all complete and utter bastards. Can't you see how frightened she is?"

Vidor made himself step toward the grouping. "Bana will care for her. She will be fine."

The girl clung to Morticia's hand, sobbing in panic. Vidor could tell Morticia felt torn about something. What did she know? What did she seek to hide from him?

"Bastard," she said again. She turned to the girl. "Let's get you to bed, sweetie." She looked at Riven. "You will help your wife have this baby or I will personally see to it you never have another child. And I think we both know I can do it."

Riven looked as white-faced as his wife, but he followed them into the tent.

The night that followed was long, noisy and not what Vidor planned. At the end of it, Riven had a small daughter with a crumpled red face, and Vidor had something new to worry about.

Outside the birthing tent, Vidor looked at Bana. "Well?"

"She is a doctor." Bana did not sound surprised.

Vidor kept his scowl. "You suspected this."

She avoided his look. "I wondered." Finally she looked at him. "The Doctor came from this galaxy. We both knew this."

She'd asked them to return her to this place. They should have listened, should have tried to help her, but Sellmin had wanted her the moment he saw her. In the years since, Vidor had judged him, condemned him for allowing lust to cloud his judgment. How ironic that he'd traveled so far, for so long, only to find himself in the same place, fighting the same weakness.

"If she is the one, you can't take her home."

"It would be different this time." But they both knew it would not.

"You have to think of your people, not what you want."

He didn't want to kill her. He couldn't release her. The fate of his people depended on him dealing with her. History could not be allowed to repeat itself.

"She might not be the one."

Bana didn't speak. She didn't have to. He didn't believe it either.

☼

When Giddioni's ship dropped off tracking, the General had a moment of panic.

Sometimes the impossible might be impossible.

And with the Leader in the mix, the odds against possible turned astronomical.

"Do you think he knew we were tracking him?" And how was that possible? The Gadi were flooding the galaxy with scan signatures. How could he pick theirs out of that mess? But he knew the answer to the question before Smith weighed in. Giddioni was a twitchy bastard.

"Which zone was he headed for before he dropped out of sight?"

"Zone Two."

Halliwell sighed. That might be where he was going or it might not be. No way to know now. He'd have to deploy cloaked ships close to all three zones.

"Try to reacquire the target," Halliwell ordered. He cut the connection and rubbed his face.

She could be dead. *Sometimes the impossible might be impossible.*

If she'd been taken because she was female, well, worse things than death could be happening to her. Three damn days. A lot could happen in three days. She was older than the other missing women. That might matter. Whoever was doing this had managed to do it on the QT for almost a year. There might be other missing women that had gone unreported. No one was keeping close track of the Dusan women, though he felt sorry for anyone who went hunting there. Those were some scary women.

He got up and paced over to the wide view port that made his ready room appear larger than it was. Kikk orbited off to his right and a big bunch of empty space was everywhere else. When he looked out on this, he felt small. He didn't like feeling small. He didn't like thinking of any of his people lost out there somewhere.

"Come on, Doc, give me a crumb, give me something to work with." What part of space was she looking at? Could she still look and feel? He remembered that moment when she'd reminded him of the Key, when he'd been aware she was a young woman and not just the Chameleon. Briggs was worried about her, and he never worried without cause. Risk was part of being in the military. There were acceptable losses, like losing people in battle. The rest were unacceptable, and he fought them with a passion.

A discreet buzz broke into his grim thoughts. It was a message from the Leader. Halliwell activated it. Voice only. Not a surprise, since he'd suspected the Leader had gone back to his Ojemba roots with this move.

Halliwell had first heard of the elusive and mysterious leader of the Ojemba from Kiernan Fyn, the alien who'd helped Sara Donovan when she crashed on Kikk. Connecting Kalian to Giddioni took too much time and a near disaster. Halliwell tried not to think of Giddioni as Kalian because it made him want to hit the Leader, and they were supposed to be allies. Giddioni was challenging enough without his other identity in the mix. If Giddioni had dusted off Kalian, it couldn't be good for anyone but Giddioni.

The report was brief, no surprises until the man made a request.

"There are many nomadic settlements and small enclaves where those who wish to avoid others reside. It will take many months to search them, and even then, there is no surety of finding the Doctor if someone wishes to conceal her presence."

A pause that told the General this was the part he wasn't going to like.

"I began to wonder if your scientists had a way to differentiate your people from ours. A way to do this from space, perhaps?"

Months. Halliwell rubbed his face yet again. If he kept this up, he'd be rubbing skin off soon. They didn't have months. And Giddioni knew it. Now that he was looking, Halliwell could see the signs of a restive Gadi people. Scientists dirt side on Kikk would appease them for a short time. Once the Gadi saw what was there they'd want it even more.

The Major would have him killed if he found out he'd shared information about the Doc's personal locater with anyone. The death would be painful and prolonged if he found out it was Giddioni. He wanted to kill himself for considering it. But, this was also an opportunity. The geeks would be able to track the data burst. Giddioni would route it through his flagship, but the geeks could track it from there to his current position. Until the Leader twitched again, they'd know where he was.

"This information can only go to people you trust absolutely. If this fell into the wrong hands…" He didn't have to spell out which wrong hands to Giddioni. He knew as well as Halliwell what his enemies would do with the information

"You have my word, General." The Leader's neutral tone wasn't that reassuring.

"How do you know one of them won't double-cross you?" He'd trained these people and they both knew double-crossing was a personal favorite.

"No one double-crosses me, General."

If that was meant to be reassuring, it wasn't. Only reason they didn't was because he beat them to it.

"I'll arrange a data burst. Just be careful with it."

"You have my word," he repeated.

Yeah, that made him feel better. What did make him feel better was the knowledge that three cloaked squadrons were positioned to monitor the three zones identified by the geeks. He also had a decoy squadron ready to go out, without cloaks, if anything twitched out there.

The geeks had been tense when the ships moved out, but there was no sign that anyone had seen the deployment. On the good news front, it wasn't enough.

☼

When Doc left the shell-shocked parents she had two desires:

to sleep and to take someone down. Riven had *seemed* guileless when he asked if they could name their little girl after Doc, but Doc wasn't fooled. Nor was she impressed. Actually, she was kind of insulted. She'd have expected Conan to know her better by now. He'd had more clues than most. She left before they could try again. Her first stop was the pit toilet for a pee and a wash. While a relief, neither soothed her lacerated feelings. She remained pissed. She stalked up to Conan.

"This is not an acceptable level of care for these girls. They deserve better. You owe them better. You owe them contact with their families—"

He brushed her comments aside as if they were a fly he was shooing away. "You are a doctor."

It sounded like an accusation, like she was guilty of hiding something from them. Of course she was trying to hide everything about herself that she could. That's why she'd hesitated to act initially. It went against her grain to give him any information about her capabilities, but it was still a relatively minor piece of information. She had bigger, much more dangerous secrets. Why did this one matter? It didn't show on his stone face, but she felt it, knew it. All kinds of alarms went off inside her head.

"EMT training is SOP for my people." She used the acronyms on purpose. The statement rang with truth because it was sort of the truth. She'd taken the training, even though she didn't need to. She did a lot of things so the wrong people wouldn't know what she could do.

He arched his brows. "EMT?"

"Emergency medical training. Babies tend to arrive when least expected, i.e. emergency."

"SOP?"

"Standard operating procedure. That means something that is *always* done. Everyone gets the training because we don't know who might need it."

He didn't believe her. She didn't blame him. She'd had to **be** a doctor to deal with the delivery. If Doc hadn't been there, mom and baby would have died. That's why she was so pissed. Even if Bana had midwife training, she couldn't have handled that birth. What she didn't understand was why did he care, why did it change things? Was death by Conan off the table just because she was a doctor? Or had it put it to the top of the list again? She never liked not knowing her options.

"Was there something else you wanted to say? Because I need to sleep. In case you didn't notice I was up all night and I'm whacked."

He *so* wanted to say something, he vibrated with it. Last night had been her deadline, and the night hadn't gone the way she planned either. They'd both have to deal.

He studied her, his usual frown pulling his dark brows together. Doc let him look. She didn't have to pretend to be tired. The bags under her eyes were so big, even she could see them. He gave a short, sharp nod and stepped out of her way. Doc started toward her tent, but a rogue flow of air stopped her in her tracks. The wind whispered out of the tree line, lifting and swirling the dead leaves at her feet into a mini vortex. It rose to the height of her knees, circling her a few times, before it moved on across the clearing. She looked up. Studied the sky. Were the clouds moving in a curve?

She tipped her head to one side, then the other. Extended her arms so the air could travel across her skin. It was still hot and heavy with moisture. The heat had been beyond bitch levels since her descent into this primitive hell. Maybe there was a reason for it. She turned her hand, trying to catch small variations in movement and temperature, trying to home in on the core of her unease.

Exhaustion was a dead-weight on her concentration. She rubbed her face. Put her feelers out and started processing what was different today from the other days she'd been here. Was it hotter? Was it possible to get hotter? The wind was heavy with moisture, depositing more than it dried as it passed over her skin. It wasn't just the intense heat. There was something else, something she hadn't felt since Mexico. The Yucatan Peninsula. Hurricane season. Then, a storm was supposed to come ashore as a tropical storm, but the bitch ballooned into a cat three just before slamming into the coast. Doc had been impressed and that wasn't easy to do. If the Major hadn't kept her on a short leash, she might have become a storm chaser. It was a total rush.

If one of those bad girls was heading toward them, they wouldn't be chasing it. It would be chasing them.

"How far are we from a coastline?"

Conan stepped into her bubble, like that would help him see what she saw. "Why?"

"Storm coming."

"We are overdue for rain." He sounded more curious than concerned.

This wasn't Earth. Storms here might not be the same, might not feel the same. So the fine hairs on her skin were sticking straight up and her brain was playing "Bad Moon Rising." It didn't have to mean what it felt like it meant.

She looked around. They used small soft-sided bottles for their moonshine, kept them in baskets by the dwarves' table. She crouched by the basket. The bottles were all deformed. Conan's shadow fell over her.

"Why are they shaped like that?"

"Pressure's dropping and fast. Where I'm from, that would be very bad." She stood up and looked at him. "Are we close to the coast? Is there ocean out there? A large body of water?"

"Yes." He nodded in the direction of the curving clouds. "That direction. We often get storms from that direction. They are not so bad."

Doc considered the situation. If the encampment got slammed, it would be a good teaching moment for Conan. On the other hand, if Conan had to evacuate his happy campers to his ship, that put a huge energy signature up there for a ship with feelers out. It was practically sky writing. Way better than a bread crumb. If the *Doolittle* got close, they'd be able to pick up her personal locater.

"This one is going to be a very big storm. You need to get your people out of here."

His brows arched a bit mockingly. "*My* people?"

"Well, I think we both know I'd be an unstable element on board that ship you claim you don't have. Besides, I like storms, the bigger the better."

Conan snorted. He looked up at the wide, blue sky for a pointedly long moment, before returning his skeptical gaze to hers. "A storm?"

"A kick your ass all over the forest storm," she corrected.

"Now you predict the weather?"

Doc shrugged. "Don't believe me. Just wait—though while I was waiting, I'd nail down anything I didn't want getting blown into next week. Or washed away—depending on how close we are to the coast. Storm surge is more of a bitch than I am."

She felt, rather than saw, doubt hit him. She was playing him, but she was playing him with the truth as she knew it. She could be wrong, but wrong wouldn't cost her anything she hadn't already lost.

"Now, if you'll excuse me, I need to check for light leaks." She used the slang for taking a nap almost absently—an indication she was mainlining her military training.

She turned and walked away. She'd wanted to stalk, but that was Conan's gig, not hers. Thankfully Bana wasn't in the tent. Doc stared at her table, too tired to climb up and lay down. She frowned. It had been a long, difficult night, but that was SOP. She shouldn't be *this* tired. She'd worked three straight days and nights on the *Doolittle,* after almost getting blown up, and had enough left in her to get hot and bothered over Hel. She was on short rations and had been pushing herself pretty hard. Lots of stress, too, but stress was her mother's milk. She fed it to her demons and got sharpened acuity in the exchange.

This was more than exhaustion. Doctor kicked on, assessing symptoms. Her head felt thick and heavy, like her neck couldn't hold it up anymore. Pulse was shallow and fast. Her throat felt dry and scratchy. Wouldn't that be a kick in the butt if she were getting a cold?

She dug into her first aid kit and found a thermometer. While she waited the requisite time, she further parsed her symptoms. She removed the thermometer and studied it.

Crap. 102? It could be a cold or an earth-based flu, but she wasn't in the Milky Way. What if she'd caught the Garradian Influenza? It was a nasty illness that was common among the indigenous peoples of the galaxy. For them it ranged to mild as head cold to relatively severe—not unlike an Earth influenza outbreak. Since the expedition had different antibodies, it was bad for them. Six of their people had come down with it and all had died inside a week. Symptoms started out somewhat mild, but then progressed into a malaria-like fever and chills. All six had gone through a symptom-free period. Everyone thought the worse was over, then found out it wasn't.

Fever had spiked again and their lungs began filling with fluid. Death had followed within twenty-four hours from resumption of symptoms. Doc felt a pang for Conan's people. The brides and the baby should be all right. They were indigenous to the galaxy, but Conan and his boys were as at risk as the Earth expedition. They had people working on an immunization and a cure, but it had only manifested in the last month. No one was sure why. There'd been significant contact between the expedition and the people of the galaxy for the last two years with no discernable ill effects.

It was possible the Gadi knew why, but if they did that information was stuck in the information screen created by the traitors among the expedition and the Gadi. Or maybe Mother Nature had PMS. It didn't matter. If Doc had contracted the Garradian influenza, death now dominated her short list of options.

☼

She was sleeping on a *table.* Vidor didn't know whether to laugh or curse. The woman refused to get into one of their beds, even when alone. She slept and still she managed to fight against him.

Seeing her like this, with her face relaxed in slumber, made him realize how much she hid when she was awake. She looked younger, almost vulnerable. He recalled the first time he'd watched her sleep. Four days—such a short time for so much to change. There was before and there was after. Would he go back to before if he could? He did not have to think about it. Even suspecting that she was the one, he would not change anything.

Tonight he would claim her. He'd searched for, and he'd found a law that allowed him to bypass the naming conventions and claim her as his wife. He was glad to have found legal precedent, but he and Bana knew he'd have claimed her without it. He would do what he needed to do to secure his people's future, and he would have her as his wife. She could not be allowed to return to her people, but there were other places they could live. To have her, he'd give up everything.

She would not react well to this claim. Now that he knew who she was, he could see how she'd done what she did to their people, though thinking about how it had happened made his head hurt. How could she be here and be then, too?

If not for the storm, he'd have given her one more day to choose. And if she'd been sharing their food, he could have used it as his medium for the compound that would make her easier to manage. He studied her belongings. Her bag was open, some of the contents tumbled onto a chair, as if she'd been looking for something. There was a box with red lines crossing and some packets of, he suspected, the food she'd been eating instead of theirs.

He took care removing the cloth Bana had given him. The compound was absorbed through the skin and very fast acting. And it took very little contact for a satisfactory result. Keeping the salve side away from his skin, he rubbed the cloth across several of the tumbled items, careful not to shift or move anything. It would be like her to notice. He also rubbed the top and sides of the red crossed box. He made no sign that might alert her to his presence. When he finished, he used as much care as he stowed the cloth.

He should leave, but the compulsion to look at her kept him there. He would have preferred her conscious compliance, but that would come in time. He fought the longing to run his finger down the side of her face. Soon he would touch her where he wanted and when he wanted.

He left as silently as he'd come, meeting Bana's questioning look with a slight nod.

He keyed his transmission device. "Evacuate the compound."

There was a single flash and everyone but he and the woman were transported to his ship.

In an interesting twist, Bana had agreed that the storm incoming might be serious. And if it turned out to be less than predicted, well, there was nothing wrong with some private time with his woman before they left the planet behind for good.

☼

Hel saw his scanners light up and knew he'd run out of time. This wasn't an anomalous energy signature. This was a whole ship, parked planet-side on Feldstar. Transport signatures followed, then it cloaked again. They'd dropped shields to transport. Were they leaving? Was Delilah among those transported to the ship? Would he be able to see her personal locator through those shields? He triggered the secure channel to Halliwell, even as he set up a hyper jump to the planet. One must play the game.

"General, I believe I've found something interesting. I'm sending it to you in a secure data burst."

"Our people saw it, too, Leader, but thank you for confirming our sighting. We're sending a squadron to investigate."

So the *Doolittle* wasn't moving? That was unexpected. Or was it? The General might be concerned about Gadi ship movements and war worries. Whatever the reason, it gave Hel an edge, *if* he found Delilah. The smaller ships lacked the scanning ability of the *Doolittle.*

"Then I won't send my people there." When Delilah disappeared, Hel wanted the General to have no one to blame but the original kidnappers. "Though you have only to say the word and I will send them in."

"Thank you." Did the good General sound relieved to believe he was backing off a rescue?

Hel missed the video link. It told him more than voice only, but Hel couldn't afford to let the General know Hel was out in the galaxy as Kalian.

"I'll wait for further news—good I hope." Hel cut the connection. He would arrive well ahead of the *Doolittle's* squadrons. He wasn't worried about them. If this was where Delilah had been taken, it was possible the hostile ship was preparing to leave. He was confident he could track them now, but that would take more time. There was a point he'd have to break off the search and return to his flagship. And if his timing was off, he might be returning to a Gadi civil war. This was why he felt anxious, not the thought of losing Delilah. If she did not return to her people, she would not succeed in her mission.

Even as he thought these things, he knew Hel sought to lie to his other identity. He felt the duality of the roles more than he ever had before. Felt their conflicting desires. In one thing only were they united: their desire for Delilah.

☼

In some ways, Halliwell was reminded of a *Keystone Cops* movie gone even more wrong than usual. There were so many different ships moving around, it was a wonder they weren't all bumping heads. Would have been funny, if there wasn't so much riding on it.

It was clever of Giddioni to phone in, but the geeks had his ship back on the grid since the data burst. Clever to bounce the signal off his flagship, but not clever enough. Even when he'd tweaked his shield, James was able to find him again.

Now, he was on course to Feldstar, where the unknown ship had dropped cloak. He'd be there in twelve hours, Earth Standard time. Their cloaked squadron was on his heels and would arrive maybe thirty minutes after him. And Halliwell had deployed a non-cloaked squadron as a diversion. It was far enough out to give the bogey the illusion they didn't need to rush. And if the rush to the scene wasn't enough, every scanner they had was pointed at the area where the unknown ship had popped into view.

It could already be gone, taking the Doc with them. If they could get close enough, they should be able to pick up her beacon. At the very least, they had a solid place to initiate tracking, at least that's what the geeks claimed. The Doc had done her part. She'd gotten the bogey to drop his pants and give them a look. They'd have gotten better data if they'd been closer, but the cloaked squadron might have more scan info on the bogey.

He'd decided to divert the other squadrons, too, though they were at the back of the pack at the moment, but they could be deployed as back-up if the bogeys didn't like letting go.

He could understand why the Doc's beacon was set to low. It wasn't designed for a galaxy. When she'd operated on Earth, even an intermittent signal might be picked up by the wrong person. Giddioni was going to have to assume a low orbit and hope to catch it on one of the constantly rotating frequencies it used.

At the moment, he was glad Giddioni had the intell to find her, and as long as they could track the bastard, he'd stay happy. And if the geeks lost him again, they'd all be unhappy together.

Twelve

The camp felt empty without his people. Vidor paced outside Morticia's tent for a while, then sat at the table and watched the opening of her tent, waiting for some sign she'd waked. As he'd paced the wind picked up, sometimes making the sides of the tents crack like whips. The wind brought some relief from the heat that had gripped the camp since Morticia's arrival. Almost he believed this was her fault as well.

This departure was coming a few days sooner than planned, but perhaps it was for the best. Morticia was unhappy with this life. Perhaps she'd be less difficult aboard ship. It had plumbing.

He looked toward her tent again. She'd never slept this long in the four nights she'd been in camp. Was she tired or was something else going on? Perhaps she'd managed to slip away? He crossed to the tent and stooped to enter, stopping just inside at the sight of her sitting on the edge of the bed. She'd shed her jacket. Her top hugged her body down to where it met her trousers. Her figure was as pleasing as he'd imagined. He looked at her things and noticed some had been moved.

Her gaze met his, but it was too dim inside the tent to see any change in her eyes from absorbing the compound. Her forehead glistened with sweat, though.

"I don't feel very good."

He took a half step toward her. "Let me help you."

"You just want to help me into your bed."

He took another step toward her, but she jumped up, swaying slightly. She used the bedpost to steady herself. Her movements had lost their crispness.

"You should stay back. I'm probably contagious—if I haven't already infected all of you."

"You are not contagious."

"You seem very sure of that. Did you do something?"

"What could I do? I have been outside waiting for you to rest so we may speak about your choice."

Her eyes narrowed. She licked her pink lips, them bit the bottom one with her even, white teeth. Desire tugged at him, low in his belly.

"Talk? Yeah, I almost believe you want to talk."

He stepped closer. She edged along the back of the bed.

"You can chase me around this bed, but you won't get me in it, Conan." She wrapped her arms around the next bedpost as if her knees had sagged. "I am ill, and you can't help me."

She rubbed the side of her face, as if it pained her.

"You will feel better soon."

Her lashes lifted, but she was in the shadows still. How far had the compound impacted her?

"If you return me to my people—"

"That will never happen. Neither of us can go home, Morticia."

Her control was less than before. He could see her struggle to think, to consider his words.

"Then I'll die."

The words pained him. "Everyone dies."

She chuckled, the sound pleasing.

"You're at risk, too."

"We will be both be fine, I give you my word." He moved closer.

She moved away. "I can still kick your ass, Conan."

He smiled. "You can try." He extended his hands in invitation.

She bit her lip, her gaze narrowing.

"I'll even let you make the first move."

"Your goons will come and get me."

"They're all gone." He smiled at her. "You told me a storm was coming and you were right."

"I'm always right." She edged toward him now and his senses leapt in anticipation. "Most people find that annoying."

His smile deepened. "Do they, Morticia ?" He shifted so that he stood dead center in the tent. She'd have to let go of the bed-post to reach him.

She frowned. "That's not my name."

He hesitated. "What is your name?"

Her frown deepened. "I don't remember." She swung around the post and sank on the bed again. "Maybe it is Morticia."

He didn't need her name, he reminded himself as he edged closer, but he wanted to know it.

She frowned. "I was going to do something."

"You were going to kick my ass."

"Oh, right." She brightened.

"I'm waiting." Again he extended his arms. He had time. The compound's effects would build for another half an hour and then subside in about two hours. The storm was still offshore. He would coax her into submission. "Come and get me."

"I think I will."

She used to the post to pull herself upright. She swayed, her body more fluid now as the drug moved through her veins. She straightened her shoulders. She tried to focus, but she probably saw two of him by now. She took a step toward him. He had to fight the urge to reach out and yank her close.

Another step. She swayed. Her knees started to buckle. He closed the gap, wrapping his arms around her. Her deadweight caught him off balance. He staggered and almost fell. He was still off balance, but her soft, supple body filled his arms and the bed was close. He pulled her tight against him, felt desire surge faster than the storm bearing down on them.

Her chin lifted, her soft mouth so close, her clear gaze—her clear gaze?

Something hard hit him in the groin. His breath whooshed out as pain exploded through his body. He staggered back, clutching himself. Her fist flashed, connecting solidly with his chin. He dropped to his knees. Through a red haze he saw she had his weapon. He reached for his transport alert, but the beam of his weapon caught him dead center in the chest. He fell back, his body jerking as the charge moved through him.

"I'd say I'm sorry, but I'm not."

He fought against it; she couldn't be allowed to return to her people…

☼

Doc lowered Conan's ray gun, swaying from relief and adrenaline. No worry she'd turn into an adrenaline addict. She was sick of the stuff. Fever may be rampaging through her system, but it hadn't killed her sense of smell. Or her hearing. And she'd been expecting him to do something. Kind of insulting that Conan thought she'd fall for something as obvious as a Mickey. Good thing she played possum better than he did stealth.

She'd considered dosing him, but then he wouldn't have felt it when she shot him.

Payback was a bitch. And so was she.

She checked his pulse and wasn't too surprised to find one. He'd keep his weapon set to stun until he subdued her, or was forced to kill her. Even if she hadn't suspected that, she wouldn't have hesitated to fire. She wasn't an assassin but she knew better than to hesitate against a larger opponent.

Conan's barbarians wouldn't leave them alone for long, not with a storm incoming. How long depended on his arrogance: huge, and the proximity of the storm: size to be determined. She knew the *Doolittle* would have been watching for her SOS, but Feldstar wasn't that close to Kikk. If they saw the ship, it would still take time for help to arrive. And if she had the Garradian influenza, it didn't matter. She was already dead.

Logic dictated she stand down. She was a scientist first. Logic should be her god. Why continue a battle she couldn't win? Even as her brain presented its case, she yanked on another pair of gloves and started cleaning the items she'd need. She used the pockets of her pants and jacket to stow stuff. There was no long-term plan, no need for a pack. Her goal was simple: evade recapture until rescue or death.

The why didn't matter, but her brain liked conclusions. Maybe I just like to win, she postulated, pausing to stare at Conan. He looked vulnerable, almost harmless lying sprawled on the dirt floor. With his systems offline, she could study him more objectively. He'd pissed her off too much to up her pulse rate, but she could see that women who didn't know him like she did might find him attractive. On Earth he'd have had no trouble getting face time with women. Why had they chosen this way?

It bugged her that she'd never know. Her brain hated unanswered questions, too. Her brain was going to have to deal. It could take comfort in the fact it wouldn't be that long before brain function would cease. Okay, so maybe that wasn't something a brain could take comfort from. It would have to deal with that, too.

She'd bet they weren't planning on coming back. Even Mr. Overconfident had to be concerned about dropping cloak and transporting so soon after having to scan for her non-existent transmission device.

Her head pounded and she ached in every joint. She considered taking some of that stuff with her, but her acuity was already degraded, and she didn't know what all the side effects were. She turned from temptation and headed out of the tent without looking back. She scanned the clearing as the building wind tugged at her clothing and hair. The empty silence was creepy, even for a cold-hearted geek. The curve of a tropical-type storm was more apparent in the cloud movement now. A rainsquall had moved through while she was in the tent. The ground was muddy, with small pools of water in every depression.

Last time they'd tracked her from space, dropping in to ring her. But, and it was this but upon which she was hanging her hope of eluding them, their tracking had been imprecise until she broke cover. She'd used a few branches to break up her silhouette last time, but she'd also kept moving. She was ill and going to get worse, not better. So this time she wouldn't run or break cover. She'd change tactics and maybe buy enough time for death or the cavalry to arrive. With any luck at all, she could report what she'd learned before brain function shut down.

Nature offered help. Mud tended to muddy a heat signature. It wasn't a permanent solution, since it was vulnerable to rain. Still, it would help in the meantime, and she needed all the help she could get. She used her knife to widen one of the muddy pools into a nice-sized wallow and played pig. The water was cool enough to feel good against her hot body. When she'd coated herself as well as she could that way, she scooped up handfuls and applied it to her hair and face.

Next, she used the knife to cut several large branches from the closest bush. Plants and trees also gave off an infrared signature, though at a different level than a live body. They were less vulnerable to being washed away and should help break up the outline of her infrared signature. She pulled out her roll of twine, cut off several lengths and she used the twine to lash the branches to her body. She stowed twine and knife, feeling like *The Swamp Thing*. That had to have been a tough gig, if how she felt was any indication.

She had a small mirror, but it was for signaling. And she didn't want to know what she looked like. What it felt like was bad enough. Her illness dragged like deadweight, on her body and her brain, as she studied the area surrounding the camp. She needed heavy ground brush, not too close to any trees. When the winds kicked up, trees tended to come down. No reason to go for an imprecise and painful death when the flu was taking care of that.

There was an area of low, dense scrub. Not completely

protected from falling trees, but it was the best there was on offer. It had the added benefit of giving her eyes on the camp. She studied the incoming clouds. Looked like another rainsquall was incoming. It should help cover her tracks. So should the rotting ground cover. She made a false trail away from her hunker down point. Just because she hadn't seen them using tracking skills, didn't mean they lacked them.

Never assume.

The clouds overhead turned darker as the storm spun closer. Be nice to get a look at weather radar. All she had was her gut, and it was telling her that out in the open was a bad place to be tonight. Branches scraped her arms and face as she worked her way into the center of the low-lying scrub. She dropped to her knees, digging through the ground debris to create a shallow depression. She pulled out her binoculars and Conan's weapon, placing both within easy reach and lay down. She scooped as much disturbed debris over herself as she could before settling in to wait. Her brain had a new question to gnaw on: who would come first?

Conan's people or the storm?

☼

Conan's boys transported him to the ship. Daylight was long gone when Delilah saw the transport flash light up the interior of the tent in a break between squalls. A few minutes later, Eamon and Cadir arrived, weapons ready and back to back, in the center of the encampment. At least she'd taught them to cover their backs. It was kind of cute that they thought that would work against her.

Doc sighted on Cadir, keeping watch while Eamon checked out the tent. She didn't think they'd see her if they stepped on her, but the weapon's lock helped her think about something other than how awful she felt.

When Eamon emerged, he showed off his rudimentary tracking skills, his *very* rudimentary skills. Her pig wallow puzzled them both. They circled it several times. Doc was glad it had rained heavily since she used it. They might have figured out she'd rolled in it. Their math skills weren't obvious, but even they might put two and two together. She needed them to believe she was gone or dead. They conferred on the evidence and concluded she'd headed toward the lake.

"Could she use the cold of the lake's water to disguise her body heat?" Cadir said with a frown.

Eamon shrugged. "Possibly. The water is very cold."

Good thing their knowledge of biology was as poor as their math. Cold tended to make the body produce more heat until it ran out of fuel. That would be why she'd piled on the branches. Between her fever and the cold rain, she'd have been glowing like a star going nova on their scans.

He lifted his wrist, requesting transport to the lake. In the pause while coordinates were configured, Eamon looked at his brother.

"There is another reason she might not have a heat outline."

That was the math she wanted them to do. Before Cadir could respond, the transport whisked them away. In the distance she heard the rumble of another squall moving in. It was going to be a long night.

☼

As Hel's ship dropped out of hyperspace just off Feldstar, he made sure the planet was between him and the last sighting of the unknown ship. He charted the low orbit the General claimed was necessary and started scanning for Delilah's beacon. He'd used the transit time to create a program that would scan all the frequencies the General had noted in the data burst. He expected to have to wait for it, but got a weak read almost immediately. He fixed on it and adjusted course. On one level he realized he was too relieved she wasn't gone, though he could not think of a good reason her captors had transported to their ship and left her behind.

As he tracked toward her position, he played with his scan

settings, hoping to crack the unknown ship's cloak. Instead he found that the *Doolittle* had been playing with their cloaks, too. He had a squadron coming in significantly ahead of the visible squadron that had deployed when the unknown ship dropped cloak.

Hel smiled. The General was a clever and devious adversary. If he'd stumbled on them, they might stumble on his settings. As soon as he had Delilah on board, he'd reset them. He started calculating their arrival time planet-side as his low orbit took him toward Delilah's location. It also brought him into the start of a new day. Her location was still dark, but not for long. He bumped his scanners to maximum. It made him more detectable, but he needed the data. He pulled up real-time imaging of the planet surface and saw the slow turn of the horizon over Feldstar's immense ocean. The sight of a massive storm made his gut clench. He cursed silently.

He'd been in one of these storms and it hadn't been this large. The white mass was almost perfectly round when viewed from space. Half of its mass was on the land, half still out over the ocean. This was bad. It meant the heated ocean was still fueling the storm. It wouldn't begin to weaken until the rest made landfall. According to Delilah's locator, she was in the worst of it, close to the center but not close enough.

She hadn't moved since he started tracking her. He turned to his heat-sensing equipment, honing in on the area with the beacon. Trees and shrubs popped out of the black background, fiercely whipped by the wind from the storm, but no discernable human shape. He tightened the focus more. He could think of one reason her body wasn't giving off heat—unless her captors had discovered the beacon and removed it. If they had, they—and she—would already be long gone.

☼

It felt odd to find clarity in so much chaos, but that's what the long night gave Doc. She'd told the General she would fail sometime, but she hadn't believed it. Calm certainty that she could think or slug her way out of anything was gone, replaced by the realization she lay in the mud, being pounded by wind *and* rain, waiting for someone else to find her. No, she needed to face facts. She lay here waiting for *rescue*. When did she become so arrogant? She could be on Conan's ship, warm and dry and dying. She'd thought it was miserable sitting out a hurricane in sub-standard housing in Mexico. She'd been wrong about that, too. Throughout the endless night, trees had bent and crashed around her. One fell so close the branches half buried her. She told herself that it boosted her infrared cover and provided some protection from flying debris. It was easier than facing the truth.

This wasn't smart. This was stupid.

Something had changed her. Even if she wasn't dying, she couldn't have gone back and worked for the Major. She'd lost her edge. But it wasn't just that. She felt different inside. She'd been changing before Conan, perhaps before she boarded the *Doolittle?* The tendrils of change reached all the way back to Sara Donovan, she realized, threading through Briggs and even taking a small pass through the General. When she went into situations with the Major as her reference, well, she was used to getting looks like the ones she got from the General. They didn't used to bother her. She knew who and what she was, but this time, it had bothered her. And the General *sensed it*. He'd seen through her and the sting of it had left her with an aching desire for his respect—something that had never happened to her before.

Hel was part of it, too. *The Leader and the spook*. She snorted, the sound lost in the roar of the storm. It would never have happened, even without the whole dying part.

And if that weren't enough humiliation, she was going to fail. She'd gotten caught like a *girl* and was going to die in the mud while experiencing every variation of miserable the universe could supply—just in case she hadn't gotten the message it was humble pie time. Pride had her trapped like she a rookie on her first op.

Nothing like a night out in a hurricane to gain a true understanding of what it meant to get your ass kicked. And that was before things got bad. She should have been freezing, but she wasn't. The heat from her body had probably boosted the storm's intensity, though the fever broke for a while, replaced by bone-rattling chills. This cycle had repeated through the night.

And that had been the warm up act.

The eye wall was the main event.

Her plan to play opossum went south when the eye wall delivered the storm surge. Luckily for her, it was only about a foot of water, and it had lost most of its oomph before it reached her. It forced her up off the ground and into the branches of the tree that almost fell on her as the water tried to sweep her legs out from under her.

It was pitch black, but the occasional lightning flash lit up her personal hell. She found she could still be awed by Mother Nature on steroids. Even *they* paused to watch the show.

A flash of lightning showed her a stray branch incoming. She tried to duck and whacked her head against the tree's trunk. And the branch hit her anyway.

At least the circle of stars only lit up the inside of her head.

☼

Hel locked his transport system on Delilah's beacon but hesitated to transport her with so much electrical activity in the atmosphere. He'd never tried it in a storm such as this one. Flash after flash blanked his heat-sensing screen as the worst of the storm passed over the spot where she lay. A failed transport attempt would not help her, if she even still lived. He had to assume the beacon could transmit after death until he learned otherwise. The General had been as sparing as possible with information about the unusual device.

He could think of one other reason besides death, that he couldn't find a heat pattern. If she knew or suspected they could track her heat pattern, she was clever enough to do something to disguise it. During her capture, she had eluded them for some distance. She would learn from that. She adapted. Her people called her Chameleon for a reason. If her captors were still in orbit, that meant they hadn't found her beacon. It also meant they were still looking for her. Scanning showed some residual energy traces lingering in the atmosphere, but it didn't mean they were still here. He had tried to play with scan settings, but there was a faster way to find a cloaked ship if it was close by.

He'd come in low to avoid intersecting with that ship and to scan for Delilah. He checked the status of the incoming, cloaked squadron, then shut down sensors and scanning, going almost dark. He adjusted his sublights, aiming for gentle lift. If a ship was there, it should be sitting in orbit just above his ship. His ship drifted into a higher orbit, the only sign of movement the alteration in light outside his front view port. Just because they weren't here, it didn't mean Delilah was dead, he told himself. If they were convinced she was dead, there would be no point in remaining—

Without sensation to give warning, his ship passed through the lower cargo bay of a large ship. He halted sublight thrust. It was a disturbing experience, no matter how many times he'd done it the past two years. He might be curious to see the bridge of this vessel, but that would have to wait. He reversed thrust and the cargo bay slid from view. When he'd once again put distance between the two ships, he lit up the scanners, turning to the heat-sensing screen with new eyes. The only reason he knew where to look for her was because of the beacon. She had to be there, but all he saw a mass of white scrub and trees moving in the wind. He focused closer. The center of the storm moved closer, too. She'd be in the clear soon.

The cloaked squadron would be in sensor range about the same time the center of the storm reached her. There would be a small window of opportunity if he worked fast.

Once the alien ship knew he was here, they'd be looking for energy anomalies, too. He'd have to go dark and hope they assumed he'd gone. The arrival of the cloaked ships from the *Doolittle* should muddy any signatures he'd left behind. He'd set course down their back trail. He checked the progress of the *Doolittle's* visible squadron. There'd soon be a lot of ships in the area. It was almost amusing. And it would further aid his retreat from the area.

He stayed focused on the foliage where her beacon still intermittently broadcast, was about to admit defeat when he saw a movement.

And a booted foot.

☼

Vidor woke slowly to pain, lots of pain. A gray bulkhead loomed over him. He was aboard his ship.

Morticia.

He sat up with a jerk that intensified the pain.

"Would you like something for the pain?" Bana asked.

Vidor looked at her through a haze of it. She'd exchanged the robe for her regular clothes.

"Where is she?" He'd tagged her, like they were all tagged. Why hadn't they found her?

"We were hoping you knew. The storm's properties interfered with our tagging mineral. Eamon and Cadir searched as long as they could, but the storm got worse very quickly."

She didn't remind him she'd told him to kill her. She didn't have to. He knew it, knew they had to find her again before she doomed their people again. He got up, wincing as his groin protested. "Heat scans?"

"Nothing." She hesitated. "It is possible she is—"

He made a sharp movement with his hand. "She isn't." He rubbed his aching head. "Any more bad news?"

"Would you consider a wave of ships incoming from the Earth expedition bad news?"

"How long do we have?"

She half shrugged.

"How long have I been out?" The pain in his body failed to completely disguise the other pain. She'd been in his arms, and now she was gone. When had she become so important to him?

"Most of the night." She rose, put her hand on his arm. "She could have killed you. She didn't."

He wanted to believe it meant something. He feared it just meant she'd wanted him to wake in pain. He pushed past Bana and made his way to the bridge. Color stained his face when his men averted their gazes and tried to hide their smiles.

"Let me see the heat signature scan data."

Eamon scrambled to get it up the screen. "This is from right after we transported you to the ship." He hesitated. "The storm has been very severe. It is possible she—"

Vidor silenced him with a violent slash of his hand. Morticia was not dead. She'd been difficult to track the first time. Movement had been her downfall that time.

"Check close to the encampment." While Eamon worked the controls, he looked at Cadir. "Where's the storm?"

"The worst of it is over the encampment."

"It's as bad as she predicted," Bana added.

Cadir pulled up real-time views for him to observe. The wind bent the trees almost to the ground. One lost its grip and was swept away. Other trees lay tumbled all over the clearing where their tents had been. Rain beat against everything with a force he had not previously seen. If Morticia was out in that—belief in her survival faltered, until he recalled how unrelentingly she'd fought capture. This woman did not give up.

"Data is up, Vidor," Eamon said, sounding subdued.

Vidor strode over the screen, scanning the areas around the camp. "Is this the latest data?"

"No, since the storm hit, the data stream has been is poor. There is much interference from the electrical properties of the storm."

"Combine all scans and replay them slowly."

The current screen flickered and jumped, as Eamon predicted. Now there was too much movement.

"It's ready."

Vidor kept his attention on one area as the first loop played.

"Keep running it until I tell you to stop," he ordered.

"The storm has a calm center that will be over the encampment in a few minutes, Vidor," Riven said. "All scanning should clear then."

Vidor leaned in, peering at the screen.

Eamon leaned in and touched the screen. "I found footprints heading this direction."

"Then she won't be there," Vidor murmured. Unless she thought he'd believe that. His head throbbed from trying to figure out how she might think. "Keep playing it."

He almost missed it during the third loop. Movement. He leaned closer and saw it.

A booted foot.

"Scan there for the tag." A pause and the scan found minute traces through the storm's electrical discharges.

"We'll drop in here," he pointed at the center where the weather was calm, but as close as they could get to where he'd seen movement. "Set your weapons to stun. You see her, fire. Don't give her time to play games with us."

☼

A softening of the deep dark on the horizon hinted the end of the long night. It would have meant more if she weren't in the freaking eye wall. The howl of the wind was so loud, she couldn't hear herself think. That was the only upside.

In the good news/bad news front, she'd had neither fever nor chills for some time.

If the fever and chills were gone, and if this was the Garradian influenza, it meant she was in the limbo between bad and worse. At some point in the next twenty-four to thirty-six hours, her lungs would begin to fill with fluid. The fever would be back, too, spiking high enough to cause convulsions and hallucinations. Neither was appealing to think about, so the wind was her friend. Maybe a tree would solve the problem for her. Time was her enemy. Stripped of all illusion, it held her in a trap of her own making.

She'd had time to wallow in regret during the breaks between the feeder bands, regret that she wouldn't see her brother again. That she let the General down.

And there was Hel. She would have liked to see him again. Liked to feel desire warm her inside and out one more time. He'd never been hers, but he'd wanted her. He'd seen *Delilah*, not the Chameleon. He'd liked her. Around him, she'd found a person inside herself she hadn't known existed. He'd made her feel real. Her personal furies couldn't be seen, heard or felt with the storm shrieking around her. Perhaps *they* waited for the fever's return to make their final move. Did *they* know how little time was left for them, too? For the first time in her life *they* didn't scare her. If *they* wanted to take her, they'd have to get in line.

A break in the storm gave her a glimpse of the eye closing on her position. It wasn't the relief it should have been. It was a window of opportunity Conan and his merry band could use to find her, if they were still looking. It was possible they'd written her off as dead or crazy and left. If she had someone to bet with, she'd have wagered Conan was still here. She should have killed him, but she'd wanted him to wake up in pain. That might have been a mistake. He was both stubborn and delusional. It was a bad combination.

All around her the storm still raged, but she caught glimpses of the eye as the clouds opened and closed. A flash that was almost but not quite lightning caught her eye. Could it be help? Brief hope flared and died before the clouds shifted again. Usually she liked being right. This time wasn't one of them.

Conan had come with the boys.

In other circumstances, she'd have put money on her ability to hide under his nose, but the storm had done a good job of stripping her cover down to the bare branches. She had his ray gun shoved into the front of her pants. It had been a bitch to lie on all night, but at least she knew it was still there. She lifted her sopping jacket and extracted it. The latest feeder arrived and began emptying its load of water on her head. Through the blur of water running down her face, she heard something new in the storm, something that sent a chill down her back.

There wasn't a freight train within a million miles of this forest. Lightning flashed and the chill turned to pure ice.

A tornado was incoming like said freight train and she was tied to the track.

☼

Hel jerked back as the alien ship dropped cloak right in front of him. They were so close, without his phase cloak, they'd have bumped hulls. Four life signs appeared on the surface in the center of the storm closest to Delilah's position. Had they spotted her? Their position indicated they had.

He kicked thrusters, backing off from the alien ship. It was risky to transport before she was clear of the storm, but he couldn't lose her now. He dropped cloak and slammed his hand down on the transport control. The four figures started toward her. Stun energy signatures tracked from both positions, then her beacon disappeared.

He turned, staring at the place she'd arrive, willing her to make it. The air silvered, then formed into a human shape. If not for her eyes, he wouldn't have recognized her. Water flowed off her in heavy rivulets, pooling around her military issue, very muddy boots. Her matted hair clung to her scalp. She was filthy, scratched and bruised. He stared at a tree branch tied to one leg. He'd never seen a women look so bedraggled—or so beautiful.

He brought up the cloak and went sensor dark. He turned back, would have smiled at her, but she gripped a weapon with both hands and it was pointed at his chest. No sign of recognition flared in her eyes or softened her stance.

"Delilah?"

Her body shuddered with cold or shock, or both.

He kept still, his voice soft. "I thought you'd be glad to see me."

She blinked once, and then again. Water ran down her face and off her jaw line.

"Hel?" Her stance softened some, one hand leaving the partially lowered weapon to rub her eyes.

He rose, taking it slow, not anxious to alarm her into shooting. He had no way of knowing what her weapon was set to.

He rubbed his scruffy chin. "I had to become Kalian to find you."

The hand holding the weapon dropped to her side. She swayed, even as she tried to smile.

"Nice timing."

"Your friends were getting close," he admitted, stepping close. The smells of the storm clung to her, hiding her scent.

"The tornado was closer." She reached out, her hand touching his chest as if she still weren't sure he was real. It slid up, a brief loss of sensation until she found his face. "You need a shave."

His hand slid down her arm, his fingers closing around the weapon and easing it out of her grasp. He tossed it onto the copilot's chair and tugged her close. "I need you."

"I'm a mess."

"You're perfect."

Her laugh broke in the middle. Her arms slid up around his neck. His mouth found hers and passion flared, as out of control as the storm beneath them. He drove her mouth open. Couldn't get close enough to her to satisfy. He pushed, with his mouth and his body until she slammed into the bulkhead. Water soaked into his clothes, and he could have sworn the air around them sizzled as if touched by fire. She whimpered, deep in her throat. He started to lift to his head, concerned he'd hurt her, but her hands at the back of his head, and her moan of protest, stopped that. One should never disappoint a lady.

He shoved his hand in her wet hair, turning her head for better access. Passion ran like a molten river between them, and then he felt her tremble and slide away. Her body going limp in his arms.

He cursed and lifted her, striding quickly to the guest quarters and laying her on the bed. Scratches and bruises marred her pale skin in the places where dirt had washed away. He threw a blanket over her, wanted to stay with her, but an alarm from the bridge sent him running.

There was nothing to be seen out his view screen, but sensors told another story. The enemy ship had dropped its cloak again for long enough to get their people on board. He'd study the data later. For now, it was enough to know that there were no life signs on the planet surface. He searched for and found brief signs of hyperdrive activation. Tracking showed the Earth ships were close. He needed to leave, but the alien ship could track and follow his hyperdrive trail, too.

A lot depended on how motivated they were to retrieve Delilah. He half-smiled. He'd left his duties, risked a civil war and an assassination to get to her. They were motivated.

He kicked on sublights. If he could put the planet mass between them before he made the jump, it might put them off his track until the Earth ships arrived to muddy his energy signatures. He looked at the course, already programmed into his system. His plan had worked as expected—until Delilah's retrieval. He wanted her. He didn't know he wanted her that much. He didn't know he'd want any woman that much. And now he had her.

The memory of how she'd looked filled his thoughts. Why did he sense that where she was concerned, nothing would ever be simple?

☼

When Vidor stalked onto the bridge after their return from the planet, no one laughed or smiled. She'd been so close. On one level he was shocked she'd survived the storm. On the other, nothing about her surprised him anymore. She'd seen them and fired. They'd fired back, but she'd vanished. They had an analysis of the ship she'd transported to: a small trading ship, typical of the galaxy—except for the fact that they couldn't find it. They'd scanned as long as they dared. It had to have gone dark. It's what he would have done.

He'd been ready to try a low orbit to see if they could track the small ship, but they'd picked up an odd energy signature, though just a short one. They hadn't had to wonder for very long what it was. A squadron of Earth ships dropped cloak close to the planet and moved into a low orbit. The trader ship had been in low orbit, too.

Then the Earth ships did something even more puzzling.

They didn't raise cloak, and they did leave. And the other, un-cloaked Earth squadron they'd been tracking altered course, though it was still headed in the general direction of Feldstar. This was the first, admittedly dubious, indication that these ships knew about, and might be able to track the trader ship that had seized the prize. The squadron's arrival would have muddied any energy signatures from the trader, but perhaps he didn't need to find it. If he followed these ships, would they lead him to Morticia?

If he'd had any doubts about who her people were, he had none now. He considered what he knew of the Earth expedition, both from their history and from studying them during their time in this galaxy. Because he'd had to pretend to be a simple trader did not mean he was one. He could devise strategy, he could react to circumstances and adapt. He frowned.

"What are we going to do, Vidor?" Eamon asked what the others were thinking.

"What we planned. Cadir will take the women, Bana and the new girl child. If you don't receive my signal, commence the attack as planned."

In a very short time he would introduce himself to her people. He would take back what was his and finish what they'd come to do—all of it.

☼

Halliwell expected Giddioni to shift his cloak modulations when he left Feldstar, but he didn't. He ordered all four squadrons to intercept the ship.

"Cloaks down. I want him to see you coming," he added. "Carey, you close enough to tell if the Doc is onboard?"

"Sorry, sir. He's got a souped-up version of what we're driving. He's just out of range and staying that way."

Halliwell spun to glare at the geeks. "Where's he heading?"

James pushed up his glasses, clicked some keys and then looked up. "He's headed here, sir."

"That's not possible. He wouldn't."

"He could still change course, but right now, he's headed here."

Halliwell rubbed his face. Now what was the bastard up to? "Don't lose him."

James paled enough Halliwell could see it. "No, sir."

Thirteen

Delilah woke to a very *déjà vu* world of hurt. *Déjà vu* sucked. So did hurting. She blinked at the gray bulkhead above her. At least it wasn't a tent, though that didn't mean the ship didn't belong to Conan. She frowned. Did she remember seeing Hel—a scruffy unfamiliar Hel who'd kissed the boots off her? Could be a hallucination fueled by wish fulfillment, but it had the feel of a real memory. Just thinking sent a nice burn all through her. She'd feel guilty about kissing him back, but the Garradian influenza wouldn't kill *him*. And she needed the memory.

She rolled to her side and let her legs drop off the side of the bunk. This helped her sit up, something she wasn't sure she could manage without some help from artificial gravity. Right now a two-year-old could take her with one chubby arm tied behind the back. Too bad she hadn't hallucinated being sick, though part of it could be simple hunger. She couldn't remember her last power bar, though she wasn't complaining about it. If she never ate one again, it would be a good thing. She held onto a bolted-to-the-wall desk when she tried out her legs. They held, but only just. She wobbled to a door and found it unlocked. It opened onto a main corridor. The cabin she occupied was a single, so not Conan's ship. The thought of him sleeping single in his double bed made her smile. It might have been an evil smile. Without a mirror it was hard to know.

Her brain spewed out the memory of her last meeting with him, if you could call anything involving a tornado a meeting.

Even by her standards it had been a bad twenty-four hours. She'd been scooped up with truly dramatic timing. So she hadn't imagined Hel. No one did drama better.

The room was small, not pretty, and arranged for utility and comfort. A towel and a small pile of clothing lay on top of the desk. The other door led to a heavenly sight: plumbing. She'd have fallen to her knees and kissed the commode if she hadn't urgently needed to apply another part of her anatomy to it. She didn't bother to pull her pants up. After four days in them, she'd be happy if she never got skin to these ABUs again. She had to tug at the spots where skin and fabric felt like they'd started to grow together.

The sight of her face in the mirror shocked her, and she wasn't easily shocked. It wasn't just the dirt and scratches, bruises and bangs. She'd lost weight, and the bags under her eyes had reached epic proportions. Nasty gash on her temple from that flying branch. If she wasn't already dying, she'd worry about infection.

What blew her mind, Hel, the Leader of all things pretty, had said he wanted *that*. Mister used-to-be-pretty-in-pink had slammed *that* against the bulkhead and kissed *that* face until they'd damn near burned a hole in the deck plating. Even her super brain had a hard time wrapping around the notion he liked her that much. Her brain was completely in denial about how much she liked him. It was just another thing to feel lousy about before she died.

She emptied the various pockets of supplies, and then kicked her ABUs to a corner, since a curb wasn't available. She had to sit down to remove her weapons strapped to various parts of her body. Kind of ironic that the only item of any use during her adventure with the barbarians was the knife. Took a few recovery minutes before she could explore the shower. Something came out the showerhead, but it wasn't water. She'd heard of ships that used a cleaning fluid to bypass the water storage problem. Their ships recycled water through a filtration system. It was efficient but best not pondered too deeply, considering where it had been again and again and again.

In normal circumstances she might have found the fluid a poor substitute for water, but her attitude had been adjusted by life in a plumbing-free zone. The fluid was warm and it was removing dirt. Enough said. She worked fast, worried it might be on a timer. She achieved squeaky clean and had time to lean against the wall for a luxurious few minutes before it shut off.

The clothes Hel had left were serviceable, comfortable and warm. They would have hugged her body four days ago, but now they hung a bit around the edges. Hel was thoughtful, but still managed to be a guy with a very good eye. Even the slipper-like shoes fit. She finger combed her hair, careful not to meet her eyes in the mirror. She didn't want to see awareness of what she was, a dead woman walking, well, tottering.

She'd played girl, pilot, scientist, a cast of hundreds. She'd been who and what she had to be when necessary. Until today doing and being what she needed to had always come naturally. Death was as natural, as inevitable as life, but she didn't know how to play this scene. She didn't know how to *be* while dying. Until this week, she'd never come up against something she couldn't go over, under, around or through.

It shouldn't be a shock to find out she was as human everyone else, but it was.

Bad enough that the flu was waiting in the wings for her final curtain, did *they* have to be creeping on stage first? It felt like someone had turned on a blender inside her head. Thoughts spun, dipped, rose and fell with dizzying—and painful—speed.

Her control was as tenuous as her life. It had been, not easy, but less hard to give her thought processes a name: *them*. When she was young they had felt like something outside, something waiting to pounce. As she grew older, she realized they lived inside her head, were as much a part of her as her hair or eyes. She'd kept the name as useful mental image, a game she played to keep from falling into the same chaos that had taken Robert.

Her parents had never understood the mental challenge they'd created for their offspring when they combined their DNA.

Both brilliant scientists, they'd easily been able to focus on their respective disciplines. Doc's brain rejected singularity in everything. Thoughts, patterns, ideas, equations, connections—it all clamored for equal attention inside her head, like a pack of hungry, snarling dogs with her trying to play alpha. Doc couldn't explain, even to herself, how she managed the data flow. Anything could spin her thoughts off true. The one way her brain helped her, it lusted for connections between those dots, searched relentlessly for them.

She felt it happening, felt her demons trying to take her to the place where Robert lived, his eyes blank, mouth slack, body twitching. Only instead of dogs circling, now it was a vortex with one, small, calm place she clung to, one place where her brain still tried to connect dots to other dots. And somewhere in that spinning mess was something important, something lost in all that mental clutter, the dross hiding the gold. Unless that was a trick, too. The need felt real, but might not be.

She clung to that center, knowing she was going to be sucked in, sooner rather than later. She knew Robert's hell, had seen him go into it and could be grateful that her sojourn there would be short. She just hoped she didn't fall in front of Hel. For most of her thirty years she'd managed to hide her fear, hide *them* from everyone but herself. The words they'd applied to Robert were haunted echoes spinning inside her head with all the other stuff: insane, mad, crazy as a loon, mentally unstable, comatose. And the worst: out of control.

Don't let them get you, Del. He'd said it to her, but his eyes told her there was no escape. She'd spent most of her life trying to control the uncontrollable. Every time she did the impossible, it was a message to them, a message to Robert. *I can do this, even if you couldn't.*

She hadn't done the impossible because the Major asked her or because people needed her or even because she could. She did it to keep ahead of *them*. Had any of it meant anything? All those years of fighting them back, of staying in control and here at the end, *they* win because she couldn't die fast enough. The irony of that didn't escape her. It shouldn't matter, but it did. It mattered more than dying.

Everything she had left inside twisted, turned, and searched for some way to control this final battle, but the flu had thrown in with *them*. She felt thick and slow and stupid. The ache in her temples didn't help. She was going to fail, but there was one last thing she could do. While she didn't have an official mission objective, she did need to report what she'd learned during her encounter with Conan's barbarians. Having a mission objective, even a self-selected one was her mother ship. She slid into it with a sigh of relief. The space was small, like a hurricane's eye, but it was a place to be while she waited to go out of her mind.

She heard the hum and felt the slight movement of hyperspace transport. She didn't know what Hel had learned about her since her capture, but knowing what she knew of him, it wouldn't surprise her to learn this ship *wasn't* on a course for the *Doolittle*. If she weren't about to die, it might have been interesting to see if she could change his mind, see if she could outwit him. He was devious, wickedly clever and unexpected. Ninety-nine times out a hundred, she knew who would win in a battle of wits or kicks. Hel was the one she wasn't sure about. It was, she admitted a bit ruefully, part of his charm. He made her inner bitch want to purr.

What she minded about spending her last hours with him was the ugly coming for her like a freight train. He did like pretty.

And she was using up coherent time sitting on the bunk. She'd have given herself a shake, but she was afraid her head might fall off, so she got up instead. The ship moved smoothly through subspace, so the problem with walking had to be her. She kept a hand on the bulkhead as she stepped out into the corridor. It wasn't pretty out there either. She looked around with interest. So this was Kalian's world. Which, she wondered, did he prefer? Where did his soul live?

It wasn't a big ship, but appeared well laid-out and functional. There was a hatch and ladder that probably led down to the engine room and cargo bays. Another small cabin and the galley were mid ship. The corridor most likely ended at the bridge. A smell that made her mouth water had her changing focus from the bridge, and following her nose to galley. Everyone deserved a last decent meal. This smelled more than decent.

The galley, like the ship, was compact and practical. Doc was more interested in what it didn't have: no fire, no nasty-looking sludge, no Conan.

It did have Hel. Doc blinked. It wasn't a hallucination. He was *cooking*.

He had his back to her and instead of Leader garb, he wore the half-pirate, half-cowboy predominantly leather uniform of the rowdier elements in the galaxy. And he wore it very well. She tipped her head to the side, the better to study the good stuff. The guy was built from top to bottom. He made her hormones sit up and take notice, even though they'd had their trash kicked as hard as the rest of her.

She propped a shoulder against the jamb. Her knees were losing the battle with artificial gravity, but it wasn't the flu doing it to her this time. That feeling came again, the one where her even her demons rolled over and played dead around him. Okay, bad word choice. Maybe she should talk instead of think.

"That smells good."

He turned, and the front was even better than the rear view. He made scruffy real pretty.

"You look better."

"I look cleaner." She tried out a wry smile. "Better" had been crossed off her list of options when she caught the flu.

He examined the clothes he'd left for her with an earthy appreciation that went well with his scruffy. Hel was there, somewhere inside Kalian. Her body knew it, knew him, but her mind recognized differences that weren't all on the surface. Ruthlessness and an attention to detail were the meet points between the two. And then there was their interest in her, which appeared to be mutual. What else did they have in common? Pity there wasn't time to find out.

"You've lost weight." He frowned.

Doc crossed the short distance to one of the chairs, sinking in with an inaudible sigh of relief.

"They didn't try to starve me." She shrugged, surprised she felt the need to defend Conan. "I didn't like the cuisine." And she didn't trust them not to use it as a delivery system for drugs. The only time it had been hard not to eat was after the food upgrade. That had smelled good.

"You cut your hair."

She touched the shortened ends. "I was trying to look less creepy."

He might have looked puzzled by that comment. It was hard to say. So much passed so quickly over his face, not to mention through his eyes. It felt like being on a hyper-fast merry-go-round. Dizzying, but nice.

"I like it."

She used to be better at controlling her smiles, but the escape of one was a small blip on a big screen full of big incoming problems.

Hel—no, this was Kalian, Ojemba leader, she corrected herself—set a plate of something in front of her. It looked as good as it smelled. The layout was sort of like a TV dinner, but it had a small bowl of soup in one section. Her fingers curled around a spoon-like utensil while her stomach rumbled hopefully. She dipped the spoon in, noticed her hand trembled on the way to her mouth. No clue if it was illness or anticipation. She just knew it tasted divine. As a last meal, it was batting a thousand so far. The soup flowed down her dry throat, soothing and warm and richly flavored.

She flashed him another smile as he took the seat opposite her. "It's good."

"I'm pleased you approve."

His intent gaze made her want to do something girl-flirty. She didn't. Not enough energy, even with the soup. She cleaned that up and started on the meat course. If this was the Gadi version of an MRE, their people needed to talk to the Gadi chef. The silence between them was comfortable, despite air thick with questions. She didn't want to break it by asking where they were headed. She didn't want to have to be anything except here. About halfway through the next section her stomach shifted uneasily. She lowered the utensil, her finger tracing its plain length so she wouldn't have to look at him.

"I didn't thank you." She looked at him through a lash veil. It helped some.

Something flared in his eyes. "I recall a most satisfactory thank you."

Color washed over her face. It kind of surprised her she could blush. Even her blood felt tired. Her smile felt, and probably looked, a bit wry.

"Your timing was impeccable."

"I would have transported you sooner, but I wasn't sure how the electrical properties of the storm would affect the beam. When they went after you, I knew I had to take the risk."

"If you hadn't, all Conan would have seen is me doing a Dorothy." Hel looked at her uncertainly. She'd been told it was hard to be funny in a different galaxy. Fine time to find out it was true. "There was a wind vortex on my six."

She'd felt the tree she'd been in starting to move from the force of the wind just before he transported her out of there.

"This Conan is the one who captured you?"

Doc nodded. "That's not his name. It's what I called him."

"This annoyed him."

"Everything I did annoyed him."

Hel's lashes veiled his eyes for a moment, then he pinned her with an intense look. "He hurt you?"

Doc shrugged. "I hurt them more." His brows arched and she

realized what he was asking. Color did a swift reappearance. “They didn’t *hurt* me.” This was so not the conversation she expected, or wanted, to have with him. “They were wife hunting.”

“Bond mates?”

“No, *wives*.”

Hel frowned. “Then they are not of this galaxy.”

“I agree.” She pushed the tray aside and leaned her elbows on the table. “Did you get a look at their ship?”

He turned, keyed something into a band on his wrist and a screen came alive in the bulkhead wall. The first shot was a recording of Conan’s ship as it dropped cloak. The screen split, giving her a view of his sensor logs scan. This one showed more detail. It was big, much bigger than she’d expected for Conan’s small band of barbarian bozos.

“Life signs readings?”

Thirty life signs appeared on the screen, so it was just the people from the encampment on board.

“It’s packing some serious fire power,” she murmured. And better-than-theirs cloaking capability.

“Does it not remind you of something?” Hel lifted an interrogatory brow.

Doc did a mental pull back, focusing on the wider view again. It didn’t just remind her of another ship. It made her brain waves explode. Data pelted her like a meteor shower. She fought for control, but she didn’t need it to see what he saw. Conan’s ship looked very similar to *their* ships. It was a bad copy, if that was the plan, but she didn’t think it was. She’d seen *this* one, no, she’d seen *a plan* for this one somewhere. It must have been fleeting or not attached to any operational necessity, because she couldn’t place it. She just knew she’d seen it. Her brain on Garradian influenza refused to make the connection for her. That wasn’t good. Usually her brain loved connections, the more obscure the better.

He swung back to face her. “Is this ship from your galaxy?”

Doc didn’t hesitate. “No, though I can see why you’d think it was.” She rubbed her face, left her chin resting on her hands. She hesitated, wishing she wasn't so far off her game. "Did the General tell you why he was so determined to stay on Kikk?"

"He gave me a reason, yes."

Doc almost smiled. One of them would have to quit being cagey. Guess that would be her. He didn't know how. "Did he tell you about the portals?"

"Yes." Some slight tension eased in his shoulders. Then the tension returned. "You think this ship is somehow related to that?"

"They went somewhere."

"Two of your years is not enough time for what you are thinking."

So the General hadn't told him all of it. He might be annoyed with her, but what was he going to do? Kill her? "We have reason to believe the portals can send people through space *and* time." This time he couldn't hide his shock. While he dealt with it, she added, "We're pretty sure the trip was out of galaxy, but no one knows for sure where or when."

She could have told him they all thought the trip was to Earth, but that would involve information not hers to share.

"The General thinks you can bring them home?"

"The General hopes." She hesitated again and wondered why she bothered. "They bring me in when a situation is deemed impossible. My skill set is...diverse." She could tell him it wasn't this diverse, but again, why bother? Whatever plan the Major had, would not be happening now.

He stared at for what seemed like a long time. His smile was slow and heart-stopping. "I am unsurprised. And surprised to be unsurprised."

Doc chuckled.

"Can you do it?"

That killed the chuckle.

"I told the General that sometimes the impossible is impossible. Time travel is above my skill set. And—" She stopped. There was the whole dying thing. It was kind of funny really. She'd done hundreds of impossible things, and she didn't know how to tell him she was dying. "I'm sick."

It was a wimp out, but surely she was allowed one. He looked almost relieved, which was odd, and wouldn't last.

Hel had wondered what was different, what felt wrong since she came on board. The sharp lines of who she was seemed blurred. Now he knew why. She was ill.

"You and your people call it the Garradian influenza." The bruises under her eyes were dark and tiny pain lines scored the skin around her eyes and mouth.

They had named it for the Garradians because they did not know where it went or when it would return.

"Sorry about the germ exchange during the kiss."

"I have had it. You only feel like you are going to die." He smiled ruefully and felt something cold track down his back when she didn't smile back. "The kiss was worth it."

"Six of our people have gotten in the last month," she paused to bite her lower lip, "and they're all dead."

His body jerked, his heart, too. "That's not possible. It is uncomfortable, but—"

"Our immune systems are different from yours." She frowned. "We were aware of the immunity problem, but it's been two years with just minor problems. This came at us out of nowhere."

"It takes many seasons for it to cycle through the galaxy." His words were absent, his mind on a frantic search for an answer, proof she was wrong. She wasn't—he couldn't think it, refused to believe it.

"I should have thought of that. Our flu viruses hit every year, but we're all on the same planet." She rubbed her temples as if they pained her.

"How long?" It pained him to ask. Her lashes lifted, her gaze met his. When had this woman become so important to him? He'd given himself many reasons for coming out here to secure her release. Failure tasted bitter in his mouth, but it wasn't as bad as the painful bite of grief. He'd known her briefly, but already he knew she would leave a hole in his heart bigger than when his bond mate died.

"Twenty-four hours. Maybe. Probably less." Her mouth had a weary droop to the edges. "General Halliwell needs this intell."

"We can give him your report when we dock with the *Doolittle*, unless you think he needs the information sooner?" Hel noted the shock in her eyes before she could hide it. "You are surprised."

Her mouth opened and closed a couple of times.

"Yes." Shock gave way to amusement, though weary still dominated the landscape of her face.

"It shocks you that I would deliver the *Chameleon* to Kikk." That word should have surprised her, but it didn't. With the shadow of death hanging over her perhaps she'd lost the capacity for surprise.

"Yes," she said again. She leaned back in her chair. Her mouth curved, the slight movement deepened his despair. "Why?"

It was a good question. That she'd expected his original plan would have amused him a few moments ago. What had happened to her during captivity didn't amuse him. The memory of how she'd looked when he brought her aboard would haunt him for many seasons. He reached out and secured her hand, lightly touched one of the angry scratches marring the smooth pale skin, felt a shift in the walls that kept his alter egos apart, felt them begin to merge.

"Why did they leave you out in that storm?"

"They didn't leave me. I left them." A flare of anger put faint color in her pale cheeks, showed she was not dead yet. "I shot Conan and used the storm for cover."

"If I hadn't had the frequencies of your personal beacon, I might not have found you in time." He hesitated, not sure he wanted to know. "For how long were you out in it?"

"All night." Her expression wasn't hostile, just closed.

"Feldstar has long nights." Her slight nod signaled agreement. "You fight hard to be free. You risked your life to be free.

I don't wish for you to fight to be free of *me*." He'd never wanted to fight with her. His mind refused to produce what he did want to do with her. It wasn't possible now anyway. He didn't want to believe she was dying, but he had to. It was there in her eyes. This was a woman who knew when to fight and what to fight. She wouldn't give in easily, but she would conserve her strength to finish her mission.

His reward was a smile, it was wan, but one of her real smiles. It reached her eyes, turning them purple for him. For those eyes to dim with death, it was wrong.

"How can I help you?"

The smile widened, then faded into weary. Her shoulders drooped, too. "You don't want to be around when I need help. It's not...pretty."

He stared at her, lifted one brow, managed to control his horror when she outlined what was coming.

"I have treatments for this in my medical kit which should help ease your symptoms."

"That's good." She looked away. "Best thing to do is get me to the *Doolittle*. They'll be able to keep me comfortable until it's over."

She was a long way from the dangerous woman who had paced the edges of the party. She looked beaten up and beaten down, but her courage shined through the battering to her body and in her bruised gaze. She could have given up, given in while down on the planet, but she hadn't. She'd fought to be free, so she could pass on what she'd learned. He knew this about her, though he wasn't sure she knew it.

She traced a pattern on the tabletop, and he knew there was more.

"There is more you wish to tell me?" He kept his voice neutral, a bit soft and saw her relief, though he didn't understand why.

"If I become delirious or incoherent, do you have sedation medication on board?"

"I do, but I hardly think..."

She pinned him with a look. "I'm dangerous when I'm in control of my mental faculties. I don't know what will happen when I'm not. It is possible I could become a threat to you, this ship, or myself." Now she looked like the woman he'd first noticed at the reception. "I'll try to give you a heads-up, but you need to be ready and willing to take me down, by whatever means are necessary."

He saw, he sensed more than she said, felt something bubbling below the surface that seemed to frighten her more than the flu, more than dying. If this was the only way he could help her, then so be it.

"I'm always ready and willing to do what I must, Delilah." He kept his voice even and saw relief wash over her face. She needed his strength more than she needed her own, so he would be strong for her. He refused to spend his last hours with her in mourning what couldn't be changed. She deserved better from him and she would receive it. "You will wish to create a report for the General while you still can."

He rose, extended his hand. She took it. He thought it would be cold, but it was hot. Already her eyes seemed deeper in their sockets. He pulled her up and into his arms, felt her body burn everywhere it touched his.

"You are very hot."

"I'm guessing you don't mean that in a guy-looking-at-a-girl way?"

"No," he said, though he didn't understand the question.

"I'd better hurry with that report." She leaned against him for a moment. "And we need that fever medicine now."

☼

Vidor found it an easy matter to track the Earth squadron of ships. As expected, they returned to the Kikk sector. He knew about the hidden outpost. He knew about all the outposts.

Was Morticia the Doctor of their history? Bana believed she was. Frustration coiled in his gut again. He'd had her and lost her. Whatever she was, whoever she was, he had to complete the mission. It was the only way to be sure. The time frame to find her was small. Once the attack began, her life would be at risk with the rest of her people, if she had returned to them. While he knew he should let her die with them, he wasn't ready to give up on securing her for himself. They might be wise and get out of his way. If they weren't wise, he would blow them out of his way. He couldn't fail. The future of his people depended on him.

Her people interested him, he could admit to himself. They did not react as he expected, did not do what he expected. On Historlet, where he had secured Morticia, they had launched a vigorous search. They'd tracked her to the capture point and also collected her ship debris in space. Her escape rig had broadcast a signal that they had destroyed, but perhaps not before her people had locked on. They'd transported close to that spot. He did not know how they tracked her to where they intercepted her. Possibly some of her people were skilled trackers. Once there, there were signs of a struggle, he had to concede.

On Feldstar, they had scanned the planet without breaking orbit and left as abruptly as they'd arrived. There was no escape rig sending a signal on Feldstar and no life signs for them to find. That might explain the short visit. If they had been looking, Morticia made sure there was something for them to see, something that brought them to the planet when he'd dropped his cloak. His ship did leave a faint energy signature when it entered hyperspace. His information was that they had this technology. Why hadn't they followed it? Instead, they'd headed for Kikk. That seemed to indicate they knew something, possibly where Morticia was?

He considered the small trader ship that had scooped her up in front of them. An impressive performance. Had it been an orchestrated effort, or had the trader scooped them all? He'd attempted to track it, but either the pilot had been lucky or clever. His energy signature had been mixed with the Earth squadrons, almost as if the pilot knew what course they'd take.

What all this told him was that he needed to take care when

it came time to act against them, to not assume he knew what they'd do. They were skilled and unpredictable. To win this, to secure his people's future, he must be better and do better than them all.

He felt Bana's presence before she spoke. "Are you ready to leave?" He knew his tone was brusque. It was not her fault, but it felt like it was.

"Of course." Her tone was its usual calm one.

He turned now. "Why are you so sure she's the one?"

Her chin tipped down, as her expression turning pensive and inward. Finally she looked up again. "I met her, just before she died."

"But—" Vidor shook his head.

"She was very old."

"Why would they let you visit her?"It made his head hurt to think about her in the past and in the present. It felt wrong.

"My mother cared for her. One day the girl who cared for me was ill." She made a half motion that could have meant anything. "Like everyone else, I thought she'd died long before. I was a child, but I remember her eyes. Her voice. Even there, on the edge of death she was...willful." She smiled at the memory. "My mother warned me not to speak of it, and I never did. I was a child, but I knew."

"What did you know?"

"That she was remarkable." A soft laugh.

He stiffened. "You know her name. You knew her name on Feldstar."

"Yes."

"Why didn't you tell me?"

"Meeting her again, like this, I understand better." Her gaze caught his now and held it. "She couldn't be forced then. You will not be able to force her now. The only thing you can do for her is to stop her from going through that portal. You must kill her."

"She escaped," he said, his voice tight with the truth of her words. "I don't know where she is."

"She'll make her way back to her people."

"Tell me her name."

"Delilah Oliver Clementyne, but she liked to be called Doc." She hesitated, then turned and left him.

She was right. There was nothing more to say, much to do.

Vidor pulled up what they knew about Kikk. A nasty, inhospitable place in an obscure corner of the galaxy. The Earth expedition had two ships in orbit there, both formidable ships with impressive armaments and skilled squadrons of pilots. The outpost was cloaked, not shielded, according to his intell.

He knew something else about her people: they liked to talk first, shoot later.

So they would talk first.

Fourteen

Doc worked on her report for the General on the bridge of Kalian's ship. It had, she'd learned, a name that, in an obscure Gadi dialect, meant: hidden warrior—very appropriate and not that different from her code name of Chameleon. It would have been funny that they had so much in common if it weren't for the dying thing, though she was glad they didn't have that in common. Those two little boys had already lost their mother. They needed to keep their father.

His fever control med was working almost too well. She'd been afraid of the flu when she should have been worried about *them*. Theoretically she knew she'd be too far gone to be aware of being carried aboard babbling like a crazy person, but she didn't *know*. What if Robert *did* know how he was? What if he was inside there, beating on the walls of his prison, screaming to get out?

When she met Hel the first time, something about him had pushed *them* back, but they weren't going anywhere this time. They knew they had her. Bits of her thoughts hung in the air, like cobwebs without mooring. She wanted to swipe them away with her hands. She clenched them on her knees, haunted by the memory of Robert flailing at nothing just before his psychotic break.

"You fear more than flu symptoms, do you not?" Kalian's voice was soft, as if he worried he'd spook her. Did she already look wild? "Is it your brother that worries you?"

Doc didn't know how to answer that.

"You could leave a message for him. You know General

Halliwell will see that he gets it."

She took a shaky breath, striving for calm amidst her inner storm. "It wouldn't matter. He isn't aware of much, least of all me."

She tried to smile, like it didn't matter, saw his eyes and knew she'd failed. What did he see when he looked at her like that? Was it the ragged edges of her sanity?

She looked too calm, too controlled. In the past, she wore her control like a skin, now she huddled in it like a coat that failed to warm. He saw something in her eyes he didn't expect: fear, a fear somehow connected to her brother. She wouldn't give up her secrets easily. In this she was like him. But he couldn't help her if she didn't tell him what concerned her. In this at least, she could trust him.

"Tell me about him," he said, when what he wanted to say was, *tell me what you fear. Let me help you.* "He is older or younger?"

"Older. Five years older." Both hands gripped her knees. "He was brilliant. And funny. A good big brother."

"Until?"

"He stopped being anything."

"What happened?"

"They called it a psychotic break." Her fingers dug deeper into the sides of her knees, her voice unnaturally calm.

"How old were you?"

"Ten. I was ten."

Hel frowned. "You were very young for such a loss."

She almost smiled. "I was never young."

"Your parents…"

"They didn't know."

"What didn't they know?" He ached to bring her close and comfort her, but he also feared to touch her. She looked like she'd shatter if he tried.

"About *them*. That *they* took him. That *they* broke him."

Hel's insides flinched as he processed what she said. Whatever she thought had happened to her brother, she feared it would happen to her. She sounded younger somehow. She looked up, the way a child might to a beloved older brother. He had to touch her then, though he was careful to keep his touch light, letting her process it and return from where she'd been. It felt like it took forever for her head to turn toward him, for her gaze to clear so that she saw him.

"What are they? Who are they?"

The edges of her mouth twitched. "They're not really a who or even a what. I do know that, though they seem alive sometimes." She sighed. "It's the way we're made. The way our brains were wired." She touched her temple. "My parents wanted geniuses and they got them, but with a twist."

He tightened his grip on her. "What twist?"

She pointed at a cup of water in the holder by the co-pilots chair. "When you look at that, what do you see?"

After a pause, he picked it up, turning it in the bridge lights.

"I see a cup. I see water in it." He looked at her, catching a flash of intense pain in her eyes, before she closed them. "What do you see?"

Her breathing shallowed and then sped up. He watched her fight her way back to calm.

"I see chemistry, physics, refracting light, thirst, reflections, memories of ops, danger, puzzles, spills…I see things that matter, things that don't. And that's just that cup of water. Everything on this bridge, the stuff out there, the way my clothes feel, the way the light refracts off your face and the metal, it all spurs ideas and associations and problems and solutions. It's why I could do what I did. It's how I did the impossible." Her lips firmed for several seconds. "But it takes concentration to manage so much input. In the end he couldn't. It drove him crazy."

Finally he understood. "The flu, you feel it is degrading *your* concentration?"

She nodded, the movement small, contained.

"This is the danger you fear, the reason for the sedatives."

"I'm creepy enough when I'm in control. You don't want to know what I'm like when I'm not." She made a face. "I don't want to know what I'm like out of control." She looked at their clasped hands, covered his hand with her free one. "I don't want to hurt you."

He tugged her out of her chair onto his lap, his arm circling her waist like it had been made to be there. She was warm against him, though not as warm as before. The fever medication was working. She leaned into him, her head nestled against his shoulder, her hair brushing his chin. She smelled of his soap, the fever medication and herself—a warm, feminine scent that stirred longings new to him.

"I do not like to lose control either." He tipped her face up, so she had to look at him. "I promise I will get you safely to your ship." Did she understand what he was telling her?

Her lips curved up in a real smile. The tightness in his chest eased.

Her arms slid around his neck and tightened in a hug, soft lips pressed to his cheek. His chest tightened. He'd been right to call her dangerous, though he had failed to realize the true threat from a woman like this. Cynical and innocent, charming and ruthless, hidden and exposed, would a man ever know all the ways she could be, even if he had the time? He wanted to hold her, keep her in his arms, keep her breathing until he found out.

"We should call the General while I'm still coherent." Her breath whispered against his ear.

He nodded and let her go because that is what she needed. Oh yes, she was dangerous, because he might, just might be willing to give her whatever she wanted, no matter the cost.

☼

Halliwell stared at the image on tracking, as if only his attention kept it on a course for the *Doolittle.* Every time he blinked he expected it to be gone. Instead the small blip tracked steadily their way, unaware or unconcerned about the four squadrons of ships close to intercepting it.

If he were going to make a move, it would be before that point. Unless he planned to somehow use the morass of the intersect point to mask his course change? Just when he thought he had Giddioni figured out, he shifted, changed in unexpected ways. That the man knew it and thought it was funny only made him that much more annoying.

"You're sure he's not heading for his own flagship? It's heading this way, too."

"He'd have to adjust his heading soon."

This didn't track with anything he knew about Giddioni, which meant it was some kind of trick or ploy. The Doc might have been able to unravel it, but he was drawing a blank.

"Is there any way he could know we're tracking him?"

The man frowned, considering the idea. "Well, our ships are heading right for him but all he needs to do to disappear is adjust his shield modulation again. I thought he would when he made the jump away from Feldstar, but he didn't. Or he could stop and hide in place. We know he has phase shields."

"I'll be in my ready room," Halliwell snapped. He had to wrench his eyes off the screen. All the way across the room, he waited for the course change, but it didn't happen. When he was inside, he pulled the tracking up again. Still no change. What was the man up to now?

As if he'd been waiting for him to go private, Halliwell got a ping on his secure connection with the Leader. He wanted to say, "Now what?", but he didn't, just opened the channel and waited.

This time the transmission was voice and picture. Only the eyes were familiar. This was Kalian. It was enlightening to see him like this.

"I have someone who wishes to speak with you, General."

The view widened to include the Doc. He almost didn't recognize her either. Scratches and bruises were luridly bright against the dead white of her skin. Only her eyes were familiar, despite being deeply sunk into her face.

"General."

The voice was the same. Something eased inside him he hadn't realized was tight.

"You look a bit worse for wear, Doc."

Her mouth twitched in a tiny smile. "Most of it is self-inflicted, sir. I had an unprecedented opportunity to observe a hurricane up close and personal. If not for," she hesitated, giving her companion a quick look, "Kalian's timely intervention, I'd have done a Dorothy to who knows where."

Halliwell wasn't so sure about that. He looked at Kalian. "I'd like to speak with her alone."

"Of course."

Halliwell expected him to look amused, that he didn't ignited in the General an ill-defined unease. If the two of them exchanged glances, Halliwell missed it. Kalian rose and headed for the rear of the bridge. A thousand questions crowded his throat. He didn't know what stopped him. Maybe it was the calm gaze in that battered face.

"I needed to prepare a report, or I'd have contacted you sooner, sir."

No duress word in the short statement. "You were so sure you could contact me, Doc?"

Again a small smile softened her face. "He surprised me, too, sir."

"You're sure there aren't any more surprises coming?"

"Yes, sir."

"Why?"

"You'll have to ask him." A rueful look. "He's an original."

Her reflection wavered and he thought the signal was going bad, but it wasn't. It was the Doc who'd wavered, shifted somehow.

"Transmitting data burst now. It's a bit random, but I was in a hurry."

"I'd prefer a verbal debrief when you're back on my ship, Doc."

She didn't blink or look away, no change in her face, so why the chill snaking down his back?

"That's not going to happen."

"I knew he was up to something—"

"I have the Garradian Influenza."

The chill turned into an avalanche.

"If you plan to allow me on board, you'll need to initiate containment protocols. Otherwise, I can stay here. Kalian isn't vulnerable to it."

"How long?"

"I'm final stage. I estimate eight to ten hours." For the first time, she looked away. "I've asked Kalian to sedate me if I become delirious, so please don't get on his case if I'm out when we arrive." She looked at him again, her expression almost amused. "I'm dangerous when I'm what passes for normal."

"We'll be ready for you when you get here, Doc." He wanted to say more, say something, change his religion to include apologies. This was his fault…

"I probably caught it before I left the *Doolittle*, when I was working in the infirmary. We're still not sure of the incubation period." A pause and then, "I'm sorry. I did make some notes on our problem. Dr. James might be able to make something of them." A shorter pause and a surprising, though wan smile. "I hate being thwarted, but I did want you to know, it has been a pleasure serving with you."

Halliwell managed to produce something that tried to be a grin. "You did warn me that the impossible isn't always possible, Doc. Don't give up on yourself yet. It's not over until it's over."

This time her grin was minus the wan. "Yes, sir."

She cut the connection, but her face stayed with him. He keyed in a call to the team working on the Garradian Influenza problem. "I need a progress update."

That was lie. He needed good news.

☼

"Do you know, I think you're the only person to ever to take a weapon from me while I was conscious?"

Delilah's voice was husky murmur in the low light of her room. Hel understood why she'd lowered the light, tried to imagine what it must be like to be assaulted by input from everything around you. Her breath rasped in and out, despite the cushions elevating her upper body. He managed a chuckle, surprising himself.

"Do you want it back?"

"Not a wise move." She nodded toward the corner. "I have divested myself of what they didn't find. You should secure them, just in case."

Hel looked at the small, but lethal pile of weapons and saw at least three knives, two hand weapons and some stuff he didn't recognize.

"Where did all that come from?"

"I'm very good at what I do." The thread of amusement in her voice tugged at his heart.

He pulled a stool close to the bed, noting she'd set up the medication system without his assistance. Her eyes showed the effects of the drug, while a hectic flush to her cheeks indicated that the fever medication was losing the battle.

"Why..." He hesitated.

"...didn't I kill them? They were too young and stupid to kill. And I didn't know where their ship was." She frowned. "I wish I knew what was going on with them."

"You are so sure there is something more to learn?"

"They aren't here by accident." She rubbed her head with her free hand, then dialed up the medication. In just a few seconds the fog in her gaze deepened and the pain lines around her eyes eased.

He secured one of her hands, feeling her pain as his own, but he couldn't use medication to ease this pain. It lived inside him, though he willed it gone. This was why he kept his lives, his worlds apart. He realized now that it wasn't about control, but about managing loss, denying pain.

"Don't die." It hurt to say the words. With his free hand he smoothed her hair back off her face, feeling the heat radiating from her skin. "Fight to live. Find a way to live. I can't...I don't want to live in a galaxy that does not contain you."

Her husky chuckle broke on a cough. "...do the impossible...not miracles..." The words cost her. This spasm of coughing was painful to watch and to hear. Her eyes had sunk deep in the sockets, the skin around them darkly bruised.

This time it was Hel who dialed up her medication. "Are *they* causing you distress?" The question felt odd, but he knew no other way to ask it.

"Some." Her mouth moved, as if she thirsted.

Hel poured water into a medical cup and held it to her mouth. Even this small action appeared to exhaust her.

"You are not your brother."

Her lashes lifted. He felt her struggle to focus on his words.

"You have fought...*them* successfully for many years." He saw in her eyes what she wanted to say and answered, "It wasn't just physical strength. If that were true, you would already be lost." He touched his temple. "You are strong here. This is why you have defeated them for so long." He leaned closer. "Use your strength to survive. The knowledge is there. I feel it here." He touched his chest. "*Live.*"

He saw, he felt her try, but despite the effort her gaze blurred more, her body slackened. Her lips moved. He leaned in. For a moment her gaze sharpened, as if she saw something he could not.

"I can't hear you. Tell me again." He almost shook her.

"...lab...outpost...Miri..."

"What are you trying to tell me? How can Miri help you?" Miri, the Garradian Key, had died long before Hel had been born, despite the long belief of his people that she would return and unlock not just the outposts, but the door to peace in this galaxy.

Her lashes drifted down, and she lapsed into unconsciousness.

His wrist control pinged a warning. He had to return to the

bridge. Hel stood, staring at her for a long moment. It felt wrong to leave her, though he could observe her from the bridge. It wasn't enough, but all he could do now was honor her last request. He gathered up the pile of weapons and secured them, then made his way to the bridge. He opened the secure channel to the General, who came on immediately. His face was set in its usual grim lines. This time Hel did not mind. He could not even find it in him to be amused that the General had all four squadrons on his six.

"I am on approach, General. Requesting landing coordinates. I will drop cloak when my ship is aboard, and your people can come aboard." He kept his voice steady and detached. The General was the last person he wished to see him lose—what? What had he lost to Delilah? There was an answer there, but he shied away from it. He could barely deal with the possibility of her death. His feelings could wait.

"Transmitting coordinates." Halliwell reached to cut the connection.

"General. The doctor said something that might mean something..." Was it a real hope or a desperate grasping for nothing?

Halliwell leaned into the screen. "Yes?"

"Something about Miri's lab? On the outpost?"

He frowned. "There are medical facilities there, but we have had limited success in getting any of the technology to work. I will check with our people—" He stopped, an odd look taking the grim off his face.

"You have thought of something?" Hel could see Halliwell struggling with his instinct to conceal against his avowed willingness to share outpost information.

"If I have, it's a chance, but a thin one. I need to think. We can talk when you are on board."

He cut the connection.

☼

Halliwell stared at the blank screen. *Miri's Lab.* He remembered the report on that lab. Was it possible the nanites discovered there could be used to cure the Doc? Nanites had cured the Key, had cured him. But they didn't even know how old the microscopic computers were, if they were dormant or defunct. No one had dared do more than look at them through the microscope in the lab. They had no documentation on what had been left, so they didn't know what they'd been designed and programmed to do. There was an inherent fear, even among the scientists, of being taken over by them. All the geeks were *Stargate* fans, so the fear wasn't a huge surprise.

Halliwell could have told them what some of them had been used for, but he'd made a promise that he intended to keep. Up until now the risk of using them outweighed the potential benefit. It seemed wrong to experiment on the Doc, but if they didn't do something, she would die. Did she think the nanites could save her life or was she delirious from the flu? There was no way to ask her now, and she had hours to live, if that. She was an asset they couldn't afford to lose, he told himself, though he knew that wasn't the only reason. He'd let her go out there alone. He owed her any and every chance to survive. And he owed it to the people he'd lost two years ago.

He keyed his intercom. "Open a channel to the outpost."

☼

Vidor found the behavior of the Earth ships inexplicable. Why had they merged at that point? They were on course for the Kikk sector. They appeared to be in escort formation, but there was no ship in the escort position. There could be a ship there, a cloaked ship. But why stay cloaked if the Earth ships could see it, were protecting it? If there were a ship there, it would have to drop its cloak to board the Earth ship.

The bridge was silent, the way he preferred it. His men had left for their ships, orbiting their targets. The wives, the new girl and Bana were safe with Cadir in a ship poised to return home if something went wrong.

He had not been himself. His focus was less clear than it had been. He knew this. Would they be as quick to judge if it were *their* women missing? Bana's words rang in his ears.

She won't be forced.

Then he'd find a way to persuade her. The right suggestion should persuade her to *choose.*

The Earth ships reached their destination, their tracking signatures disappearing one by one as they merged with the larger ship. No other ship dropped cloak. Had he been hoping for a sight of the trader that scooped her up?

Probably.

He tried to remember what it was about her that convinced him she was unclaimed by any man. She was of an age to know about men, but the way she'd moved had showed little awareness of her essential feminine core. Even Bana had agreed she seemed untaken. But this did not mean some other man had failed to notice her. It amazed him she'd lived so long without collecting many men.

If she wasn't aboard her ship, his chances of finding her in time were slim to none. If she were on her ship, he could tag and transport if their shields were down. Unfortunately, unusual activity by the Gadi had both Earth ships orbiting with shields up and weapons hot. If he did nothing, she would die with her people.

There was risk in exposing himself to them, but the success of their mission did not depend on his presence aboard this ship. All sixteen ships were fully automated and programmed to continue attacking until disabled, destroyed, or ordered to stand down by its pilot. He did not anticipate much resistance. Their ships were superior, but each ship was equipped with a smaller drone ship, preprogrammed to return survivors to Keltinar.

Nothing, not even the quest for wives to rebuild their civilization, could be allowed to interfere with their mission. If history could be changed, they would do it, though it cost them everything. But while they waited, he could open a dialogue with her people. As Bana liked to point out, he was here to learn.

☼

Halliwell wearing a medical face mask, waited in the cargo

hold, feet planted, arms crossed, while he watched Kalian's ship appear. Security cameras had been disabled in the bay. Halliwell wanted as few witnesses as possible just in case the nanites did manage to cure the Doc. The hatch at the side of the ship lowered, becoming a ramp. At the top Kalian waited. He'd done something to his eyes, so even those weren't recognizable anymore. Those eyes looked past him.

"Where is your healing team?"

Halliwell closed his fingers around the cool surface of the test tubes in his pocket.

"I have something to try before we involve anyone else." Halliwell also had a concealed side arm. He didn't trust Kalian, wasn't convinced he'd have brought the Doc home if he hadn't thought she was dying.

"The lab." The words were flat, but the man couldn't hide the flare of hope in his strange eyes.

"The lab." Halliwell paced up the ramp, without waiting for an invite. It might be too late, even if the nanites worked. "We should hurry."

"This direction."

Even worried, Halliwell was human enough to look around and like what he saw. It was a side to the man he hadn't expected. In other circumstances, could they have been…friendly? No, he decided, but he might have respected him. Respect was better than friendship between two warriors.

Kalian led him into a small, dimly lit cabin.

"The light bothered her eyes," Kalian said, as if Halliwell had asked a question. He turned the light up just enough for Halliwell to see the bed.

Two strides put him at the bedside. Even the low lighting couldn't hide what the flu had done to the vibrant, dangerous woman who'd left the *Doolittle* four short days earlier. She'd looked bad when they'd called him, but now she looked worse. The only color in her face was the dark circles under eyes sunken into her skull and two patches of fever flush on her cheekbones. Even her lips looked bloodless. The blanket over her chest barely lifted with each shallow, painful breath. She was almost out of time.

Halliwell realized he had no idea how to administer the nanites.

"What do we need to do?"

The "we" was reassuring, though Halliwell was loath to admit it. He pulled out one of the tubes. The thick, yellow goo looked unimpressive.

"What is it?" Kalian sounded as dubious as Halliwell felt.

"We call them nanites. Microscopic computers."

"You believe they will help her?"

"That's what I hope." Halliwell hesitated, but he'd gone this far. "I've seen the Key heal using them, but these might be inactive. We don't know how old they are."

"If the Key were here, she could heal Delilah?"

"She healed me after the battle." Halliwell flexed the arm that had been broken, while he processed the fact that Kalian called the Doc, Delilah. He hadn't even known her first name.

"We need to get them into her body to work."

"That's the plan." Not a good one, since he didn't know how to do that. He should have brought a doctor or a geek with him, but he didn't want them to know or wonder why he'd been willing to take this kind of risk. If the Doc survived, they needed to maintain her cover. The Major had a long reach, and there was also the problem of the leaks aboard the *Doolittle*.

Kalian held out his hand. "We can use this." He pointed to a device that somewhat resembled an IV, though this one had no visible needles. A tube reached down to a band wrapped around the Doc's forearm.

"Right." It took considerable resolve to hand Kalian the tube. He curled one hand around his weapon as he watched him pour the yellow goo into the device. After a pause, the tube changed from clear to yellow as the fluid flowed down the tube toward her arm.

Kalian looked at the empty tube, then at Halliwell. "What will happen?"

Halliwell remembered his healing. "I…glowed and the pain left. It was fast."

They both stared at the Doc. In his mind, Halliwell followed the progress of the nanites into her body. They'd go into her bloodstream and spread. Could they move fast enough to repair the damage? He looked at the scratches and bruises, hoping for some sign of healing, but saw nothing.

"Perhaps they no longer work," Kalian said, his voice edged with grim.

Halliwell pulled out another tube. "Let's give her more."

Kalian added a second tube and then a third.

"She does not glow."

"Do you have a way to look at her vitals? Heart beat, temperature? Stuff like that?" They *had* to work. He'd been so sure…

Kalian left the room and returned with another small device. He attached this cuff to her arm and a HUD similar to the equipment in a hospital appeared at the head of her bed. They both stared at it.

"Do you know what these readings mean?" Kalian asked.

Halliwell shook his head. "I guess I need to get one of the docs in here." He started to turn.

"Wait."

Kalian's voice halted the turn. Halliwell turned back, his gaze sweeping the prone figure. At first he didn't see it. Still no glow, but one of the bruises on her face began to fade, leaving the spot clear and unmarked. Next the wound on her temple healed, though without a glow.

Kalian laid his hand on her forehead. "She is cooler. Her fever is breaking."

Halliwell yanked off the mask and bent over her. "Doc? Can you hear me?"

"There is much damage. Perhaps it will take time for her to awaken."

If she did. Could the nanites complete the job? What if all they could manage was superficial healing? She hadn't glowed. He'd been hoping for a glow.

"Her breathing is easier, better."

Halliwell touched his radio, calling the small medical team he had standing by, his gaze on Kalian, still not sure the man wouldn't try something.

A crooked smile flashed briefly on his face. He brushed a finger down the Doc's cheek and then stepped back.

"I prefer not to be seen by your team. When you have cleared this area, I will take myself and my ship off the *Doolittle*."

"Just like that?"

He shrugged.

Halliwell hesitated. "Thank you."

"I did it for her." Kalian gave a wry smile and faded away as the sound of booted feet on the ramp echoed down the small corridor.

Halliwell stared at the spot where he'd been, his thoughts spinning with that last remark. *I did it for her.* Maybe the bastard had changed.

☼

The lift to his quarters was private, never used by anyone but Hel. He'd shed the trappings of Kalian before leaving the hidden bay where he stored his ship. It should have felt better to be back, to be himself. In the past, there'd been relief, even if part of him missed the freedom that came from being Kalian. But not this time. While still reluctant about pondering it too deeply, he did know he'd left something of himself behind with Delilah. He didn't want to know what, didn't want to face the realization that his political maneuvering interested him much less than before he'd left his flagship. She'd altered him in some basic, uncomfortable way. He needed to ponder this, but not now, not when his insides still felt raw and sore.

The lift doors slid back and he stepped out. By the time he realized something was wrong, it was too late. The pain of the energy blast was almost a relief. If he died now, at least there would be no more pain.

Fifteen

Doc woke up hungry. The white ceiling above her didn't look like heaven, hell or anything in between. It appeared to the infirmary on the *Doolittle*. It seemed she had failed to die. If she had to fail at something, she'd picked the right thing.

No more pain and her head felt clear and *quiet*. She poked around and found *them* still there, but lined up like dogs that had graduated obedience school, instead of slathering hounds from hell. Memories formed in a neat line. Her transition from Hel's ship to the *Doolittle* was missing from the line up—as was the reason her demons were behaving.

She could theorize with some confidence that Hel kept his promise and returned her home. Who knew the Leader had a white hat in his pretty closet?

No equation, hypothesis, theory, premise, supposition or wild guess filled the blank between dying and being alive. Without sufficient data it was pointless to speculate, so she sat up instead. She felt good and wasn't plugged into anything. Everything worked but the hospital gown. That would have to go.

A small locker set into the bulkhead held the clothes that Hel had provided. She fingered the material, more memories returning in a neat line, like French schoolgirls in a *Madeline* book. She did a mental shudder. Since when did she use fictional schoolgirl analogies? She gave a small shake. It helped, though she still felt far from what passed for her normal—not that she was complaining. Her normal wasn't that great.

She exchanged gown for clothes. They fit better this time. How had she put *on* weight? She'd been unconscious for—as she thought the question, the answer scrolled across the inside of her brain like it was a heads up display: 14.4 hours.

That couldn't be right. A mirror over a sink showed her a face devoid of injury. Not even a scar remained to tell of her time in the eye wall of that storm. No IV bruises on her arm. How could she know how long she'd been out? The question made her mentally wince. Behind the wince was the sense her brain was trying to get her attention. It always had her attention, so why did it think it needed a mental wave now?

Even by her liberal standards, it was strange.

She had questions, but no one in the infirmary could answer them. And she was hungry enough to eat her own arm. In the interests of her appendage's continued well-being, she needed food, but she'd stand out like a sore thumb in the alien clothes. One thing hadn't changed while she was out: a dislike of standing out. Luckily, her quarters weren't far from the infirmary. Outside her room, the hall was empty, though she heard voices in some of the rooms she passed. She took a lift to her level and palmed open her quarters. It was comforting she hadn't been locked out or moved out. Her weapons, last seen aboard Hel's ship, were piled neatly on the bed. An indication the transfer of her person had been friendly?

She stripped off the alien garb, grabbed a quick shower, strapped on her weapons and then donned fresh ABUs. Her ID tag was gone, but she didn't need it to get into the cafeteria. It was a bit disorienting to be back in a tech/metal environment after her adventure in primitive, though she still had to fight the urge to hug anything plumbing related. MREs couldn't come close to her almost last meal on Kalian's ship, but they trumped Conan's sludge by light years. She started eating, expecting her stomach to have problems with resuming normal eating, but her stomach reacted just fine.

It shocked her how fast she went from relaxed to alert when

the two MPs stopped in front of her. She didn't pull a weapon because they were "her" guys, but that didn't mean she didn't want to pull something.

"Doctor Clementyne? General Halliwell would like to see you in his ready room, ma'am," one of them said, his tone cop-neutral. Both had hands close to their weapons, as if they weren't sure she'd go quietly.

Had her abrupt departure from the infirmary been perceived as dangerous? And if it had, why? Last she remembered, she and the General were on their way, well, she wasn't sure what to call it. A state of mutual neutral, maybe? Two MPs were both over—and under—kill. No way could those two bring her in if she didn't want to be brought, but she'd have gone without the escort.

"Can I bring my brownie?"

That got a slight reaction from the two men. Very slight. And the lights overhead flickered once. Doc looked up, then got up, her brownie in hand.

"How long has that been happening?"

"I wouldn't know, ma'am." One of them gestured toward the doorway. "The General is waiting."

☼

It was a surprise to awaken in his quarters aboard his flagship. It wasn't a surprise to find he'd been detained. A security cuff secured his arm to his bed. Hel turned his head, unsurprised to find his cousin, Glarmere standing by the bed.

"This is an interesting move, even for you, cousin," Hel said. Was the man acting on his own or with support of the Council? Based on the fact that Hel was alive and still in his quarters, probably on his own for now.

"I need your access codes."

Hel arched his brows. That would never happen.

"I'll kill you if you don't give them to me."

He'd kill Hel once he got them. Hel stared at him. Glarmere looked edgy. How long had he been waiting for Hel's return? And how had he gotten into his quarters? Hel didn't ask. Questions exposed weakness. Glarmere had already exposed his flank, revealed he was acting alone at the moment. If he had enough support in the Council, he'd already be in control of the fleet.

"Everyone dies."

"There are worse things than dying."

Hel doubted his cousin had the stomach to act for himself. He shrugged.

Glarmere's face twitched. He hadn't expected this. The man had known him since they were both small and still he didn't know Hel at all. Time was limited. Once the ship reached the outpost, the Leader would have to emerge from these quarters. Even if Glarmere succeeded in taking control, he wouldn't have a smooth transition. The people on this ship were Hel's. If ships were now en route to support Glarmere, they were still at least a day out or more. Hel had checked his ships positions before coming aboard. None had moved. Glarmere wouldn't have risked ship movements while Hel was unsecured. And Hel had made sure the most unreliable ships were two to three days out—unless he'd miscalculated some loyalties? That was possible.

He'd miscalculated the security of his quarters. Again.

Almost, Hel wished he'd stayed on the *Doolittle.* Was he losing his taste for political maneuvering? None of it seemed as critical as it had a few days ago. This wasn't about life and death, well, it was about his death, but the stakes weren't galaxy-wide high. This was a power play, pure and simple. Was this what had added to his dissatisfaction? For many long years, they'd battled to survive, battled to find a way to defeat the Dusan. They'd succeeded and this was the result?

It was beneath them, a disservice to the people who'd given their lives to preserve their freedom. It should have made them better, not the same or worse.

He realized something else as he stared into his cousin's less-than-scary face: Glarmere could do nothing worse, could not cause him more pain than he felt right now, knowing Delilah was forever out of his reach. He'd avoided facing this, but with death hanging over his head, he owed it to her and to himself to face this one truth. Somehow, during their interactions, she had secured his heart in a way no other woman had, and that included his bond mate. He'd cared for her. He longed for Delilah. He always would.

Death would be a mercy.

☼

The MPs flanked her on the journey through the ship. It told her the General considered her a risk, but didn't tell her why. The light malfunction came with them. This made people look up as they passed. She liked that. The MPs attracted too much attention. She munched her brownie and mulled, but the only thing she could think of was that maybe the General thought she had Stockholm syndrome. She hoped she was wrong. Surely he didn't think she'd bond with bad guys in four days?

One of the MPs palmed open the door to the General's ready room, and then they followed her in. Unless they needed to know who she was, which they didn't, this was starting to feel like an arrest.

The General looked up, his face impassive, even by his standards.

"Doctor."

Not a lot of information to pull out of the single word, but his body language indicated unease and distrust. How had she managed to piss him off while she was unconscious? She came to attention and saluted.

He studied for almost a minute. "How do you feel?"

She had a not normal impulse to say, "With my hands, sir, just like everyone else." She managed to quell it. Didn't want to get shot over a bad joke.

"I feel fine, sir." What did he want her to say? Usually improvisation wasn't a problem, but even improv actors got a jumping off point.

"You left the infirmary."

That was his problem? "I was hungry."

"You could have asked for food to be brought to you."

"I'm sorry?" She made it a question because she couldn't ask the ones she wanted to ask with the MPs playing audience to their very boring word play. "I feel great and I didn't want to bother anyone."

"So you checked yourself out? Without telling anyone?"

"I didn't see anyone to tell." Someone had to break the verbal stalemate before they bored each other to death. "Have I done something wrong, sir?"

Annoying people wasn't unusual, not knowing why was.

He hesitated, his gaze still boring into her. "What do you remember?"

She didn't look at the two MPs but she felt their presence. "Not much." Her programming to hide was stronger than her current need to know.

"Sit."

One of the MPs pulled out a chair the furthest from the General. Suspicion and wariness were buried deep in his steely gaze. She wanted to reassure him, but she didn't know how. She could tell him she was better than fine, but she didn't know why she was better than fine or how the cacophony inside her head had been tamed. Somebody had done something. That was obvious, but who and what? Could she be a risk and not know it?

He sat down and the silence drew out. While she met his gaze with outward calm, she poked around inside her head, looking for clues. It wasn't as easy as it should be. Even tidy, there was a lot to examine in there. Her brain before almost dying had been like a meteor shower. Now it resembled a huge multi-lane highway. Ideas were lined up, proceeding through her thought processes in neat lines, but there were a lot of lanes. They all thought they were of critical importance, so finding the one that mattered at the moment wasn't easy.

"Do you feel in control, Doctor?"

More than she ever had her whole life. "Yes, sir."

Another long pause, then he nodded to the two MPs. "You're excused."

When the door slid closed behind him, he lifted a stun weapon onto the table, his hand resting on the handle. Black ops fought to come online. Doc did tense, but she kept her hands in view. She could react before him if necessary. She just didn't know why she'd need to.

"Did I miss something while I was...away?"

"Before you lost consciousness aboard Kalian's ship, you mentioned Miri's lab. Do you remember that?"

She shook her head. The last thing she remembered was Hel urging her to live. The lights in the room flickered once and then again. They both looked up. Then the General looked at Doc.

"Did you do that?"

"How—" *Miri's lab. Nanites.* "You used nanites to heal me."

As soon as she said the words, her brain connected the right information stream and brought it to the front of the line. That's what was different. The nanites were helping her control the flow of information and the way her brain dealt with its lust for connections and information. She was better than fine, though telling him how much they'd changed her wasn't a good plan when he looked ready to shoot her.

He nodded, his hand twitching on the handle.

"You're afraid I'm going to go bad SF movie whacky and take over the ship?"

His lips twitched then, but firmed. "I just need to know you're fully in control of yourself." His gaze narrowed, turned searching. "You are different."

"Maybe I'm just relieved to not be dead, sir." He was right, though. She felt different, had been changed before the nanites came on board. What they'd done to her, well, she was sorting through that now. She was surprised he'd picked up on her differences. He was a General, but he was also a guy.

His gaze plowed into hers, seeking for the indefinable something that even Doc would have had a hard time explaining. She felt the difference to her toe nails—but she felt *like* herself. Truth was, she felt like she was who she'd been meant to be. There was still a lot to process, but one thing was clear, almost dying *had* changed her almost as much as the infusion of nanites. She'd been pretty cavalier with her life up to now. It gave her an edge going into an operation and that edge felt gone. She wanted to live, which was odd, since she hadn't known she wanted to die. The Major wasn't going to be happy about that, but like her, he was going to have to deal.

After a pause, he nodded. "I guess I can see that. You gave us quite a scare, Doc."

"Us?" It unsettled her to think of the General discussing her with anyone. Made her feel exposed and vulnerable. She didn't like either of those things.

"Kalian assisted."

The General worked with Kalian? She'd like to have been a bug on that wall.

"As far as the infirmary staff knows, the Garradian Influenza was a false alarm." He hesitated. "When you disappeared from the infirmary..."

"I can see where that might make you uneasy." She thought she knew about weird, but she didn't. She was aware and involved in her conversation with the General, but she was felt herself absorbing information at a tremendous rate. The nanites were learning how to communicate with her, though it wasn't as smooth as either side would have liked and still indirect. She'd think questions and her mind would flood with images or equations or data. Some she understood. A lot she didn't. That was new, too.

The nanites were taking her questions, the ones she'd had before she got sick and the ones she had now, and processing them as information requests. It felt a bit like ants swarming, but tidier. Each question was in one of the memory lanes, with information flowing both ways. It was...extraordinary and very efficient. She could get used to efficient. She slotted what she was learning into priorities and then got distracted when she wondered how many nanites they'd used to heal her and a HUD popped up between her and the General.

She blinked. It didn't help. "That's a lot of nanites, sir. Did you tip the whole test tube in me?"

The general's grim visage cracked. "You didn't glow. And you were pretty far gone. Didn't seem like they were working."

Doc stiffened. "So you what? You dumped two test tubes in me?" The General didn't look at her. "Three?"

He twitched. *Three test tubes of nanites?* Doc looked at the HUD, surprised there was room inside there for her. No wonder he was worried about her control. Maybe she should be worried. She was amazed. The little buggers had been dormant for years but had kicked into high without too much trouble.

"Can you control them?" He appeared as fascinated with the view as she was—or he still didn't want to look at her.

The answer didn't come in words. They were still trying to integrate their systems with hers, but she felt reassurance, felt her control, though she couldn't have explained how.

"Yes." The word sounded hesitant, because she wasn't sure if she'd stay in control. There were a lot of them buzzing around in her system. The light flickered overhead again.

"Are you doing that?"

"No, but I don't think it's a problem." A control problem is what she meant.

She got his Look. "And you know this how?"

"The...Key interacted with this ship, sir. Installed upgrades. I think those nanites are talking to mine. They're both learning." And trying to teach her at the same time. It was multi-tasking gone ballistic.

"Why would they need to learn? They were created by the same person, weren't they?" His frown was something to see. His hand twitched on his weapon again.

"The Key's nanites came to her through the womb, from her mother. They experienced things these hadn't." Her palms tingled and she looked down, shocked and not shocked, to see golden beads of light emerge from her skin, then sink from sight again. The rate of information exchange sped up and then knowledge...

expanded inside her head like a garden bursting into bloom all at once. It hurt, but for Doc it was a "hurts so good" pain.

She sat in a chair in the General's ready room, but she was also in the ship and on the outpost and riding an invisible shockwave through all the other outposts. She was here, but everywhere. She could feel why and how they'd helped her mental malfunctions but the exchange wasn't one way. For one, very odd moment, she could "see" how her brain looked to them. If they had a concept of a mother ship, her brain was it. She couldn't understand everything yet, but they believed she had the capacity.

She felt their—satisfaction wasn't the right word, because they couldn't *feel,* well, she was pretty sure they couldn't feel, but her IQ aided them in ways the Key hadn't been able to, even enhanced by the nanites. She'd lacked the education and the IQ to process what they were trying to share with Doc.

They were downloading into her brain too fast, but she didn't stop them because her brain loved having every single data stream maxed out. For the first time in her life, *they* weren't the enemy. The cacophony settled into a happy hum and with it, the pain dialed back to a faint throb at the temples.

"Doctor?" The General sounded wary.

Doc blinked, peering through streams of data. Was this what it would be like to be inside a computer? "Yes, sir?"

"You're glowing."

She tapped into a security camera and studied herself. He was right, though pulsed was a more accurate description.

"Sorry, sir." She concentrated on dialing that back and saw the beads sink back into her skin. First he wanted her to glow and now he wanted her to stop. There was no pleasing the man. "I thought you wanted me to glow."

That earned her another Look.

She, or they, and her with them, were deep inside the ship and she sensed a tap on the video line to this room and others. She followed them back to the source. Went into the computer and locked it down just by thinking about it. Genius gone nova.

The analogy seemed apt. She'd changed from one thing to something else, something better. Okay, with three test tubes of nanites, maybe she'd gone *super* nova.

"I found your security leak, General. I've resolved the problem, and I'm assessing what information has been compromised."

She was having so much fun, it surprised her when red suffused his face, a mini, less happy version of a star going nova.

"What? Who?"

"Neil Caldwell, assistant to Ambassador Rockley." She directed some resources to sifting through his computer for any indication of other accomplices. He had to be part of a network. He'd been part of the transfer that brought her to the *Doolittle*, so he was either a new recruit or replacement.

"You can prove this?"

"I have created a report on the trace and sent it to your computer." Doc felt an unscientific thrill of pleasure. This was way better than fine. This was ass-kicking cool. Be even better when the General quit wanting to shoot her. It was almost painful to sit so still. She and her new peeps wanted to move, to dance and sway. Maybe do some lip synching. Karaoke was out of the question, unless the peeps had also fixed her inability to carry a tune.

Halliwell keyed on his intercom and sent his own order—one to quietly arrest Caldwell. "Any other security breaches I should know about? Accomplices?"

Doc sent some of her new peeps searching through the ship for other signs of tampering and Caldwell's accomplices.

"Working on it, sir."

He tugged at his military knot. "Good. I think." He swallowed. "You sure you can control them?"

"There is an ethics subroutine in their programming. They can't attempt me, ship, world, or galaxy domination." She grinned and felt them quiver in response. Did they have a sense of humor or were they learning it from her? The ache eased some more though she still felt super nova on the inside. Doc wasn't surprised by the ethics programming. The original Garradians had freaked over their own abilities and how that technology might be used and abused. It was what had prompted them to lock and abandon the outpost and their galaxy.

"Okay." He tried to smile, hesitated. "Can they help you with the portal problem?"

"We need to talk about that," she saw something that made her sit up and take notice, "but we have another problem." She activated a HUD again, this one a view of the galaxy.

"What am I looking at, Doc?"

That he was calling her Doc again seemed promising. She held back a smile, reminding herself she didn't do warm and fuzzy. She didn't get attached.

"Doc?"

It was so obvious to Doc what the HUD showed, it took her a minute to realize her clarity came from the peeps. She honed in on one of the outposts and enlarged one of the ships they'd found when they pinged the galaxy during her nova thing. It looked like the one Hel had caught on tracking at Feldstar. The nanites did a compare and confirmed that. All sixteen looked alike, though there were the expected small differences. No two ships could ever be exactly alike. The peeps were able to pull up more data than Hel's ship had. None of it was good.

"That's a ship." Halliwell stood and moved closer to the HUD. She could have shifted the HUD to him, but he'd left the ray gun when he got up. The further he got from the gun, the better for her.

"Sixteen ships, sir. One strategically positioned near fourteen outposts and one incoming to this outpost." And number sixteen was positioned near the outer edge of the galaxy.

"Why didn't I know this?"

"They're cloaked." Had these ships been in the galaxy as long as Conan? She asked the question and the peeps tried to find an answer. It was nice and also painful. Hopefully they'd work on that. "These are the people who took me, and the other women, captive."

Halliwell tensed. "You think their arrival here is related to our missing people?"

He'd read her report. That helped.

"Yes, sir."

"The people you think can't be retrieved?"

Doc hesitated.

"I need answers, Doc."

"I'm trying sir. There's a lot of stuff you need to know, but when you ask me questions, it slows things down." It hurt, too. Each question sparked a response or responses from the nanites. Those responses launched offshoot thoughts and ruminations. It was orderly, but still a sort of controlled chaos. She was having trouble keeping up with her own brain. Verbally it wasn't possible to keep up. "I'm sorry to do this, but could you let me talk and not ask questions? I just need some time to process what I'm learning."

He opened his mouth, must have realized he was about to ask another question and closed it.

"For just a moment, I need to put the portal and your team to the side. I'm working it, though." For the first time, it seemed possible she could do something about that. Her thoughts, combined with the nanites help, had produced hope. He nodded again and started to pace. At least he wasn't talking. Data continued to arrive, even as she worked on how to tell him what she was seeing and learning.

"Sixteen ships. There were sixteen guys in the encampment. Only thirteen women missing. That has to be their entire contingent, otherwise more women would be missing. Single life signs per ship except the one." The HUD changed to show the ship positioned at the outer edge of the galaxy. This one probably held the non-combatants. At least they were trying to keep them safe. But one man per ship? "Ships automated? It's possible." Talking was almost painful, even in short hand. It was so *slow*. "Weapons and shields better than ours, but not sure we are a target or the outposts. Could be both."

Halliwell made a strangled sound.

"Sorry, sir. It's an odd experience." Downloading and uploading, processing, filtering, sifting. "There are more hangers, more ships, but we can't access them unless I can figure out how to unlock the rest of the outpost. Manufacturing facilities, too. I always wondered about that. That stuff didn't appear out of nothing."

General Halliwell growled and kicked up the pace of his prowling.

"Sorry, sir. Still processing."

As the words left her mouth, the nanites delivered another round of data.

"Give me a few more minutes of incoherence and then you can talk again." She finished with a rueful smile and got a grimace in return. She was ready to talk portal when she got an unexpected warning from the peeps.

"We're being scanned, sir." The HUD changed, focusing on the ship now within sensor range of Kikk and their ships. She didn't need the nanites to postulate that this was Conan's ship.

"Can they penetrate our shields? Why aren't I getting a warning from the bridge?"

"They aren't sensing it—"

Doc stopped as she saw—or felt—the scan hone in on her. Light passed down her body and changed color.

"Did you see that, sir?"

"Yes. What the hell is it?"

He leaned forward, covering her hands with both of his, as if to hold her in place.

The peeps provided the answer.

Scan has found alien compound.

Purpose?

Assessing. A pause. Possible *marker, identification tag.*

Not incapacitating?

No. Eradicate?

Can remote transport be initiated through our shields?

No.

Monitor for now.

"Doc?"

"Apparently Conan tagged me with some kind of tracking compound sometime during my stay." She frowned. "I didn't eat or drink anything of theirs. Was probably in the soap. I did wash my hands several times." It made a kind of sense. If everyone in the compound was tagged, then mass remote transport could be triggered in an emergency. No hostiles scooped up. And it would shorten the time the cloak would need to be down. For a moment she wondered why they hadn't found her before Hel, but the answer came with the thought.

Minimal contamination. The storm's electrical properties masked it.

It was almost clever. Which didn't fit with their clunky bride hunt. There was nothing to say this was only place they were hunting. If they targeted multiple galaxies, they'd end up with a more diverse DNA mix. It would be interesting to think about if she didn't have more pressing issues on her front burner.

"Is it dangerous?"

"No, but it means Conan knows I'm back."

"Is that good or bad?"

Why did he think she'd know? She sighed, bit back what she wanted to say and settled for, "Last time I saw him I rejected his proposal of marriage, used my knee on his groin and shot him with his own gun."

The General looked like he was trying not to smile. Doc was glad when he managed to suppress it. Smiles weren't his thing.

"Let's hope he likes his revenge served cold. Any other bad news for me?"

"The portal and your people."

He tensed, erasing all smile indicators.

Even with a plethora of data, this was giving her a normal

headache. It didn't make sense. "I've been assessing the files of the people we know went into the portal, and I found something odd."

She put photos up on his big screen, leaving up the Conan-tracking HUD that hovered between them like a ghost, though she did move it to one side.

"Those are the people who went through the portal."

"I know," he grunted. "I look at them every damn day."

"It's far fewer than I expected." Three scientists and a military escort of four. Seven men. No women. "Why so few? Why no women?"

She'd have thought evacuating the women would have been a high priority, considering how the Dusan treated female captives.

He stared at the pictures. "Because we won. That halted the evac."

Okay, but...she could understand why they'd send soldiers through first, but only if they didn't know how the portal worked. Surely Smith knew the downside of portal travel?

Questions almost choked her, but she knew there might not be answers. Reports had been filed, but the final minutes of the war were confused and chaotic. The Kikk outpost had come under fire. People who knew things had died. Accuracy was not possible. She brought one picture to the front of the screen. "Dr. Smith, he's the one who told you that travel through the portal and back was possible."

"Yes." A pause. "You still think he was wrong?"

Doc shook her head. The peeps had pulled up his notes, which were interesting and troubling. As the General had said, the skill set he'd postulated *could* solve the portal puzzle matched hers in almost every detail. All they'd left out was the black ops/ass-kicking part. "Not wrong. The Garradians wouldn't have, couldn't have created the portal to be one-way. But returning was very uncertain, and his notes that I've been able to access feel incomplete. I don't understand why he'd go through with it when it was a long shot, or why he'd sell it as a sure thing."

Halliwell frowned. "We were trying to keep assets from the Dusan that they could use to get to Earth. He was one of those assets."

"But you must have had another option for the noncombatants?"

"I was going to use one of the Garradian ships to get them the hell out of here, but he convinced me it wasn't necessary. I let him convince me because we couldn't afford to deplete our resources." He rubbed his face. "We needed every ship we had."

Memory turned his visage grim again. No one had expected to survive the battle. Yet more issues for the General's guilt trip.

"Would he have known that?"

Halliwell shrugged. "I didn't tell him. Wasn't need to know, but anyone with half a brain should have known."

Doc frowned. Smith had more than half a brain, but that didn't mean he knew military strategy, or had any basic common sense. The real question was what had he believed about the portal?

"What's your problem, Doc?"

"I'm not sure." She paused, studying the various threads, looking for the one that was making her gut twitch. Waves of impatience didn't help as much as the General thought it would. She considered what she knew and translated it into non-geek. It was second nature to her now. She dealt more with non-geeks than geeks, so didn't get to speak geek that often anyway.

"It took the Garradians years to map the galaxies connected to the portal. They sent research devices through first, retrieved them with special beacons. When they finally sent people through, they carried these beacons that allowed them to be retrieved, but learned even then retrieval wasn't precise. The greater the distance, the greater the variable in outcome, both in going and in returning."

Words tried to push out, as the various connection rates between ideas sped up, but she needed air first.

"We know the last person to use the portal traveled to Earth. Everyone assumes that's where Smith and his people went, that they traveled somewhere into Earth's past, but there's been no sign of them in our history." And if he thought he was going into Earth's past, why the security detail? She was pulling data directly from the outpost at an impressive rate. She felt a bit like an Overlord of the universe, but didn't mention it to the General. He was still looking twitchy.

"That doesn't mean they aren't on Earth. They were under orders to be careful about affecting the timeline."

"Careful is fine, but *no impact* is almost impossible. Plus, there *are* signs of impact on Conan's society. And then there's the fact that the portal settings have been changed."

"Changed? How do you know that? You haven't been down there yet."

She shrugged. "You gave me very thorough help with the nanites, sir. According to current readings, anyone going through the portal right now would be sent to a dwarf galaxy about 300 million light years from this one. The people there call the planet Keltinar." That had to be where Conan and his barbarians came from, though their current reality didn't resemble the data the Garradians had collected on them as much as she'd have expected. Of course, their civilization should change over that length of time. But they'd gone a long way from where they'd been when the Garradians studied them to Conan and his bride hunt.

"Did they go back or forward in time? When were they sent to?"

"Back, though how far is difficult to calculate, there's a lot of differences between their concept of time and ours—" She and the peeps ran some numbers and came up with an estimate, though one with a large margin of error. "I'd estimate maybe one hundred of our years...could be less, but probably not more than that."

She rubbed between her brows. Her brain, even with upgrades, didn't like questions it couldn't answer and this was a biggie. Why would Dr. Smith strand himself in the past on an unknown planet? He was the resident expert. How could he not know the risks? And if he didn't do it, then who had? She'd wondered if someone used the portal after the last Garradian left, but the peeps insisted that the portal had been locked and remained locked until unlocked by the Key. So either Dr. Smith had changed the settings or someone else had changed them, either accidentally or maliciously.

Her brain charged off in all four directions, trying to find theories to support or disprove any of them. It was a kind of murder, but one without an obvious motive. If you wanted to kill someone, there were easier, faster ways to do it. She couldn't see where anyone had benefited from it, though she'd be the first to admit she lacked critical data to postulate any kind of theory.

"Is it possible one of the geeks messed with the settings *after* it was unlocked?"

"They were under orders not to." Halliwell looked grim, but he sounded a bit winded.

"I wish I could talk to someone who meant to go through, but didn't. Or someone who saw it happen. There's no clear account about what happened in the portal room that day." There were a lot of holes in the play-by-play. Again, by design or intent? Maybe there was a need for her black ops persona in this operation—though she couldn't see how Smith would have known that.

"Major Loren was in command of the outpost defenses, but he died just before it ended." He rubbed his face tiredly. "What does it matter? You can't bring them back."

"I didn't say I couldn't bring them back."

The General spun to face her, his body leaning over her. His gaze bored into her. "What are you saying, Doc?"

"Traveling great distances and spanning a lot of time is seriously imprecise, even if I could use a beacon for *my* travel, and finding them without beacons is impossible." They wouldn't have arrived on Keltinar together, unless they went through at exactly the same moment. Seven guys couldn't fit through the door at the same time. "But a short distance, short time? When we know exactly where they will be? That's possible." If her calculations were correct and the peeps seemed to think they were.

The General's eyes widened. "You think you could go back two years and stop them from going through?"

She grimaced. "That's not a good idea."

"Why not? You just erase it. It never happened."

"It *did* happen. If we change *our* past, we risk changing our future."

"So?"

"Didn't you see *any* of the *Back to the Future* movies?" First he looked surprised, then grim again. Last came the scowl. "It's the law of unintended consequences. We have no idea what impact any of those people would have had on our current time line. Reintroducing them into the timeline *will* change it and not necessarily for the better."

"How can letting them live their lives, like they should have, be bad for the timeline?"

"What if one of them gets drunk and has a hit and run and kills me? I cease to exist, can't come and figure this out, creating a time paradox. While I've never experienced one, the scientific consensus is that they are *bad* and should be avoided at all costs. Or at least when possible."

"Okay, changing the timeline is bad. I get it." He didn't look like he did, but he was trying. "Why tell me about it then?"

"What I propose is that we keep our future intact by jumping them over the past two years. I go back to just before they go through the portal and bring them to here and now. Inserting them into the *current time* stream now should be more benign, or at least less risky. They could still mess up the future. There are always consequences to every action, but at least it wouldn't impact the *known* history, the *known* past. They'll lose two years, but it's better than living out their lives on an alien planet a hundred years before they were born or risking a time paradox." She paused. "Well, it will be if I can do it."

"We're back to the technology that we still haven't accessed." She nodded. "Why didn't it become active two years ago when the outpost was unlocked by the Key?"

"It wasn't locked by one person. According to the nanites, it was locked down in stages."

"So if you can't unlock it—"

"I can't bring our people home and we'll be facing fifteen alien ships with better cloaks and weapons than our two ships. And there's the Gadi ships heading our way." They could withdraw and let Conan and the Gadi duke it out, but Doc didn't suggest it. The General wasn't leaving until there was no chance of bringing his people home or he was dead. And if he were dead, technically that would be not leaving.

"Can we use the alien threat to bring the Gadi back into our camp? Or at least put them between us and the aliens? They won't want the outposts taken over or destroyed."

"They're outgunned, too. And if the Leader isn't in control of all his ships…"

"So even if you manage to bring my people back, they might be coming back here in time for yet another battle or two?"

Maybe he hadn't understood her report. His screen changed. Doc walked over to the diagram.

"This is a preliminary plan for an intergalactic ship designed by Dr. Smith. I knew I'd seen it somewhere before, just didn't remember until I connected his name with the memory." Technically the peeps had made the connection, trying to answer her mental question, but telling him that might make his eye twitch. She pulled up the scans for Conan's ship and put it next to the diagram. "This is the scan of the alien vessel."

A long pause while he studied both diagrams. "They're almost identical."

"Many of the specs are different, of course. That's to be expected considering the time involved." Though she'd have expected more variation than this in the plus-or-minus one hundred years—unless they only recently found the plans and built the ships.

"There are similarities to our ships, too." The General sounded reflective.

"He was part of the research team on Earth that created our ships." Their team had used some, but not all his ideas.

Halliwell rubbed the top of his head. "I haven't had a lot of sleep in the last five days, Doc. Break it down for me. Why does this matter? Other than as more evidence our people went where these people come from."

That sentence was almost painful to hear.

"If Dr. Smith did contaminate their society, then stopping him from going there should eliminate *this* alien threat. They don't get his plans, they won't arrive in *these* ships, nor will they know so much about *us.* Bringing our people home should alter *their* future." Which wasn't nice, but they had shot her. That wasn't nice either.

"Why would he? Why would he contaminate their society?"

Why did he think she knew what Dr. Smith thought or wanted?

"Maybe he wanted to come home." Doc frowned. What would she do in similar circumstances? If she had the knowledge to come home, she'd try. She wouldn't have sat on her ass and waited for someone to figure things out and rescue her. Been there, done it once. Didn't want to do it ever again.

Would Smith have known how far into the past they'd gone? Doc could see settings on the portal, but she was looking at it with the peeps help. She knew where and pretty close to when. What had Smith seen when he looked at it? What had he thought he knew and what had he actually known? And why had he lied to the General? She couldn't believe a scientist of his stature didn't know what a long shot it was to go and be brought back. Had he counted on her figuring this out? If he'd known the only way to get them back was to stop them from going through, why not mention it in his notes? Why the emphasis on skill set? If that had been her, she'd have left step-by-step instructions, the *for dummies* version so anyone could do the job.

If he hadn't changed the portal settings himself, then he'd believed he was going to Earth, in the past. His actions took on a sinister cast, if that were the case. He could have seriously impacted their past with just what was in his head—*if* he'd known how far into the past he was going. That was a reason to leave fuzzy instructions behind. He wouldn't want anyone to figure it out. But why leave a scientific shopping list that brought her to the galaxy?

She was ninety-nine percent sure he went to Keltinar. She'd have been one hundred percent sure, but she didn't believe in absolutes. She couldn't think of any reason he'd want to go there or how he'd know about it.

"Uh, Doc?"

Doc blinked and refocused on the General. "Sir?"

"You're glowing again. And what's that?" He indicated a HUD once again hovering over the conference table. And he had his hand curled around the butt of his weapon again.

It looked like a movie graphic on steroids, with equations and graphics and maps flowing in and out of view. If that was what was going on inside her head, it was a shock she didn't have more than a slight headache. She looked down. She wasn't just glowing, she was *glowing.*

"Sorry, sir." She reined in the glow and the HUD. His grip didn't relax.

"So you think we can change the alien element and then all we'd have to worry about is the Gadi."

"If we get access to the stored ships, the Gadi will be less aggressive." She frowned. "Some of the manufacturing facilities were on other planets, and they were found and used by the Dusan and the Gadi, but there is a facility here on Kikk, on the ocean floor like the last one. One geared to manufacturing their latest stuff. The ships are better than the ones we used last time.

There are more weapons and shields we could bring online to protect the outpost, too."

"They had shields? Why would the Garradians lock the shields?"

That was the problem with doing the impossible. People started expecting you to *know* the impossible. "Maybe they hoped the outpost would be destroyed. Maybe they thought the cloak was enough. It doesn't matter. It is locked."

"And you don't know how to unlock it."

That question prompted a good news/bad response. "That would be yes and no, sir. I know *how* to do it, but *I* can't do it."

Halliwell paced toward her, stopping to lean on the table in front of her, his face inches from hers. "What?"

"The rest of the outpost requires someone with a specific genetic string to complete the unlocking process."

He shook his head. "What?"

"I think we assumed that the Key's nanites were the unlocking mechanism, but it was more likely a *genetic* string. It was in her DNA."

"So this new key could be anywhere, anytime, which makes the odds of us finding someone with that specific genetic string, what?"

"Not as bad as you're thinking. The people who lived on this outpost were all related to people in *this* galaxy. It's possible that a descendent of *our* Key could have unlocked the outpost, too, but we found it first. Think about it. The legend of *a* key could have been the knowledge that there were two keys. Or several keys." She frowned. "These people know so little about the Garradians, it's embarrassing."

"Didn't you ever play gossip when you were a kid, Doc?"

Doc blinked. "I was never a kid, sir."

He twitched. "Well, trust me. It doesn't take long for information to become distorted and lost." He rubbed his face. "So you think there might be someone in this galaxy with the correct genetic string? How do we find him? Or her? Or them? And persuade them to help us?"

The peeps and the outposts had extended her reach unbelievably far, but telling him that might make him twitch again. Or have him diving for his gun.

"I can use the outposts to search—"

There was a transport wash, and an internal *voila* from her nanites. When the wash and *voila* faded, Helfron Giddioni stood there.

The General didn't look like he appreciated the irony of Hel being the second Key to the outpost. She had a feeling Hel would. He loved irony.

☼

Vidor took up an orbit on the far side of the Kikk moon. He did not require the cover the moon provided, but it would prevent an accidental collision of his cloaked ship and an Earth ship. There was much activity around the two Earth ships, but no sign of interaction with the hidden outpost somewhere below. He had to assume they used direct transport to move back and forth. His scan had detected her aboard the ship called the *Doolittle*. Much information about the Doctor had been deliberately concealed, but Bana had proved to be a surprising resource.

The woman, Doc, had failed to settle into their world. Had fought to leave and failed at that, too. Had eventually been isolated, deemed unstable, though Bana said she had seemed lucid when Bana met her as child. If she was *the* Doctor—and like Bana he was now sure she was—it cast an interesting light on the past, on the conflict that eventually tore through the fabric of their world, that brought them to this reality, their current need. If he succeeded in stopping her from coming to their world, he did not know what would change, but he was sure his longing, his desire for her would not be one of those things.

If Bana were right, if she must be persuaded, then he would persuade her to come with him. He wouldn't confine her to a life, a world she did not want. He would give her not just a universe, but as many as she wanted. They would live aboard ship and travel.

She'd have plumbing.

There was also the problem of wives for Eamon and Cadir. He'd sworn to provide them when he claimed the doctor for himself. He would fulfill his word on that matter as well. His men would return home with wives and the hope of children.

☼

"I appreciate the rescue, General, but it might not have been a wise move to take my side in the current dispute." Hel seemed unperturbed by his abrupt removal from his ship.

"Rescue? You were in trouble?"

He's the one. It wasn't a question, but Doc's peeps took it as one.

There are others, but he's the one you want.

Because he's the better match? The closest you could grab?

You like him.

It was like having the General in her head, only without the judgment. She couldn't even pretend they didn't know what they were talking about. They were in her head and *they* weren't in denial.

"That would explain your fleet's movements our direction," Doc said, watching about half the fleet now heading toward their outpost on a HUD inside her head. Her voice pulled Hel around to face her.

Satisfaction flared in his eyes, but his voice was neutral. "You look...well."

She had to smile at him. "I am well, thank you."

See, you like him.

Okay, so I like him. He saved my life.

The sudden silence said more than words—or thoughts. What had the peeps been doing since the Garradians left, besides getting too smart for their circuits? Aware the General was glaring at her, Doc tried to pull on a more professional persona, but she did wonder what Hel was thinking—and what he'd think when he found out why he been yanked onto the *Doolittle.*

Hel forced his gaze and his thoughts from Delilah, striving to still the rumbling of his stomach. Glarmere had lacked the stomach to torture him directly, but had hoped hunger would make Hel reasonable. The man had much to learn about winning battles, wars, and knowing his enemies. He'd been clever about breaching the security in the Leader's quarters, but that had been his single—and last—clever act.

The General keyed his radio and ordered a tray of food. Hel nodded thanks as he slipped into a seat halfway between the General and Delilah. As his thoughts spun with names of possible traitors and questions about why he'd been snatched to the *Doolittle*, he studied Delilah from under lowered lids.

The contrast between his last sight of her and how she looked now was stunning. All traces of her ordeal were gone from her skin, but the marks had been more than erased. Her pale skin shimmered in the ugly lighting so common on the Earth ships. Her dark hair almost seemed alive, as it shifted with each subtle movement of her head. Her eyes gleamed, the color of them changing and giving him glimpses of that lavender that told him she was as aware of him as he was of her. Her mouth seemed fuller and more inviting, and it appeared she had to fight to keep the edges from tilting up in a smile. She was once again dressed in military garb and the lines of her body were alert and still dangerous, but he also sensed a lessening of tension in her that was apparent now that it was gone.

Before, even when she was still, she didn't seem to be *still*, he realized now, perhaps caused by the demons inside her head? Did this change mean this had somehow changed? With the General sitting at the head of the table like a storm waiting to break loose, Delilah avoided looking directly at Hel, but he knew, he *felt* her studying him, too. Whatever bond connected them, it had grown stronger with each contact and each separation.

He regretted letting her go, but logic told him she'd be dead if he hadn't. A pity logic did not seem to mitigate a bone deep longing for everything to be different in his life and hers. It felt like they belonged together, though people in both their galaxies would vehemently dispute this. Even as something in him pulled him toward her, a deep panic made him want to flee. He did not recognize this sensation. He had not felt this pull from the mother of his son's. Everything in his life had taught him that this level of need was a weakness to be rejected with every fiber of his being. So why did every fiber of his being pull toward her? She could cost him everything he wanted: his position, his power, his freedom and he had to struggle to care.

Hel ate as much of the food provided as he could manage. It lacked many things, a pleasing flavor being the one he missed the most, then lay down the eating utensil and pushed the tray away. He needed to find out why he had been brought to this ship; the rest would have to wait.

"I am surprised my ship did not detect the transport signature."

Halliwell shot a look at Delilah, though Hel could not call it an alarmed look.

Delilah had a fleeting questioning look, followed by an almost imperceptible shake of her head that made her hair shift, the strands stroking her cheek. His fingers tingled, remembering the feel of her skin. His fingers clenched into fists, and it took willpower to relax them again. It was almost amusing, the way none of them asked the questions teaming in the silence. For Hel, not asking was his only power play. He was on their ship; for all he knew, he'd exchanged one jail for another. Without the power of the Leadership behind him, what did he have to bargain with?

"There's been no mention of your arrest in the diplomatic channels."

Why did Halliwell look at Delilah before he spoke or after and sometimes both? Something had shifted in the power balance between them, though Delilah's aspect was that of respectful soldier.

Hel shrugged. "I am being kept in isolation to make me more reasonable. Glarmere hopes he can force me to resign, thus sparing him the ugly process of deposing me."

The edges of Delilah's mouth twitched. "He doesn't know you very well."

Hel smiled. "No, he doesn't." That she did both delighted and terrified him.

"What did you do?"

Halliwell's words and tone were not diplomatic, and Delilah gave a slight wince.

"I engaged in illegal communications with you, General."

"Oh. Sorry." He blinked and almost managed to look sorry.

"It was necessary. Glarmere was in contact with someone on this ship as well."

"We know." This time Delilah didn't look at the General. "We're rolling up the network, both here on our ship, on the outpost, and on the *Apollo.*

"I was in this process, as well, which is why Glarmere was forced into open action," Hel admitted. Though breaking Carig would take time. His hatred of Hel's family line was wide and deep.

"So at the moment you're a man without a galaxy." The General was unable to hide his satisfaction, though he did look guilty almost immediately.

"Nor am I in control of the Gadi fleet." Hel said with quiet force. The General needed the reminder that this made his ships vulnerable, too.

"Can Glarmere order the fleet to attack?"

Hel hesitated. "Not without my codes or action from the Council."

"But some of your ships are heading this way." Halliwell activated one of their HUDs.

"The loyalties of these ships' commanders were in question before my capture," Hel admitted. "Glarmere may have convinced them of the necessity to act sooner, rather than later. And if he delivers the outpost, many on the council will not censure his methods."

"Made a lot of enemies, have you?"

The General was going to have to decide who his friends were before it was too late.

"As have you, General—at least among my people."

The General's scowl deepened. "I agreed to allow your people on the outpost—which they haven't done yet."

"You were going to give the order," Delilah's voice cut into the exchange, "perhaps go with your people to see the outpost?"

"I was."

"So if the order doesn't come?"

"Glarmere won't act until the other ships are in position to assist him." Hel hesitated. "He had help getting on my flagship, but most are loyal to the position and to me. They won't act without proof I have been legally deposed." He hoped. He hesitated. "Do you intend to withdraw from the galaxy?"

"Not without my people," Halliwell growled the words.

Hel tensed. "I am useless to you as a hostage."

The look Delilah sent the General was interesting. It looked similar to one a woman gives her mate or a mother gives her child. He reacted like a small boy, sighing and finally nodding. Hel looked at Delilah now that he was free to do so. He kept his expression bland, though his eyes ate her up. Purple flickered in her eyes, as if she felt their nonverbal communication as deeply as he did.

"Your rogue ships aren't our only problem," a hesitation and a quick glance at the General, before she added, "Hel."

The General might have growled. Hel ignored him because Delilah was more interesting. She didn't move, but the General's HUD changed. He stared at the ships, counted them and noticed their positions. As if she knew he needed it, the HUD zoomed in on one—the ship he'd scanned at Feldstar. He looked at Delilah, a brow arching.

"As you previously noticed, their shields and weapons are better than yours and ours."

"But they are not positioned to attack our ships—" He stopped as he realized what he'd seen. "They are after control of the outposts?"

"Or they plan to destroy them. There's no way to know."

"They must see my ships approaching this outpost."

"I know." Delilah frowned. "Bit unsettling that it doesn't appear to worry him. That makes me think this is a hit-and-run operation. Up to now, his cloaks have kept him hidden from us."

It was true he hadn't seen the ship on Feldstar until it dropped its cloak. "These ships are still cloaked?" A quick nod from Delilah. "How is possible that you see them?"

"You dumped *three* test tubes of nanites into my system. I've acquired several interesting new abilities since you saw me last."

Hel tensed. "You've gained access to the rest of the outpost."

The General growled again, and Delilah shot him an impatient look.

"Sir?"

He didn't look happy, but he did nod.

"We haven't gotten access to the rest of the outpost," she hesitated, her gaze intent as it met his, "but I did find out how to do it." Now she looked almost amused.

He didn't ask the question, because his brain was starting to make some connections that would explain his arrival and the General's growling, but he wanted her to say it out loud.

"The first tech was unlocked by the Key."

He knew this.

"It was a *genetic* Key, in something we call DNA. The rest of it also requires a specific DNA string. Another genetic Key."

No wonder the General looked like a ticking bomb.

"Me." His smile was slow, but wide.

"You were the closest," the General snapped.

Why did he suspect he was not the General's choice?

Delilah stared at the ceiling, trying not to grin.

"The nanites picked you," the General added, as if to keep

Hel from getting ideas about Delilah's interest.

It was too late for that.

"The nanites remain inside you?" The question gave him breathing room to think about being a *Key*. The irony was delightful and terrifying. For an answer she turned her palm up. Golden beads of light emerged from her skin, then sank out of sight.

The General looked as uncomfortable as Hel felt. "She glowed?" For the first time Hel noticed the weapon lying on the table close to the General's seat.

"She glowed."

It did not sound as if the glowing made the General happy, but perhaps nothing could.

He had many questions, but would ask none of them in front of the General. He forced his mind back to the salient point: they needed his help. Was it true there were others out there with the correct DNA string? His power was not absolute, but finding others would take time and time was in short supply. Hel felt this, and he was sure they did, too.

"Currently the outpost has some weapons online and a cloak, but no shield. If you unlock the technology that would bring additional weapons and a shield into play, not just for this outpost, but the others." She hesitated and her gaze strayed to the General. "It's not just about our protection. This is your history, your heritage that might be destroyed or taken over."

"It is true that outsiders to this galaxy have been unwilling to share control," Hel said, with pointed emphasis.

"You have every reason to be suspicious, Hel," Delilah said, before the General got his mouth open, "but keep this in mind. We arrived in this galaxy openly. Once we'd sorted out the players, we took sides. We fought *with* you against the Dusan, and we haven't gone covertly around the galaxy kidnapping young women and forcing them into marriage."

She gave both men the kind of look only a woman can give a man. Even his mother might have quailed from it.

"And the distrust between our peoples has been *deliberately* fostered and fomented by traitors on both sides. But we've moved past that. Haven't we, sir?"

The General looked like he might choke on the words, but he managed a, "Yes."

Hel jumped from frustrated to amused in a heartbeat. Halliwell reminded him of Lorin, caught in mischief.

"Of course." Hel could be gracious. It made him look good to Delilah and annoyed the General at the same time.

"And you don't need to worry, Hel, because you'll have joint control of the outpost from now on, won't he, General Halliwell?"

"Of course." It came out through gritted teeth, but at least he said it.

Hel could appreciate his problem. He had teased the man at every opportunity.

"I appreciate the effort, General Halliwell." He said it sincerely and seriously and got his reward—Delilah's smile of approval.

The General might have snorted. It was difficult to hear anything negative while basking in that smile.

"While we're all enjoying being good friends, the Gadi ships are getting closer, and the clock is ticking with these ships from Keltinar," the General pointed out, going from grouchy to pragmatic with an abruptness that left Hel feeling a bit impressed.

"Keltinar? You know where they originate?"

"We're pretty sure we know they're from Keltinar," Delilah said. Before Hel could ask the next question, she answered it. "We think that's where our people went and they're here because of them, because of us. That might be why they are targeting the outposts." She frowned as if the words didn't feel right to her.

Hel blinked, mostly because he didn't know what to do or say to that.

"The doc said you noticed their ships are similar to ours."

"Yes. I did wonder—"

"If we lied about the level of our deployment in your galaxy." This General he hardly recognized added, "I would have thought the same thing. The similarities are disturbing."

"Dr. Smith, the scientist who traveled through the portal, had a design for a ship that is uncannily similar to the Keltinar ships. And he was involved in the design of ours." Something still bothered Delilah. It was there in the almost absent way she said this.

"Which would explain the similarities and the differences." Hel didn't have access to their design specs, but he had scanned their ships. He frowned. "They have been in the galaxy for some time. They started abducting women several seasons past. Is this deployment a reaction to your escape?"

"I don't think so. I felt their clock ticking when I was with them. I think they've been multi-tasking, learning the players here, getting wives, waiting for a trigger of some kind."

The frown between her brows made her seemed more human, less remote.

"What concerns you?" Hel asked.

"Well, logically, if they had an issue with us, it should be related to Dr. Smith's trip through the portal two years ago. So either they-re late and don't know it or—"

"—the trigger is something else. Someone else," Hel finished for her. "You fear that we, that what we plan to do, is this trigger?"

"I don't know what to think." Her wry gaze slammed into his. "Something I'm not used to."

"Is this more of that time paradox stuff?" The General was getting frustrated again.

Delilah's smile was half-hearted, abstracted. "Possibly, sir."

Hel almost asked her what it was, but he did not wish to distract her, too. He looked at the HUD. Was this Conan character only after the outpost? But he had no way to know Delilah was on this ship. He'd made sure he stayed cloaked both arriving and leaving to protect her.

"At least his arrival is not related to you," he shot a look at the General, "Delilah."

They both stilled. There was no other word for it.

"He knows I'm here. He tagged me when I was dirt side with him." She held out her hands, palms up and random spots on them glowed red. "He can track my movements on this ship. And possibly on the outpost."

"But surely your nanites can deal with this contamination?" Hel's gut tightened at the thought of the barbarian tracking Delilah's movements.

"They can, but if he can't track me that might be the trigger. Or provoke him to premature action." She rubbed her head and sighed. "He hasn't attacked yet. That's probably a good thing."

"You need to unlock the outpost before he does, Doc," the General said, his face unsurprisingly grim. "It'll be a short battle for all of us if you don't."

Sixteen

"We can provide proof you weren't involved in the plots, if you think your people will believe us," Doc said, trying not to stare too hard at Hel in ABUs and boots. Men in uniform were hot. And a man in uniform you were hot for? Well, the combination was downright explosive. And it had been her idea. She'd pointed out to the General that they'd attract less attention on the outpost if he were dressed like their people.

He paused to consider her words, but he was as good as she was at hiding his thoughts. She wondered what his IQ was. He'd been quick to grasp the essentials. His mind was agile to the point of frightening. So why wasn't she afraid of him?

You like him.

It was a rhetorical question.

No it wasn't.

Okay, fine, but the answer is more complicated than like or dislike. And I don't have time to sort it out now.

She sighed. How could she expect the peeps to tell which questions needed answers and which didn't, when she didn't know? She had a weird, knee-jerk reaction to the word *like* in relation to Hel. It was an anemic word and the emotions he roused in her weren't anemic, but there was no point dwelling on it. There was no future in it and a lot of risk—the kind of risk she wasn't used to dealing in. The realm of feelings weren't in her skill set. On some level she so wanted to deny, she knew that the level of pleasure she'd felt at his sudden appearance could result in an equal or greater level of pain when they both returned to their respective worlds. She'd done pain when Robert lost his battle with *them*. It wasn't a place she wanted to go again. She did understand that one was not always given a choice, but it didn't stop her from trying.

Hel shrugged, drawing her out of her thoughts. "There is much that will happen in the next few days. The outcome will determine many things about my future and yours."

So he didn't want to think too much either. It was kind of funny, that their level of denial was yet another thing they had in common. The General had finally quit hovering and let her brief him on the basics of the plan to retrieve their missing people and eliminate the alien threat. She'd added her usual qualifier about the law of unintended consequences.

It still bothered her that she didn't know very much about what had happened two years ago, but at least she'd considered all the possibilities that she reasonably could, and prepared for them as much as one could prepare for the impossible and a possible time paradox—which meant she was much less prepared than she liked to be. And at least she could go knowing she'd done all she could to help the General mind the store while she was gone. Even taking out the distance factor, she wouldn't be able to return that close to her departure time, but if she was successful, any problems with Conan and his boys should just go away as if they never happened. She might not remember him when she got back.

She tried not to worry about how success might change her current reality, tried not to think about possibly returning to a life without the peeps. No matter the impact on *her* life, she had to go forward. She promised the General she'd try to bring his people home. He'd brought her home. She owed him this. Even the peeps didn't know what would happen. The Garradians hadn't used the portal to try to change time. It was, in fact, one of the reasons they'd locked it. She felt no sense of judgment from the peeps for what she was attempting. Maybe they didn't want to get blown away either.

"Do you fear you are this trigger, Delilah?"

Hel breaking into her thoughts was a relief. She needed to think less, if she could just figure out how to do that.

"No." She frowned, remembering Conan's reaction to finding out she was a doctor. She wasn't the only doctor with the expedition, and she couldn't think of any reason she'd go through the portal to Keltinar. She'd maxed out her brain trying. On the other hand, there was that law of unintended consequences and the many things she didn't know. "Though I never say never."

It was part honest assessment, part superstition.

Hel zipped up his vest and hung the loaded P-90 on the hook off the front. With the cap on, he'd exchanged his leader persona for jarhead. And they called *her* chameleon. The weapons added to the uniform made her skin sizzle. She could almost hear her peeps noting and assessing this phenomenon. It was a good thing she could multi-task.

Her peeps went on the alert. "We got incoming."

"Gadi?" Hel went from jarhead to something even more lethal with the word. Doc didn't know you could get more lethal than a jarhead, except maybe her.

"No. It's Conan. He's popped out in a smaller ship, a kind of shuttle I'd guess. It's more benign than a fighter craft." She tapped into ship's systems. "He's asking for medical help."

"He knows you are a healer." Hel didn't sound surprised.

"Why would he want to see me after I shot him? That's nutty."

"He hopes," Hel said, his tone quiet but firm.

Doc's radio earbud activated. "Doc?"

"I see it, sir."

"Can you get on a video link with me? He'll be here before you can get to my ready room."

Doc looked at the video screen, saw the General already there. "I'm here, sir."

He frowned. "I can't see you."

"Oh, sorry. I took us both off the video screen as a security measure." Well, the peeps had. Yet another cool thing they could do. She loved them. At the thought it almost felt they wiggled with delight. Was that possible? The General twitched, letting her know they were visible again.

"Is that the man who kidnapped you, Doc?"

The picture taken from his transmission popped into view, but Doc had already seen him during her tap.

"Yes, sir."

"What does he want?"

Doc blinked. "Um, medical care?"

"He wants you," Hel said, his voice flat.

"Because kneeing someone in the groin and shooting them with their own gun is foreplay?" She looked at Hel, then at the General. "I was his worst nightmare. I can't see Conan risking his whole obscure plan for a *woman*."

"I left my ship, exposed my flank and may have lost my position as Leader to rescue a *woman*," Hel said, his voice still devoid of inflection and too low for the General to hear.

Doc looked at him, tried to think of a response and couldn't.

He likes you.

Now is not the time.

"What's his plan? And what's our move?"

Doc felt an unfamiliar frustration stir in her chest. "I don't know." And she hated admitting it. She *always* knew what to do. Didn't make her right, just proactive.

Hel's mouth twitched. "He needs to see a doctor. He should see one." He half-turned to her. "He should see you."

"Why?"

"It will distract him. And perhaps he will talk to you, tell you why he is here."

"That makes sense." Halliwell frowned, as if surprised.

"He wouldn't tell me anything before. What makes you think he will now?"

"You escaped him. Force failed. Now he must persuade."

"It won't work."

Hel's smile was almost tender. "We know that, but he does not. He is arrogant. Information can only be helpful to us."

"Fine." Why was she so annoyed? She almost glared at Hel. Didn't it bother him to have her talk to Conan? She frowned. Did she want him to be jealous? Was she having a girl moment in the middle of an op? "At least while he's on this ship he won't be firing on the outpost."

She gave in to the temptation to study herself via the ship's security cameras. And saw what she always saw: a pale woman in ABUs, minus Morticia's vamp factor, but loaded with creepy. Hel made her feel like a girl, but she still didn't know how to *be* a girl, and she sure didn't want to be one around Conan.

"We need to get you a security detail—"

"I will accompany her."

Hel still had that odd, flat note to his voice. Maybe that was his version of not happy with the situation, but being pragmatic? Doc felt her ire go down at that thought. He'd left his position to hunt for her and even more significant, he'd *set her free* after finding her, and he'd done it before he found out she was sick.

Halliwell's objection was automatic, but Hel was ready for him. "Perhaps you have others you wish to know about this situation?"

"He's right, sir. We need to contain the flow of information as much as possible. Briggs would be a good second choice."

Halliwell huffed, but finally nodded. "Do we take him to the infirmary or can you treat him in the shuttle bay?"

Doc had a sudden memory of two girl-less guys on the planet. Could Conan be multi-tasking with this visit? "Shuttle bay, sir and no women anywhere near."

He tensed. "You think he might—"

"I'd rather take precautions, sir. He's three women short of a full complement. I'd like to keep it that way."

"But, how could he get himself and three women off my ship?"

Doc could almost see his hackles rise. She'd put her nanite peeps up against his tech any day. Her peeps did not disagree. If they could have puffed like cats, they would have.

"On it, sir, but let's limit our exposure until we're sure."

☼

Vidor was not surprised when the Earth ship gave him permission to land. Two fighter ships appeared on either side and escorted him toward the *Doolittle*, toward the bay where he was to land. They did not concern him. He had no reason to fear them. His weapons were superior in every way. He had predicted they would talk to him and he'd been right.

He settled his shuttle where indicated and shut down his engines. She was still onboard, he could track her progress through her ship, and soon they would surrender her to him.

☼

Doc had to arrange for medical supplies, so she missed seeing Conan's arrival in person. She did watch it through the security monitors because she was curious and always would be. He strode down the ramp from his shuttle craft, his hard gaze sweeping the bay with a look that was cool and thorough. He moved with more arrogance, more authority, more confidence. If she'd had any doubts that he was the leader of his people, he put those to rest.

What, she wondered, made him so confident? Okay, so he had the military advantage, but what did he plan to do with that advantage? It wasn't just about her. No one went to all this trouble to get a girl. She didn't realize she'd tensed until Hel touched her shoulder.

"It bothers you to see him again?"

He'd been worried that Conan had forced himself on her, she recalled. He hadn't, but not for lack of trying. That didn't explain her reaction. He didn't affect her sexually, but he did bother her, she had to admit. She was unable to be indifferent, her preferred response during an operation. The question was why? Doc tried to be strictly honest with herself, because she knew no one else would be. Was it ego? She'd never had to be rescued before. He hadn't *beaten* her because she'd have died, so technically it was a draw.

Okay, it bothered her that he saw a female when he looked at her, but his...unpredictability also made her twitchy. She may not know that much about sex and men, or how they related to women, but she usually could predict how someone would react until she met Conan. Maybe it was his inexperience running into hers? It was almost funny, but she couldn't summon a smile, let alone a chuckle. It could be an alien thing. She had trouble predicting what Hel would do, too. Her gut twitched, as if she were close to figuring something important out.

"What is it? What troubles you?"

She circled the idea like a vulture, afraid it would move if she settled in too fast.

"I can't figure him out, I can't predict what he'll do and plan for it." Her words were as careful as her thoughts.

"Perhaps it is because your cultures are so different."

Doc frowned. "But our people contaminated their culture. There are things we do have in common, things we *should* have in common."

Hel looked thoughtful, but what he thought was not clear on his face. "You believe they should be...less alien than they are?"

Doc half-smiled. "Sounds a bit whacky when you put it like that but yes. Even taking into account the lack of contact as both our societies developed and evolved, I'd have expected more points of contact than we have."

"This troubles you."

"Because it feels wrong. It feels like I'm missing something." She met his gaze, felt her concentration fracture and reform into something different. She smiled at him. She could because she'd taken them off the video feed again. She did it because she needed to smile at him. It was more fun than the endless circling of her thoughts. "I hate missing things."

She'd missed him. It hadn't been two days since she passed out on his ship and it felt like forever.

A smile formed on his mouth as he processed the shift in her focus and followed her into the subject change. "As do I." He smoothed a strand of hair off her face, tucking it behind her ear. "I expected to miss you, but—" He finished with a rueful shrug.

Doc matched his rueful and raised it a grin. "I know. It's crazy. It's hopeless."

"Yes." The word suggested agreement, but the tone, the look in his eyes didn't.

She wanted him to kiss her again, but she didn't know how to make that happen. And then she didn't have to do anything. Hel did it. He stepped in, bringing them together. The cool press of the wall at her back reminded her of the kiss on his ship and her blood heated in anticipation. The sense of the peeps watching was a bit unsettling, but she forgot about them the minute Hel's mouth settled onto hers. She sank into the kiss, sank into sensation without a whimper. *This* was what she needed. This was what she wanted. She wanted him, not just for this moment but for always.

She'd only wanted one other thing in her life and she hadn't got that one either.

☼

Doc requested a medic to assist because she wanted to be able to work fast. Conan was a primitive man to his toenails, but she would not make the mistake of underestimating him. Everywhere they went, primitive man had managed to survive and thrive. Primitive didn't mean stupid. When the Hel-induced fog faded she realized she needed to be unexpected, too. When did she forget that? He might think he had her figured out. She needed to show him he never would. She did a mental flip through her various personas. Which one would he hate? She stopped at one. Considered it. She didn't do it that often, it was a bit too close to who she was, but in this case, that might be a good thing. She was so wrong for him.

"What?" Hel's voice broke into her thoughts.

Doc realized she was smiling and it wasn't a nice one. She made it nice for Hel. "I need to change. Tell the General I'll hurry." He looked uneasy—which made her feel more right about her decision—but let her go, left with the medic.

Doc didn't have a lot of wardrobe options, but she could work with what she had on hand. She always did. She stripped down to her military drawers and pulled out the borrowed scrubs. Not as severe as she'd have liked, but they'd work. He'd seen soldier, might be expecting that. She used water to plaster her hair back off her face and found her computer glasses. A little makeup on her mouth took the pink out of her lips. She didn't have time for contacts, but the peeps popped in to dim the intensity of her eye color. She let her inner geek seep out, added a stethoscope around her neck to complete the bland ensemble.

She booked it double time to the secondary landing bay, flashing her ID to the men flanking the door. She took it as a good sign that they both winced at the sight of her. She removed all signs of girl from her walk as she entered. Her peeps extended her view in interesting ways, allowing her to see and assess her impact on everyone waiting inside the shuttle bay. As impacts went, the ratio of output to reaction was well within the satisfactory range.

Predictably, Briggs looked amused without indulging in a lot of muscle play on his face.

The General blinked. For him that was like a dead faint.

Hel, well, he was himself. Inscrutable on the surface, but she felt his amusement as if they had a personal Internet connection.

It took Conan a few seconds to recognize her, to ping on her like radar on a target. He surged to his feet, his injured hand cradled against his chest. As amazing as it seemed, he *had* come here for her. His body language screamed it, and just in case she didn't get the memo, his eyes telegraphed it. Her hackles rose and her peeps went on full alert, but none of it showed on the outside as she minced in his general direction, no sign of recognition on her face.

Conan scrubbed up pretty well, though he still favored leather in his ensemble. He'd done everything but shave. The guy could have walked into any bar on Earth and gone home with a threesome. Maybe they ought to offer him a free subscription to match.com. Give his email to Russia or the Philippines.

The next thing she noticed, he'd lost that simmering frustration that had ruled on Feldstar. This man knew his next step, knew his purpose and felt ready to embrace it.

She'd have to do something about that.

She paused by Briggs.

"Doc."

It didn't surprise her he didn't ask her what the hell she was doing. He didn't blink when she gave him a prim smile. He might have winced. The General saved her having to approach him.

"Doctor." The tone had a question buried in it.

"General." His lips twitched, but from humor or ire, Doc couldn't tell. "My patient?"

She saw him decide to trust her. It felt good. He stepped back, gesturing toward Conan. Doc directed her attention to the male medic waiting by a medical setup. He winced, too, though he was too nice to look openly horrified at her androgynous geek from hell ensemble. Conan didn't frown. Didn't move. Just watched her approach from under hooded lids.

"What seems to be the problem, corporal?" Her tone was devoid of inflection of any kind. She held out her hand for gloves and got them. She used the explanation time to yank them on, her body language oozing dull and brisk.

She added safety glasses and then moved in for a look at the laceration. Even as her attention shifted to Conan's injury, she could see their tableau through the security cameras in the bay. The General had kept security to a minimum. Both Hel and Briggs were armed and at full alert. She looked a bit like a dumpy blob standing in front of Conan, thanks to some slight padding around the waist. She could have done it without the padding.

People saw what you wanted them to most of the time. She held out her gloved hand for his injured one. Her silence did not appear to bother him. She knew he studied her with an intensity that might have been unnerving to someone not locked in stolid. Doc lifted the temporary bandage applied by the medic and eased his fingers back so she could see the injury better.

She did her doctor thing and he acceded to each question without comment. "You're lucky. No tendon damage." She looked at the medic, giving him a cow blink before saying, "You're right, corporal, he needs stitches."

He had the equipment already set up. Doc lowered Conan's hand to the tray with its sterile field at ready. She did the job with the fussy precision of an old man. When they finished, Doc squeezed out a "thank you" for her assistant as she stripped off the gloves and tossed them on the tray. He seemed relieved to step back. He gathered up the medical debris and rolled it and himself out of the bay with an eagerness he couldn't conceal. Doc waited until the doors hissed closed to turn back to Conan. She pushed her stool back enough to put space between them. She planted her feet wide, resting her hands on her knees, careful to make her pose unfeminine. When she looked at him, her expression was more neutral than Switzerland. Channeling her dullest professor, she lifted both brows in a mute question.

His mouth twitched at the edges, but in a smile or frustration, she couldn't tell.

"You look well."

She didn't know how to take that. "Well" hadn't been what she was going for.

"Plumbing and chocolate on tap. I'm blooming awesome." The contrast of bored tone and the sassy words got a choke out of one of the men watching her.

His rueful smile was charming. "I have plumbing." He gestured toward the ship at his back.

Doc took her time studying the ship. She redirected her gaze to Conan, and said, still in her flat, professor tone, "I believe I mentioned before that size does matter?" She paused, giving him a chance to mention his big ship. He didn't, so she added, "As does the truth."

He stiffened. "What have I told you that is not true?"

Doc arched her brows again. "That you didn't have a ship." Her gaze drifted past him to his ship. "Looks like a ship. Flies like a ship. You just called it a ship. That would make it…a ship."

"It is true I did conceal certain information from you when we were on Feldstar. I had no reason to trust you."

"You still shouldn't. Not after shooting me, kidnapping me and taking away my plumbing for four long days. And nights."

He gave a look that bordered on frustrated. "You are very attached to plumbing."

Having to sit to pee made most women that way. "So?"

"There are other things that are important."

"True, but decent plumbing makes everything important better." While it was fun to torment him, the plumbing causality loop wasn't getting them where they needed to go. She shifted gears without losing her flat tones. "You went to a lot of trouble to talk to me."

His gaze narrowed. "It was no trouble."

"If you'd gone any deeper, you'd have lost the use of your fingers."

He tried to look puzzled. Didn't do it very well.

"When you cut your hand. On purpose." He opened his mouth, possibly to deny it, so she arched her brows. "Please don't insult my intelligence by pretending that was an accident." She smiled the prim nasty smile. "You're lucky I didn't order some tests into places you didn't know you had."

His eyes widened. His lids hooded his gaze. His sigh was pointed. "Is your General the leader of your people?"

"He is the leader of our people here."

"I wish to negotiate with him."

So what? Time to sweep the woman aside and let the real men talk? He wasn't even good at making third contact with her.

Or was this fourth? She didn't know whether to count the near Dorothy moment as contact or not.

"I'll get him for you."

His nod didn't border on arrogant. It owned arrogant.

She did *boring walk* to the General, felt Conan's gaze hooked into her ass every step it took to get there, the way it had been on Feldstar. She hadn't like it then, didn't like it now. She paused by the three men, made sure her voice was pitched low and asked, "Can I kick his ass, sir?"

"What did he do?"

"Everything he could to annoy me." She took a deep breath. It wasn't that calming with Conan still in sniffing distance. "He wants to talk to you."

☼

Vidor watched her walk away, saw her stop by her General, knew they watched him as she spoke. Was her General wise? He was a soldier. It was there in his bearing, in the authority he wore as easily as his uniform.

She respected him. That was clear. Her relationship to the other two men was less clear, though he sensed connections between them both. The big one, the older one was protective. The other soldier felt something, too. She had not looked at him, nor had he looked at her, but there was something about him that made antagonism prickle on the surface of his skin. Next to the three of them, she looked small, and absurdly fragile. He'd taken her captive, but these men had sent her out alone, had put her at risk of capture and still she gave them her loyalty. Perhaps it was a female weakness.

Her aspect, her clothes, everything about her irritated, which is what she'd planned. She tamped out all that was female, hoping to provoke him. He would not be provoked. She was strong. He knew this, but despite her strength, he'd been able to tag her. He could track her. She would not be able to leave this ship, except with him, and to a destination of *his* choice. He would not be able to go home, but she would not trouble his people.

It was a fair trade. They both lost something, gained something.

As predicted, their technology was more advanced than anything here. He did not desire to go to war with any of them. If he could accomplish his mission, he'd be happy to leave this galaxy behind. The past year had been long and tedious.

Her General approached now, with the two men flanking him, their demeanor protective. She did not come with them. Perhaps she did understand some things.

She can't be forced.

Bana's words echoed in his head. He must persuade her people that she *must* leave with him. It was the only solution. Her General's gaze bored into Vidor in way that reminded him of his father. It took effort to meet it.

Vidor recognized the power play. He crossed his arms, arched his brows in an unspoken request to be introduced to his companions.

Her General ignored it. "I understand you want to talk to me."

Vidor nodded once.

"Then talk."

"I want my wife."

The stone face changed not at all. "Your wife?"

Vidor hesitated, then his gaze shifted to hers. "My wife. Delilah." No one moved, but he felt tension in their stillness, an infusion of menace filtering into the air around him. "Oliver." He paused. "Clementyne. Doctor Clementyne. Though she prefers to be called Doc."

Despite the risk, it was a relief to name her.

Her General knew how to use silence. He waited many long moments before lifting a hand, crooking one finger. Delilah came, though in no great hurry.

"Are you married to this man, Doc?"

She let her bored gaze trail over him, from top to bottom. "No."

Vidor ignored this byplay. "I have named her my wife. If you withhold her from me, I will destroy your ships." He looked at her, hoping to catch her unaware. "The ship that carried you from Feldstar scanned my ship. You know I can do this." He expected threats. He got silence. He answered as if they had threatened him. "My ship does not require a pilot to attack. If I do not return within the designated time, it will carry out my final orders."

"You will die with us," her General said, his voice almost indifferent.

"Everyone dies."

Delilah's brows arched. "Original."

He ignored her. "In addition to my wife, I require two more of your females."

"Two more females." The tone was flat, the menace in the air spiked again.

"Young. Comely. Fertile."

"Can I kick his ass *now*, sir?"

She had not moved and her tone was calm, not unlike the calm before the storm that had ripped Feldstar apart.

"I'm tempted to let you."

"You can choose to save your people, or die with them." He looked at her now, ignoring the others. He held the power position. Surely they could see this? "If you attempt to leave this ship, if you try to transport to the outpost, I will know it. My ship will also know it and attack."

"I'll bet there's a deadline. He likes deadlines, sir."

"Is there a deadline?" Her General sounded calm, looked calm, but he wasn't calm. He couldn't be calm.

"I will give you four hours to identify the females and contact me to arrange transport."

"Hours."

Delilah's tone was odd, the look she exchanged with her

General different as well. He sensed currents, but he had them cornered. They had no room to move. Their currents, how they felt did not matter. What they did, that was what mattered now.

"Why don't you want me to go down to the outpost, Conan?"

Before this day finished, she *would* say his name.

Seventeen

Doc could feel the three of them staring at her as they left the bay. She tried to ignore it, but it wasn't easy. When she couldn't stand it anymore, she turned and glared at them.

"What?"

"You started a war?" The General sounded more dazed than surprised.

"You're taking *his* word? An alien from another galaxy? I do stealth. I am *covert.* There is no way I'd start a big, noisy war. *If* I went to his planet, which I also dispute."

Briggs arched a brow. It was very Spock of him.

"Okay, *if* I went there—which I didn't—I might—*might*—have given them a nudge if I thought it would help me."

Hel blinked.

"I said I was sorry." She put her hands on her hips. "Is it my fault he can't forgive and forget?"

Hel frowned. "Why would someone exile Delilah to Keltinar?"

"I don't know." Halliwell turned his attention on Doc. "I thought *Smith* went to Keltinar. How the hell did you end up there?"

I didn't, she wanted to say, even when the peeps weighed in on Conan's side. Okay, so the evidence was compelling. "He did go to Keltinar."

"You both went to Keltinar, but somehow failed to meet? Hell, maybe we've all been to Keltinar." He rubbed the top of his head, but his hair wasn't long enough hair to ruffle. "I feel like my head is going to explode!"

"I know the feeling." Doc knew she sounded like a sulky six year old—an unfamiliar sensation.

No one said anything more until they reached the General's ready room. Their arrival coincided with Conan's return to his ship. Doc stared at the tracking screen.

"He thinks we don't know about the other ships." There ought to be a way to use that. Her brain and her peeps began sifting through possibilities.

"Doc." This through gritted teeth.

She looked up. "Sir?"

"What makes you believe it was Smith who contaminated their society? We have evidence it was *you*."

"From a guy flying in a ship designed by *Smith*."

"You've seen his design specs."

"A cursory look. It would take more than some vague knowledge of his design to make those ships happen." Given enough time she might be able to come up with an FTL—faster-than-light—drive, but ships were about more than drives and design. There was plumbing and air filtration and weapons and material. There were tons of things she'd never needed to know that she'd need to know to design and manufacture a ship. She could multitask, but build ships *and* start a war? She dedicated half a thought stream to the idea and had to admit it wasn't totally outside the realm of her possibility. Enough of a long shot she felt comfortable not admitting it, though.

"You've taken more than a cursory look in the last few days. As much as it pains me to say this, you haven't gone there yet."

It did look like it hurt him to say that. And what she had to say wasn't going to help that.

"I'm not the person who contaminated their society." He opened his mouth, probably to scream, so she rushed into an explanation, though she was pretty sure it wouldn't explain anything. "If I did go there, I'm a different version of me than the one they met. Or will meet."

His mouth worked for a few seconds. "And you know this how?"

"Well, for one thing, this version of me met Conan. If he'd met me before, he'd have remembered me, so it was a first for him, too. And if I'm the reason they came here, then meeting me, capturing me, has already resulted in an altered me. Even knowing I went to Keltinar and started a war makes me a different me from that me. If I were to go there now, it would create a reality different from this one. Not that I plan to go. Sir."

The General stared her for what felt like a long time. "I should have retired, but no, I had to make this trip one last time."

At least he didn't shoot her. Of course there was still time for that. Neither Briggs nor Hel dared look amused, though Doc sensed they were. Briggs could afford to be amused. He didn't have to figure it out. Hel just had a dark sense of humor. It was another reason she liked him.

Halliwell took a breath that might be meant to be calming. "What the hell did you just say?"

"You need to understand, sir, that all I have are theories of how time works, and how it might be changed. No one I know has traveled through time." She frowned. "Well, except me, but since I haven't done it yet, technically, I still don't know anyone who's done it. And I'm still not sure I did it." Okay, that didn't come out quite the way she'd wanted.

Her peeps and her thoughts circled what they knew. It didn't help that much. There was a chicken or the egg problem with the set up, no question. Though, just because Conan hadn't mentioned Smith, didn't mean they hadn't met at some point. There was no way to know what impact their separate trips through the portal had made on the present reality. It was even possible that they'd both traveled through the portal, but not met. Time could have split into divergent realities. There was no way to *know*.

She rubbed between her brows as her peeps helped her organize her thoughts. Once again, it sounded better inside her head than out loud.

The General blinked. Maybe that's all he could manage.

What bothered Doc the most, she realized, was Smith's notes on who could help solve the problem. That act took on a more sinister cast, with this new twist. Had time split, merged or become...fluid? Could opposing goals make time lose cohesion? She and time did have an uneasy relationship. Was it possible it was a side effect of time becoming unstable as different...forces...sought to fix it?

"I can only theorize, sir, but Conan is here on a ship that *Smith designed* and he's looking for *me*." His eye twitched. Doc's did, too. "Maybe we can exist in disparate realities because time is fluxing, and it will remain that way until the disparities are resolved." Now he looked at her like she was crazy. Also fair. She felt a bit crazy. "Maybe I have to go through the portal and stop him from going through *and* stop someone from sending *me* through to make time gel again."

"If you transport to the outpost, Vidor Shan will attack," Briggs pointed out. "He has the ability to destroy the outpost before you can go through the portal."

Hel shifted in his chair, then leaned forward. "What if you don't go down, don't go through the portal? Won't that change the past? Change him and his ships?"

"That changes *my* part of our time problem, not Smith's. He still goes through, he arms Conan and sends them here." It was hard to argue a point that wasn't scientifically sound. And sounded totally nuts. "I think it's like a leak. We have to plug it in both places."

"First time is Jell-O and now it's a faucet?" Doc might have made a face. The General rubbed his face. "And you think this will work?"

Doc shrugged. "I hope it will work. I refer you to my previous statement about the difficulty inherent in doing the impossible or knowing the unknowable."

"Didn't work last time," Briggs pointed out. "Someone got the drop on you and booted you to another galaxy. How do you know it will be different this time?"

"Because I'm not the same person. That's the problem with trying to game time, if that's what someone is trying to do. There are always variations. Like me meeting Conan."

"But how can you be sure you're a different you?" the General asked with another eye twitch.

"If I had nanites when I went through that portal, I would have won that war and come home."

Damn straight.

When had her nanites learned to swear? She didn't ask where. She knew that. When this was over, she needed to find out how sentient they were.

"That would be the war you didn't start?" Briggs arched a brow again. He was almost as creepy as she was when he wanted to be.

Halliwell rubbed his face again. "This is what you meant, isn't it? This is a time paradox?" Doc nodded. "No wonder no one likes them." He rubbed his head again. "So how do we get you to the outpost without starting another war?"

☼

The General had detained Hel to threaten him with dire things if he misbehaved while on the Outpost, taking long enough that Hel was able to watch Delilah unobserved for several moments as she geared up once again. He liked her like this, liked the dangerous aura that she donned with her clothing and weapons. Liked the change in the way she moved. He'd always liked danger and dangerous creatures—which made him wonder why had he gone into politics? The reasons were getting harder and harder to remember.

She wore headphones connected to something call an iPod. Their president had sent him one of these as a gift. Hers seemed to be loaded with more interesting content than his. She swayed, as if to music, as she strapped various-sized holsters to various parts of her body. She picked up two of their pulse weapons, spun them several times, then tucked them into slots high on her waist. Two projectile weapons went into holsters riding low on her hips.

A larger, longer weapon got slung across her back. A smaller P-90 got hooked to a clip on her vest. She added magazines for her projectile weapons to pockets. Food and water packets also went into other pockets.

"Can you still move with so much armament?" he asked, half-amused, half-fascinated. She didn't hear him, so he stepped closer and she spun to face him, yanking the plugs from her ears.

"Sorry. The music pumps me up, gets me locked and loaded."

"You can move," he gestured with his hands, not sure how to describe her gear.

Her grin was a bit crooked. "Not much slows me down." She pulled on a rigid hat, with an odd-shaped projectile coming out of the side and what looked like eye protection that could be lowered. She strapped it under her chin. "I don't always go in quite this geared up—on the surface."

Hel recalled the pile of hidden weapons she'd removed on his ship and wondered again how she could take a single step.

"It does not inhibit your flexibility?" The word was unfortunate. It conjured up thoughts of other places where flexibility was useful.

She grinned, as if she sensed his thoughts. "Hopefully, you won't have to be surprised by what I can do like this and with this."

His attention sharpened. "You play a mind game, too?"

"I can think of three reasons why Smith didn't outright ask for me in his memo on how to rescue him. He didn't want to be that obvious. He didn't dare ask for Chameleon because he wasn't supposed to know it, or—"

"He did not know who you are," Hel provided the second. "Could this be an attempt to expose the Chameleon?"

Doc shrugged. "It could be a lot of things. If someone is trying to get at the Chameleon, this has got to be the most convoluted and clumsy attempt ever. Now if they wanted to mess up Keltinar, it looks like I was a good choice. Though Smith seems to have played a part in that as well. His part *could* have been an accident. We know what happened to me wasn't."

Hel considered her words and came back to, "I still do not understand the gear. Would it not be better to be more covert?"

"I thought about that, but if they do know about Chameleon, they'd expect covert. I figure freaking scary might throw them off their game, confuse the issue a bit. If they did take me out as I came through the portal, all I need is for them to hesitate for a second, and I get them instead."

He could not help but enjoy the way her mind worked. "You would have been an excellent Ojemba."

Her brows arched. "A girl in your Ojemba? I'm shocked." But her grin was pleased.

So he would not grab her and kiss her, he addressed his other concern. "You believe your nanites will be able to fool his scanner into believing you are still aboard this ship?"

"I hope so. But just in case the illusion isn't perfect, the distraction might help."

The General had almost had a heart attack when she'd suggested bringing Vidor Shan back aboard to meet some possible wives for his two men. She'd also proposed the General invite the prospective husbands aboard. Her mind was as quick and devious as a Gadi. He liked that about her, too.

"But they aren't here," the General had said, when he got his voice back.

"He thinks we don't know that," Delilah had pointed out. "It will put him on the defensive. Point out that it isn't reasonable to expect any women to volunteer for this duty without meeting the men in question. Keep pushing. Keep him off balance. Give us time. If we can unlock the outpost's shields and defenses, we change the board, the game. He thinks he's got us boxed in. He needs to realize we're not that easily boxed."

"How superior are his weapons?"

Hel was coming to recognize the look on her face when she was communicating with her nanites. She'd frowned.

"Just enough to beat us."

"Does the locked tech put us ahead?"

She'd shaken her head. "If we bring the ships online, can get them manned, we'll be evenly matched. Without them, he has the edge in numbers."

"But he'd have to bring his ships here. It gives you time. Gives us time."

Her smile had been a bit crooked. "Too much time and too little. Did I mention I hate irony as much as time paradoxes?"

The General had lost his ability to be amused by this. Imminent destruction did that to some people, Hel knew.

"He'll want to see you if he does come back aboard," Hel pointed out now.

"He won't be surprised if I refuse to see him before I have to. And not getting what he wants will be good for his character." She stowed the last magazine and turned.

"How will you know the illusion is successful? That his ship is no longer tracking you?"

"When Conan doesn't open fire?" She grinned. "My nanites will give me a heads up."

"Could the nanites disable his ship, if you could get them on board?"

She tipped her head to the side for a long moment. "Not in time. There are technical incompatibilities to work through."

"Incompatibilities?"

"His technology is from another galaxy. The nanites are programmed to learn, to bridge those types of gaps. One reason they were designed was for first contact situations, for travel through the portal, but it takes time for them to learn to talk to alien tech, and they won't know how much time until they are onboard."

She turned toward the door leading out into the hall, but he stopped her with a hand to her shoulder.

"I wish you did not have to go through. It feels...personal."

"His scientist shopping list was pretty detailed in my direction," she admitted, "but if someone wanted to take me out, a bullet is a lot quicker and more permanent than messing with the space-time continuum." Her lips pursed, her brow furrowed. "In a way, someone did kill me. Sending me into the past was a death sentence of sorts. But I wasn't the only victim. If this were a mystery, we have the means and method, but no clear motive for a move on me, Smith, or Keltinar."

Did she know she rubbed between her brows when her mulling went deep?

"Their world got pretty messed over with the war and all—which I still don't think I started. There's evidence their girl population got dramatically reduced and who knows what else happened because of the intrusion. The butterfly effect."

Hel frowned. "I do not understand."

She created a HUD with a small creature with delicately fluttering wings.

"There is one theory that says this insect's wings fluttering can impact time. If that's true, dropping a whole human into a world could do a lot of damage."

Meeting Delilah had changed him, changed his world. There were things he thought would never change, wants he would always have. Now he was not so sure.

"We don't know that Smith wasn't a victim, too. We don't know who tampered with the portal settings yet. It could be someone from the future, which makes my head hurt thinking about that. Regardless, all roads lead to the portal. And that means we need to unlock the outpost and I need to go take a look. Conan's clock is ticking again. Before it hits zero, we need to be able to protect the outpost. It's my way home again."

"I should go with you. You should not go alone. Again."

"That's sweet, but not a good idea. I can't even imagine what would happen if you accidentally got stuck someplace where another you existed."

She had succeeded in doing something none of her people had done before: she'd made his head ache. "You should not go alone," he insisted.

"I'm always alone. I'm used to it."

That made his heart hurt worse than his head. He smiled and nodded, but knew he'd find a way. She was not going through alone. Not this time. Not ever again.

☼

Doc had been worried about transporting among members of the expedition, but her peeps took them to another destination. They ended up in a room no one knew existed. It looked a lot like the other spaces they'd explored on the various outposts, but this one had a circle marked out in the center of the room. All kinds of tech consoles circled it. She couldn't see a door anywhere, which would explain why their people hadn't found it. The peeps did their equivalent of a dance of joy at being in this place. The data transfer rate spiked again, but they knew her limits better. No pain this time. They also knew her mission brief and could answer questions she hadn't asked or thought to ask. Some of the concepts still baffled her, but she had a feeling if she could stop and think she'd get there. Stopping wasn't on her agenda at the moment, though.

If clocks still ticked, then they'd be ticking like crazy right now.

"You need to stand in that circle and be scanned," she said. Hel looked so good, it made it hard to keep her mind on the problem at hand, well, that part of her mind dealing with her feelings. She could still compartmentalize, but it felt odd, thinking *and* feeling.

He strode into the circle without hesitation. He had some brass ones, when neither of them knew what would happen next. Without warning, beams of light came down from the ceiling, hitting the edges of the marked out circle. The lights changed color several times and then stopped.

Hel looked a bit bemused.

"Are you all right?"

He patted himself, seemed reassured to find all of him still there. "I seem to be."

"Are you in?"

"I believe so." He flexed his fingers and Doc saw his skin flicker with beads of light. Did he know he'd picked up some peeps, too?

Before she could ask, a hologram formed at the edge of the circle.

"Welcome back, My Lord."

Hel stared at the hologram for several seconds.

"Thank you." Hel glanced at Doc, drawing the hologram's attention to her.

"Welcome, Lady, to our city."

"Thank you." Doc gave a tentative smile, unsure about hologram protocol. "I'm glad to be here."

"Your makeup is unfamiliar to us, but you have been integrated. How is this possible?"

Gold light flared on Doc's skin as her peeps opened a dialogue with the hologram. She felt their questions, many of them the same as hers.

The hologram spoke again, "Only he may operate the systems."

"I don't know how to operate them. I wish my lady to do this."

The hologram was silent, perhaps searching information databases. "You may assign her to control the systems if she becomes your *ma'rasile*. Is this your wish?"

"How will that give me access?" Delilah asked, but the peeps were faster than words. The answer came on the heels of the question. She needed to stand in the circle with Hel and have the Key DNA string added to hers.

That's a bit bad SF movie, peeps. Did they chuckle? Could they chuckle? Reassurance fluttered through her. She'd retain her present form and identity, but would receive the ability to operate the outpost—though Hel would have veto power. He'd be the primary, because now the outpost had keyed on *him*. That was interesting. She had questions, and they had answers, but she needed to focus on the task at hand. She'd never felt time pushing her like this, like a hand at her back. Was it another sign that time was out of whack? How could she know what normal was, if time was changing around her?

"Delilah?" Hel's voice broke into her nanite dialogue. "Is there a problem?"

"He must agree to take you as his *ma'rasile*." The hologram almost sounded annoyed with her. She gave Hel a look that would have been sappy if she'd been a real girl. On a hologram it was a bit creepy.

"I agree."

He looked amused, which made Doc suspicious, but also awed at his trust. Unless he already knew he was primary? Could he sense his peeps? Communicate with them? She happened on an information packet in her head and realized why he was amused.

"It's like a marriage?"

He shrugged. He shrugged better than a Frenchman. "I have heard of a *ma'rasile*, though I believed it was a legend, but yes, it is similar to what you call marriage and what we call a bond mate."

Delilah stopped the peeps telling her what was different about the rite. She didn't want to know. It might stop her from doing what she needed to do. She pushed the marriage/bonding part to the back of her mind and focused on her mission brief: getting control of the outpost.

"Okay. Let's do it."

The hologram looked annoyed again. "The correct response is, I agree."

Okay, that was almost bitchy. "I agree." She arched her brows at the hologram.

She sniffed. "Step into the circle."

Doc locked her gaze onto Hel's, felt something ripple through her that had nothing to do with her mission objective. *Marriage.* She wanted it to be real, not a necessity. She wanted him to want it to be real, too.

"You don't have to do this, Hel," she heard herself say. "Maybe I can help you control it if you don't want to, you know, get bonded. I'd understand."

His smile was slow and potent. "I want you."

"Oh." She didn't have to see her smile to know it was goofy. "You know, don't you, that you can stop me if someone orders me to do something you don't like. You get a veto on anything I do."

"That is good to know." The smile faded. "You don't trust the General?"

"I trust him. But the people he takes orders from? Not so much. Like yours, our leadership is subject to change." She stepped toward him, not noticing she'd crossed into the circle, as her peeps delivered another round of data. "This is your heritage. You're a direct descendent of the man who locked it." She tipped her head to the side. "You look like him."

He pulled her closer, his half-mast lids over his hot gaze making her pulse skitter.

"You can see him." His grip on her shoulders was gentle but possessive.

Not anymore. I can only see you. She may have nodded. Or not. She did lean in, hoping he'd take the hint. He did. Her lashes drifted down as his mouth covered hers. The heat came first, slow and warm and wonderful. The sizzle on her nerve endings was new, but it was nice, too, as they connected on a cellular level. The blaze of passion was there, in the background, waiting for its time. This wasn't it. This joining, this moment was all about magic. And wonder and...*love.*

She loved him. The thought should have scared her. He *wanted* her. He didn't love her. It didn't matter. This is what she'd missed when Robert fell, this love without conditions or expectations. If he wanted her, she'd stay. If he didn't, she'd let him go. She could wish, but not demand. She could hope but not expect.

She loved him.

She eased back, so she could see his face. She needed to see his face. She rested her palm against his cheek, loving that she could do that. For this moment, she had the right. He covered her hand with his, holding it there. The combination of rough and soft fascinated her. And his strength. She felt his strength. He was her match in every way.

"Sara said I'd like you." Doc felt her mouth curve with happiness as the half-forgotten memory came back to her. She'd thought it a throwaway comment, but now she wasn't so sure. A giggle bubbled up from inside. "Even if it's just temporary, you got your alliance mating."

The hologram snorted and Doc realized that the glow had faded, or moved inside them. She still felt lit up.

"A *ma'rasile* is not temporary, Lady."

Doc looked at Hel, found his expression one hard to categorize. "I didn't mean to be disrespectful."

"It is not disrespect, Delilah. I thought your nanites had explained?"

"I stopped them. Wasn't need to know." Now she wasn't so sure.

He pulled her hand away from his face and turned the wrist up, showing her the inside of his and hers. Both wrists now sported a delicate, silver pattern, like a tattoo. It was intricate and lovely. Side by side, it was clear they completed each other. Doc touched it.

"It's in my skin."

"Yes."

"It's amazing." She realized she still resisted knowing, understanding. "It's permanent, isn't it?" She looked at him, almost afraid of what she'd see in his eyes. She didn't expect gentle understanding.

"See how it glows? When we move apart, it will fade. If it disappears—" he hesitated.

Doc lifted the block in her mind, knew the answer. "We die." She took a shaky breath. "That's pretty permanent."

"Are you angry?" His tone was neutral.

"No." She didn't hesitate and was glad about that. How could she be angry? She loved him. "Are you okay with it?" *Did you know*, she wanted to ask, but was afraid of that answer, too.

"I am pleased, most pleased." He hesitated, started to say something more, but Doc's radio crackled.

The real world waited, even if the timing sucked.

"How's it going down there, Doc?" the General asked, his tone gruff, worried.

She turned her hand so that she held his, brushed her mouth across the back. "It's going great, sir. I mean, we're in."

Eighteen

"He is *not* going through that portal with you, Doc." The General was not happy. He should have been doing cartwheels of joy. The outpost had shields. They had access to the new ships.

"Sir. He has to go with me."

"Won't that up the paradox issue? There will be two of him there."

"I'm aware of the risk, sir, but we might have to unlock the portal again. In the past. I can't do it without him. And since he's on another planet…" The truth was, she didn't know what she'd control and what she couldn't control in the past. The peeps weren't sure either, since none of the Garradians had tried what she planned. She considered telling him that Hel had veto power, but she didn't want him to kill the Leader and not just because she'd die, too. Mentioning they'd gotten married wasn't in her game plan either.

Hel stood a few paces away, amused and unsurprised. He'd made it clear he was going through with her, bonded or not. No one had ever had her back before. No one had wanted it. She liked it. Maybe too much.

What if it affected her concentration? She always had skin in the game, but this was the first time she'd cared about someone else's skin more than her own. Not that it made a difference to the outcome. Their skins had to be in the game together. They were married. They'd live or die together, succeed or fail together. Thinking about that made her feel funny, so she focused on something that annoyed her.

How had someone gotten the drop on the other her? It couldn't have been Smith. He was a geek for Pete's sake. She'd considered letting whoever waited for her think he had her, to find out what his deal was, but that only worked in books and movies. Real bad guys didn't pause to reveal their evil plans. They just did them. She'd never paused to enlighten a target. She had a strict shoot first, ask questions later policy. The good thing about shoot first, it eliminated the need for questions. Most of the time talking was overrated. This time she needed answers though. If someone had access to the portal in some other time, they could keep trying to mess with their timeline. That made her eye twitch some more. Damn time paradoxes. Why did time seem to have a personal beef with her?

"Won't that change things? He wasn't there last time. Or he wouldn't be here now. Would he?"

"That's true." At least she hoped it was. How was she supposed to know? Even her peeps winced. "But I think everything we can safely do different is good." Doc considered this and decided it felt right, even if she lacked data to back up her hypothesis.

"I thought we should try to keep things the same?"

"If you pitched a losing game, you'd keep your *team,* but you wouldn't do the exact same things the next time you played the opposing team, would you?"

The General was orbiting Kikk, but she could still feel him thinking.

"No." A pause. "You sure about this, Doc?"

"As sure as I can be, sir." Doc was used to sounding sure on uncertain data. The General wasn't. Maybe she should give him something else to think about. "You should deploy Colonel Carey and his team."

"Can they do this without your assistance?"

She looked at Hel. He shrugged. She saw the hologram out of the corner of her eye. "I think I might have some assistance I can send over for them." She cut the connection and turned to smile at the hologram. The hologram looked from Doc to Hel. Her holo-gaze stayed with Hel. That hologram seriously needed some other interests. Maybe some hot guys in uniform would prove to be a good distraction.

☼

It always felt good to have earth beneath his feet again, but *this* earth felt particularly good.

Hel had waited a long time to be on the Kikk Outpost, to be in control of the legacy of the Garradians. It was not what he'd expected in some ways; in others it was what he thought it would be. He could feel the sleeping power seeping up from this tranquil setting, feel it around him, settling into his bones and sinews.

It was a city on an island in the middle of the vast ocean that dominated most of the planet's surface. Tall buildings were sprinkled amidst a forest, the imposing stone buildings connected by a series of deceptively peaceful walkways. This was a place primarily for the study of war and defense. No one knew how long it had been since the Garradian evacuation, but he did know he was the first of his kind to be here in a very long time. That the buildings stood, almost unchanged was a testament to their ingenuity in both creating this research facility and in hiding it.

As he would have expected from his people, the structures were dignified and pleasing to look at, though they lacked the evolved aesthetics of current Gadi architecture. The expedition must have many of their people working here, but they saw no one as they walked toward the shoreline and the building that housed the portal. It was hard to pass by the buildings. He longed to go inside and see the paintings he'd heard about, thumb through the books they'd left behind. He wished to know why his ancestor had left the galaxy and his family. He wished to know this past that had been shrouded so long in mystery.

The Key had revealed some of it, but had left many questions unanswered.

He was a Key.

All had moved so quickly, he had not had time to think, to

consider this, to consider Delilah. Her jacket sleeves hid the mark, the pattern that made her his. No one could take her from him now. They were joined, bonded for life: *ma'rasile.*

She had not told the General. It was a wise decision. The General had many things to concern him right now. Vidor Shan's ships. Gadi ships. Time paradoxes. Their bonding would make the General more difficult to manage, though he was impressed with how well Delilah managed him.

"Have you known the General long?"

"Less time than you and you shouldn't be so amused about it," Delilah said, her lovely lips twitching as she tried not to show her own amusement at the General's difficulties.

They were well suited. He had a sudden memory of thinking this about his first bond mate. He had cared for her, missed her, mourned her as their culture required. What he felt for Delilah exceeded those feelings. He'd seen something in her eyes when she'd looked at him during the ceremony. It had filled him with satisfaction, with pleasure.

She wanted him.

He'd known she desired to mate with him, had felt her interest, but her self-sufficiency made him uneasy. She didn't need, she didn't want to need. In this she was like him. She had changed. He had changed. Instead of discomfort at the idea of this change, he felt…relief. She needed him. He needed her. He could admit this now that he had her anchored in his life.

"My sons will be pleased." He paused to look at her. "They liked you very much."

"I'm a stepmother." She blinked several times. "Wow."

"This pleases you?" He felt a sudden anxiety. Not every woman could mother another woman's children.

"It does." Her smile was without guile. "I never thought I'd have children. They're great."

She feared to doom them to the same mental problems experienced by her and her brother, he realized.

"But you no longer need to fear." The nanites had cured her

problem. They should do the same for her children, could they not? He would like to see her carrying his child. A girl who looked like her mother. It was the first time he could recall desiring a daughter.

"No, I don't." Her eyes widened again. "Your mum?"

"She likes no one, not even me." He smiled at her. Got a smile in return that stopped the breath in his chest. It was possible he more than needed her. There was no word in standard for this feeling, this ache in his chest that was both pleasure and pain. Only in Gadi. He must teach her Gadi so he could tell her.

"I can live with that if you can."

He grasped her hand, took a quick look around to make sure they were unobserved and raised it to her mouth. "We will live with it together."

Her smile widened, but there was a shadow in her eyes.

"What bothers you? Do you not trust me?" The ache in his chest became more pain than pleasure.

"I do, it's just," she hesitated, bit her lip, then said in a rush, "I've loved my brother, Robert. And I lost him. My parents died, too." She shrugged, but her eyes gave her fear away. "I must have abandonment issues. Or maybe its fate I don't trust. I don't trust that I won't lose the people I love."

"If we go, we go together," he reminded her. "What is this love, you speak of?"

She stared at him, first startled, then relieved. She turned and started walking again. "I'll make you a deal. If we survive our adventure in portal time travel, I'll try to explain love to you."

☼

The General had cleared the whole building, not just the portal room, prior to their arrival. An elevator-like device took them deep underground where the portal waited, so innocuous it had been mistaken for a doorway at first. Its accidental discovery caused many problems for the Key, though it was also a convenient way to travel to the other outposts in the galaxy.

Doc could smell the scents of the people who'd been there

lingering in the air, and she also smelled the stone they'd used to build the room. Like everything else in the galaxy it was a bit different from what she was used to. The ventilation was subtle, but present. She felt the air circulating, felt it slide across her skin. The air was chilly, from being so deep underground and the stone walls. The floor was stone, too, the craftsmanship almost too nice for such a pedestrian space.

Hard for her to believe two years ago something had happened here that had sent her out of the galaxy and into the past. She brought black ops online, felt her peeps adjust, too. She glanced at Hel.

"Can you talk to them yet?"

"Talk to whom?"

"Your peeps. The nanites."

He almost broke out in expression. "I have these nanites?"

"I saw them on your skin after you plugged in as the Key. And I think some of mine went into you during the wedding." Black ops flickered as bride tried to do a comeback. Doc benched her. "If you can talk to them, then we'll have secure communications during the op." He gave the impression of being a bit boggled. "Just relax and let them talk to you."

"I do this how?"

"Ask a question. Something easy. Like, are you there?"

A pause, then his eyes popped wide. "I have nanites."

"Excellent."

"How does this help us communicate?"

"The nanites communicate with each other. That means they can pass on messages as fast as we can think them."

His eyes widened. *What's a wedding?*

Doc felt heat surge into her face. She hadn't expected this downside to their secure communications. "I'll explain that later." Not to mention control her thinking better. "Let's take a look at this bad boy." She stepped forward, her gaze traveling across the consoles on each side. She felt their readiness to respond to her, but it was the portal she was interested in right now.

It looked harmless, a simple doorway in a wall, with flat screen TV-looking panels on either side. She'd seen these screens, seen the maps in her mind, but this was her first look at them in real time. She ran her hand up the jamb, careful not to get even a toe over the threshold. This was not the moment to have an accident. It was just as advertised. Looked like a door, but the inside was densely dark and looked the same no matter where she stood in the room. That was creepier than her.

The panels on either side were portal controls. Dominance shifted to the side you were interacting with. Maps on the left opened portals to the other outposts in this galaxy. Pick a planet, touch, and step through.

Maps on the right were a tad more complicated. She studied this side, felt the capabilities beneath the simple surface. Keltinar rotated in the center, a listing of the settings in Garradian down both sides. It was strange to know how to set it, but to not *know*. The science behind it was beyond her understanding, though she sensed it had something to do with what she and others sometimes called folding space. She felt the lack of precision between their concept and hers, but couldn't bridge that gap right now.

She might be smart enough to get it, but the language barrier was huge, even with the nanites helping out. The words were there in her head, but the principles, the science behind the words was, well, alien.

Science assumed that atomic numbers were universal, but that assumed everyone used the same symbols, or at least similar representations of those symbols. The Garradians didn't use the same symbols or the same computer language they did. The first Key had been able to "talk" to the outpost because of her nanites. What upped the difficulty factor, the Garradians had gone far beyond what they'd achieved in their scientific understanding. They'd dealt with concepts Earth scientists could only dream about or hadn't yet thought of. In this room, with their knowledge swirling inside her head, it was like being in kindergarten. Well, she'd never attended kindergarten, but she'd bet it was like that.

With enough time, she thought she could understand it. Most of it anyway. How ironic. *Enough time.* She had time, lots of it, and was running out of time. Talk about a freaking paradox.

She didn't have to touch the maps to reset the portal. It was safer to think it anyway. Touching was risky. She worked with her peeps, watched the map reform into a new pattern, a new setting. Since they planned to travel portal to portal the settings were easier to adjust.

"That should do it."

"This does not look like Kikk," Hel observed.

"It's not. We'll travel to the past through another portal in the outpost system, and then come here via simple transport. It won't let you time travel to the same portal, even with a time difference." She'd picked the closest planetary portal to minimize any time/space distortion. Gristal was in Dusan space; a risk, but a necessary one, she and her peeps agreed. What they knew about the portals two years ago indicated it *should* be uninhabited, but there was always that law of unintended consequences she lived with.

"And our return?"

"The peeps have activated beacons in themselves, which means in us. When triggered, we can enter the portal and return to present time Gristal. We'll return close to this time, but it's not precise. Then we do a normal, non-time travel trip back here."

"How much time variation?"

"As much as a week. As little as a couple of hours."

"So we might have to wait a week in the past?"

"That's why our packs have survival supplies in them." She sighed. "I was hoping I'd never have to eat an energy bar again."

"And if we have only a few of your hours?"

"Then we'll have to work fast. We should go in weapons hot, but set to stun. I want us to be ready for anything. If someone is waiting for me, they might figure out I'd have to arrive via another one of the outpost portals and attack there."

"You are sure we should use stun?"

He was a guy after her own heart: never leave an enemy behind you.

"We have questions that need answers." She had several syringes of a special truth drug, developed just for the Major, which should encourage a useful exchange of information by whoever was targeting her.

"You ready?" He nodded. She took a breath and tapped her radio. "General Halliwell? Requesting permission to proceed."

Before he could respond, the consoles around her lit up like a carnival sideshow. Doc stared at the HUDs popping up over each console, but she didn't need to look at them. Data flowed into her through the peeps.

"Looks like Conan has figured out where I am. We got incoming. Brace for impact."

Her radio crackled. "Get the hell out of here, Doc. We'll try to hold the fort until you get back."

The ground shook as Conan's first salvo hit the shields he wouldn't be expecting. Hel grabbed her arms and the edge of the portal or they'd have been knocked to their knees.

He pulled his ray gun at the same moment she pulled both of hers. His smile curled her toes in her military-issue boots. Pirates might look like that before they boarded a gold-packed merchant vessel way back when.

She nodded. "We have to go in together, or we'll arrive on the other side as corpses. And we have to back in." For whatever reason, the portals all faced the same way, so you had to exit the same direction you entered. Doc never liked to have her back to an open doorway.

He nodded crisply. One of the consoles blared a warning of more incoming missiles.

She bent her arms, weapons pointed up, elbows tucked in

against her body, so they'd both fit through the opening.

"When we get there, go out right and I'll go left. On a three count. One. Two. Three."

Shoulder to shoulder they stepped backwards together into the opening.

Doc was glad she'd passed on a last meal; she'd heard portal travel made you queasy. She figured this would be worse, since they were going back in time. It sucked to be right. Didn't suck to not be barfing up lunch as lights stretched green and gold on either side of her. She looked down—or it felt like she looked down. Not sure if she could since she didn't know what state her body was in at the moment. She felt pulled in one direction, then another. Then the pulling angled, like she'd been pulled off true. Her stomach didn't like any of it. She sensed other anomalies in their passage, but lacked the ability to put them into words.

She was traveling through time. Holy foxtrot sierra.

Doc tended to swear in military jargon when she went black ops. It felt more natural.

The lights began to shrink again and so did her body. She had a slowing sensation, though what had happened didn't feel like movement. She was weapons ready when she reintegrated—or whatever the foxtrot hotel happened.

The Dusan squad leader wasn't ready.

Hel dove right as requested. She dove left, passing under his body, hit the floor, rolled onto her back and fired at two bogeys from her two ray guns. Before they hit terra firma she'd twisted and rolled again, her line of fire tracking toward new targets.

There were a lot of targets in a small space.

Hel fired in multiples, too, their flashes creating a satisfactory crossfire that had to make them tough to see. A couple of them got off a few shots before they cleared the room.

Doc didn't do a victory dance. She kept one gun trained on the door, the other on the downed bogeys. With a thumb, she kicked her ray gun from stun to kill and fired at the downed men as she moved through them.

This was not an enemy you wanted waking up and coming in at your back.

With an impressive lack of fuss, Hel adjusted as quickly, taking a position on the other side of the door. They were so integrated, all she had to do was think, and he got the message. They didn't even have to use hand signals.

She palmed open the door, went through firing and they cleared that larger room, too. This room had consoles and HUDs that came on for them, even as she followed Hel to door number two. Data flowed into her head via the peeps as they stacked by this door. They had successfully traveled back in time, though she didn't know exactly *when* they were yet.

There'd been no report of Dusan coming at the Kikk Outpost via the portal, but that didn't mean they hadn't tried. This was also a deeply buried portal room on this small outpost. Looked like the Dusan troops had been working their way down from the surface and had reached the portal seconds before their arrival. Several ships waited on the surface with more troops. The next door led to a lift or elevator. Doc kept a weather eye on it while she studied the various HUDS, trying to determine *when* they were.

Halliwell had briefed her as comprehensively as possible on troop deployment before, during and after the battle two years ago—no, *now*. She'd read about the battle, but seeing it this way, seeing the Dusan fleet arrayed against her people made her throat close up.

"Holy foxtrot sierra." She found the planet where Hel had been, making the move on the Key that had so pissed off General Halliwell. Locating him was a quick way to figure out where they were in the timeline. She found the two phase cloaked ships closing on the two Dusan battle cruisers.

"We don't have much time. The General will order the evac sometime in the next hour, I think." It was horrible to see it, hard to fight the impulse to engage. These were her people, but this wasn't her fight. This wasn't her time. She might endanger the victory. *Some victory.* Hard to believe anyone survived alive.

She looked at the life signs readings. The Dusan up top must know their people were dead, since they communicated through transmitters inside their heads. She didn't want them on her heels either, but she might not have time to deal with them before they had to go through that portal.

"Can we lock the portal behind us?" Hel asked, following her thought processes.

"I don't think so. You're not keyed to these locks."

He grinned and shrugged. "Then we will need to watch our backs."

At least the Dusan weren't moving yet. They couldn't without direction from the Supreme Leader, she realized and he'd been a bit distracted about this time.

"We should go now."

"I agree."

They didn't need to talk out loud, but Doc did like the sound of his voice, the reminder she wasn't alone.

"The Kikk portal will be under guard, but I don't know if they'll be friendly." She switched her weapons back to stun. "They *will* be super trigger happy with the outpost under attack."

They picked their way past bodies to the portal. If someone was waiting for *her*, or anyone coming through, they'd be focused on the center, about chest high.

"What do you wish me to do?"

She considered the problem, let him see both scenarios play through her head.

If one of them stood, it would pull the attention of anyone waiting, but it also upped the risk of getting shot. She didn't want to get shot, sure didn't want Hel to get shot. It was inconsistent with loving him. And it changed the working dynamic.

If the portal were guarded by regular jarheads, they'd be using live, projectile based ammo. No stun guns there. Hel wore body armor, so he had a good chance of surviving. While they were shooting at him, she'd be shooting at them.

If they were using stun weapons, he'd be out, but alive and in pain later.

If they both crouched and backed into the portal, it would be awkward, but it should take any guards a second or two to sight on them. All Doc ever needed was a second, two were a gift.

She looked at him, brows arched. Felt like it should be his choice. While she waited for him to process her scenarios, she did a mental assessment of trajectories, cross-fire options, risk assessments, bogey numbers and deployment possibilities. The bogies had the consoles for protection. A lot depended on how much they knew about the Chameleon, what they'd be expecting.

If she was expecting someone like her to come through that portal, she'd bring riot shields and she'd shoot to kill. She'd know that the first shot was the one that counted. If they missed they wouldn't get a second chance. Only they hadn't killed her, they'd banished her to Keltinar's murky past. So someone *had* been shooting with a stun gun.

"I wish I could see it—"

The sudden shift inside her head made her stomach lurch again, as the peeps enlarged her view. She'd done this before, she remembered now. When she'd first met the peeps, when they'd pierced Conan's shields. As before, she wasn't just in one portal room, but in all of them. There weren't security cameras. There were life signs detectors. Doc mentally homed in on Kikk. The view started aerial, masses of life sign dots swarmed against what had to be the first line of Major Loren's outpost defenses.

"Delilah?" Hel sounded distinctly uneasy, in a very guy, very macho way, of course.

She held up her hand. Talking wasn't possible. Too much of her mental resources were in this. She moved her view, like she'd move a mouse, over the outpost, swooping down on the building that held the portal. The swoop made her stomach drop, like a carnival ride.

She shifted inside, then headed down though the levels, though she took it slower this time.

"I do not wish to hurry you, but the Dusan are on the move."

Suddenly she was there. It felt there, but looked like a floor plan inside her head. Seven life signs. Four of them were behind the four consoles closest to the portal entrance. That had to be the jarhead detail. Two dots were behind one console by the lift, one on the other side, also near the lift.

No way to tell which was Smith, but Doc was sure the lone dot was him. She felt it in her gut and she always believed her gut. There was one other interesting item of note there. The portal settings were set to Earth, not Keltinar. That ruled out accidental option. Someone in that room would change the settings in the next hour unless they stopped them. She yanked out of the outposts, back to the present. It hurt like she'd rung her bell.

"Did you see it?"

Hel nodded, his eyes on the HUD that tracked the approaching Dusan. The lift bringing four of them was almost to their level. Doc had left the doors open, so they had a clear shot. They backed to the edge of the portal. Doc flicked both weapons back to the kill setting. Pointed both at the soon-to-open door. Hel matched her moves, having extracted a second ray gun.

"I'll take the side with four. When we come out of the portal, you'll want to dive for the wall. That should give you a clear shot down the channel behind the consoles where our bogeys are."

The door slid open. These Dusan were weapons hot, though not as weapons hot as they should have been. Light sprayed from their position by the portal into the confines of the lift.

It was overkill, but Doc didn't mind overkill when it worked. She flicked her weapons back to stun and looked at Hel. "Shall we go kick some scientific ass?"

Nineteen

The difference between the two travel times through the portal was the timing. This one was a whole lot shorter. Time travel took longer, which felt both wrong and ironic.

Hel was on her left as they arrived back on Kikk. He went right and Doc went left, once again passing under his body. Her peeps spiked into the portal as soon as they arrived, expanding her view as she hit the floor. It wasn't as good as looking through a security camera, but it didn't hurt.

Her stun ray hit the first jarhead in the chest. As he went down, that gave her a clear shot of jarhead number two with ray gun number two.

Her back hit the stone wall with a thump, but she'd prepped for it. It didn't affect her aim or her timing. The two geeks dropped before they had time to look startled.

Doc rolled to a crouch, prepared to back Hel up, but he'd done his work well. The lone bogey still conscious was Smith.

"You said you wanted to talk to him before we shoot him." Hel had both ray guns pointed at the doc's chest.

Smith looked scared—until Doc got to his eyes. She spun to cover their six and caught a guy coming out of the portal. He wasn't Dusan or a jarhead. He went down just as hard as they did.

The silence in the portal room was a stark contrast to the distant—but not distant enough—sounds of the battle raging on the island's surface. Inside her head, she could see the battle playing out, knew each explosion ended a life or lives.

Doc flashed a look at Smith. "Anyone else coming?"

He didn't answer. He didn't react at all. That was unexpected. He was a geek. He should have peed his pants. Doc studied Smith. He was as curious about them. His gaze flicked between them. Finally he settled on Hel.

"You are the Chameleon."

That answered two of her questions. She thought of a response, but Hel said it.

"You're not supposed to know that."

She felt his protective instinct like a warm wave. He didn't want Smith to know she was the Chameleon. Sweet, but dangerous for him.

Smith didn't react. Again.

Doc felt his curiosity, felt the detachment in it, as he studied her now. Neither of them was real to him. Neither of their lives meant anything to this man. She saw it in his eyes. On the outside, he looked like a middle-aged scientist, with a bit of wear around the edges—as long as she didn't look into his eyes. They reminded her of her eyes. Hyper alert, cool, assessing everything. His training went beyond his PhD.

She felt Hel get it, too, saw him tighten his focus on Smith.

"I'll cover him and the portal while you secure his friends."

Doc pulled out flex cuffs and started securing wrists and ankles, beginning with the jarheads. They were the most dangerous. She needed DNA tests, she decided and the peeps agreed. She patted them both down, but didn't find anything that shouldn't be there. The two geeks weren't armed with anything but their intellects—which was also a comment on those intellects. Maybe Mensa should also test for common sense. Started a DNA test on them, too. Before she could check the portal guy, she got a warning from the peeps.

Incoming.

Doc kept a weapon trained on Smith, the other on the portal. Hel got the alert, too. Feet braced she fired at the moment of arrival and another body fell out of the portal. They both fired at the next one. No time to play eeny, meeny, miny, moe with Hel. She waited a few beats, but that seemed to be it for now.

Who were those guys and where had they come from? She crouched to cuff and search them, and the peeps went in to test their DNA, too. Their weapons were very interesting. Stun/ray guns, but the design sleeker and lighter than the ones they'd brought back in time with them and they had more buttons. Doc held one up so Hel could see it.

"You ever see anything like this?"

The first crack in Smith's calm appeared. He twitched when she tossed it to Hel. He caught it easily, managed to study it without losing his focus on Smith.

"Nice." He fiddled with the settings and pointed it at Smith, who visibly paled. It upped Hel's hotness factor by twenty. Doc didn't fan herself, but she wanted to.

Smith kept scanning the area, as if he expected someone to pop out of the walls or ceiling. She'd been told this place was too deep for transport in or out, but she never believed what she'd been told.

Time to cuff and search him. Her gut told her to approach him with caution.

"Hands on back of your head," Doc said. After a hesitation, he complied. "Move to center of the room and kneel."

He didn't like it, but he did it, his eyes killing them with each step.

"Now lay on your stomach, hands still behind your head."

He didn't move. "You are making a mistake. If you don't return my weapon to me, you will regret it."

"I could taze you. It hurts like a bitch, and you don't get to pass out."

He complied, his eyes now lit with a murderous glow. Doc cuffed his ankles, then his wrists. When she'd searched him—depriving him of a couple of thumb drives and another über ray gun—she added some peeps for DNA analysis and put some distance between them again. One weapon indicated confidence in the outcome, or he'd trusted his backup too much. And he'd thought he had the element of surprise on his side. He had to be the one who'd got the drop on her and that pissed her off.

"We need him conscious," Hel reminded her.

She gave Hel a look, while her brain considered what else she'd learned about Smith. He might look paunchy, but when she patted him down she learned it was all muscle. Guy was built like an ox. She'd suspect him of being on the Major's payroll, but if he was, she wouldn't be here. The Major was a miser with his resources. Besides, he had an über ray gun. If he worked for the Major she'd have one, too.

His gaze flicked between them. It was like looking at her eyes in the mirror. Creepy.

"Who are you?" Doc asked the question without any real hope he'd answer.

"Doctor Tobias Smith."

His DNA said he was more than that. How could he be a mix of Gadi and Dusan? The two bogeys had close to the same balance in their DNA. The jarheads and the scientists were from Earth.

A faint crease formed between Hel's brows. *How is that possible? There has been no intermarrying for seasons past counting.*

"The Chameleon works alone." For a guy tied up and kissing floor he was pretty confident.

Hel nodded to Doc, like they hadn't been peep-talking. She holstered her weapon and pulled out a syringe.

"That isn't necessary. Ask your questions. I'll answer them."

"But will you answer them truthfully?" Hel asked, skepticism adding a hint of texture to the cool indifference of his voice.

"If you are the Chameleon, you will know if I'm lying."

He had a point. Major called her a human lie detector—when he wasn't calling her names not fit for polite company. Doc kept the syringe out to keep the pressure on.

"Let's start with something easy. How do you know about the Chameleon?"

A slight smile, a hesitation as he considered his answer. "The Major could not resist the urge to write his memoirs."

The chill heading down her back wasn't because the air started to circulate again. She didn't waste breath asking how he knew what he knew, not with the portal at her back, the portal she'd used to travel back in time. The Major she knew didn't write anything down that didn't have a built-in destruct code, but then he decides to write his freaking memoirs sometime in the future?

"You're not from Earth." It wasn't a shock. Not after the DNA test, but he didn't know about that. Doc let amusement trickle into her voice when she added, "And you believe he told the truth?"

The first hint of uncertainty crept into his expression. *Cause and effect.*

One of the jarheads' radios crackled. Doc grabbed it and listened to Major Loren giving the order to begin the evacuation through the portal. They were running out of time.

How is this possible? Hel's crease deepened, while Smith watched them with increasing frustration.

Unless Conan succeeds in blasting it out of existence in two years, there's no reason to think this portal couldn't outlast all of us. It's been remarkably durable so far.

It was annoying. They could leave the jarheads and scientists where they lay and risk the time line, or they had to figure out how to manhandle ten bodies through the portal into the future without losing their upper hand. It was complicated by the fact that she and Hel had to travel together. And she couldn't guarantee they'd all arrive at the same time, upping the challenge factor by a number she didn't have time to run but was sure to be astronomical.

She crouched with care in front of Smith. Those flex cuffs wouldn't have stopped her. He still looked convinced the situation would spin his direction. Hel caught the thought and focused on both lift door and portal, though he wasn't obvious about it. Guy might talk if he thought he'd soon have the upper hand. She wouldn't. Wouldn't write any foxtrot memoirs either. And if she made out of this, the Major wouldn't be doing it either.

"Who are you really?"

His eyes showed awareness of how they were alike. He almost smiled. "I think you know."

It was the truth. "Why mess with our past?"

"I didn't."

There was a measure of truth in the statement, but a large helping of lies, too.

Doc looked around. "I don't see anyone else in this room from the future."

"The changes aren't permanent," Smith said, quickly, as if he needed to delay them, his gaze studying places without doors again.

"So you messed up our lives for the hell of it?"

For the first time, he hesitated. "Time is persistent. Like water seeking to be level, *true* time asserts itself."

That sounded like the truth, but she wasn't reassured. She knew that look. He was hunting. Did that make him a good guy or a bad guy? He'd been careful not to reveal his real name. Did that mean he was afraid they'd go mess with his life? That they could?

"It's a trap," Hel said it aloud, plucking the thought from Doc's head.

"He's using the time instability as bait," Doc finished. Unless the Chameleon was the bait? Or was she part of the prey? This trap had been fashioned for her, too.

Now Smith looked concerned. "How—" He stopped, but not in time.

"We're gifted." Doc didn't have to exchange significant looks with Hel. They were synched better than her iPod to iTunes. It was time to go.

She yanked out a knife and cut the restraints off their people. It wasn't a great plan to leave them behind, but it was their only option. "Why bring Keltinar into the mix? Why speed up their technology development?"

His slight smile sent another nasty chill down Doc's back.

"I slowed it down."

"Hotel foxtrot sierra." She looked at Hel. "We gotta get back."

"We'll take the time travelers with us."

"You can't—"

Doc pulled a stun weapon and shut him up. He'd done it to her or he planned to do it to her.

Topside the battle went quiet, like someone had clicked a switch. Maybe someone had. The battle shouldn't be over yet. Doc activated a console as a HUD. Nothing moved anywhere, in space or on the outpost. It was as if they'd been frozen. A sudden, painfully bright beam of light filled the room. She snapped her shaded visor down and had a Luger in her hand without even thinking about it. When the light faded, two figures stood by the lift doors.

"That won't be necessary," a cool, calm voice said.

Doc couldn't tell if they were male or female. Their faces, their clothes, their miens were bland beyond weird. It didn't take much thought to conclude they were Smith's prey, but that didn't make them the good guys.

"Who the foxtrot are you?" She didn't lower her weapon. Instead, she grabbed one of the future weapons they'd taken off Smith's buddies. Hel still held the one she'd tossed him.

"We are here to deal with the time violators."

Doc flicked her safety off. "You'll notice this is a projectile weapon, so your shields won't protect you."

"You do not know this."

He or she was right. She lifted the future weapon. Only one reason Smith and his boys were packing them. "But this one will."

They might have paled. Hard to tell when they had skin whiter than hers.

"Who are you?" Pale gazes flicked between Doc and Hel,

curiosity lighting their pale gazes with animation.

"The ones with the weapons," Hel said.

"And the upper hand," Doc finished. "Who are *you?*"

"We are time wardens. We detected an instability and tracked it here."

"And how do you fix this instability?" Hel asked the question. Doc felt his need to keep their attention away from her.

If this was a Chameleon trap, which of them had set it, Smith or the self-declared time wardens? Doc wasn't getting heavy truth vibes from them either. How much did they *know?* Her peeps hackles rose with hers.

"We must collect the contagion and reset time."

"Why should we believe you?" Doc asked, sensing something from them, but not sure what.

"We are not allowed to affect the time stream. We protect it."

"Then you should already know who we all are, shouldn't you?" Hel arched his brows, his lips almost twitching at the chagrin that marred the blandness of their expressions.

Good one.

"It is not that simple."

"Nothing ever is," Doc agreed. "When I don't know what to do, I start shooting. It returns things to simple." She didn't want any of this bunch at her back when she left. With a flick of her thumb she brought the future weapon online. "Too bad I haven't had time to figure out the settings."

Okay, that time they did pale.

The truly weird part for Doc, now that time was frozen, she could feel its fluidity, feel the pressure for it to seek its proper level.

"We are here to remove the interlopers." Light crept from them to engulf Smith and the bogeys who'd come through the portal. Neither the jarheads nor the geeks were included in the selection. And the light stayed well away from Doc and Hel. The time warden added, a slight tremor in his or her voice, "We have no issue with you or your companions."

They didn't know that she and Hel were out of their time.

"You must surrender their weapons." This came from the other warden.

The gleam in their eyes told Doc all she needed to know. Besides, it was against her religion to surrender a weapon.

"You first," Hel said, his future weapon pointed at the he or she on the left.

Unlike her and Hel, they had to look at each other to silently communicate. Their pale gazes turned back to them.

"You won't remember this meeting. Once we leave, this event will cease to exist."

They were bluffing. Doc felt it to her core.

Doc arched her brows. "Then we have nothing to worry about." Unlike them, she could make everything she said sound like the truth. "And neither do you. Once time resets, the weapons will cease to exist here."

They didn't like that. What was more interesting, they weren't sure that the weapons would vanish.

"If we use the weapons," Hel put in, "won't that create another instability you can track?"

One of them nodded. It seemed unnatural, like they didn't do it that often. They exchanged looks once more, and then light flared again and when it faded, the two creeps and their time traveling prisoners were gone, leaving the jarheads and the Earth geeks with Doc and Hel. Time unfroze with their departure, the battle once more heading toward its big finish.

How much had changed, or would change when the reset occurred? And when would it happen? What created a trackable instability? Could the wardens track them back through time? She didn't feel watched, but she felt time building toward something. Doc spun toward the portal, the peeps already entering their coordinates with her mind and preparing to activate the beacons.

Would they be returning to a time different from the one

they left? How different might it be? Neither the geeks nor the jarheads would regain consciousness in time to go through the portal before the battle ended and if they did? They'd arrive two years into the future. No one would be traveling to Keltinar. Halliwell would not have spent the last two years worrying about his lost people. Would he have returned on the *Doolittle* or retired? Doc would not have traveled to Keltinar, and she would not have started that war that wasn't her fault. Conan would have bigger guns, but he had no reason to come to this galaxy.

What she didn't know, what kept her from diving into the portal was the question of how it would affect her, the peeps and Hel. Would she have come to this galaxy without Smith's specific shopping list? It seemed unlikely. The Major liked to keep his assets close.

They could stay, even as her mind latched on to the idea, her mind also pointed out the problem: if they stayed, they risked creating a time instability and bringing the wardens back. They had to go through, they had to go back, no matter what the consequences.

At the opening, she looked at Hel. "Things might be weird when we get back."

His brows arched. She wasn't sure what he'd do if she told him everything, so she just said, "Just don't be surprised by what we find on the other side."

His smile was both wry and tender. "I have been surprised almost every minute since your people arrived in this galaxy, Delilah."

Doc pulled her sleeve up and looked at the mark of their bonding. "I know you don't know what it means, but when we say we love someone on my world, it's big. I want you to know I love you. Whatever is on the other side, that won't change." She so hoped that was true. Could she love someone she'd never met? *Time is persistent.* She hoped Smith was right about that.

"We have a different word for it, but it is the same for me."

Her mind and heart swirling with worry and love, Doc

stepped into the portal with Hel.

Doc tried to notice if anything was different from the first time as they went forward in time , but it looked and felt the same. Stomach still lurched and protested. The lights thinned and bent the same. And then it stopped and they were back on Gristal, but *when* were they back?

Doc looked at Hel. He looked at her, his brows arched in a question she didn't have an answer for. She stepped out, surreptitiously checking for anything that might be missing, such as her *ma'rasile* mark. It glowed on her wrist, a beacon of hope in a life that had been neutral on the subject of hope.

"I still carry my *ma'rasile* mark, as well."

Doc frowned. "I still remember them. Do you?"

Hel matched her frown and raised it to a scowl. "Yes."

"Perhaps it takes time to fade. Or maybe they aren't as powerful as they thought they were."

Doc liked that option best. She tapped into the outpost. Everything looked the same as when they left, but minus the Conan shooting at them part. Had they arrived before they left? Conan's ship lurked behind the Kikk moon and his other ships hovered over the outposts, including this one. Were they about to meet themselves coming through the portal? It was almost too weird to deal with. Doc's gut kicked into high gear. She turned and stared at the portal that would take them back to Kikk. She couldn't get a sense of *when* it was. She needed contact with the General to get a fix on the date and time. Was this an instability that the time wardens could track?

"I'd sure like to bypass this part of the trip," she muttered.

"This forgetting could happen at any point," Hel pointed out. It was very guy of him to take the logical approach, very girl of her to find it annoying. "We must return to Kikk."

Of course he wanted to get back to Kikk. He'd been trying to get there for most of his life. They could still be in the instability, she supposed. She could wish she'd paid more attention in time travel class, if there'd been one to not pay attention in.

"You are giving me a headache, Delilah." Hel grabbed her hand and lifted it to his mouth. "Let's go home."

Home. With her free hand, she touched Kikk, bringing it to the front and center, while her mind replayed images of all her time with Hel. So few meetings to feel so safe with him, to feel like she belonged somewhere. To believe they could have a home together. He was right. First things first. She fixed her mind on the things she wanted: a life with her *ma'rasile,* her husband. The power to walk away from the Major and his imperatives, to live her own life. Any life with Hel was a huge unknown, but having *a life* with him was worth holding on to. She anchored her thoughts on these things as they made the leap.

She'd do this last thing and then she'd be free to be who and what she wanted. She owed it to the General. The Major? She'd paid any debt to him a long time ago. She'd do it and somehow, some way, she'd do it without losing what mattered the most. She felt the peeps dig in, too.

"Ready?"

"Weapons out?"

Doc nodded. Kikk should be safe, but she still never assumed.

Together they backed into the portal. All seemed as it should be until the last moment when a bright golden flash went through her like an electrical charge.

She had time to think, *those freaking foxtrot lying time freaks* before she fell into a deep, dark place.

Twenty

Doc woke in the *Doolittle's* infirmary feeling some serious *déjà vu.*

She loathed *déjà vu.*

Her brain felt like it had been in a blender, but *they* were quiet. Blender was better than *them.* So why did it make her gut kick in fear? Where was she? *When* was she? Why was she thinking when?

She sat up. No one shot her. That was good. She felt fine, better than fine physically. Mentally was another story. Why was she in the infirmary? Inside her head it felt like a two-year-old was trying to build a space ship with the little bitty Legos. She swung her legs off the side and had no trouble getting upright or staying there. The cubby for her clothes held ABUs. Why did that feel wrong?

"Ma'am?"

Doc turned and found Lieutenant Simmons in the doorway. Her look of patient resignation was familiar but something was different between them. Doc felt it, even as she felt uncertainty about how it should be between them.

"Lieutenant." Doc never asked questions she could get other people to ask. If someone knew what you didn't know, they could lie to you. People lied to her a lot.

"You shouldn't be out of bed, ma'am." She bustled in and began ripping the bedding off, in direct contrast to her statement. "How do you feel?"

With my hands. She'd had that thought before. When had she started doing lame stand-up routines, in or out of her head? "I feel fine."

Almost absently she rubbed her *ma'rasile* spot, drawing Simmons attention to it.

"That's a cool tat. Didn't notice it when they brought you in."

"It reacts to my mood," Doc improvised. "Only shows when I'm happy."

She got a skeptical look from Simmons and tried to look happier. Simmons turned back to the bedding.

"I'll get Captain Evans. He wanted to know when you woke up."

Doc felt her gut jolt. *Captain Evans?* She'd seen him die when he tried to push the suicide bomber out of the Gadi reception hall, hadn't she? If that hadn't happened, what else hadn't happened? And why did she remember stuff that hadn't happened? The time freaks said she wouldn't.

She shouldn't remember them either.

Through the spinning, shifting blocks in her head, she reached out and found the peeps. They'd had their bells rung, too—if they had bells. They'd protected her from whatever the freaks had tried to do, she realized, kept her in the same time slipstream the freaks used to move through time without affecting it. *They lied.* It was so not a shock. What else had they lied about?

She looked at her *ma'rasile* mark again. And why did it itch like crazy? Why was it still there? *Did you protect him, too? Where is he? Does he remember me?*

Answers flowed into her head as her link with the peeps was reestablished. They couldn't reach Hel, couldn't connect with him, but he must have moved physically closer. They'd been separated. That's why she'd been unconscious. The peeps had managed to extend the *ma'rasile* link so they didn't die, but they hadn't been able to keep her conscious. Hel had probably lost consciousness, too. Inside her head, she saw the approach, not of nine Gadi ships, but the bulk of their fleet, twenty–five ships, including Hel's flag ship. Was he in charge or was Glarmere? Was Glarmere a problem in this timeline?

Time is persistent. That would be comforting if she knew in what direction time wanted to be persistent.

The *Doolittle* was on high alert, though Doc couldn't tell from the data stream if they expected to be attacked or were just being careful. The kind of data she needed was inside the General's head, not in the computers or on the HUDs. And she had no idea what her relationship with him was like in this altered timeline.

"Doctor Clementyne?"

Doc switched her view from internal to external. It was Captain Evans, and he was alive and well. Did that mean there'd been no reception on the Gadi home world or just no bomb? Had she changed things or had the time freaks?

"Captain." Doc stayed in neutral. It was the only place she knew to be. Because the peeps had protected her, she hadn't lived this Doc's life for the last two years. She wasn't complaining at what she hadn't lost, but it did leave her with a huge information deficit. If the bombing hadn't happened, then she hadn't helped out here and didn't know these people. *She'd never met Hel.* If he didn't remember her, that could be interesting.

"How do you feel?" He projected calm competence as he pulled off his stethoscope and listened to her heart.

"I'm fine." What was she supposed to feel?

He eased back, studying her with a look she'd used herself. There was a pause, possibly for question or questions from her, but she didn't know what to ask.

"You're a medical doctor, so I won't bravo sierra you. I have no clue why you collapsed or why you woke up. Do you remember what happened?"

"No." It was a form of the truth. What she didn't know could fill a novel. What she did know was the stuff of fiction now. *She was married to a man she'd never met.* Okay, she didn't know they'd never met. The reception could have happened, but there was no record of the trip or transport in the ship's logs. "How long have I been…here?" She'd planned to say "unconscious" but what if she hadn't been out the whole time?

"Five days."

She was into the ship's systems, so she knew the date. In the other timeline, she'd been Conan's prisoner right now. So that hadn't happened either.

"Oh."

"I understand you transported down to the outpost to do some research and collapsed." His gaze turned keen. "You don't remember any of it?"

"I remember transporting to the outpost." This was the truth.

He sighed. "We could run some more tests, but they've all been negative. Have no reason to think that's going to change."

"You're releasing me?" Doc let a little hope creep into her voice. Normal people were always happy to get out of the infirmary.

"If you promise to let me know if you feel faint again."

"I promise." If Hel kept heading toward her, she should be fine—unless they went to war with the Gadi and the *Doolittle* left the galaxy. That would kill them both. If he still had his mark. He had to, didn't he, if she did? She needed to know how bad things were, and she wasn't sure she had the access to find out. Her peeps were on all of her questions, they were tapping into the General's quarters, ready room and communications, but she'd rather go through the data when she was alone. If things were as messed up as she feared they were, she needed privacy to cuss.

"I've informed the General you're conscious. He'd like to see you, if you feel up to it."

That was oddly polite. Just who or what did the General think she was? And what mission objective had brought her to this galaxy?

Doc trotted out her bravo sierra smile. She'd like to know more before she met him, but he was the General. No matter how politely couched, the request was still an order. "I'd like to shower first."

"I don't think he'll mind." He smiled. It was a nice smile.

When he left the room, Doc took a cautious sniff of one arm pit. No, the General wouldn't mind the time for a shower.

Doc didn't rush her ablutions, even if she only got two minutes of water from the head. It was disconcerting to find her hair long again. *Morticia's return.* It was a time anomaly her peeps couldn't explain. Someone had left clean drawers with her ABUs. She wondered if she'd been armed with her usual stuff when they found her and what they'd done with it if she had. It was hard not to feel naked, despite the clothes. She was still lethal, with or without weapons, but Doc preferred to be over armed whenever possible.

While she dressed, her mind and her peeps went over priorities and plans. First up, she needed to talk to Hel. He should be on his ship. She'd been returned to her ship so he probably had, too. Strong probability Glarmere had used his collapse to take control of the fleet. Based on scan data, the fleet had started heading toward Kikk five days ago.

So how did she get to Hel?

She could steal a ship with a phase cloak and board the flagship.

That left her with a pissed-off General at her back. And a huge black mark on her record. She wasn't sure which bothered her more. In the other timeline, she'd forged an uneasy something with the General. She didn't want to lose that, but she'd die if she got yanked out of the galaxy. That would end the uneasy something, too. Best case would be to get him on board with her talking to Hel. Sara had told him all her secrets, and she'd had some seriously freaky secrets. He'd kept her secrets and then some. He was an honorable man. He knew when to talk and when to keep quiet. It went against her grain to talk, to ask for help, to need help, but her time in the other timeline—this line of thought made her eye twitch—had knocked her pride around a bit. She'd needed a lot of help and both Hel and the General had delivered it.

There was risk. The General she'd known had been shaped

by the two years that had been erased. This one had lived a different two years, but both of them had known Sara Donovan. That hadn't been wiped out by the reset.

The law of unintended consequences? Or time having a laugh at her expense?

It was possible that her leaving those people behind had impacted this future in unexpected ways, just as she'd warned the General. Was it possible that concern for his lost people had made the General and their diplomats more conciliatory toward the Gadi in the previous time line? That by changing the stakes, she'd changed the dynamic of their interaction with them now?

There was no sign of any back door manipulation and scheming on the *Doolittle.* Neil Caldwell, the man who'd been implicated in the bombing of the Gadi reception, wasn't even on the ship. Based on the peeps delving into the diplomatic data, the relationship with the Gadi had been pretty much static since the end of the battle: locked in a state of mutual distrust and steadily escalating posturing. What intelligence info she could tap into indicated increasing pressure for the Gadi to kick them off the Kikk outpost and out of the galaxy. Why they hadn't done it sooner could only be conjectured. No need to wonder why the expedition didn't want to go. Even with most of the tech locked, there was still some cool stuff to study on Kikk.

In this time line, was Hel still waiting to see if the Key would return on the *Doolittle?* If he believed the Key would never return, or that the expedition was close to figuring out the tech, he'd act. He had no reason not to and lots of reasons to go for it. Hel didn't, couldn't know he was a Garradian Key, though without talking to him, she didn't know how to use that information. Or how much to share with the General. His first reaction would be to keep Hel as far away from the outpost as possible. Or get the foxtrot out of the galaxy.

The other question she had, could *she* access the outpost and unlock it, since her DNA had been altered? Her peeps knew the reset had reset the locks down there. They didn't know what she could or couldn't do, just that the Key DNA string was still there.

If she could unlock the rest of the tech and the wrong people found it out, she'd be as at risk of exploitation as the original Key had been. And even if this Hel didn't know her, it still felt like a betrayal. She'd promised him he'd have a stake in the outpost. And she wasn't sure the tech would be enough to stop a war with the Gadi or be enough protection against twenty-five ships.

And then there was the risk of dying if she and Hel got too far apart or his enemies managed to kill him. Or if her people thought she was crazy and sent her home. Death was always on the table during her ops, but this one had a lot of death running through it. Felt like the Grim Reaper was coming at her from every direction.

The irony was, she didn't want to live without Hel in her life, but she didn't want him to stop living when she did. He had two sons who needed their father. Two sons who didn't remember her.

They like you.

She'd been a mom, step-mom, for a few hours. She'd been desired by a man who'd seen past her scary surface, who'd found a person inside her she didn't know was there. Doc liked that person, wanted to *be* that person.

She loved him.

She might not get him.

Her chin lifted. She did what she had to. She could do it again. And when she was done, she'd figure out how to go on living.

Despite her worries and wrapped in all-she-didn't-know concerns, Doc was glad to head out of the infirmary. She passed by an open door. Stopped. And backtracked.

This room was a larger treatment room with several exam tables lined up in rows. Several people sat or lay on the tables, but only one caught her attention.

Conan.

Time is persistent.

What was he doing on the *Doolittle?*

His gaze followed one female, switched to another, his look assessing.

He was girl hunting in this reality, too? Or maybe it was just the persistence of Conan and not time? *Was he tagging women on this ship?*

The peeps brought back a resounding yes. He'd managed to touch about five women, including Simmons. It shouldn't have been a shock to realize Doc was still tagged. How did he plan to get them off the ship? Could he transport them through their shields? The peeps had no answer for that question.

As if he felt her gaze, he turned and pinged on her. His gaze flicked up and down before returning to her face. Doc didn't let recognition show, but it didn't matter. She saw it in his face, in his eyes. If something had to be the same between the two timelines, this wouldn't have been the one she'd have chosen.

While Doc added him to her list of concerns, he got up, cradling one hand against his chest, and strode toward her. That was way too familiar. She had to look up when he stopped in front of her, but it didn't intimidate her. She could kick his ass in this timeline, too, if she had to. Her chin lifted, her expression locked in calm and bland.

"I am Vidor Shan." He held out his hand.

Cringing inside, Doc let him take hers, knew the moment the new round of compound hit her system. It went against the grain to offer even a version of her name to him.

"Doctor Clementyne."

A tagged nurse hove into view on his six. "He's waiting to see one of the doctors, ma'am. A laceration on his hand."

Doc made the mental shift to physician. "I'm a physician, Lieutenant. I can take a look, if everyone else is busy."

The nurse looked doubtful. Doc handed the girl her ID tag.

"You can scan my ID and verify my credentials." She knew Conan hadn't stopped looking at her during her exchange with the nurse. She made herself look at him. "If you'll go back to your station I'll be with you in a few minutes."

He didn't move. What a shock.

"I wish you to care for my injury."

A familiar headache started behind her eyes. A ton of responses trooped through her mind, but all of them reflected her previous knowledge of him, their previous interaction.

"If you don't go back to your station, I'm going to leave." She was keeping the General waiting and pissing him off even more. Of the two, the General had more power to make her life miserable. The steely determination in her voice must have got through his Cro-mag skull. He did as she asked, though he kept her in his sights the whole way. She went to the nurse's station, where the gal was scanning her ID.

"What's Con—his story?"

The nurse looked a bit startled, but at least she didn't trot out any privacy crap.

"Just a trader who cut his hand. Asked for medical assistance." She snuck a peek over her shoulder at him. "He's pretty hot, isn't he?"

Doc managed a bland smile. "Yeah." She'd known he'd do well around Earth women. Nice to be right about something.

The girl looked a bit surprised when Doc's credentials popped up on her screen.

"It's nice of you to help out, ma'am." Questions cart wheeled through her eyes, but didn't come out her mouth. Maybe she was too happy for the help to risk ruining it.

Doc headed for Conan, the nurse on her six. She pulled on gloves while her assistant exposed the injury. Self-inflicted just like last time. She was so tempted to order some invasive tests, but her peeps were bringing her disturbing news about the changes in his ships technology—though the numbers were the same, same in ships and guys. No girl brides this time though. Probably not a good idea to rattle his cage when he had the power to blow them out of the sky. So the automation factor hadn't changed. But their targets had. They weren't after the outposts this time.

All sixteen ships were strategically ringing Kikk. Reminded her of when they had her ringed on Feldstar. Doc had a sense of them hanging back, perhaps waiting until the expedition had duked it out with the Gadi? It's what she'd do, and had in similar—though on smaller scale—situations.

The Gadi would win, that was a given, but they'd be weakened for when the stronger ships moved in. Conan had the fire power, but the Gadi had more ships.

And she had a bargaining chip to use with the General and Hel.

Just for that, she'd forgo ordering Conan those tests.

She realized Conan and the nurse were chatting. *Small talk.* The tension in Conan's arm and hand eased, though Doc felt his pulse sputter when she asked a question he didn't like. Wow, she'd always though small talk was a necessary evil, something to get over with, but this was enlightening. It was an interrogation without drugs, the big light or the water board.

When they finished, Doc thanked the nurse and let her remove the debris and leave before she looked at Conan, this time looking for differences. There weren't many. Some small things in his clothing and less seething frustration in his manner. When Doc was sure the nurse was out of earshot, she said, "She was flirting with you, you know."

His brows arched. "Flirting?"

"Indicating interest in you as a man. She liked you."

His gaze tracked her way for several seconds, then returned to Doc.

"This flirting is how your people show attraction?"

Doc half-nodded, half-shrugged.

"Is this how *you* indicate interest?"

"No." It was the truth. She had no clue how to flirt. She took a fake look at her watch. "And I'm late for an appointment."

"I am free to leave?"

Doc signaled the SOs. "Of course. They'll escort you to your ship."

She started to rise, but he halted the movement with his hand on her arm. Doc fought the urge to flip him on his back and put her foot on his throat.

"You do not wish to know how we show attraction?"

Doc stared at him for a ten count. It wasn't wise. It wasn't smart, but she said it anyway. "No."

Instead of looking pissed, he smiled. It was more charming than she remembered, but it still left her cold. "You do not speak the truth."

Instead of an answer, Doc looked pointedly at his hand on her arm. He slid his hand down to her hand and lifted it to his mouth. Doc couldn't hide the jerk of rejection she felt at the touch of his mouth against the back of her hand. She knew, saw in his eyes, that he thought her reaction was something else. Typical guy.

She got her hand free and left, aware he watched her until she turned into the hallway.

Can you keep an eye on him, she asked the peeps. She got an affirmative. When she had a minute, she needed to talk to them about sentience. Did they tell her they weren't holding their breath?

She felt them flowing through the ship, flowing through her, as she headed for the lift that would take her to deck where General Halliwell waited to talk to her. It felt good to be connected, to be plugged in again. She expanded her view to the outposts, before tightening her focus on Conan's big ships. Smith hadn't been kidding when he said he'd slowed them down. Their cloaks and weapons were bigger and better. Seriously better.

She saw Briggs heading her way, his long-legged gait a bit rolling, like he walked the deck of a ship, not a space ship. Did he know her? Did she still know Sara?

To her relief, he checked when he saw her. "You don't look like you fainted." The hint of derision in his tone was a relief, as was the concern he couldn't quite hide.

"Don't feel like it either." Relief flooded in. Finally someone who knew her and wasn't scared of her. "Are you heading anywhere in particular right now?"

"Commissary."

"Can I ask you something?"

His face didn't change, but she could feel him considering her request. His nod was a bit wary. He was such a guy.

"Do you…trust me?"

He hadn't expected that question. To her relief he didn't do derisive or take it lightly.

"Yes."

That he also didn't hesitate warmed her where she didn't know she'd been chilled. Her smile was the one she'd learned from being with Hel.

"Thank you."

He shrugged, a bit uncomfortable and not wanting to show it.

"Could I persuade you to take a detour with me? General Halliwell wants to see me."

"Why?"

He could have been asking why she needed him or why the General wanted to see her. She assumed it was the first.

"I need someone who knows me at my back when I talk to him, someone who can vouch for me." Briggs wouldn't like it either, but he'd know she wasn't crazy. At least not until he heard what she had to say. Then she'd find out how much he really trusted her.

Another pause for reflection and he shrugged. "All right." He hesitated again. "Known him longer, Doc."

"I'm not asking you to choose sides." She hoped it wouldn't come to that.

"Good."

General Halliwell waited for her in his ready room. He looked the same, except for his eyes. They regarded her with barely disguised dislike. It hurt more than she'd expected, as life delivered her yet another loss. The look eased when he saw Briggs, one brow arching.

"I asked him to come with me, sir."

His gaze returned to her, expression blanked out now. "You afraid of me, Doctor?"

She missed the friendly Doc he'd called her before. A slight, almost sad smile edged her mouth, despite her resolve not to go there. She needed his belief, not his friendship.

"No, sir." Not strictly true. She was afraid he might have her confined. He'd believed Sara, she reminded herself. She trusted him. Doc had to trust him, too. And convince him to trust her.

"Fine. Sit." His glance included Briggs, though they both showed a bit of puzzled around the edges. Without waiting for her to speak, he leaned forward, pinning her with a look. "I don't know what your mission is, Doctor. Don't want to know."

He didn't know her mission? She didn't know her mission. It wouldn't be anywhere she could find it either.

"Can you finish it before the Gadi get here? Because you're running out of time. If they attack, we will have to abandon the outpost and possibly the galaxy."

Without responding to his question, Doc turned to Briggs. "Will you tell the General how we met?"

His brows arched, but he answered the question instead of asking the one in his eyes.

"Captain Donovan introduced us."

"Did she tell you how we met?" Doc prayed that hadn't changed.

"You delivered Donovan's baby."

"*You* delivered Miri?"

"She went into labor while driving to Area 51. I happened by at the right time." In the face of the general's surprise, Doc added a touch defensively, "I am a trained physician." She'd hoped that the rigors of medicine would help her with *them* but it hadn't been enough.

Doc looked at the General again. Now he looked puzzled, but slightly less hostile.

"What's all this about, Doctor?"

"You don't like the Major." He jerked when she said the name, his glance flicking to Briggs. "I don't much like him either. He doesn't matter here. Not now. I have some information that's going to make the hair on the back of your neck stand on end. I can prove some of it, but most of it, not a hope."

☼

The itching brought him out of the deep well. Something was wrong. Menace thickened the air around him and a deep sense of loss hollowed out his chest. He lifted his lids, taking his time, to make sure he was alone. He was in the medical ward, a private room. For a moment a memory flickered in his mind. A flash of light and falling rubble…

The itch broke his concentration. He rubbed at it, relieved to be alone, though he had a feeling it wouldn't last. Why wouldn't his wrist stop itching? He looked at the spot and found a strange silver pattern embedded in the skin. What—

A *ma'rasile* mark.

He'd heard stories, legends about these deep mating bonds, but he'd never—how did he know what it was? Why was it there? Memory taunted again, a fast flash, an impression of a stone room that left him wanting more. How was this possible? He had not left this ship for a season. He'd been in conference with his commanders, discussing the *Doolittle's* return to the galaxy. And then…nothing.

He needed to remember, if he didn't…something was wrong…the persistent itch taunted him with what stayed just out of memory's reach.

A door swished open, snapping Hel's eyes closed. Footsteps approached.

"He still sleeps."

Hel recognized that petulant, too imperious voice. Glarmere. His cousin on his mother's side. Memory twitched again, as annoying as the itch.

"I need him awake. I need his command codes." His companions did not speak. "Watch him. If he wakes, get the codes, then kill him."

He swept out, the door hissing behind him as if it was annoyed, too.

Hel lifted his lids a fraction, careful to keep the movement slight.

What he saw sent a different jolt of shock through him.

☼

Something in her neutral gaze awakened a sense in Halliwell that he'd been here, doing this with her. She knew Briggs, knew Donovan. She kind of reminded him of Donovan, he realized. Maybe that's what he remembered. She had the same air of not expecting much from those around her. And he could see why people called her Morticia. All that long, dark hair and pale skin, not to mention a butt load of creepy.

That she didn't like the Major made her smarter than he'd thought. That Briggs trusted her helped some. He may not know her mission, but he could guess: alien weapons.

It was the reason they were still here. He didn't know why her handler thought she could succeed where their top scientists had failed. He'd come, postponed his retirement, for one reason: to protect his people. They'd stumbled into the war with the Dusan. This one could be avoided.

His official orders were to defend the outpost and to aid in negotiating peace with the Gadi. Nothing could make peace happen now. The reason Giddioni had held off attacking this long was his hope that the Key would return. The Key had stayed put. Once the Leader knew, the peace would be over. He couldn't risk his people with a commander who didn't know the issues and might waste lives holding out for the impossible. For two long years the scientists had claimed they were close to cracking the technology. Some of them had admitted they'd made no progress at all—the ones who knew the Gadi meant business this time. The others were too stupid to live, which wouldn't stop him trying to save their lives.

"Sir, the Gadi fleet is the least of your problems." She turned to his built-in HUD, but paused. "May I show you something?"

He nodded, though he knew the movement was short and sharp, suspicious.

She pulled a keyboard toward her and started typing, her fingers creepy fast on the keys. The screen resolved into a map of the galaxy. She typed some more and ships popped out in places there weren't supposed to be ships. One of them lurked behind the Kikk moon, but the others were close enough to hyper-jump into weapons range without a lot of fuss or time. The deployment looked a like the one he'd used against the Dusan.

"What the hell?"

Briggs leaned forward, too, exchanged a worried look with him.

"These ships are from a planet called Keltinar. It's in a dwarf galaxy about 300 million miles from here. What you need to know right now, what you need to understand, is that these ships have better armaments than both us and the Gadi."

He stared at her, tried to think of something to say except "what the hell?" and couldn't.

"What are they waiting for?" Briggs wanted to know. It was a good question. And then he answered it himself. "They're waiting for us to fight it out with the Gadi. Then they'll pick off the survivors."

"That was my take on them as well," she said.

"Why am I finding this out now?"

"Well, I have been unconscious, sir."

Right. To hell with his orders. "We can start the evacuation. Leave." Something on her face sent a chill down his back. "What?"

"That might trigger an attack. Their leader has been aboard this ship for several hours and—"

"What?" The word came out as roar this time.

She tapped some more and pulled up video from the security cameras. It showed a tall, primitive-looking type in the infirmary.

"His name is Vidor Shan, and he claims to be a local trader needing medical care. He's not."

"How do you know this, Doctor?"

"That would come under the heading of hard to explain or prove, sir."

The screen split into some kind of scan, life signs but something else. His ship, people on his ship, but showing some kind of contamination.

"He's tagged six of the women he's come into physical contact with. Used an alien compound. If he can punch through our shields he could track and transport them, and we'd be leaving people behind."

He felt his gut jerk. He didn't leave people behind. His head buzzed. He shook his head to clear it. "How could you know this? You've been awake, what, an hour? Less?"

Her gaze met his, a look in them that didn't track with what he knew of her, what he'd felt at their last meeting. Something was different about her. She was the same, but not.

"I'm one of the women he tagged." A hint of color stained her pale cheeks. She shrugged. "Apparently creepy doesn't put him off. It should. So he's clever but not smart."

He fought back the impulse to crack a joke about the Major and a sense of humor. What struck him with blunt force was the realization of how young she was, when she let her creepy shell go down. She was...lovely. If this man wanted women, of course he'd want her. That she didn't know this surprised him almost as much as what she'd just told him.

"How did you know you'd been tagged?" Briggs asked the question, his tone mildly curious.

It was the question Halliwell should have asked. Her answer was another kick in the gut.

She turned her palm up and beads of light rose out of her skin.

"How the hell did you get nanites?"

Her gaze slammed into his, a look in them that left him winded and baffled.

"You gave them to me, sir."

"What?" He felt stuck on roar.

"I'm aware you don't remember it, but you did it to save my life. I'd like to return the favor."

"I saved your life?" He tried to sound outraged, angry, anything but what he felt. "And when did I do that?"

"Two days from now. In another timeline. Which brings us to the things that I don't have a hope in hell of proving."

☼

Doc wasn't surprised to be confined to her quarters. Wasn't shocked she'd been escorted there by four, very well armed jarheads. It wasn't enough of a guard, but Halliwell couldn't know that. This Halliwell lacked critical experience with Doc. He'd weathered each information blow pretty well, considering how crazy she sounded. At some point, Doc had felt a shift in him, a point he started to believe her, even though he didn't want to.

Briggs had blinked a couple of times and grinned when she told them there was a bond between her and the Gadi Leader. She didn't mention it was a marriage bond. Doc did necessary dangerous things, but she had a strict policy against waving red flags at angry bulls with the power to order her shot. At the end, the General started thinking again. She'd give him time to come to terms with it all, time to come to her conclusions. If he didn't, well, the jarheads outside her door couldn't stop her leaving this room, this ship, if she had to.

Some part of the General must know he had limited ability to stop her. He was one of few people who did know what the peeps could do. He'd known it when he'd grilled her about their options. And he'd still sent her to her room. Did that mean he trusted her or that he wanted her to go off book? She couldn't read his mind, so she decided to read her email. Someone had tried to lock her out. They couldn't. They'd tried to get into her email, too, she noticed. Couldn't do that either.

She had an email from the Major. Didn't want to read it. If she survived, she'd send him a resignation. If she didn't, he'd get the memo. The email from Sara she opened.

It was chatty and fun. She'd been to see the new *Star Trek* movie. It was about an alternate time line and how crazy was that, but also very fun.

Fun. Yeah, Doc was having a hilarious time.

She rubbed her face, managed to craft a response that didn't include a wail of anguish. Curious, she pulled up their emails for the last two years. It was a relief to find them much as she recalled. At least that hadn't changed.

She closed down her email and turned to her room. It looked like she remembered, devoid of personal details that gave people insights into who she was. She opened a cabinet and found her weapons. Did that mean she'd gone down to the outpost without them? That wasn't like her if she had. On the upside, she could put them on now. She stopped at the visible ones. Not part of the plan to get shot by a jarhead.

With some reluctance, her brain circled and landed on the subject of Hel. It had been hard to explain events to someone who knew her. How hard would it be to convince him if he didn't know her? The *ma'rasile* mark itched. Was that from missing him, or from wanting proximity? It had gotten more defined with every light year the Gadi ships got closer to the outpost, but now the ships appeared to have paused a hyperjump away, just like Conan's ships. Would there be a last diplomatic effort or was this the prelude to battle?

Whatever it was, the General was out of time.

As if he'd heard her thoughts, she got her summons back into his presence. What it meant that she still had an escort she didn't know.

☼

She was too well informed, knew stuff she shouldn't. *Donovan trusted her.* Briggs agreed it was crazy, but crazy didn't make it bogus. She hadn't been near Miri's lab. He'd checked. She hadn't been on the outpost long enough to do much of anything before she'd collapsed into a still medically unexplained coma. The thoughts of any kind of link with Giddioni made him want to hit something. The thought he might be a prisoner on his own ship helped. But none of it solved the basic problem.

If she was right and this Vidor Shan character could pluck the tagged women off his ship, then he had a problem. He couldn't leave. He couldn't stay. His only way out was with Gadi help and that was a long shot. She hadn't sugarcoated any of it, he'd give her that. They were in a tough spot, even if the Gadi came down on their side again. They'd expect access, possibly a complete withdrawal from the galaxy by the expedition. His bosses would be pissed. Good thing he was retiring after this deployment.

Asking the Gadi for help made his gut burn, no question about that.

He looked up as the doors slid back, the SO detail delivering the Doc back for round two. He used the power of his eyes while he waited for the detail to leave the room. This appeared to amuse her for some reason. He thought about calling her on it, but there was no time. If the Gadi attacked before contact could be made, they were screwed.

"Why do I have the feeling you have a plan, Doctor?"

"I always have a plan, sir."

When she laid it out, Halliwell almost couldn't find his voice to ask the question. "You go in alone? That's your plan?"

"Yes."

It wasn't right.

"Anyone you could send would just slow me down." She almost smiled. "I require a high level of autonomy. It allows me to be functionally flexible, and I don't have to explain anything I don't have time for."

"You shouldn't be alone."

"I'm always alone."

Some emotion, and not a good one, flickered in her eyes before she masked it.

"If it can be done, I'll do it. If I can't do it, it can't be done."

It was arrogant, the words were arrogant, but her tone was resigned.

"How long…" He trailed off, not knowing how to ask her when he should give up on her.

"The impossible takes a little longer, but if the Gadi start shooting real missiles…" She finished with a shrug, too fatalistic for someone so young.

"What if Vidor Shan tracks you?"

"The phase cloak should block his tracking capability."

He made one last try. If he could get Shan off their back, he'd retreat without hesitation. "Donovan was able to affect Gadi systems using her nanites. If you got on board Shan's ship, couldn't you do that, too?"

"The nanites were designed to aid in first contact, but Vidor Shan is from a different galaxy, with different tech. It will take time for my nanites to learn to talk to their tech. And if the Gadi attack before I take him down…" She gave him a sympathetic look. "I did consider all possible variables. This is the one with highest probability of success. And it's not that high."

If having her board the Gadi flagship alone and trying to convince Giddioni she'd met him in another reality was their best hope for survival, they were screwed.

Twenty-One

Doc didn't let it go to her head when she was able to board Hel's flagship with no discernible problems. Fate could pull the rug out later. And the law of unintended consequences was sure to have a go at her, too. She spiked into their systems with no muss and no fuss. Her peeps were as curious as she was. All that time in a test tube.

They were sentient. She'd always known it, but had to ask when she was about to put her life on the line again. Lucky for her there were only three defined personalities, one per test tube. If all of them had been individually sentient, the vote might have taken too long. They'd worried they were bothering her until she pointed out she'd always had multiple personality disorder.

I'm always alone, she'd told the General, but this time the peeps had her back in a way no human could or would. They'd taken to the phase cloak like ducks to water and adapted something similar for her personal use. It wasn't a total phase, because she didn't want to accidentally shoot out of the ship into hard space from say, firing a weapon. Actions always had reactions.

Each light year closer to the Gadi flagship had eased the itching around her marriage tattoo. That had stopped when she'd come aboard. Hel was on this ship and he was close. He had enough surviving nanites to achieve a minimal connection with hers and together they made her a map. That he still had nanites gave her some hope he might remember her, though she'd been unable to communicate with him. Doc was eager to see him and terrified like she'd never been terrified before and that included her thirty year battle with *them*.

Would she be stuck in limbo, forever bonded to a man who didn't want her, who maybe had never wanted her?

She finished gearing up, and the peeps made her a hole in the phase cloak. She stepped out into a little-used storage bay. No surprise it was pretty. Their garbage compactor was probably pretty. Also no surprise it was empty. That had been the plan.

Doc carried a stun hand weapon, had a stun rifle strapped across her back. Was packing some doubles for Hel. Also had some projectile weapons, but it didn't seem like a good idea to go in shooting-to-kill when her mission was semi-diplomatic. It was a pity that the future weapons had disappeared when the creeps messed with them.

It was easy to avoid contact with the crew on the first few decks, but as she got closer to Hel's location, crew contact increased exponentially, though the people she saw looked more like goons and mercenaries. And they weren't that pretty.

There was no guard outside Hel's room, which felt wrong. The door was secured, not a problem for her peeps. Three life signs inside. Doc pulled an extra ray gun and prepared to drop cloak. Her peeps popped the lock. She stepped over the threshold. Saw two guards, weapons pinging on the open doorway and puzzled looks on their seriously goon-like faces. These two were not Gadi. They made the mistake of looking at each other when the door slid closed again. Doc dropped cloak. Then she shot them.

Hel lay unmoving on the bed. Her wrist tingled as she moved closer, the mark turning intensely silver, a mini *ma'rasile* dance of joy? He had a setup attached to his arm that looked much like the one he'd used on her when she was sick on his ship in the other timeline. If they were sedating him, she hoped it didn't take long to get him alert again. She reached out to shut it off.

Arms closed around her.

Her feet left the decking.

Her back slammed against the bed.

A long, strong body pinned her down.

She could have put up more of a fight, but her body liked being flattened into the soft mattress by Hel, it liked the feel of him, the smell of him and wanted to taste him right now. His hands shackled her wrists, holding her arms above her head, igniting a now familiar system meltdown.

"You are a female."

No sign of recognition in his face or eyes. It was kind of embarrassing she was still turned on. Though he wasn't completely indifferent either. It took all she had to keep her face blank and calm. There were several smart ass retorts she could have made, but she didn't. "Yes."

"You are an assassin."

"No."

"I do not believe you."

Doc looked for changes in his face. Other than the dislike and suspicion, which was new, he seemed the same. She felt an odd desolation quiver in the center of her chest. He didn't recognize her. He didn't like her. Hello, law of unintended consequences. Maybe she could hook up with a new law. This one wasn't working that well for her.

A frown pulled his brows together.

"Why are you here?"

Did he sound a bit less hostile? Or was she hoping he was less hostile?

"The General sent me."

"You jest."

"I never jest about the General. He doesn't like it." She wanted to close her eyes and inhale him back into her soul. His face loomed over her, his mouth was so close his breath puffed against her skin. The edges quivered, as if her comment amused him. She tried to calculate the distance, tried to use math and science to get some emotional distance but proximity to him had put key processes offline.

His leg hooked over hers, though she'd made no attempt to free herself. She shifted against him, though not in flight or fight. In the back of his eyes, tiny flames flickered and steadied. She didn't read anything into it. He was a guy, and she was technically a girl. Her heart pounded against his, but he didn't seem worried. Maybe he thought she was scared. This Hel didn't know how dangerous she was. Or that fear wasn't her primary emotion around him.

He didn't know her.

But their bodies did, hers knew him right down to her DNA, and not just because she was his *ma'rasile*. If she didn't get black ops girl back online, bride might derail the mission. No matter how lovely it felt to be with him in this bed, it wasn't a good idea to consummate her marriage to a man *who **freaking** didn't remember her.*

The tough talk, the mental shout, helped. Fortunately her DNA had a little pride left.

"Why would the General send you here, except to kill me?"

"That would be a waste of resources."

He frowned. "I do not understand."

"Well, isn't that your cousin's plan? Take your ship, your position, your life?" She gave a small shrug. "I would be redundant."

His body jerked, his gaze narrowed to sharp points. "What do you mean?"

"Your cousin, Glarmere, is running things, isn't he?"

"How could you know this?"

Doc couldn't help it. She'd learned it from him. Her mouth curved into a smile meant to be provocative. "I know a lot of things I shouldn't."

He almost smiled, but caught himself in time. Did that mean her Hel was in there somewhere? He could be pissy over being imprisoned. That would make her pissy.

"Why are you here?"

"To ask you a question."

"You sneak onto my ship, shoot my guards, risk your life to ask me a question?"

It did sound a little crazy when he put it like that. His body shifted, removing all doubt he was unaffected by her proximity. Doc tried not to let it go to her head.

"I might have two questions." His brows pulled together in what could be the start of a frown, so she added, "What? It's not like you have something else to do right now."

That stopped the frown in its tracks. His body shook with the chuckle he refused to allow past his lips.

"What is it that you wish to ask me?"

Doc stared at him for a fifteen count, because he was being a bit of a jerk. "Just wondered if you'd like help taking back your ship?"

He tensed. "You have an assault force waiting on your ship?"

"No."

He was off her in a move so sudden and graceful, she was impressed. And he took her two ray guns in the process. That was the second time he'd taken weapons from her. But since it was in two different time lines, it wasn't a habit yet. And she'd let him take them, so technically he hadn't taken them. Doc straightened slowly into a sitting position. Now was not the time to get shot with one of her own guns. She curled her feet under her.

It looked relaxed. It wasn't.

His expression was assessing, a bit amused. It reminded her of her Hel in the infirmary when he had tried to figure her out.

"Your General sent one woman to assist me."

She shrugged.

He looked amused, but not convinced. "So General Halliwell returned with the *Doolittle*. I wondered if he would. And the Key?"

She shook her head.

"This I expected."

Doc felt a stab of jealousy. He'd wanted the Key for more than her unlocking capabilities. Had he ever wanted her?

"Miri's Key will never return to this galaxy." Her voice had a bit of an edge to it. Not a surprise, since this was her first time in the jealous zone, well, in this timeline. She might have been jealous of Hel's first wife. That part of her brain that was always curious, moved in to study this with scientific detachment. The rest of her was glad to hand it off to the study department. It wasn't pertinent to the situation. And it was a bit embarrassing.

His gaze hooded. "Then we have no reason not to take back what is ours."

Doc slid her legs free, letting them hang off the edge of the bed, the shift in her center of gravity, not visible to the human eye. "That's not exactly true. I can think of two reasons for you to rethink your strategy."

One of the guards moaned. Hel didn't take his gaze off her as he fired on one, then the other. Their bodies jerked as the blast hit them. Something about them bothered her, her frown deepening as she connected the dots.

"You waste your sympathy on them." His tone was politely scornful. "Their function was to persuade me to surrender my command codes when I awoke."

"Are they Dusan?" If one needed someone tortured, the Dusan were the go-to guys for that.

"A few of them survived the battle."

If they were wired like the others had been, they could expect company soon.

"Does the Council know who your cousin's friends are?"

He checked the ray gun settings and shot her a look. "You should have killed them."

"I wasn't sure it was an operational necessity. And my presence is sort of diplomatic."

"Diplomatic?" His open skepticism didn't bother her. His inability to truly *see* her did.

She had to stop reacting to him, she realized. This mission, this moment needed the Chameleon; it needed the Major's creature. Somehow she had to find her way back to the person she'd been before she met him. It was just another role, another persona to put on. She could do this.

"The General wishes to form a new alliance for our mutual benefit and survival."

Hel stared at for several long moments, and then he threw his head back and laughed.

It was a first for Doc. He done many things in her presence, but laughing wasn't one of them. She almost forgot to be Chameleon as warmth and charm softened the arrogant lines of his face. No surprise he had a lovely laugh, a beautiful sounding laugh. He did everything well—except getting a clue.

But the Chameleon could get past that.

When he sobered, he wasn't Hel. He was his people's Leader, a man of power bringing it to bear on her. He leaned in, his voice soft but lethal. "We do not need anything from your expedition but your departure from our galaxy."

Doc shrugged on black ops and bumped it up with Chameleon on top of her game, let it settle in place while she had a short stare down with this Leader.

"I can see why you'd think that."

A flare of pupils was his response to her changed mien, but she knew he was on full alert. He had her ray guns, so he thought he had the upper hand.

"Since your systems are unable to detect the sixteen alien vessels that have invaded this galaxy of course you'd think you're still the dominant force in the galaxy. Only you aren't. The alien vessels can kick you and your fleet's collective asses with half their weapons tied behind their backs."

Several thoughts flashed through his eyes. Doc didn't need to see them to know what they were. He feared they'd unlocked the tech on Kikk. He suspected a trick, a trap, a ruse to stave off their attack on the expedition ships. And he was worried she might be telling the truth.

Doc offered him an olive branch, though a small one. "We managed to upgrade the scanning capability of the available technology."

Relief was fleeting, distrust not so much.

"The alien ships are from a dwarf galaxy about 300 million light years away, specifically from a planet called Keltinar. Based on their current deployment, we believe they plan to wait until we've had our battle, hoping your numbers will be depleted—which they would be—making their ultimate victory that more certain."

"Your ships could withdraw."

No indication whether he believed her in the flat calm of his voice.

"That was the plan. General Halliwell isn't in love with the idea of saving your ass again." It was provocative, but he deserved it. "But the leader of these ships infiltrated the *Doolittle*, disguised as a simple galactic trader, and tagged some of our people. General Halliwell's concerned that if we try to leave, these ships will breach our shields and take our people. As you know, we don't leave our people behind." Did he know this? Or was that a last timeline thing?

"People?"

"Women. He managed to tag six women before we were able to limit his access."

His stare was long, his thought process unclear.

"He tagged *you*."

"Yes." He'd given her the perfect lead-in for his next surprise.

"This is why your General sent you here? Did he hope I could be manipulated by a woman?"

It was Doc's turn to laugh. "You think I came here to ask you to rescue *me*? Not bloody likely."

Okay, it was good he didn't know he'd rescued her once already.

"And excuse me, but aren't you the one currently locked

in a room on your own flagship? And wasn't I the one who breached *your* security, opened *your* locked door and took out *your* guards?"

Not her brightest diplomatic moment, but still satisfying. He looked disconcerted, and then he surprised her by grinning.

"But thanks to you, that is a temporary situation." His face shifted to something that hovered between Leader and Kalian. "Why did General Halliwell send *you*?"

Doc tensed. She couldn't help it. Moment of truth time did that to her. She'd never jumped into anything slow—in this time-line—so she yanked her sleeve back and held up her arm.

"Look familiar?"

He took the hit with a sight widening of his eyes and a little loss of color.

"You've been unconscious for five of what we call space days."

He didn't move. Didn't blink. Impressive. He was like the male version of her. No wonder the General didn't like her.

"So have I. Our return to consciousness was triggered by our coming back into closer proximity to each other."

"How is this possible?" His voice was hoarse and not in a happy way.

Had she expected him to grab her and plant one on her? Maybe. Hoped anyway. She was pathetic.

"It's a long story. And while we're sitting here chatting, your cousin is preparing to attack the expedition. If he fires on the *Doolittle*, there will be no alliance. The General will assume I've failed in my mission. Which will start another war for your people, though this one will be shorter, since you're seriously out-gunned by Conan."

"Why should I trust you, trust this information?"

Doc waved her arm at him. "Hello. If you die, so do I."

"You are a woman. That is worse than no help."

She might have to kick his ass. But would that kick hers? Just how close was their connection? Maybe a little demo was in order.

On her internal HUD, her peeps flagged three bogeys closing on their position. She mentally initiated Plan A—she'd never needed Plan B but always had one—and worked out her timing.

When the bogeys were five seconds from the door, she shifted her gaze over his shoulder.

He half-turned, realized it was trick and stopped the move, his hand tightening on the trigger.

One second of displaced focus, but that's all she needed.

Bright light tracked toward where she'd been.

She hit him midsection.

They went down and Doc made sure he was on the bottom this time. And that she got her weapons back.

She flicked both to "kill" settings and rolled to the side as the door slid open.

Three shots. Three kills.

Nice of them to fall back so her peeps could shut the door.

Hel was still staring at the door when she put the knife to his throat.

"Still think I'm better than no help?"

No surprise his voice was a bit constricted. "I may have been hasty in my judgment." A pause. "If you kill me, you will die as well."

She knew that. She was just making a point. Doc lifted the knife off his throat, spun it easily between her fingers and sheathed it.

He looked at her, really looked at her. He didn't see the woman he'd unleashed yet, but he saw her as a person and not just an annoying female. It was progress of a sort.

His hand ran down her back and came to rest on her butt. Heat flared in his blue eyes. "Have we mated?"

It was either kick his ass or jump his bones. Doc jumped to her feet instead. Called it Plan C.

He followed her up in a move as graceful and fast as her own.

"What are you called?"

She looked away to hide another flash of pain. He couldn't help it. It wasn't his fault. That damn law of unintended consequences.

"Doc. People call me Doc." She needed to be content with what she had. The peeps kept *them* at bay, keep her mind clear and orderly unless they decided to leave, too. She almost laughed at herself. She was the toughest, bad-ass coward she knew.

"And what do *I* call you?" He stepped close, his body heat against her back, his breath against the side of her neck. Was this a real move, real interest, or something else? She wanted real, but he didn't trust her and she couldn't trust him. Not now, maybe not ever again. It didn't matter, it couldn't matter. She owed him. He'd saved her life. She'd find a way to save him, to save the *Doolittle* and then she'd find a way to free him from their so-called marriage. She owed him that, too.

"A pain in the ass?" How ironic. In the other timeline, Hel had known her name and she'd kept it from Conan. Now Conan knew more of her name than Hel.

Somewhere Fate was laughing its ass off.

☼

Hel fought against the uncomfortable sensation that somehow he had disappointed this woman. Why should he care? She was his *ma'rasile* by accident, not by choice. It shocked him how freely she shared her weapons with him, that she turned her back on him with no evidence of unease. If he ended her life, he would die as well, this was true, but he would keep his eyes on *her*. Trust did not come easily to him and trusting a woman? As this one had said, not bloody likely.

She adjusted the straps that secured her weapons, and he realized he was not suffering by having to watch her. There was strength in her, an innate grace that pleased, and she wore danger as easily as she wore her military uniform.

He liked danger. He loved women. As Kalian, he would not be her reluctant mate, but as Leader? She would not fit their ways, any more than the Key would have. In many ways she recalled the Key to his mind. Both were cool and confident, but with some deep sorrow in their core that he sensed, rather than saw. She hid everything that mattered to her. She was not just dangerous, but she was, Hel suspected, one who attracted danger. Or was it that she sought it out? It was not a good quality in a mate.

He wished to take her to bed, not to take his bridge with her at his back.

A memory, more felt than seen, tried to break free of restraint in his mind, but couldn't. Was she part of what he sensed he'd forgotten? How could she have any part in his life when they'd never met, when they'd had no chance to meet? She was his *ma'rasile.* This still astonished him. Despite what he felt, this was a truth he could not escape. He'd felt his strength return, felt the itching ease around the mark about the time she'd come onboard his ship. In this she did not lie. Somehow, some way, a permanent bond had been forged between them.

A long story.

He wished to hear this story, but first he would take back his ship.

"What is the cost of your *help* in taking back my ship?"

"We work together to defeat Conan and his boys, to protect your people and mine."

"My fleet helps your two ships in exchange for what?"

"Access to the outpost?"

Her diplomatic skills were poor. Or she knew this would never be acceptable to him.

"Control of the outpost." He would settle for no less than their due.

She shrugged. "The General likes the idea of joint access."

Since Halliwell did not like anything, he doubted this.

"We will allow you the access given us the past two of your years." He let his disdain show. "And now I suppose you will withdraw your assistance."

The look in her eyes was impossible to decipher.

"You suppose wrong."

"Because you are my *ma'rasile*?"

"No." Her tone invited him to drop the discussion. She started to turn away from him.

He grabbed her arm, forced her to look at him. "Why would you help me except to save your own life?"

Her chin lifted. "That's my business."

"If I am to trust you, you will make it mine."

Her lips tightened and he thought she would refuse him.

"I owe you one, okay?"

He frowned. "I do not understand."

"I pay my debts."

"What debt could you owe me?"

"It's part of that long story. If we survive, maybe I'll tell you."

Her tone said, probably not.

"And if we try and die?"

She shrugged. "Everyone dies." An odd look altered her face. "Living is the hard part."

In his head he heard a voice pleading with someone to live, to fight. His voice? Even as he thought this, the voice faded into that closed place in his mind.

"Is there a plan?" He must clear his head, his thoughts, and focus on the task at hand.

Her sudden grin hit him like a blow.

"I always have a plan."

That was not what he'd meant. He'd assumed General Halliwell was at the helm of this move, but this woman would be hard to steer. There were clues her mind was unusually agile. Curiosity and his attraction to danger had gotten him into trouble more times than he could, or would count, but he was unable to cure the addiction to both. Still, he was a man. Men did not ask. He arched his brows. It was an acceptable compromise.

"You're such a guy."

But she did not look displeased. He thought she bit back another grin. Perhaps it was just as well she held it back. The sight of it made him feel strange and unsettled. If he were to wrest control from his cousin, he needed to be settled. He did not know what to expect from her, but what she did was not something he could expect.

She turned her palm up and a schematic of his ship appeared above it. It spun in the air between them.

"We're here." This place on the layout lit up, painted in red. "Your bridge is here, isn't it?"

The proper place lit up. "Yes." How did she manage this… magic?

"I've already messed with your surveillance cameras so no one can see us once we leave this room—the feed on this room is running on a loop so your cousin thinks you're still sleeping by the way—and I've closed off all access to the bridge except for this route—" It lit up on the hologram. "Locked down access in or off the ship and disabled all transport devices. Oh, and cut off communications." She looked at him. "Did I miss anything? Any system they can use to come after us?"

"Can you disable bridge controls?" He wasn't sure if it was a serious question. Surely she jested about this?

"Did that with the lockdown. Don't want them starting a war without us." She paused, then added, "Why hasn't he attacked yet?"

"He has…had control of this ship, but cannot order the other ships to attack without my command codes." This was not strictly true. If the other ships' commanders had been co-opted, and they took back the outpost, the Council might forgive their action—if they didn't find out Glarmere had used Dusan mercenaries. All who knew this would have to die in "battle."

"Right." Her gaze flicked to the goons Glarmere had assigned to persuade him to surrender those codes. He could not fault her timing. "I can see why you were playing possum."

He did not know this word, but forgot to ask what it meant when her expression shifted.

"What?"

"Nothing." She shifted her shoulders as if she were uncomfortable. She turned back to the hologram, as if she sought to deflect more questions.

Life signs were added to the schematic.

"What's the mix of friendly to unfriendly along our route?"

He might have looked puzzled.

"How can I tell who is on your side? Don't want to shoot the wrong people."

He considered this, studying her hologram carefully. "It appears that all that support me have been confined." Glarmere had brought his support onboard with him. He'd brought Dusan mercenaries onto his ship. "My cousin's forces number sixty. We are outnumbered. Perhaps you wish to reconsider your participation."

Her brows shot up. "That's not outnumbered. That's an opportunity to excel."

He frowned, the question coming from deep inside. "Who are you?"

"I'm their worst nightmare." She pointed at life signs that were now highlighted in red. "So those are the bad guys?" He nodded. "And you're okay with shoot to kill? Cause I hate leaving bad bogeys behind me. They have a nasty habit of popping up when I least want them to."

"I, too, prefer not to leave enemies at my back." She would have made an excellent Ojemba. The sense he'd said these words, or thought them before, got lost before it could fully form.

"Does this plan work for you, Leader?"

"It is acceptable. You will do what I tell you."

She looked more curious than annoyed. "Why do you get to be in charge?"

"This is my ship." Her mouth moved as if to open. Instead she bit her lip. Heat flared in his midsection. "You have something to say?"

"Not anything I haven't already said."

He might have been a prisoner, but it was her fault. He

grabbed her wrist and turned it over. Knew he was not himself, but couldn't hold back the words, the worry behind them. "This weakened me."

Expression, all hint of warmth and life, drained from her face, like blood from a mortal wound. He looked into her eyes for signs of pain and found worse than pain. He found nothing.

"When this is over, I want a divorce."

Why did it feel as if he'd killed something that mattered to him? "Divorce?"

"You gone from my life. For good."

"That is impossible. The bond is permanent."

She checked her projectile weapon, with deadly decisiveness, angled it so it was pointed down but ready to deploy. Her voice was icy cold. "The impossible just takes longer. Let's get this over with. I'll catch your six, *Leader*."

He knew he should say something, but did not know what. Instead he turned to the door. It slid back for him. He took a quick look out.

"Our path is clear." He stepped out.

"Got three bogeys, next corner." She shifted to his side to clear her sight line.

He wondered how she knew this, but lacked time to ask. He brought his weapon up and the three "bogeys" went down without firing a shot. He paused, frowning. He'd heard this sound before, the soft pop, followed by the thud of a body hitting the ground.

"Is there a problem, Leader?"

He shook his head, tried to shake the weight off his heart. It refused to go. He'd been…not himself. If they were to die…

He looked back, but down, not able to look into the chill of her blue eyes. "It was unworthy of me to blame you for this."

Silence greeted his words. He forced himself to look at her. There were signs of a thaw, though it tightened the vice in his chest to see wary so dominant in her eyes. They'd flared with lavender he remembered now, when he'd lay on top of her in the bed behind them. Nothing flared in them now.

She half-shrugged. "I'm used to it."

She shouldn't be. He wished to say more, to make things right between them again, but was not sure it was possible. It had been wrong since she arrived, and he feared this was also his fault.

"We should hurry. At some point, your cousin has to notice he isn't in control of *your* ship."

Doc felt the shift when Hel apologized but shoved it to a brain stream off the front line. Felt a bit Scarlet O'Hara about deciding to think about it later. That was new. If she'd ever compared herself to a fictional character—and she hadn't—she wouldn't have expected it to be Scarlet. Of course, this was an altered timeline.

Glarmere knew they were coming, despite or because of Doc's spanners in his works. He threw what he could at them. Put someone onto trying to break her hold on the ship's systems. They were pretty good, but they didn't know what they were up against. She'd been focused on many things since going nova with the peeps, but even with her mind running multiple data streams, she had time to feel their power flowing in, around, through her and this ship. The feeling of power wasn't unfamiliar. Her track record of doing the impossible had made her arrogant. Events in the other timeline had dented arrogant, but falling in love with Hel had changed her in ways she was still trying to process.

The power was nice, the ability to basically toy with Glarmere was nice, too, but none of it satisfied when put up against what she'd lost. All those peeps in her system made her more, not less, aware of her humanity in a way she'd never felt before. All the things she could do only made her more aware of what she couldn't do, what she couldn't have. Watching Hel's six didn't help either. Maybe she should have insisted on taking point. Mental whining depressed her and the peeps, so she pushed it off the front line, too.

They had about one hundred yards left to navigate. Now she was deep enough into the ship's systems to sense Glarmere's attempts to take back control. Not that he was doing it himself.

He had people for that.

"Your cousin's an asshole," she said, as a large Dusan mercenary tried to get his tree limbs around her. The bigger they were, the harder they went down. This one made a dent in the decking when he face-planted into it. It should have taken her three moves to take him down, not one. Had the peeps boosted her physically, too? She rubbed the blood from the side of her mouth. She'd caught the edge of his fist as he went down. It healed as her fingers wiped the blood away.

She caught Hel staring at her.

"What are you?"

Okay, that hurt. Her chin lifted. "Your cousin's worst nightmare." Her peeps gave her a heads up. "He's trying to lock us out of the bridge."

Someone was trying to cut controls through the panels. She had C-4. They could blow the door, but it was a delay they couldn't afford. Doc sprinted to the door and put both hands on the other side of the wall from Glarmere's only smart goon. Beads of light lit up her arms and hands and then the wall.

"Flash bang in my top pocket, right leg. It—"

"I know what it does."

"Oh, right." He had been on the receiving end of one just before the battle with the Dusan started. "Get ready." Doc's warning was terse. "Toss it when the door pops."

In her mind she saw the goon positioning his cutters on the wiring. Power surged through her, through her peeps and into that wiring. As the metal tip of his cutters connected with the wires, that power went into the goon. The force of it threw him back several feet, knocking down a couple of other goons in the process.

Cause and effect. Had to love them.

The door popped open and Hel tossed in the flash bang. They both looked away, covered their ears. First came the flash. Then came the bang. Then they went in. The results were predictable. Doc put some moaning goons out of their misery in one direction. Hel worked in the other direction. They met in front of the command chair. The man crouched in it, his eyes spinning in the sockets and reeking from voided bowels, wasn't too pretty anymore. Doc wasn't convinced he'd ever been pretty. His eyes were too close together.

"I take it this is your cousin?"

"On my mother's side."

That was pretty defensive. Doc hid a smile. "You can't choose your relatives."

"Just your friends."

There was something in Hel's voice, something new that pulled her attention his way, though not her weapon. She found it in his eyes, too, though she didn't know what it meant. Her life experience had not given her this kind of knowledge. And she didn't have time to learn what it meant.

"We've cleared most of the hostiles. I can release your people and tweak your scanning system before I go."

"Go? Where?"

The sharpness in his voice and the frown were a surprise. She'd have thought he'd want her off his ship ASAP.

"Back to the *Doolittle.*" And then onto the outpost. They needed the ships and enhanced shields before Conan started shooting. Halliwell wanted her to try to unlock it before they brought Hel into that mix. She disagreed with the General and made the mistake of saying it. He'd ordered her not to tell Hel he was a Key.

"You are my *ma'rasile.* You must remain with me."

Okay, not exactly a declaration of love. Not even first cousin to a declaration of love. She pulled out a couple of pairs of flex cuffs. "If you aren't going to kill him I should put these on him."

"I wish him to stand trial for his crimes."

"Right." She quickly secured Glarmere, her peeps helping her out with the smell. "You should have full system control. I've kept the areas with bogeys locked down, but you or your people can access them."

She kept her gaze off Hel, though she knew he watched her, as she went to scan control and pretended to adjust the settings while her peeps did the upgrade. As soon as she finished, warnings blared as it detected the alien intrusion.

"They've shifted into attack position." But they hadn't powered up weapons systems. Were they still hoping the Gadi and expedition would go at it first?

"We are too late?" Hel's voice came from closer than she expected. Warmth bloomed along her back.

"Not yet, but you'll need to attack soon."

"Attack?" His hand on her shoulder turned her to face him. "I thought we were to be allies again?"

Doc waited. Her Hel would get it without the long explanation. He had a wonderfully devious mind. What did this man have?

"We are to pretend to attack as a diversion?"

She couldn't stop the smile any more than she could stop breathing.

"If you start moving your fleet into attack position, that will give us time to deploy small phase cloaked ships, each with a small attack force. We plan to board and neutralize their weapons." If she and her peeps could figure out how do to that in time. She'd be an attack force of one and would go in ahead of the others. Halliwell had wanted her to target any ship but Conan's, but Doc didn't dare. They didn't know how automated their systems were. It was possible he had override authority. And it was always good strategy to go after the top of the command structure.

"You are going on one of these ships."

She looked at him. "If we can't stop Conan, we'll die anyway."

"You plan to go alone. I will go with you. I will catch your six." His smile was wry, a bit crooked for a guy so into perfection.

She'd been hoping he'd say that, though him going with her onto Conan's ship wasn't part of her plan. "And who will mind this store while you're gone?"

"This ship, all our ships have commanders. They will follow

my orders, once they learn Glarmere has brought Dusan mercenaries aboard the Gadi flag ship."

"I don't have time to wait—" Before she finished, his crew began to flood the room. They checked at the sight of the Dusan, their pretty faces unexpectedly grim. The one in the prettiest uniform and with a decided air of command approached Hel.

"Leader. I am pleased to see you are well." His gaze flicked toward Doc, but did not stay there. In addition to pretty, the Gadi were polite.

"You will wait while I brief my commanders." Hel had no problem looking at her, she saw. Just in case she was inclined to protest, he added, "You cannot move freely through this ship without me."

She could, she already had, but she didn't tell him that.

Twenty-Two

Hel angled in the co-pilot seat so he could see his *ma'rasile.* Her skin was smooth and pale, her features flawless. She was younger than he'd first thought and beautiful, despite her military wear. The thick, dark braid hung almost to her hips. When he'd pinned her to his bed, she'd smelled uniquely female, the scent enticing to a man long focused on everything but a woman. Had he thought he would not want her? His temporary detainment must have clouded his judgment. She'd gone quiet since they boarded her ship—he looked around—a Garradian ship that should belong to the Gadi.

"You remember our bonding."

Her perfect lips tightened into a perfect pout. The look she slanted at him was her only response. He began to object, but saw their course. "We are not returning to the *Doolittle?*"

"Not enough time for detours."

He wanted her to look at him. She did not wish to look at him. What did she seek to hide? There were other ways to find out. He watched her closely as he said, "The General wishes me to go with you to the outpost?"

Her lashes flickered. She made some adjustment to ship's controls.

"He ordered you not to tell me what you know."

She kicked up the speed of their descent toward Kikk, the edges of her mouth almost curving up until she stopped them.

"He forgot to say something about not *showing* me the outpost."

She laughed now, the sound a soft caress across his skin. It had more than humor in it. He felt their connection, something beyond the *ma'rasile*.

"I have a knack for finding loopholes when it's an operational necessity," she admitted.

The ship slowed now, moving into a high orbit above the planet. She adjusted the controls and turned to face him.

"You are not going to land this ship?"

"We're running out of time." She hesitated, which was usual for her, he sensed. "I need to—there might not be time later—oh, what the foxtrot."

She leaned in, putting her mouth against his. Fire surged into his veins at the contact, his memory kicking against the closed door. He knew this. He knew her. She pulled back, breaking the contact. He reached for her.

"Good-bye, Hel. And good luck." She hit something on the panel, and he felt transport grab him.

"No—" The light surrounded him, enclosed him and when it receded, he stood alone in stone lined room somewhere in the Kikk outpost.

He should have felt triumph. Instead he felt empty. *Delilah.*

☼

Doc knew when she dropped the cloak to transport Hel, Conan's systems would see the tagging compound and he'd go for her like a barbarian on a bride hunt. Normally, she'd have done all she could to thwart him. Thwarting was good for his character, but they needed to talk, so thwarting would have to be back-burnered. It was no shock when he took the bait. His transport had more of a physical yank than theirs. She felt stun energy try to pierce her peep shield and fail, before she got dropped onto a transport pad on what she presumed was Conan's ship.

She was upright before the transport wash faded, fighting the urge to pull something and shoot. She was alone in the room, though that wouldn't last. He hadn't yanked her here to ignore her.

The peeps dived into the ship's guts, their curiosity a match for hers, while she studied the surface. There wasn't a lot to see. The space was small and sterile. Lots of shiny metal and blinking lights. Not friendly. Not that a warship should be *welcoming*. The *Doolittle* could do big and bad when necessary, but it gave off pragmatic vibes, lived solidly in the functional zone. This place had a seriously hostile thing going, like a gangbanger strutting his stuff outside his hood.

She didn't recognize the writing on the single control station and the data streams flowing across several screens didn't match anything in the Garradian database that the peeps had downloaded into the unused parts of her brain. As expected, they found it alien and fascinating. They loved a challenge. No timeframe on when they'd crack the computers, but she sensed confidence. Of course, they could have caught it from her. She'd always considered overconfidence a strength, but now she wasn't so sure.

There was an exit that had refused to open for her when she circled the room, but now it slid back with an angry hiss. It seemed even the doors had attitude. Conan stalked through it, checking at the sight of her upright and conscious. He pulled his weapon with a speed that might have impressed Wyatt Earp. She wasn't Wyatt Earp.

The weapon was huge like his ship.

Time is persistent.

It seemed size issues were as well.

He'd changed his trader gear for a uniform that tilted toward leather and high-topped boots, but with an official spin. He looked like a cross between a pirate and an early Captain Kirk. He had the "I'm so cool even my poop smells good" walk down pat as he paced toward her, his boots hitting the metal decking in measured beats.

Doc auto-calculated the time to intercept. Helped keep her mind off wanting to kick his ass. He stopped in front of her and smiled. The nurse might have found it charming, sexy even. One of her thought streams started pondering the mysteries of sex and attraction again. On the surface, they had a lot in common. They both liked to shoot people and each other. That was almost two things in common. But not enough to get past the intergalactic differences and the fact she was in love with a guy who couldn't remember her name.

"Doctor Clementyne."

He just had to rub it in, like he sensed it was a sore spot. It brought back wanting to kick his ass. "Captain. Or are you a Commander?"

"There is nothing comparable in Standard for my rank. You will have to call me by my name."

So he still had name issues. This was the point she should think, *interesting*, only it wasn't. His fierce gaze narrowed, the ping tightening like a laser on her face. A slight frown pulled his brows together. His gaze swept up and then down.

"You are a soldier?"

Her answer was half-shrug, half-nod. Hard to deny the obvious.

"But you are a doctor."

She shrugged again.

"I require you to remove your weapons and leave them on the deck."

He thought he had the upper hand. Not as cute on him as it had been on Hel. It went against the grain to give them up without a fight, but he wouldn't answer questions if she took him out and if his automated ship had a dead man's switch, well, that would be bad, too. Now was not a good time to realize just how much she wanted to shoot him for what he'd done in the other timeline. She forced her thoughts into another track so she wouldn't give into the impulse.

She'd figured out some of what was the same between the two timelines—her wanting to shoot him—now she needed to figure out what was different. A big difference was him here and now. Why would he be here? With her and Smith gone from his past, there was no reason for Conan to come to this galaxy, not even for a girl hunt. As she'd previously noted, there were better galaxies to get girls.

That would be one of the things they needed to talk about. So she shed her visible weapons, taking her time, giving it a strip edge that darkened his gaze and hopefully scrambled his brains a bit. Doc wasn't worried about winding him up. She was worried she didn't have it in her to wind him up enough. He'd need to be seriously distracted if he wasn't going to see through the war games ruse.

She watched him through half-mast lashes. So far, the flow of blood away from his head was within expected parameters. And she hadn't flashed any skin yet. She ran the numbers. How long it would take before the Gadi would start the war games? She estimated the time it would take the teams to get to the ships and launch and then board the alien ships and take them down. No matter how she figured it, it was too long for her to keep Conan so distracted he didn't notice it wasn't a real war.

It left her on the high wire, juggling what she didn't know—the peeps couldn't connect to the *Doolittle* through Conan's cloak, so she was working blind—while trying to keep him interested enough to spill his guts. She wouldn't be working from her strengths. A pity she didn't dare shoot him. She was much better at shooting than vamping.

When the last weapon clanked against his decking, he used his foot to shove them away from her. He urged her to back away from the pile with a wave of his big gun. He crouched and picked up her hand gun, studying it with a guy-like interest. When he looked at her, he might have been impressed. She didn't know him well enough to be sure.

"Impressive."

Okay, maybe she did know him well enough. She didn't respond, not even a shrug. It wasn't that she didn't know what to say, it just seemed a waste of time to state the obvious.

He gestured toward the still open doorway with his gun. Looked like he wasn't going to pat her down in this timeline either. She tried to look cowed. Wasn't sure she succeeded. It was a tough look for someone who'd never seen a live cow. She proceeded as directed. His silence, as he followed her through echoing, empty corridors, didn't bother her. Talking was overrated when there was so much to see.

The ship was interesting. She studied all they passed, increasing her data streams to accommodate the input. She felt a kick of memory at the sight of the octagonal hatches, added it to her other observations—no, not *her* memory, but something from the Garradian outpost's database. She flipped through the files as she walked where he directed, somewhat aware of his gaze boring into her back every inch of the way.

Everything about this ship shouted, *I'm a big, bad, very lethal ship.* What it didn't shout was: *I'm a Keltinarian ship.*

The Garradians had documented their trips through the portal, had made observations about the people and surroundings they'd observed on those journeys. It had been a long time since any Garradian had studied Conan's world, but there was always something that a defined civilization clung to, even as they moved forward. Just like the Gadi liked pretty and the Dusan didn't, the Keltinarians had certain design preferences that peeked out here and there, but on this ship they were overpowered by another influence. Her brain found a match: *Saratarius.*

The name meant less than nothing to Doc. The star map did. Saratarius was about twice as far away from the Garradian galaxy as Keltinar—in the opposite direction. How had Saratarian technology found its way to Keltinar?

☼

In other circumstances Hel would have lingered on the outpost. He'd waited long enough to get here, but all he could think about was how to get to Delilah. He knew what she'd done. He knew why she'd done it. He did not like it. They were *ma'rasile.* They worked together now. The time she'd saved was negligible when compared to his ability to assist her. The necessity now was to get to her, to cover her six as she had covered his.

He felt the increase in capabilities as his brain made contact with the nanites, expanding his memory beyond the moment when she'd kissed him. He remembered everything from a past that hadn't happened. His first sight of her at the party. The explosion, her caring for him, her delight with his sons and that strange game they'd played, the way it had felt to hold her, to kiss her. He rubbed at the *ma'rasile* mark. *I'll tell you later*, she'd said. Now, when it might be too late, he heard the suppressed hurt in her voice. She hid many things, but she'd never been able to hide everything from him. They were meant to be together, belonged together, with or without the *ma'rasile.* He'd been slow to recognize what his instincts had told him the first time he saw her. The threat she posed had always been to his heart.

Before they'd gone through the portal that last time, she'd said she loved him. Was it possible this was that Standard word for what he felt, what he'd never expected to feel for any woman? He recalled the look in her eyes, eyes that were expressive for him and no one else. She'd come to him and he'd failed her. How could he have forgotten her when he bore the mark of their bonding? As he thought the question, his nanites provided the answer. There had not been enough of them to protect him from the effects of the time reset. They'd condensed to protect his memories of Delilah, recognizing their importance to him even before he'd known this. Delilah's kiss, combined with unlocking the outpost had boosted the number in his system, had helped him remember *everything.*

He had to get to her before it was too late. She deserved to know the truth, even if she still wanted this divorce that wasn't possible. If they were going to fail, if they were going to die, he wanted to be with her. It was strange to feel the nanites approval for his course of action. They felt alive and separate, but also part of him. He requested and received immediate transport back to the ship they'd used to travel from his flag ship. As soon as he came on board, he heard General Halliwell trying to make contact with Delilah.

He did not know Hel was the one who'd sent instructions on how to access the ships in the hidden bays. He did not know Hel had unlocked the outpost, not Delilah. He did not know it was Hel who'd requested the evacuation of the outpost. If they failed the self-destruct would destroy the outpost. He could not, he would not, allow it to fall into the hands of the enemy. It did not seem wise to disabuse the General of his misperception just before a big battle. If he were annoyed, he would be distracted. While the General did his part, Hel would help Delilah do her "impossible."

The impossible takes a little longer.

He steered the ship onto an intercept course with the alien ship, was unsurprised he could not make contact with her outside the cloak. From the previous timeline, he recalled using his phase cloak to breach the hull of the alien vessel. This should restore communication between them.

On tracking screens, the newly discovered ships rose like small insects from the planet surface, then fanned out to intercept the other alien ships they were not supposed to know were there. What the General didn't know, what Hel could not tell him, was that he'd also discovered a cache of medium-sized, but powerful war ships. What they lacked in weapons, they made up for in maneuverability.

From the outpost, he'd contacted his fleet. Even now, small crews were heading to the outpost to pilot these ships. Invisible to Earth and alien ships, they'd also rise from the planet, also on intercept course with the alien vessels. He prayed they would be in time. Even with them, in a head-to-head battle with the alien vessels, the victory outlook was not certain.

An opportunity to excel, according to Delilah, Hel recalled with a slight smile. There had been a time when he'd been considered a draw a win. Not anymore. It seems he'd been infected with her unwillingness to give ground. Somewhere, while living in two different time lines, he'd started to believe the impossible *was* possible.

☼

They stopped on the bridge. It wouldn't have been Doc's choice as a prisoner destination, but Conan seemed unconcerned as he did his usual stalk to a panel and activated a view screen.

"So you can observe the coming battle," he told her.

It was very Emperor of him, even if he hadn't seen *Return of the Jedi*. Was he trying to depress her? He'd tried that on Feldstar without much success, and it hadn't had plumbing.

"Bet this ship has plumbing."

"Plumbing?" His habitual frown deepened.

"When you've had to do without it, you don't take it for granted."

He looked at her, baffled now dominating his expression. He tried—and failed—twice before he managed, "The Gadi ships will soon be in attack position. They will open fire on your ships."

Doc wanted to say something about his ships in position, but she wasn't supposed to know about them. She sifted through what she wasn't supposed to say or know, looking for something she could say to get the conversational ball rolling. She needed to know why he was here. That meant she had to interrogate him. Since he had that big gun, she'd have to use small talk. She was better with bright lights and water boards. Drugs were good, too, but his ship might not react well to her usual stuff.

She offered, "Nice view."

He frowned. It brought back a lot of memories. None of them good. Doc resisted falling into the Feldstar pattern. She wished she could bust his chops for the lack of originality. This altered timeline stuff was crap. She turned from his baffled gaze to study his bridge.

It was more interesting. Large screens were angled for optimum viewing from his command chair. No crew positions, confirming her single pilot automation thesis. The chair was big, freaking throne big and designed to intimidate. She walked around it, taking her time. Conan got on her six, maybe hoping to close the gap, but Doc knew how to stay out of reach without looking like that was what she was doing. It was a gift.

It still irritated him. "Stand still, woman."

"You stand still."

He stopped, his frown a puzzled one, rather than the irritated one. "You fear me?"

Not bloody likely. "You kidnapped me. You're pointing a gun at me. I'm maintaining a comfort zone."

He looked at the gun as if surprised he still held it. Then he looked at her, as if assessing her threat potential. Doc kept black ops buried deep, though she wasn't stupid enough to try to look harmless. She tried for the middle ground, a place she wasn't that familiar with.

His study of her was unabridged and very male.

"Take off your jacket."

Doc arched her brows. "Are you going to look at my teeth, too?"

The scowl came back. "Is there something wrong with your teeth?"

"There will be if I keep gritting them." She unhooked the front tabs on her jacket, taking her time. Her Gypsy Rose Lee lacked that certain something, but Conan didn't look like he minded, prompting her to ask, "How long have you been on your own on this ship?"

It was need-to-know. If it were as long as she suspected it was, she wouldn't have to work that hard to get his motor running.

"How did you resist the stun in my transport?" he countered. He held his weapon more loosely now, as if he'd lowered her threat level. It seemed he didn't believe his own eyes.

"I'm gifted."

At least he'd quit chasing her around the command chair. It was such a cliché.

She slung her jacket over the arm of his chair, since there was no sign of a coat rack. She met his gaze with a measure of caution—like a bucket load of it. He lowered his chin, his eyes sparking with something she didn't examine too closely, because she didn't want to. There were some things it was better not to know. The tee shirt wasn't snug. That would show off the hand gun strapped low on her back but this one did give away the fact that she had a shape. She was girl, even if she sometimes forgot about it. Her pants were baggy enough to frustrate him, but so far he hadn't tried to get her out of them. She appreciated his restraint.

"Lot of fire power here just to get girls, when all you needed was an email account."

He looked baffled. She wasn't surprised. Intergalactic humor was as different as their tech. Did he even have a sense of humor? Didn't remember seeing one the last timeline, so wasn't holding her breath this one.

"Getting girls, as you put it," he said, trying to narrow the gap between them and failing, "is a side benefit and not the main event."

She nodded to the view screen. "That's the main event."

He nodded, a bit of shrug in the move. He wasn't as good at it as she was.

"I don't understand." That wasn't wholly true, but suspecting was different from knowing.

"Weren't you headed for the Garradian outpost when I intercepted you?"

"You're after the outpost?" Okay, on one level it wasn't crazy. Everyone was after the outpost, so why not Conan. But… "How do you even know about it?"

"Everyone in this galaxy is aware it exists," he pointed out, with more than a hint of male superiority.

Doc studied him for a moment, while she considered her response. "But you're not from this galaxy. Three hundred million light years is a long way to come for a place that barely has the lights on and no welcome mat out."

His gaze narrowed. "How could you know how far I traveled?"

"I told you, I'm gifted. Why would you come so far? What,

you couldn't build one in your galaxy?"

It was his turn to hesitate, before he offered, "It is our right."

Could a Garradian or two have migrated to his planet? Could he be a Key? She was going to have to let him touch her. She needed a DNA sample. Hopefully it wouldn't go to his head. Better for her if his blood headed the other direction.

"Your right? You're not from here." She shifted his direction, hoping it looked accidental and not planned. This girl stuff was so not her skill set. He almost leapt the gap. His hand curled around her wrist. Maybe she didn't need the skill set. Guys like Conan thought everything was foreplay.

"This place, this battle was foretold in our prophecies."

The peeps went in. That was good. He wasn't letting go. That was bad. His gaze pinged on her mouth. If he tried to kiss her, she might lose focus and kick his ass. Be good for his character, but not the plan. A flash of light over his shoulder lit up his view screen.

"It appears the battle has begun."

He spun, maintaining his grip on her wrist, but his gaze pinging on the opening salvos of the war games. It looked pretty real from here, but what would sensors and tracking tell him?

The peeps were still burrowing in, making some headway, but they weren't there yet. It was almost as if the computers knew about peeps and had planned to thwart them.

Conan released his hold on her and sank into his chair. It lit up like a carnival ride. Lots of lethal looking bells and whistles.

"What are you doing?"

"While it would be entertaining to watch," his gaze flicked up and down her body, "I find I am impatient to claim all that is mine."

"If you join this battle, my people will fight with the Gadi."

"But they won't know I'm in it. I'm going to take out your ships' shields, take what I need—" Doc didn't need to be a genius to know he meant the women he'd tagged, "—and let the Gadi eliminate them. And when they stand down to celebrate their victory, we will attack."

As plans went, it was a pretty good one, and he wasn't totally stupid, which meant he'd notice when the *Doolittle* and the *Apollo* didn't blow up from the Gadi fire. And, recalling his temper, it didn't take a genius to figure out what he'd do about it.

☼

Hel's nanites connected with Delilah's as soon as he stepped onto the ship's decking. His instinct was to head for the bridge. The nanites wanted him to go to engineering. Delilah was at the top of this ship. Engineering was near the bottom. Seven decks would separate them.

After a brief mental struggle, Hel turned toward engineering. He could not fault their logic, much as he wished to. If the alien realized the Gadi and the expedition were play fighting, he would leap into the battle. Her nanites had not seized control of the ship's systems, as she'd hoped. They had identified a target in engineering. He'd secured some of their C-4 from Delilah's supplies before leaving her ship. It was a good plan, except for one small problem.

Explosive charges at that point would cause a cascade overload of the FTL drive that would destroy the ship. He could set a timed trigger, but if their ruse was exposed, he would have to initiate detonation. This ship would be destroyed, but the others in the alien fleet would still be battle worthy, and he had no way to let the other teams know of the weakness without getting clear of the still functioning cloak. His chances of making it up to the bridge, freeing Delilah without triggering the dead man's switch, and then making it to their ship and clearing the cloak, not to mention radioing the other teams in time for them to deploy charges, was a level of impossible even Delilah might find challenging.

He could not save her and save his fleet and her people. He could not destroy her, without destroying himself.

His nanites sent the plan to hers. Her answer came back

without even a hesitation.

Do it.

He frowned. He would—with a slight variation.

"Any word from the Doc?" Halliwell asked, though he already knew the answer. He'd been looming over communications since his last, unsatisfying communication with her. Didn't take him long to figure out she'd gone aboard the alien ship by herself. He just wished he thought of it before she did. Then he could have ordered her not to do it. He was going to bust her to private if he got her back on this ship. And that was before the courts-martial and to hell with the Major. He'd find a way to put her ass in jail.

"Something coming in, sir." The COM officer tried not to sound relieved. "It's a secure data burst to us and our teams."

"Can you read it?"

"Running it through decrypt now."

A map appeared on the HUD, with instructions. Halliwell stalked over to it. What it told him made a cold ball form in his gut. His teams had minutes to get onboard the alien ships, deploy charges and get the hell off. And the Doc might have less than that. At least the Leader was on his own ship this time.

"Those ships twitch, I want to know about it," he ordered. Doc thought she'd fixed it so Vidor Shan couldn't transport their people, but that didn't mean he couldn't blow them out of space in the time it took his heart to beat twice.

Doc took the hit internally, no sign on her face that she knew she was going to die. *You've got to try to save him*, she told the nanites. *He has two little boys who need him.* And then, *I'm so sorry I'm taking you with me. If you can get away, now would be the time.*

The thought of doing this without them, of her mind bringing back *them,* was a harder hit than dying, so she didn't fight it when they ignored her. They'd had a lot of years to figure out what they believed, what was right for them. And they knew what they could do and what they couldn't. They had run out of time to take control of the ship. She felt them withdrawing, coalescing inside her again. It was amazingly comforting.

They brought knowledge with them. The ship was a mix of Keltinar and Saratarius tech, but no indication why or how in the ship's databanks that they'd been able to access. And they had Conan's DNA results, too. Those were as puzzling as this ship. Conan had no Garradian DNA, but he did have the DNA string that would let him unlock the outpost. It had to have been added by someone, but who? Who had given them the so-called prophecies? She needed answers and she needed to distract him. The teams needed time to get on and off the other ships in Conan's fleet. It was the only way to save Hel's people and hers.

"Why am I here?" She stepped between him and the view screen, trying for a sexy pose, but not sure she managed it. It was embarrassing, but did get his attention.

"You will be my *ma'rasile.*"

Okay, the fact that he knew that word and what it meant set off enough alarm bells inside her head to qualify for going nova again. This was all wrong. Had someone been hinking with time? Had the time creeps messed up again? It might be the wrong move, but she needed him off balance, angry at her and not thinking about the battle outside.

"That's going to be a problem, *Vidor.* I'm already someone else's *ma'rasile.*" She held up her wrist, so he could see the mark on her wrist. It wasn't itching, which meant Hel wasn't off the ship yet. Damn it, what was keeping him? Her peeps gave her the answer. He'd sent the ship and message out of the cloak without him, planted the charges and—

"In point of fact, the woman belongs to me," Hel said from the open hatch.

—made it to the bridge in record time. Doc let him get away with the chauvinism in his tone because she was so glad to see him—and totally pissed he hadn't left.

Conan spun, his very big gun lifting and firing, before Doc could say or do anything. The beam hit Hel and splattered into millions of tiny lights, defused by the nanites in his system. She gave him a look, erasing it when Conan spun back to her. He grabbed her wrist and studied the now shimmering mark.

"How is this possible?" Conan looked surprised and pissed. It didn't bother her. If she had to be pissed, then he might as well be pissed, too. They could all be pissed together until they died.

"He's gifted, too," she said, her mind already moving on. "What happened to the women in your world?"

But she knew. It was there in the database. The Saratarians were rabidly anti-female. The Garradians who'd observed their culture had predicted its demise from female eradication over the course of several generations unless they modified their behavior. Instead, they'd managed to infect Keltinar.

"Did you forget you need women to have male babies? That little girls grow up to be son producers?"

"It is not your concern, woman."

She got in his face. "It is my concern. You're about to destroy *my* people out there. Why? You don't know how to have a discussion? Make a little diplomacy? You came here packing attitude and big-ass weapons without even thinking about it. We've done nothing to you. Why do you feel the need to blow us to hell and back? How and when did we become your enemy when this is the first time we've met?"

"It is in the prophecy!" He got back in her face. "We come here. We destroy the enemy. We take back what is ours."

"It was never yours! You're from another freaking galaxy! How could it be yours?"

He opened his mouth, closed it, opened it again. "It is in the prophecy."

"Show me. If you're going to destroy my people, I want to see why."

Hel had the detonator switch in his hand, she felt his watchfulness, heard his questions in her head. *What are you doing?*

She couldn't tell him what she didn't know. She was following her gut. It surprised her when Conan complied. His fingers moved on the arm rest and one of the screens came alive with scrolled words. Thanks to her peeps adventures in the ship's guts, she could read Keltinar, at least enough to get the gist of the so-called prophecies.

"What are they?" Hel asked, his gaze still on Conan.

"They're notes, scientific notes."

"Garradian?"

"No." She didn't mention the DNA string out loud. Not good for Conan's character, but Hel plucked it out of her head.

"What's going on?" Hel asked it, Conan looked it.

"I think someone else slipped the time creeps' leash." If they were the good guys, which was hard to believe. How did one go about creating an instability that would attract their attention? Could she already have done it? Time felt wrong, out of synch, messed up. And she felt something else: watched.

She looked up, not because she thought the time creeps were watching from above like God. She just wanted it clear who she was talking to. "Do you hear me? You blew it again!"

Conan started to look relieved they weren't getting married.

"Enough of this, woman. I will do what I came to do."

Do it, Hel. Got a light nod. *How long?*

Five of your minutes. At her mental *crap,* he added, *I thought we might make it off. Sorry.*

Five minutes. She could distract him for five minutes, couldn't she?

"You won't get the portal. If you do this, the portal will be locked forever. He's the true Key and he's made sure you can't get at it." *You did, didn't you?* She got an affirmative, Hel style. She looked up again, yelled at the ceiling. "Do you feel the shiver down your spine, time creeps? If the portal is destroyed, you'll be out of work!"

Four minutes. Had minutes always been this long?

"You seek to deceive me." Conan hit something on his chair. "I will destroy your ships and then you will die, as well."

☼

Halliwell took the news that the alien vessels were going weapons hot with his customary calm. Waiting was always harder than engaging. Damn, he was glad he hadn't retired. Always better to go out fighting.

"Pick a target and prepare to fire all batteries."

He'd sent a data burst through the satellite relay to Earth.

"Gadi ships are going weapons hot as well, sir."

Halliwell hoped to hell they knew who to shoot at.

"Time to alien weapons hot?"

"Three minutes."

☼

Three minutes.

Delilah sought to delay the alien. Hel stepped forward to help her.

"You think we do not know about your ships? That we are not prepared for this battle?"

That drew the alien's attention off his bond mate. Hel felt a flicker of approval that could have been Delilah or the nanites.

"Look at your scans. Look at our ships. Are any of them damaged?"

The alien looked and this time he saw the ruse.

"What ships? I am alone."

His face chilled to ice, his resolve to attack hardened, but Hel had another card to play.

Two minutes.

With a little boost from the nanites, the extra phase cloaked ships now appeared on the alien's scanners, two poised to fire on each of the alien's sixteen ships.

"Nice." Delilah smiled her approval. Was there something more in her eyes? "Maybe that will yank some time creep tail?"

One minute.

If they did not appear soon…

Hel felt it before he saw it, felt it tingle across his skin as time halted and the glowing light appeared. Out the view screen he saw an energy beam halt half way to its target. The two figures in the time stream looked almost annoyed.

"How is that you remember us?" one of them asked.

Delilah shrugged. "You must have muffed your reset. Shoddy work is so embarrassing, isn't it?"

Why did she seek to annoy them? Was it good she succeeded?

"You sought our attention, now you have it."

Their body language was wrong. What did they have to hide?

"Someone is messing with time again. Did Smith escape your leash?"

"We have detected no instability."

She stared at them for what felt like a very long time, her head to one side.

"You're lying."

"You are understandably distraught—"

"What I am is pissed." Delilah cut them off, her voice flat and cold. "I don't know why I didn't see it last time. The look. The attitude. I grew up with it. You're my parents all over again."

"What look?" One of them asked the question, before Hel could. He heard wary in the voice and knew Delilah was right, but about what?

"The scientist look. I've used it myself a few times. You aren't minding time. You're messing with it, using us as your lab rats. You're using us for some sick, twisted experiment."

Hel saw the truth of it in their eyes before they turned remote again.

"It does not matter. We will reset Earth time so far back, you will be a child again."

Hel moved instinctively toward her. "Delilah?"

If he lost her again—he couldn't let that happen. They had to stop them—

He saw her light up, realized he glowed, too. Felt the internal nova. The nanites that had protected them last time exploded in a rage that equaled his, and also Delilah's. He had not realized the nanites could feel rage.

He reached for her.

She reached for him.

Fingertips touched, slid together and gripped…

They were yanked into a vortex of light. It spun and dipped around him, around her. Time whirled around them, broken pieces like flat mirrors bending and turning in the vortex with flashes of his life and hers, flashes of other lives, other times. They spun faster and faster. It tried to pull them apart. He wouldn't let it. He knew his grip bruised her. He didn't care.

Light built.

Exploded.

Into darkness without bottom.

☼

The blackness faded to gold, taking her to a place that streamed like a transport beam. Doc still had her peeps sending her data. She was in a sort of energy field, but whether it was a cell or a protection wasn't clear. Hel was here, too. She couldn't see him, but she felt him, felt the nanite connection, though direct communication was offline. To one side, the streams of gold were vertical, instead of horizontal. Could it be a control panel of some kind? Some peeps flowed toward it, unaffected by the energy field that immobilized her. As weird as it was, she felt as if she went with them. Incoming data spiked, knowledge exploding in her head.

She was in time's slip stream. She, Hel and the peeps had almost destroyed the fabric of time, had almost ripped it to shreds. Somehow the peeps had held it together until they'd been able to pull all of them free of time's drag. Or maybe time had ejected them. *Time is persistent.* Equations and data streamed through her head at an incredible rate. She could *feel* time flowing, sensed its ebb and flow as if it were a part of her. She recognized it on some subterranean level, as if she and time had always been connected.

A figure emerged from the flow, taking shape in front of the vertical data stream. He didn't look at her, his attention on the data stream.

Dr. Smith?

That he was black ops something was clearer now that he wasn't playing scientist. Could he be a merc? A mercenary? As if he sensed her scrutiny, he finally turned, a slight frown between his sandy brows, as if something about her puzzled him.

"I need to know how you almost destroyed time." There was an authority in his voice that hadn't been there before.

Doc shrugged.

He looked at her then, a frown upping his stern factor by ten.

"Who are you?"

He didn't know who she was. The relief might have taken out her knees, but it was hard to know for sure with the energy field pinning her physical body in place. "So you can go mess with my past?"

He frowned. "It's not that simple. Time is—"

"Persistent. And so are you."

Nothing slight about this frown, though he erased it.

Did that mean he didn't remember her? Had the time creeps reset his time line, too?

He'd tried to trap the Chameleon, she reminded herself, so he had to remember her, didn't he? The time creeps remembered her and Hel, though what they knew about them was still an unknown.

The peeps quivered with unease as they flowed back into her body. Smart peeps.

"You should not be here."

"And yet here I am." Not that she planned to stay. Her peeps almost had control of the field. This was future tech, but it was *Garradian* future tech. Her peeps were connecting with the grandpeeps and both sides were happy about it.

"I cannot release you until I identify the contamination and correct it."

"You don't want to fix anything."

He gave her a black ops look. Funny how that never changed.

"Sometimes it is necessary to—" he hesitated, as if trying to find the right word "—delete a feature so that time can be stabilized."

They were a "feature?" No, she realized, he was lying about stabilizing time. Doc felt time smoothing out around the slip stream. Perhaps it was relieved it still could.

"You're just mad we got the drop on you." She felt the click as she and Hel connected again, felt her ability to breach the field increase as they combined their peep power.

Smith stiffened, whipped back to the data stream control or whatever that was. "What are you doing?"

Doc didn't answer. People only explained themselves in the movies. Besides, it ought to be freaking obvious. They were getting out. He stared at her through a field starting to flicker like a bad circuit.

"I will learn who you are."

I will learn who you are. She thought he knew who they were, not precisely, but ballpark knowledge. His body language said he lied, but he sounded confident. This place wasn't a time machine, it was a time tracking station, according to the peeps. It tracked instabilities, not people or planets or galaxies. She saw, or maybe she felt the threads of time moving past the slip stream that protected them. It wasn't a movie. It was a river, a jumble of galaxies and planets and countries and lives. Finding them in that mess would be like trying to find a pebble in the Mississippi River when it was at high flood stage. That would be why the time freaks had used instabilities to play with time. But that didn't explain Smith.

She didn't understand most of the data delivered via the peeps, but what she did get, gave her hope. He'd have a better chance finding a needle hidden in the Garradian galaxy. She mentally plucked some of the threads and saw him wince. She gave him her Morticia smile. "Good luck with that."

He tried to fight them. She felt him fail. He spun away into a mix of light and dark. Did he cry out? She wasn't sure. The field holding her in place faded. She was falling again. Faster this time and not through darkness, but back into the stream of time. It was cold, then hot…

Twenty-Three

Doc didn't want to open her eyes. It took a few heartbeats to remember why.

She sniffed. No cordite, so not a post bomb moment.

She was upright. Holding onto something hard and cool. She took a peek. A marble sink. A Garradian marble sink.

She was in a bathroom. A Garradian bathroom.

There were worse places to be, worse places she'd been.

She still had the peeps. She could feel them in her head, though they were as rattled as she was. Almost destroying the fabric of time twice had that affect.

She lifted her lids. Saw her face, her body in a mirror over the sink.

She was wearing a *dress.*

That was new.

Not that she'd never worn a dress, but wearing one in this galaxy was new. It wasn't just a *dress*. It was a modified *Morticia dress*: black and clinging with sleeves that had drifty points that stopped at her knuckles. It wasn't long. She never wore long dresses. If she had to lift them to kick it filled her hands with something besides knives or guns. She touched the a-bit-lower-than-her-usual neckline. What was up with that? This dress was fitted—she felt her back and sure enough, no gun snugged into the curve of her lower back. She yanked at the skirt, feeling out of proportion relieved to find a knife strapped to one thigh, a small, but lethal hand gun strapped to the other. Minimal was better than nothing. The heels went with the dress, but holy foxtrot they were high enough to be a different kind of weapon.

Her hair was shorter than last timeline, but longer than the hair cut before that. It brushed her shoulders, utterly straight and about the same length as Cleopatra's was supposed to have been, but sans the bangs. She didn't do bangs. Got in the way of a gun sight if she didn't keep them trimmed.

Her makeup was exotic and a bit creepy.

What was going on? Where was she?

She studied the bathroom, not able to fully appreciate the nice accoutrements. Situational awareness the size of a bathroom was not helpful, even if it was a nice bathroom. The stone walls looked familiar. This had to be the Kikk outpost. The peeps wanted to help, but they were fetal in a dark corner of her brain. Okay, outpost, dress—could be a party. But why was she packing creepy with her other armament? What was her mission objective? Did she have a mission objective? She hadn't at the last party in this galaxy, two timelines ago.

Her heart thumped again—hard—as she froze on another thought.

She pulled up her sleeve and turned her wrist to the light.

It was bare. It was gone. Her *ma'rasile* mark was gone.

Her hand wrapped around the spot.

It is what you said you wanted. The peeps sounded reproachful.

I did. I do. It's just—

You like him.

Her chest felt tight, like something wanted to explode out of the center. It wasn't tears. She didn't do tears. Okay, she'd had a rotten couple of timelines and maybe she'd earned a good cry, but that didn't mean she'd do it. She'd escaped Smith, but not the law of unintended consequences. She needed to get a new law to live by, but until then, well, Hel was better off not bonded to her. She was dangerous and creepy. His sons needed him more than she did. People didn't die from their heart shattering into millions of pieces—not that hers had. It felt like it had, but it hadn't. It was a biological impossibility.

She could stay in the bathroom and whine, or she could go find out where she was and why. Her brain made the case for leaving. Her heart voted for whining. The brain won. Whining made her head hurt.

She resisted the impulse to pull a weapon as she eased the door open onto an empty bedroom. She did a quick search of the pleasant space, found her stuff neatly stowed. She had a window, so she looked out. It was still light enough to tell that she'd been quartered on the Kikk outpost. Be nice to know why. Be better to curl up and die.

A tap at the door to the corridor almost put her on the ceiling. She had her weapon in hand without being aware she'd grabbed it. A little time shifting and she turns jumpy? *Get a grip, girl*, she ordered as she eased up to the door.

"Yes?"

"Doc?"

Briggs. She sagged. "Give me a minute." She stowed the weapon and shrugged on a persona that went with her clothes. Then she opened the door.

Briggs was in his dress uniform. He looked good.

His once over was thorough and appreciative enough to bring a half smile to her face, despite the hollow core in the center of her chest where she used to have what passed for a heart. He held out his arm, so she took it, pulling her door closed. It appeared they were going somewhere together, somewhere that required the dress and dress blues. She could do this. She could bluff it out. They walked in silence for the length of a semi-medieval corridor. It reminded her of an upscale castle—one without the damp and the gloom. No suits of armor either.

"Can I ask you something, Doc?"

She looked at him, wrapped in exterior calm. "Sure."

"Are you all right?"

Okay, maybe her exterior wasn't as calm as she thought. "Why wouldn't I be all right?" At least her voice sounded the same, cool and too much like her mum.

He stopped, turning to face her, forcing Doc to face him right when she could have used a hair screen while she figured out what he was talking about.

"If you don't want to do this, screw Giddioni and the alliance."

Doc's jaw sagged about the same moment the hole in her chest started to close. *Time is persistent.* She felt a smile tipping up the edges of her mouth, despite a reminder to herself that this didn't mean Hel remembered her. The peeps were still too rattled to do any research for her.

Briggs sighed. "The General said you like him." He shook his head, like he couldn't believe it.

Doc made a face and shrugged. "At least we know I'll be bad at whatever it is an alliance mate does." Doc still wasn't a diplomat, probably never would be.

He looked more cheerful. "That's what the General said."

They resumed their walk toward the party—if it was a party. Had to be a party. She was wearing a freaking dress. With all the practice she'd had with working in the dark, she should be better at it by now. The crowd murmur built as they approached open double doors. Men in pretty uniforms stood on each side. Did that mean the party was hosted by the Gadi? Did that mean the Gadi were on the outpost? In possession of the outpost?

The food smell reached her first. It smelled great. Had to be a Gadi party. Doc's nose quivered. As far as she knew, she hadn't eaten great food in this timeline. And she had no equation to help her do the math on how long it had been since food had hit her stomach.

People smells came next, some of them not quite as good as others, though none of them rampantly unpleasant. No one had obvious BO, though the mix had an alien tinge to it. Her eye didn't twitch. Maybe she was getting the hang of the time paradox crap. Or her eyelids were just tired of twitching. They reached the entrance and paused. Doc could feel Briggs longing to retreat as keenly as she felt her own. If she hadn't spotted Hel, she might have given into it.

He looked *good.*

You like him.

What's not to like? She'd never have asked that question of the General. He'd have a long list. The peeps just agreed with her. As if her thoughts had summoned him, General Halliwell appeared on her two o'clock, wearing his dress blues and stone face. At least he'd left the thunder cloud in his quarters. Something in his eyes told her they were friends again, which further eased the chill of the reset. She felt those tendrils again, those roots connecting her to both men and hopefully to this time. She was as adaptable as anyone she knew, but she'd had it with adapting—at least adapting in the dark.

Briggs came to attention. Doc did a variation more suited the dress and killer heels.

"It's not too late to change your mind."

It was too late two timelines ago, but telling him that would make *his* eye twitch. She smiled, channeling her mum's calm and cool.

"I'm good, sir." It was almost true. She'd almost destroyed time. Had no clue what day of the week, month or year it was, or why she was wearing a dress. Or if Hel remembered her. But he wanted her enough to do that alliance thing—unless she'd done it. Her chest hollowed out again.

The general's gaze sharpened, his voice dropped. "It's happened again, hasn't it?"

She nodded. He'd seen through her before. That he still could wasn't as big a shock as it should have been. She smiled, a cool and confident one. "I have no clue what this is all about, sir."

Before the General could respond, a Gadi man slithered up to them, undressing her with his close-set eyes. *Glarmere.* Perhaps he was the reason she'd decided to pack creepy. She felt a sudden longing for a flash bang. She could hope time was *that* persistent.

"My lady. I am Minister Glarmere." His gaze ran over her again, leaving a slime trail.

Were there laws about beating up on a Minister? A cool, male hand cupped her elbow and every nerve ending in her body perked up. They might have done the Macarena.

Hel.

Time slowed in a nice way as she turned her head to look at him. She felt the air rasp in her throat as she inhaled his scent, felt the electrical current passing between them where his skin met hers. There was an internal buzz as both their peeps tried to reconnect. Physical contact helped them, though both sets were rattled.

"Delilah."

That's all he said, but it told her all she needed to know right now: *he wanted her.*

She didn't know if he remembered her, didn't know if he remembered everything that had happened, but right now it was enough to know *he wanted her.*

She kept her façade, taking her cue from him. She didn't want to look away. She did. She looked at Glarmere, met his close-set gaze, then let her gaze trail over him with the same thoroughness he'd used on her, though she didn't do the slime trail and her scrutiny had a hearty measure of lethal. She gotten some practice with Conan and she used what she'd learned. He was almost Hel's height and was pretty in an oily way, but he lacked Hel's presence, his clarity of purpose, his hotness factor, and the eyes were just too close together.

Did Dusan mercenaries lurk in his life somewhere?

Time is persistent.

Last timeline their *ma'rasile* had made Hel vulnerable to his cousin, but that wasn't an issue this time. Her gaze made it back to Glarmere's. She let out some lethal and saw him pale. She added a tiny, very tiny wrinkle of the nose, just in case his ego didn't get the memo that messing with her was a bad idea. Now color surged into his face. He was easier to wind up than Conan. Before he could implode or explode, hard to say which way a guy like that would go, another Gadi man edged in close, riding in a bubble of self-importance.

"Minister Carig," Hel murmured, bending close so that his breath ruffled the hair covering her ear.

She shivered, wondering when the wedding was. It took a couple of blinks to focus on the new player. Hel wasn't the only one made vulnerable by the sizzle between them. These men would use any advantage they could find against them.

Carig was about her height and darker skinned then Hel or his cousin. Doc hadn't realized they had variations, since Carig had missed the other party, not wanting to get blown up. Was he still plotting or just frustrated and bitter? Were there rumblings among the expedition for him to tap into this time?

Time is persistent.

She didn't see Neil Caldwell, but that didn't mean he wasn't here somewhere.

She had a sense, perhaps from the knowledge the peeps had downloaded from their time in the slip stream, that this reset was dang near back to square one. Where did that leave Dr. Smith? She didn't see him anywhere either, but that didn't mean he wasn't somewhere.

"I don't see Dr. Smith, General Halliwell?"

Hel's fingers on her arm contracted once. The General frowned.

"Who?"

"Tobias Smith?"

"Never heard of him." His gaze asked a question she couldn't answer in this place, but she let her gaze tell him the question was related to the time reset. His nod was almost imperceptible. He was a good, no, make that a great man. He'd…saved her in his way, as much as the peeps and Hel. It had started with Sara and Fyn, continued with Briggs and finished here. She was officially a real girl.

Time is persistent.

Flinging him back into his own time wouldn't stop Smith

from trying again. It was the one thing she knew for sure about him, almost the only thing.

Time is persistent.

As if to add emphasis to that thought, Doc saw Conan. Freaking Conan. He strode toward her scattering pretty Gadi guys like they were bowling pins and he was the ball. Just looking at him made her headache. Just how persistent was time? She couldn't see a bandage on his hand. Was he playing tag again or had he arrived like he was supposed to this time? She wanted to ask who he was, but what if she already knew?

The General shifted, blocking her view, and said in a low voice, "His name is Vidor Shan. He's from another galaxy. Said he was curious."

The General's tone said he didn't believe Conan. Doc didn't either. The peeps wanted to help out, but they were lucky to connect with each other. Clarity would have to wait.

At least the party was interesting enough to distract. Her gaze glanced off Glarmere, Carig and Conan, before finding Hel again. Even without Dr. Smith, it was the most interesting party she'd ever attended.

☼

Doc wasn't sure when she realized Hel was steering her, not just through the crowd, but some*where*. Since they'd met every Gadi person in the room, and he wasn't pushing her into another timeline, Doc didn't fight him. The limelight was not SOP for her, so she was happy to get out of it. The door was hard to spot. A tapestry hung down, but Hel found it and nudged her through it, then slipped inside after her. It was a small room, a small office maybe. It had a desk and shelves, though it was way nicer than her office on the *Doolittle*—well, the one last timeline. She didn't know if she had an office in this timeline.

She trailed a finger along the smooth edge of the desk, feeling the subtle changes in the grain. She'd been longing to see Hel, to talk to him, but now they were alone, her heart fluttered with an unfamiliar panic.

"Delilah."

Just her name, but his tone pulled her around to face him. Her lashes lifted, taking more time than needed to connect with his deep, blue gaze. This was the moment for the law of unintended consequences to pull the rug out. She leaned against the desk, maybe gripped it with both hands. She knew she looked calm, because she knew what calm felt like on her face, knew each muscle in her face was where she wanted them to be, knew they gave nothing away. Her heartbeat too fast and her eyes ate him up, so he wouldn't be fooled by the calm. Even if he didn't know her, he *knew* her.

She needed to break the silence, so she did. "Glarmere isn't going to be Leader, is he?"

Hel's perfect mouth curved. "No."

Doc's throat dried, as the heat in his eyes ramped up. Maybe she didn't need him to remember. This was good…

"I remember the first time I saw you. At the party, you paced like you were looking for a way out."

"I'm lousy at parties, unless I'm supposed to shoot someone. Then I'm good."

Not the best quality in an alliance mate.

He took a step toward her. "I remember the first time I kissed you. And the second."

Color stung Doc's cheeks as she remembered them, too. A current of something formed between them. She swallowed.

"I had influenza." It sounded better than, "I was almost a corpse."

He took another step. "I remember that, too. I almost lost you." He stopped bare inches from her, trailed a finger down her cheek and across her mouth. "I remember hurting you."

She lifted her shoulders in a slight shrug. "Your cousin was trying to torture you. I'd have been cranky, too."

"That was not what unsettled me, and you know this."

She gave a tiny, happy shrug. Maybe she smiled. "We have a tradition on my planet called kissing it better."

His mouth curved up. "We have this tradition as well." He leaned closer. "Where does it hurt?"

She touched her chest, just above the vee in her Morticia dress where her real girl heart pounded. "Right here."

He bent and kissed the spot, his mouth lingering for an endless second against her skin. Her heart almost stopped. Her breathing did stop. If he hadn't lifted his head, she'd have passed out. As it was, she saw stars. He slid his arms around her waist, pulling her close and her stars went nova. A hand cupped her chin, tilting her face up to his. Not that she fought him. Just in case he wasn't sure she was with him, she parted her lips in invitation.

"When we were about to go through the portal, you said you loved me. We have something we call—" The Gadi word was unfamiliar to Doc, but the look in his eyes gave her a translation. "Could this love, be similar?"

She nodded, but it didn't seem enough. "If yours means I never want to be where you aren't, then yes, it's the same."

"Then I also feel this love for you. Even for my sons' mother, I have not felt this, Delilah. When I realized our *ma'rasile* was gone..."

The pain in his voice and face brought back the echo of her pain.

"I know why you did this, but I ask you to reconsider, to be my *ma'rasile* again."

There were good reasons to say no, but Doc couldn't look into his blue, blue eyes and say anything but, "If that's what you really want."

She eased up on her toes, just to give him a little hint that kissing would be nice about now. Before he could take the hint, her wrist tingled. She looked and found her mark back.

We could not wholly remove it, the peeps admitted. *We would have told you if...*

Doc smiled because she couldn't help it. "I'm going to make a lousy Leader's whatever."

"I no longer desire to be a Leader. I served my people when my skills were needed for war. I am ill-suited for peace." He looked around. "I think we should live here with my sons and learn together about this place."

"I could do that, but who will lead your people?" Then she got it. "Naman." Hel nodded. "He'll be good. He learned from the best, after all." She stiffened. "Does this mean we don't have an alliance mating between our people? Or do I have to stay with him?" The law of unintended consequences better not be messing with her.

"You are my *ma'rasile*, Delilah."

"But will this mess up your alliance mating creds?"

"If we announce my retirement prior to the ceremony, yes. Once it has happened, then you may choose to remain with the Leader or come with me."

She gave him a slow smile. "Well, I'll have to think about it, won't I? Do I keep my position or the guy?"

"Permit me to aid your decision."

He bent his head towards hers. It felt like it took forever for his mouth to find hers but when it did…

Her toes curled in her mile-high shoes. It was an unintended consequence, but one she didn't mind.

Doc thought she knew about going nova.

She thought she knew about going super nova.

She didn't know anything.

But she was learning.

Epilogue

The facility showed few lights as midnight passed them by. Doc didn't check her watch. She didn't need to with the peeps in her head.

She fired the grapple over the wall at the same time as Hel. They went up the wall side by side, though she let him reach the top first. They were evenly matched in everything, but he was a guy. First mattered more to him than it did to her. They dropped silently onto the grass on the other side. No dogs, though there were motion detectors. The peeps helped them fail to detect their motion. They went ghost and reached the side of the building without a confrontation with the single guard. He was inside flirting with one of the nurses.

The peeps hacked into the building security and messed with the cameras, while Doc popped the locks the old-fashioned way. She did like to practice every now and again. Inside it was just a matter of avoiding the night staff. They took the halls less traveled to the third floor. Had to wait while a nurse did a room check. Drifted down the hall to the right room. This time Doc let the peeps pop the lock. They liked to practice, too.

The room was dim, a small nightlight giving a soft glow from the bathroom. He lay on his side on the bed, straps on his arms and legs to prevent him from hurting himself. Doc worked quickly, Hel assisting with the Gadi IV device. She extracted the test tubes and added them one at time.

It was kind of funny that it freaked her peeps out a bit, letting themselves out of the tubes. They were quick to point out that another Doc was out there somewhere, too. Time paradoxes were still a challenge for all of them.

"If he does not wake soon..." Hel's gaze strayed to the doorway.

They had to leave undetected. The space-time continuum might depend on it. For sure they didn't want to attract anyone's attention with a time instability.

He didn't glow. He did stir, his lids fluttering several times before staying up. His brows drew together in a familiar frown.

Doc turned on a small, hooded flashlight, letting some of the light hit her face.

"Hello, Robert."

Other Fabulous Books by Pauline Baird Jones

The Key

An Air Force pilot—the best of the best to be assigned to this mission—Sara Donovan isn't afraid to travel far beyond the Milky Way on an assignment that takes her into a galaxy torn apart by a long and bitter warfare between the Dusan and the Gadi. When she accidentally discovers a mysterious, hidden city, it brings her closer to the answers she seeks – about her baffling abilities and her mother's past.

Out of Time

What happens when a twenty-first century woman on a mission to change the past meets a thoroughly 1940s man trying to stay alive in the hellish skies over war-torn Europe? Melanie "Mel" Morton is an adventure reporter, who lost her grandfather in World War II. Enter Jack Hamilton, sexy octogenarian, genius/scientist and former WWII bomber pilot. What he tells Mel sends her on her craziest adventure yet—straight into the past to save her grandfather's life—and change Jack's future, if she doesn't accidentally end it. All Mel has to do is outmaneuver the entire German army—and not fall in love with Jack. Unfortunately, eluding the German army is the easy part...

Do Wah Diddy Die

Luci Seymour—sexy & free spirited—returns to steamy New Orleans in search of the father she's never met. She finds murder, mayhem, love and adventure when her timing puts her directly in the sights of an elderly hit couple and a con man's last scam.

The Spy Who Kissed Me

Isabel "Stan" Stanley's mother has been hoping a man would fall in Stan's lap. But when a handsome spy dives through the sunroof of her car in a hail of bullets, Stan's sure this wasn't what momma had in mind. Bad guys beware. Stan's packing a glue gun and she knows how to use it. Sort of.

A Dangerous Dance

His whole career, Remy Mistral has fought for reform in a state where corruption is an art form. Now is his chance to quit talking about reform and make his move to change things, but two things stand in his way. One is a woman, the other a killer.

The Lonesome Lawmen Books:

The Last Enemy

Two men need her. One needs her dead. Romance author, Dani Gwynne is plotting her own survival, working against time, terror and her fear of heights. Deputy US Marshal Matt Kirby is the lawman in charge of finding her—and stopping the hit man hunting her. With the clock ticking on a macabre game of hide and seek, Dani must defeat a killer who won't stop until he gets what he wants—or destroys them all trying.

Byte Me

Deputy US Marshal, Jake Kirby, is a top tracker who always gets his fugitive. Now he's hot on the trail of a gang of cyber-thieves with an unusual agenda. That trail takes him to Colorado and a bar managed by the sexy, mysterious Phoebe Mentel. Instant attraction complicates this high tech chess game between two people who don't know how to lose and are afraid to love.

Missing You

Denver Homicide detective, Luke Kirby is looking for peace and quiet in the mountains above Denver. Instead he finds a beautiful and mysterious woman bringing a storm of trouble for them both. Too bad she can't remember what, why or who.

Lonesome Mama

Debra Kirby's boys aren't lonesome lawmen anymore, and now the long time widow finds herself pining for a bit of adventure and romance in her life. When Donovan Kincaid (introduced in *Missing You*) offers a plane ride to a friend's wedding, neither expects to run into trouble—and the "Lonesome Mama" gets more than she wished for.

Non-Fiction:

Adapting Your Novel for Film

A nuts and bolts guide to adapting your novel for film.

Managing Your Book Writing Business (with Jamie Engle)

This helpful handbook outlines basic and important information every author needs to know about the publishing industry and the the "business" of writing.

Made Up Mayhem

A quick and dirty guide to writing the suspense novel.

Author Pauline Baird Jones

Pauline Baird Jones is the award-winning author of nine novels of of science fiction romance, action-adventure, suspense, romantic suspense and comedy-mystery. She's also written two non-fiction books, *Adapting Your Novel for Film* and *Made-up Mayhem,* and she co-wrote *Managing Your Book Writing Business* with Jamie Engle. Her seventh novel, *Out of Time,* an action-adventure romance set in World War II, is an EPPIE 2007 winner. Her eighth novel, *The Key* won an Independent Book Award Bronze Medal (IPPY) for 2008 and is a 2007 Dream Realm Awards Winner. She also has short stories in several anthologies. Originally from Wyoming, she and her family moved from New Orleans to Texas before Katrina.